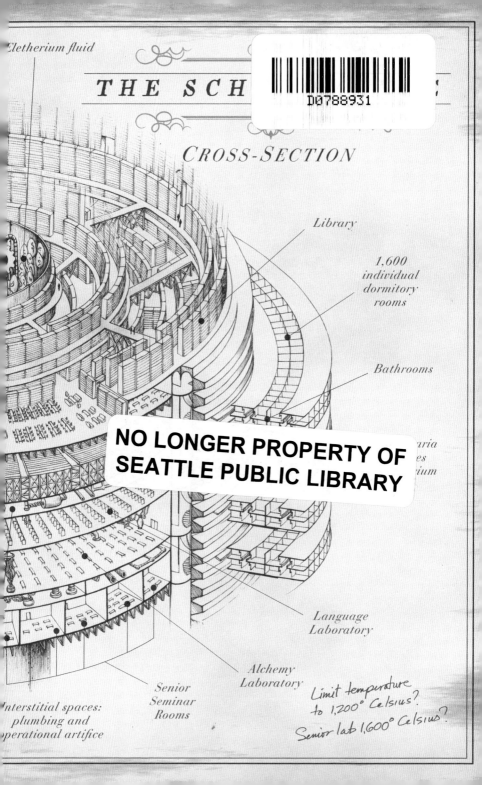

Eletherium fluid

THE SCH[...]

CROSS-SECTION

Library

1,600
individual
dormitory
rooms

Bathrooms

[...]aria
[...]es
[...]rium

Language
Laboratory

Alchemy
Laboratory

Senior
Seminar
Rooms

Interstitial spaces:
plumbing and
operational artifice

Limit temperature
to 1,200° Celsius?
Senior lab 1,600° Celsius?

BY NAOMI NOVIK

THE SCHOLOMANCE

A Deadly Education
The Last Graduate
The Golden Enclaves

Uprooted
Spinning Silver

TEMERAIRE

His Majesty's Dragon
Throne of Jade
Black Powder War
Empire of Ivory
Victory of Eagles
Tongues of Serpents
Crucible of Gold
Blood of Tyrants
League of Dragons

THE GOLDEN ENCLAVES

NEW YORK

THE GOLDEN
ENCLAVES

A NOVEL

✦ *Lesson Three of The Scholomance* ✦

NAOMI NOVIK

Copyright © 2022 by Temeraire LLC

All rights reserved.

Published in the United States by Del Rey, an imprint of Random House, a division of Penguin Random House LLC, New York.

DEL REY and the CIRCLE colophon are registered trademarks of Penguin Random House LLC.

Hardback ISBN 978-0-593-15835-7
International ISBN 978-0-593-59769-9
Ebook ISBN 978-0-593-15836-4

Printed in the United States of America on acid-free paper

randomhousebooks.com

2 4 6 8 9 7 5 3 1

FIRST EDITION

Book design by Simon M. Sullivan

THE GOLDEN ENCLAVES

Chapter 1
THE YURT

THE LAST THING Orion said to me, the absolute bastard, was *El, I love you so much.*

And then he shoved me backwards through the gates of the Scholomance and I landed thump on my back in paradise, the soft grassy clearing in Wales that I'd last seen four years ago, ash trees in full green leaf and sunlight dappling through them, and *Mum,* Mum right there waiting for me. Her arms were full of flowers: poppies, for rest; anemones, for overcoming; moonwort, for forgetfulness; morning glories, for the dawn of a new day. A welcome-home bouquet for a trauma victim, meant to ease horror out of my mind and make room for healing and for rest, and as she reached to help me, I heaved myself up howling, *"Orion!"* and sent the whole thing scattering before me.

A few months—aeons—ago, while we'd still been in the midst of our frantic obstacle-course runs, an enclaver from Milan had given me a translocation spell in Latin, the rare kind that you can cast on yourself without splitting yourself into bits. The idea was that I'd be able to use it to hop around from one place to another in the graduation hall—all the better to save people like enclavers from Milan, which is why she'd handed me a spell worth five years of mana for free. You couldn't normally use it to go long distances, but time was more or less the same thing as space, and I'd been in the Scholomance ten seconds before. I had the hall visualized as crisp and clear as an architectural drawing, complete with the horrific mass of Patience and the horde of maleficaria behind it, boiling its way towards us. I was placing myself at the gates, right back where I had been when Orion had given me that final shove.

But the spell didn't want to be cast, putting up resistance like warning signs across the way: dead end, road washed out ahead. I forced it through anyway, throwing mana at it, and the casting rebounded in my face and knocked me down like I'd run straight into a concrete wall. So I got back up and tried the exact same spell again, only to get pasted flat a second time.

My head was ringing bells and noise. I crawled back to my feet. Mum was helping me up, but she was also holding me back, saying something to me, trying to slow me down, but I only snarled at her, *"Patience was coming right at him!"* and her hands went slack, sliding off me with her own remembered horror.

It had already been two minutes since I'd been dumped out; two minutes was forever in the graduation hall, even before I'd packed it full of all the monsters in the world. But the interruption did stop me just banging my head against the gates repeatedly. I spent a moment thinking, and then I tried to use a summoning to get Orion out, instead.

Most people can't summon anything larger or with more willpower than a hair bobble. But the many summoning spells I've unwillingly collected over the years are all intended to bring me one or more hapless screaming victims, presumably to go into the sacrificial pit I've incomprehensibly neglected to set up. I had a dozen varieties, and one of them that let you scry someone through a reflective surface and pull them out.

It's especially effective if you have a gigantic cursed mirror of doom to use. Sadly I'd left mine hanging on the wall of my dorm room. But I ran around the clearing and found a small puddle of water between two tree roots. That wouldn't have been good enough ordinarily, but I had endless mana flowing into me, the supply line from graduation still open. I threw power behind the spell and forced the muddy puddle smooth as glass and staring down at it called, "Orion! *Orion Lake!* I call you in the—" I took a quick glance up at the first sunlight and sky I'd seen in four years of longing for them, and the only thing I could feel was desperate frustration that it wasn't dawn or noon or midnight or anything helpful, "—waxing hours of the light, to come to me from the dark-shadowed halls, heeding my word alone," which would very likely mean he'd be under a spell of obedience when he got here, but I'd worry about that *later,* later after he was *here*—

The spell did go through this time, and the water churned into a cloud of silver-black that slowly and grudgingly served up a ghostly image that might have been Orion from the back, barely an outline against pitch darkness. I shoved my arm into the dark anyway, reaching for him, and for a moment, I thought—I was *sure*—I *had* him. The taste of frantic relief swelled through me: I'd done it, I'd got hold of him— and then I screamed, because my fingers were sinking into the surface of a maw-mouth, with its sucking hunger turning on me.

Every part of my body wanted to let go at once. And then it got worse, as if there were any room for that to get worse, because it wasn't just one maw-mouth, it was *two,* grabbing at me from both sides, as if Patience hadn't quite finished digesting Fortitude yet: a whole century of students, a meal so large it would take a long while eating, and meanwhile Fortitude was still groping around trying to feed its own hunger even while it was being swallowed down.

And it had been blindingly obvious to me back there in the graduation hall that we couldn't possibly kill that monstrous agglomerated horror, not even with the mana of four thousand living students fueling me. The only thing to do with Patience was the only thing to do with the Scholomance: we could only push them off into the void, and hope they vanished away forever. But apparently Orion had disagreed, since he'd turned back to fight even with the school teetering on the edge of the world behind him.

As if he'd thought Patience was going to get out, and in some part of his stupid brutalized brain imagined that he could *stop* it getting out, and therefore he had to stay behind and be a hero this one more time, one boy standing in front of a tidal wave. That was the only possible reason I could imagine, and it had been stupid enough without shoving *me* out the gates first, when I was the only one of us who'd ever actually fought a maw-mouth before. That made it so unutterably stupid that I needed him *out,* needed him *here,* so I could scream at him at length to impress upon him exactly how stupid he'd been.

I clung to that rage. Rage made it possible for me to keep holding on, despite the heaving putrescence of maw-mouth trying to envelop my fingers, sucking on my skin and my shielding like a child trying to get through a candy shell to the better sweetness inside, trying to get to *me,* trying to get to every last bit of me so it could devour me down to staring eyes and screaming mouth.

Rage, and horror, because it was going to do that to *Orion*, Orion who was still there in the hall with it. So I didn't let go. Staring down into the scrying puddle, I hurled murder at it past his blurry, half-seen shoulder, casting my best, quickest, killing spell over and over, the feeling of a lake of rot sloughing away from around my hands each time, until I was gulping down nausea with each breath I took, and each casting of *"À la mort!"* went rolling off my tongue on the way out, blurring until the sound of my breathing was death. All the while I kept holding on, trying to pull Orion out. Even if it meant I'd heave Patience out into the world with him and spill that devouring horror into the cool green trees of Wales right at Mum's feet, my place of peace I'd dreamt of in every minute I'd been in the Scholomance. All I'd have to do was kill it, after all.

That had seemed utterly impossible five minutes before, so impossible I'd just laughed at the idea, but now it was only a low and trivial hurdle when the alternative was letting it have Orion instead. I was really good at killing things. I'd find a way. I even had a plan laying itself out in my head, the clockwork machinery of strategy ticking coolly away in the background of my mind where it never stopped after four years in the Scholomance. We'd fight Patience together. I'd kill it a few dozen lives at a time, and he could pull the mana out and feed it back to me, and together we'd create an unending killing circle between us until the thing was finally gone. It would work, it would work. I had myself convinced. I didn't let go.

I didn't let go. I was pushed off. Again.

Orion did it himself. He must have, because maw-mouths don't let go. The mana I was pouring into the summoning spell was coming out of the graduation supply that was still unending, as if everyone in the school was still putting mana into our shared ritual. But that didn't make any sense. Everyone else was gone. They were out of the Scholomance, hugging their parents and telling them what we'd done, sobbing and treating the wounds they'd taken, ringing all their friends. They weren't still feeding me power. They weren't *meant* to be. The whole idea of our plan was to sever all connection to the school: we wanted to cram it full of mals and break it off the world and let it float away into the void like a putrid balloon full of writhing malice, vanishing off into the dark where it belonged. It had been going when Orion and I had made that last run towards the portal.

As far as I knew, the only thing keeping it anchored to reality now was *me*, still clinging to the line of mana coming out of the school. And the only person left in the Scholomance to feed me that mana was Orion. Orion, who could capture mana from mals when he killed them. So at least in that moment, he must still have been alive, still fighting; Patience hadn't swallowed him up yet. And he must have felt me trying to drag him out, but instead of turning round and helping me to pull him through, he drew away from me instead, resisting the summoning. And the horrible sticky mouthing over my hand pulled away, too. Just as if he was trying to do the same thing my dad had done, all those years ago: as if he'd reached out and grabbed a maw-mouth and pulled it away, letting it have him instead of the girl he loved.

Except the girl Orion loved wasn't a gentle, kind healer, she was a sorceress of mass destruction who on two occasions had already managed to shred maw-mouths apart, and the stupid bloody fool could have tried trusting me to do it again. But he didn't. He fought me instead, and when I tried to use my summoning hold to *force* him to come, abruptly the bottomless ocean of mana ran out from underneath me like he'd taken the plug out of the bath.

In an instant, the power-sharer on my wrist turned cool and heavy and dead. In one more, my wild profligate spell ran sputtering out of gas, and Orion slid out of my grip as if I'd been trying to hold on to a fistful of oil. His outline in the scrying pool vanished into the dark. I kept desperately groping for him anyway, even as the image began fading out at the edges, but Mum had been crouching beside me all along, her face stricken with worry and fear, and now she grabbed me by the shoulders and threw all her weight into shoving me over and away from the puddle, likely saving my hand from being cut off at the wrist as the spell collapsed and my bottomless scrying well returned to being half an inch of water pooled between tree roots.

I went tumbling and rolled back up onto my knees in a single smooth motion without even thinking about it: I'd been training for graduation for months. I threw myself back at the puddle, fingers scrabbling it into mud. Mum tried to put her arms around me, begging me desperately to stop. That's not why I stopped, though. I stopped because I couldn't do anything else. I didn't have an ounce of mana left. Mum caught me by the shoulders again, and I turned and grabbed at the crystal round her neck, gasping, "Please, *please.*" Mum's whole face was desperation; I could feel her longing to get me away, but then she shut her eyes a moment and with shaking hands reached up and undid the chain and let me have it: half full, not enough to raise the dead or burn cities to the ground, but enough to cast a message spell to scream at Orion with, to tell him to throw me back a line and let me help him, save him. Only it didn't go through.

I tried and tried, shouting Orion's name until the crystal and my voice were spent. I might as well have been shouting into the void. Which was where the whole Scholomance had presumably now gone. Just as we'd so cleverly, cleverly planned.

When there wasn't even enough mana for shouting, I used up the very last dribbles for a heartbeat spell, just trying to find out if he was still alive. It's a very cheap spell, because it's stupidly complicated and takes ten minutes, so the casting itself makes almost all the mana it needs. I cast it seven times one after the other without ever getting up off my mud-soaked knees, and stayed there listening to the wind blowing in the treetops and birds making noises and sheep talking to each other and somewhere in the distance a little running stream. Not a single echoing thump came back to my ears.

And when at last I didn't have mana left even for that, I let Mum lead me back to the yurt and put me to bed like I was six years old again.

The first time I woke up was so much like a dream that it hurt. I was in the yurt with the door open to let in the cool night air, and outside I could faintly hear Mum singing, the way I had in all my most agonizing dreams for the last four years, the ones that always ended in a jolt when I tried desperately to stay in them for a few minutes more. The truly awful part of this one was that I didn't want to stay in it. I turned over and went back down.

And when I couldn't sleep anymore, I just lay on my back in bed staring up at the billowing curve of the ceiling for a long time. If there had been anything else to do, I wouldn't have gone to sleep in the first place. I couldn't even be angry. The only person available to be angry with was Orion, and I couldn't stand to be angry with him. I tried: lying there I tried to think of every savage cutting remark I'd have made to him if he was here right now. But when I asked Orion *what were you thinking*, I couldn't make it come out angry, even inside my own head. It was just pain.

But I couldn't grieve him either, because he *wasn't dead*. He was busy screaming while a maw-mouth ate him, just like Dad. People do like to pretend maw-mouth victims are dead, but that's just because it's unbearable to think about it otherwise. There's nothing you can *do* about it, so if someone you love gets eaten by one, they're dead to you, and you might as well pretend it's all over. But I know, I know *from inside,* that you don't die when a maw-mouth eats you. You're just being eaten, forever; for as long as the maw-mouth lasts. But knowing didn't help. I couldn't do anything about it. Because the Scholomance was *gone.*

I hadn't moved when Mum came in a while later. She put a small tinkling handful of things into a bowl, saying softly, "There you are," to Precious, who made a squeak that meant gratitude and started cracking seeds. I couldn't feel sorry I hadn't thought about her, small and hungry. It was too far away, and I was too far down. Mum came and sat down next to my camp bed and put her hand on my forehead, warm and gentle. She didn't say anything.

I fought her off a little: I didn't want to feel better. I didn't want to get up and go on in the world, agreeing that it was in any way acceptable for the world to keep going itself. But lying there under Mum's hand, unimaginably safe and comfortable, I couldn't help but feel stupid. The world was going on anyway whether I gave it permission or not, and finally I sat up and let Mum give me a drink of water in the lopsided clay cup she'd made herself, and she sat on the bed next to me and put her arm around my shoulders and stroked my hair. She was so *small*. The whole yurt was so small. My head brushed the roof at the edge, even sitting on the camp bed. I could have made it outside on one good jump, if I were stupid enough to leap out into the unknown where anything could be waiting to ambush me.

Of course, that wouldn't have been stupid at all now. I wasn't in the Scholomance anymore. I'd set the students free, and jailed all the mals in our place, and then I'd broken the school off the world with all of them crammed hungry inside to gnaw on each other forever. So now I could sleep for twenty hours without a care, and I could go bounding out of my yurt with a song in my heart, and I could do anything and go anywhere in the world I wanted to. And so could everyone else, every last child I'd shepherded out of the Scholomance and all the children who'd never even have to go.

Except for Orion, gone into the dark.

If I'd had any mana left to do anything with, I would have imagined the possibility of doing something for him long enough to try some more. But since I didn't, all I could imagine was going for help to someone else—his mum maybe, who was on track to be Domina in the New York enclave— and asking her for mana so I could do something, and that was where my imagination broke down: looking her in the face, someone who'd loved Orion and wanted him home, and asking her for mana, for any of the ideas that became obviously stupid and useless as soon as I had to persuade someone else to believe in them. So I did the only thing left to do, and put my face in my hands and cried.

Mum sat beside me the whole time I was weeping, sat *with* me, caring about my misery without pretending she was feeling it too, or hiding away her own deep joy: I was home, I was alive, I was safe. Her whole body was radiating gladness out into the universe, but she didn't try to make me join in or smother my own grief; she knew I was deeply hurt, and was so sorry, and ready to do anything that she could to help me, when I wanted it. If you'd like to know how she told me all that without saying a word, I would too. It was nothing I could ever have done myself.

When I stopped crying, she got up and made me a cup of tea, picking leaves out of seven different jars on her crammed-full shelves, and she boiled the water with magic, which she'd never ordinarily have done, just so she didn't have to go outside to the fire and leave me alone yet. The whole yurt filled with the sweet smell when she poured the water in. She gave it to me and sat down again, holding my other hand between both of hers. She hadn't asked me any questions, I knew she wouldn't ever push, but there was a gentle silence between us waiting for me to start talking about it. To start grieving with her, for something that was over and done. And I couldn't bear to.

So after I drank my tea, I put the mug down and said, "Why did you warn me off Orion?" My voice came out hoarse and roughed-up, like I'd run sandpaper up and down the inside of my throat a few times. "Was this why? Did you see—"

She flinched like I'd jabbed her hard with a needle, and her whole body shuddered. She shut her eyes a moment and took a deep breath, then turned and looked at me full in my face in the way she called *seeing properly*, when she really wanted to take something in, and her own face went crumpling into folds along the faint wrinkle lines that were just beginning at the corners of her eyes. "You're safe," she said, half whispering, and she looked down at my hand and stroked it again, and a few tears dripped off her face. "You're *safe*. Oh my darling girl, you're safe," and she heaved a massive gulp and was crying herself, four years of tears running down her face.

She didn't ask me to cry with her; she looked away from me in fact, trying to keep her tears from me. I wanted to, I wanted so much to go into her arms and feel it with her: that I was alive and safe. But I couldn't. She was crying for joy, for love, for me, and I wanted to cry for those things too: I was home, I was out of the Scholomance forever, I was alive in a world I'd changed for the better, a world where children wouldn't have to be thrown into a pit full of knives just for the hope they'd make it out again. It was worth rejoicing. But I couldn't. The pit was still there, and Orion was down in it.

I pulled my hand away instead. Mum didn't try to hold me. She took several deep breaths and wiped her tears away, packing the joy out of the way, tidy, so she could go on being with me, then she turned and cupped my face with her hand. "I'm so sorry, my darling."

She didn't say why she'd warned me off Orion. And I understood why at once: she wasn't going to lie to me, but she didn't want to hurt me either. She understood that I'd loved him, that I'd lost someone I loved, in the same horrible way that she'd lost Dad, and my grief was all that mattered to her now. It didn't matter to her to tell me why, or persuade me that she'd been right.

But it mattered to me. "Tell me," I said through my teeth. "*Tell me.* You went to Cardiff, you got that boy to bring me a *note—*"

Her face crumpled a little, miserable—I was asking her to hurt me, to tell me something she knew I didn't want to hear—but she gave in. She bowed her head and said softly, "I tried to dream you every night. I knew I wouldn't be able to reach you, but I tried to anyway. A few times, I thought you were dreaming me back, and we almost touched . . . but it was only dreaming."

I swallowed hard. I remembered those dreams too, the faint handful of near-touches, the love that had almost made it to me despite the thick smothering layer of wards blanketing the Scholomance, the ones that blocked every possible way that anything could get in—because otherwise mals would use that way, too.

"But last year—I did see you. The night you used the linen

patch." Her voice was a whisper, and I hunched up, back in that moment and seeing it with her eyes: the little cell of my room, me on the floor in a puddle of my own blood, with the gaping ragged hole in my belly where one of my especially charming fellow students had shoved a knife into me. The only reason I'd survived it had been that healing patch she'd made me herself, years of love and magic worked into every linen thread she'd grown and spun and woven.

"Orion helped me with it," I said. "He put it on me," and I stopped, because she'd dragged in a gasping breath, her face twisting into the memory of a horror worse than my lying on the floor bleeding out.

"I felt him touch it," she said raggedly, and even as she was speaking, I knew I was going to be sorry I'd asked. "I saw him, so near you, touching you. I saw him, and he was just— *hunger*—" and she sounded *sick,* she sounded like she'd been watching a mal eat me alive, instead of Orion kneeling on my floor and pressing healing into my torn body.

"He was *my friend,*" I said in a howl, because I had to make her stop, and I stood up so fast I cracked my skull hard into a crossbar and sat down with my hands on top of my head with a squawk and started crying again a little from the jolt of pain. Mum tried to hold me, but I shrugged her arms off, angry and dripping, and heaved myself off the bed again.

"He saved my *life,*" I ground out at her. "He saved my life *thirteen times,*" and I gasped on a breath of agony: I'd never have the chance to catch up now.

She didn't say anything, didn't argue with me, just sat there with her eyes shut and her arms wrapped around herself, breathing through it in shudders. She only whispered, "My darling, I'm so sorry," and I could hear she truly was, she was so very sorry for hurting me with this supposed truth of what she'd seen in Orion that I wanted to scream.

I laughed instead, a horrible vicious laugh that hurt me to hear it in my own ears. "No worries, he's gone for good now," I said, jeering. "My brilliant plan took care of that." And I went out of the yurt.

I walked around the commune for a while, staying in the trees just past the limits of where anyone had a pitch. My head ached from crying and banging it against the roof and from pouring an ocean's worth of mana through my body, and from four years of prison before that. I didn't have a handkerchief or anything. I was still wearing my filthy sweaty leggings and T-shirt, the New York T-shirt Orion had given me, threadbare with four holes and still the only wearable top I'd had left by the end of term. I pulled up the hem and wiped my nose on it.

I wanted to go back to Mum, but I couldn't, because I wanted to ask her to hug me for a month, and I wanted to scream at her that she didn't know anything about Orion at all. What I really wanted was to not have asked her in the first place. It was worse than if she'd told me she'd foreseen it all, and if I'd only listened to her warning, instead of pulling him into my magnificent scheme to save the whole school, he'd have made it out fine.

I could guess what Mum had seen: Orion's power that let him pull mana out of mals, and the empty well inside him because when he took the power, he gave it *away*. The power so terrifyingly vast that it had forced him to become exactly the kind of stupid reckless hero who'd face an entire horde of maleficaria alone, because for every moment of his life, people had made him feel like a freak unless he was putting himself out in front of them.

He'd been the most popular boy in the Scholomance, but

I'd been his only friend, because when everyone else looked at him, that was all they saw: his power. They pretended they saw a noble hero, because he'd tried so hard to fit himself into that picture, and they loved the picture: that made his power something *for* them, something that would help them. The same way everyone looked at me and my power and saw a monster, because I *wouldn't* play along with what they wanted. But they'd loved Orion only in exactly the same way they'd hated me. Neither one of us were ever people to them. He just made himself useful, and I refused to.

But I'd never imagined that *Mum,* of all people—who'd never let me see a monster in my own mirror, even when the whole world was trying to convince me that was all that was there—would look at Orion and see his power, and decide that *he* was a monster. I couldn't bear it that she hadn't been able to look at him and see a person. It made it feel like she was lying about seeing *me* as one.

So I could have gone back to scream at her, to tell her the only reason I was alive for her to dream of was because Orion had killed the maleficer who'd gutted me, and had risked his own life spending the night in my room killing the endless stream of mals who'd come to finish the job. But the way I really wanted to prove her wrong was by having Orion walk up the path to our yurt next week, the way he'd promised he would, so she could see for herself that he wasn't either the terrible power she'd glimpsed or the gleaming perfect hero everyone else wanted him to be. That he *was* a person, he was just a person.

Had been a person. Before he'd got himself killed at the very gates of the Scholomance, because he'd thought it was his job to make a way out for everyone else but him.

I kept walking around as long as I could. I didn't want to feel anything as small as being tired and filthy and hungry, but

I did. The world did in fact insist on going on, and I didn't have the mana to make it stop. Precious finally came and got me, darting out from underneath a bush to pounce on my foot when I circled back closer to the yurt again. She refused to let me pick her up. She ran away from me a little way towards the yurt, and sat up on her haunches and gave me a scold, her white fur practically glowing in an invitation to the large number of cats and dogs who roamed the commune more or less freely. Being a familiar doesn't make you invulnerable.

So I followed her back to the yurt and let Mum give me a bowl of vegetable soup that tasted like it had been made with real vegetables, which might not sound very exciting to you, but what do you know. I couldn't help eating five bowls of it, even seasoned with agony and sour resentment, and almost all of a loaf of bread and butter, and afterwards I let Mum coax me to the bathhouse. There I spent a full hour in the shower, very much against commune rules, trying to dissolve into the hot water I was gluttonously consuming. I wasn't even mildly worried that an amphisbaena might erupt out of the showerhead.

Claire Brown turned up instead. I had my eyes shut under the spray when I heard the shockingly familiar voice saying, "So that's Gwen's daughter back, then," not with enthusiasm, and deliberately loud enough to be overheard.

It didn't make me angry, which was odd and uncomfortable; my supply of anger had never run dry before. I shut off the shower and came out hoping to find some, but it didn't work. The showers let out onto a big round dressing room, only that had also shrunk while I'd been away. The commune had built it when I was five, and my toes knew every weird uneven inch of the floor, so I knew the cramped little room with its one bench was the same place, but it still didn't seem believable that it could be. And there on the bench was Claire, with Ruth Marsters and Philippa Wax, waiting together in their towels as if I'd been in their way even though there were two other cubicles.

They all stared at me as if I were a stranger. And they surely had to be strangers, too, even though they did look and sound almost exactly like the women who collectively be-tween them had told me ten thousand times or so that I was a sad burden to my saint of a mother. Everyone who lived here had a reason, something that had driven them to shut themselves away from the rest of the world. Mum had come to live here because she wasn't willing to compromise with selfishness, but these three women, and a lot of the other people here, they hadn't come here to do good, they'd come here to have good done for them. And they'd looked at me and saw a perfectly healthy child, with this magical being lav-ishing love and attention and energy upon her, and they all knew what it would have meant to them to have that same unbounded gift, and here I was, apparently sullen and un-grateful, soaking it up to no good end at all that they could see.

Which wasn't an excuse for being nasty to a miserable lonely kid, and just because I understood their reasons didn't mean I was ready to forgive them. I should've enjoyed it so much, I should've spoken to them with contempt: *That's right, I'm back, and I've grown; have any of you accomplished anything in the last four years besides horrible gossip?* Mum would have sighed when she heard about it, and I wouldn't have cared. I'd have floated out of the bathhouse on a cloud of mean greedy pleasure.

But I couldn't do it. Apparently, if I wasn't going to be angry at Orion, I couldn't be angry at anyone.

I didn't say anything to them, and they didn't say anything

to me, or to each other. I turned and dried off with their silence behind my back and put on the clothes Mum had left
for me on the hook next to my shower stall: actual new cotton knickers fresh from the cellophane, and a linen shift with
a drawstring at the neck, big and loose enough to fit me; one
of the people in the commune made them for medieval reen-
actors. A pair of handmade sandals from one of our other
neighbors, just a flat sole cut out of wood with a leather cord.
I hadn't worn anything this clean in four years, except the day
I'd first put on Orion's shirt. The last clothes I'd grudgingly
bought were a couple of pairs of lightly used underwear off
a senior at the start of my junior year, when there just wasn't
enough left of my last pair to cast make-and-mend on them.
New underwear went for insanely exorbitant prices inside:
you could've bought an all-round antidote potion for a pair
of unworn pants, and now here I was with untold riches.

I couldn't enjoy them any more than I could enjoy a round
of delicious payback. I put them on, because it would have
been stupid not to, and of course it felt better, it felt wonderful, but I looked at the ragged filthy ruin of Orion's shirt,
which wasn't fit for anything but the bin, and feeling better
felt worse. I tried to make myself chuck it along with the rest
of my old things, but I couldn't. I folded it up and put it into
one of my pockets—it was so worn thin, half made of magic
at this point, that I could get it to the thickness of a handkerchief. I cleaned my teeth—new toothbrush, fresh minty
paste—and walked out. It was dark outside by then. Mum
had a small fire going outside the yurt. I sat down on one of
the logs next to the pit and after a bit, I cried some more. It
wasn't original or anything, I realize. Mum came round and
put an arm around my shoulders again, and Precious climbed
into my lap.

I spent the next day sitting blankly by the dead firepit. I was clean, I was fed, I was sitting outside in sunshine and a brief shower—I didn't move—and sunshine again. Mum puttered around me quietly, handed me food to eat and tea to drink, and left me alone to process. I wasn't processing. I was trying very hard not to process, because there wasn't anything to process except the raw horrible truth that Orion was somewhere off in the void screaming. I could almost hear him, if I thought about it too long: I could almost hear him saying, *El, El, help me, please. El.*

Then I looked over, because it wasn't just in my head anymore. There was a small odd bird standing on the log right next to me: purple-black, with an orange beak and bright-yellow marks around its head, and a big round beady black eye it tilted up towards me. "El?" it said to me again. I stared down at it. It stretched its head out long and made a sound like a person coughing, then straightened up again. "El?" it said again. "El? El, are you okay?" and it was Liu's voice: not exactly the same sound maybe, but the accent and the way she'd have said the words; if it had spoken from behind me, I'd have thought she was there.

"No," I told the bird, honestly. It tilted its head and said, "Nǐ hǎo," and then, "El?" again, and then it said, in my voice, "No. No. No." Abruptly it took wing and darted away into the trees.

We'd had an agreement, me and Aadhya and Liu: I was going to go and get my hands on a phone, as soon as I made it out, and text them both. They'd made me memorize their numbers. But that had all been part of the *plan,* and I couldn't make myself do any of it.

It had been a perfectly good plan. I had the Golden Stone sutras all ready: they were snugly bundled together with all my notes and translations inside a soft bag I'd crocheted out of my last threadbare blanket, to pad them inside my painstakingly carved book chest, which had itself been bundled into my waterproof shower bag. I'd slung it on my back when the gears first started to turn. They were the only thing I'd taken out with me, my prize—the one truly wonderful thing I'd got out of the Scholomance. I would have swapped them for Orion if some higher power had made me the offer, but it would've taken me two heartbeats instead of one to agree.

The plan was, if I made it out alive, I was going to hug Mum half a million times, roll around in grass for a while, hug Mum some more, and then take the sutras and head to Cardiff, where there was a decent-sized wizard collective near the stadium. They weren't powerful enough or rich enough to build an enclave of their own, but they were working towards it. And I'd have offered to take the mana they'd saved up and build them a little Golden Stone enclave outside the city instead. Nothing grandiose, but a space good enough to tuck their kids in at night and keep them safe from whatever stray mals had been left behind by the purge.

Orion hadn't been part of the plan. Yeah, it had occurred to me that he could find me in Cardiff, if he came looking. But he would have been landing in his own parents' arms and the wider embrace of the united New York enclave. They'd all have fought him leaving with every clinging vine of sentiment and loyalty they could wrap around him. So I really sincerely hadn't expected Orion to come: I'm good at pessimism. And I hadn't *needed* him to come, either. I'd been ready to go on with my own life.

I don't know that I'd even needed him to make it out alive.

I had been fairly sure before we began on our objectively lunatic plan of escape that I'd end up dead myself, and at least half the people I cared about along with me, with Orion topping the likely list. If our plans had gone pear-shaped, if the maleficaria had broken loose from the honeypot illusion and started slaughtering us, and we'd all had to run for it, and in the chaos he'd been one of the people who hadn't made it out, I think I'd have cried and mourned him and gone on.

But I couldn't bear this. I couldn't bear that he'd been the *only* one who'd died getting all of us out. Getting *me* out. Even if he'd chosen on his stupid own to turn round and face Patience, even if he'd chosen to shove me away, still being the hero he thought he had to be to be worth anything. I couldn't bear for that to be his story.

So I wasn't okay. I didn't go and get a phone, and I didn't try to call Aadhya and Liu. I didn't go to Cardiff. I just sat around, inside or outside the yurt mostly at random, and kept trying to change it in my head, play the whole thing out again, as if I could change what had happened by finding some better set of things I should've done.

I can say from experience that it was very much like when you've been humiliated in the cafeteria or the bathroom in front of a dozen people, and because you couldn't think of any clever comebacks at the time, you keep daydreaming about all the viciously witty things you might have said. As Mum had pointed out to me several times during my childhood, really what you're doing is bathing yourself endlessly in the humiliation all over again, while your tormentor sails on perfectly unaffected. She was right, and I'd known it even then, but knowing had never stopped me before. It didn't stop me now. I stayed stuck, going back and forth on the rails, trying to find a way to shove the train that had already arrived off the tracks somehow.

After a few more days of trying to rewrite history on the inside of my own head, I came up with the magnificent and highly original idea that maybe I could do it on the world instead. I went into the yurt and dug up one of my old notebooks from primary school that Mum had saved in a box, and I found a blank page towards the back and scribbled a few lines down, something something *l'esprit de l'escalier.* The idea felt very French, just like my best and most elegant killing spell, and if that doesn't sound like a recommendation to you, I can't imagine why.

I can't tell you what I was thinking when I started creating a spell that would let me literally alter the fabric of reality. That sort of thing just doesn't work on a long-term basis, no matter how powerful you are. Reality is more powerful, and it will eventually bounce your attempt off, generally disintegrating you personally along with it. But you can certainly have a nice long run—at least from your own perspective—in your own personal fantasy universe, and the longer you go and the more power you have to keep it going, the more havoc you'll wreak on yourself and others in its final implosion. And if I'd stopped long enough to think about it, I'd have *known* all that: both how useless it would ultimately be and how much damage I'd do if I tried it. But I didn't. I was just trying to find an exit from the agony, like I was in the maw-mouth with Orion, mindlessly desperate to escape.

Mum found me looking for the next line of the spell, which I was almost certainly going to find. I'm very bad at writing spells of my own devising unless they cause vast amounts of destruction and terror, and then I'm absolutely unmatched. Her tolerance for the grieving process didn't extend to watching me tie the whole planet into knots and eradicate myself along the way. She got one look at what I was writing and tore it out of my hands and threw it into the fire, and then she went down on her knees in front of me, caught my hands tight, and pinned them against her chest. "Darling, darling," she said, and then she freed one of her hands and put her palm against my forehead, pressing hard between my eyebrows. "Breathe. Let the words go. Let the thoughts go. Let them slip away. They're already going, out on the next breath. Breathe. Breathe with me."

I obeyed her because I couldn't help myself. Mum had almost never used magic on me, even when I was exactly the howling furious storm of a child that any other wizard parent would have been spelling into calm every other day. Most wizard kids can fend off their parents' coercion spells by the age of ten, but when I was four and screamed because I didn't want to go to sleep, I got three hours of lullabies, not a spell to make me go quietly to bed; when I was in a kicking rage at seven, I got understanding and space and patience, even when what I would've liked much better was a screaming match and a good dose of soothing potion. I don't actually advocate for this approach—in retrospect I still think I would quite have appreciated a dose of soothing potion once in a while—but it did mean that I wasn't any good at blocking Mum's magic, at least not instinctively, and instinct was the only thing I was running on in the first place.

Anyway, Mum's magic feels good, because it's only ever meant to be good for you, and I leaned straight into the relief of it. By the time I did manage to wrench myself loose, she'd knocked the beginnings of the spell out of my head and also made me feel better enough that I could recognize I'd been doing something incredibly stupid.

Not that I was grateful for her help or anything. It only made me feel worse knowing she'd been perfectly right. After she let me go, I was too unwillingly calm to storm off into the ongoing rain, but I also didn't want to do anything unendur-

ably horrible like talk about my feelings or say thanks for saving me from unmaking myself and blowing up the commune
if not half of Wales. I had to find another way to escape, so I
got out my book bag and took out the sutras.

Mum had gone to the other side of the yurt to wash pots
with her back turned, to give me space. But after a while she
glanced back and saw me reading and said in her peacemak-
ing voice, which I both loved and hated passionately, "What
are you reading, love?"

Of course I wanted to boast of them and show them off,
but instead I just muttered surly, "It's the Golden Stone sutras.
I got them at school," except I didn't finish the sentence because Mum made a noise like someone had stabbed her repeatedly and dropped the plate she was cleaning to thump on
the ground. I stared at her, and she was staring back, wide
and terrible and frozen, and then she fell to her knees and put
her hands over her face and literally howled like an animal on
the floor.

I panicked completely. She was in roughly the same state
of hysteria as I'd been myself, half an hour before, but I'd had
her for help, and she had me, and I'm not very useful unless
you're under attack by an army of maleficaria. I hadn't any
idea what to do. I literally ran round the yurt twice looking at
things wildly before getting her a cup of water. I begged her
to drink it and tell me what was wrong. She just kept keening.
Then I got the idea she had been poisoned by the washing-up
liquid and tried to test it for toxins, found nothing, decided I
had to cast an all-heal, didn't have enough mana, and started
doing jumping jacks to build it, all while she wept. I must
have looked a proper twat.

Mum had to pull herself out of it. She gulped a last few
times and said, "No, no," to me.

I stopped, panting, and went on my knees facing her and

caught her shoulders. "Mum, what is it, just tell me what to do, I'm sorry. I'm sorry." I forgave her everything, I forgave her for not loving Orion, I forgave her telling me to keep away from him, I forgave her for making me feel better. None of it mattered in the face of this upheaval, as if my awful half-written spell had somehow already begun to take the whole world apart underneath me.

She made a slow drag of breath that was a moan and then said, "No, love. Don't. It's not for you to be sorry, it's me. It's me." She shut her eyes and squeezed my shoulder when I was going to say something inane like no it's all right, and then she said, "I'll tell you. I'll have to tell you. I have to go to the woods first. Forgive me darling. Forgive me," and she got up like an old woman pushing herself off the floor slowly and went outside straight into the pouring rain.

I sat on the bed hugging the sutras to me like a stuffed bear, still in a restrained panic that only stayed restrained because Mum did go into the woods all the time, and came out again with calm and healing and care, so some part of me could cling to the hope that she'd come out with them again this time, but nothing like this had ever happened in my life, and the bad things in my life were always my fault. I nearly cried when Mum did come back, only an hour later, wet through with her dress plastered in tissue-paper bunches to her legs and muddied all up the front and over her face like she'd lain in the dirt for a while. I was so desperately relieved to see her, all I wanted was to hug her.

But she said, "I have to tell you now," and it was her deep, far-off voice, the one that only comes when she's doing major arcana: when a wizard comes to her who's trying to be healed of something really awful, a deep curse or magical illness of some kind, and she's telling them what they have to do, only this time she was telling *herself*. She took my hands for a moment and held them, and then she pulled my face down and kissed me on the forehead like I was going away, and I was half sure that Mum was about to tell me that she'd been wrong all these years and I really was doomed after all to fulfill the prophecy of death and destruction and ruin that's been hanging over my head since I was a tiny child, and that I had to leave her forever.

Then she said, "Your father's family were from one of the Golden Stone enclaves."

"The ones built with the sutras?" I said it in a broken whisper, not really a question. I'd known my father's family, the Sharmas, had once lived in an enclave—an ancient strictmana enclave in the north of India somewhere—that had been destroyed a couple of centuries ago during the British occupation. The Golden Stone sutras were old, old Sanskrit spells, and I knew they'd been used to build a whole slew of enclaves in that part of the world, ages ago. So that was a bit of a coincidence, but it didn't seem anything bad. I was still terrified: I could feel something absolutely horrible was coming.

"Enclaves are built with malia," Mum said. "I don't know how they do it, but you can feel it when you're there, if you let yourself. All of them, except the Golden Stone enclaves. Your father told me about them."

"But, that's good, then," I said, high and begging; I held the sutras out to her like an offering. "There's no malia in building them, Mum. I've read all of it, I can't cast it all yet but I'm sure—" but her face was crumpling in as she looked down at the beautiful book. She put out her hand over it trembling, fingers hovering a little bit away as if she couldn't bear to actually touch it, and then they curled back into her palm again without even brushing the cover.

"Arjun and I, we wanted to build a new golden enclave,"

THE GOLDEN ENCLAVES ✦ 29

she said. "We thought, if we could only show everyone a better—" She cut herself off and started over, in a familiar way: she always reminds people not to explain when they're trying to ask forgiveness, not to offer excuses until they're invited. "We wanted to build a golden enclave. We wanted to find the sutras," she said, and I think maybe by then I was beginning to understand, but my head was going blank, full of white noise. "We thought our best chance was there in the school, in the library. My darling, I'm so sorry. We cast a summoning spell. We summoned the sutras, and we left the payment open."

Chapter 2
THE GARDENS OF LONDON

"WE THOUGHT IT HADN'T WORKED," Mum said. "We thought they'd just been lost or destroyed."

I'd already sat back down on the bed by then. I was still clutching the sutras to me. Maybe the right reaction should have been to set them on fire, but at the moment they felt like the only thing in the universe that I could rely on.

I'm not sure if it was better or worse than Mum telling me that she had changed her mind about me and was now convinced I was in fact doomed to go mortally evil. I've been preparing myself to hear that my entire life. It would have smashed me into pieces, but I was braced for it. I wasn't ready to be told that Mum had, that she and Dad had—I didn't even know what to call it.

Summoning is like make-and-mend. There's a basic version of it in any given language, which you then elaborate on, depending on what you're asking for and what you're offering up in return. You can use a summoning to get almost anything you want—including unwilling sacrificial victims— as long as the thing you want exists. But you have to pay for it—and more than what the average wizard would call its fair market value. If you do a summoning and you lowball the offer, don't put enough mana in or make enough of a sacrifice, then you lose whatever you *have* put up, and the summoning doesn't work anyway.

But there's another way to cast a summoning. You don't have to put in any mana or make an offering at all. If you don't, if you just leave the payment wide open, you're offering anything and everything you have, including your life. Or, in this case, offering to have one of you spend a dragged-out eternity screaming in the belly of a maw-mouth, and offering to have the other crawl out of the Scholomance gates alone and sobbing to bear and raise your child.

And you're offering up the life of that child herself. That handful of cells so completely dependent on your body that you *can* offer her up without even realizing you're doing it. Making her *a burdened soul* as my great-grandmother colorfully put it in her prophecy, signed onto the family mortgage from birth, a vessel to be filled up with terrible slaughtering power and a hideous destiny of murder and destruction, the balance for your pure idealism. All of you paying together, just so that one day that child will earn a chance, just a thin sliver of a chance, to jump up and grab a copy of the spellbook you're after, off a library shelf at school, to accomplish your dream of generosity and freedom.

I still had my arms wrapped around the sutras, my fingers tracing the embossed pattern in the leather without thinking about it. I'd known that they were a windfall, luck beyond anything I'd earned; I had just held on to them all the tighter, and never asked questions. And now it turned out actually I'd been paying for them my whole life, without ever having agreed to it up front. I'd been paying in the single worst moment of my life: when I'd had to face the maw-mouth in the library, the one that had been waiting at the end of the stacks after I'd made that jump and got the sutras off the shelf. The last chunk of my parents' debt.

I suppose I'd had a choice about that. I hadn't had to fight the maw-mouth. I could have let it go and kill several dozen freshmen instead. I could have paid off the debt of my parents' courage with that cowardice, sending a pack of children to go down screaming into ten thousand years of hell, and set the balance right that way. I'd paid with my own screaming instead. I didn't want to remember, but I couldn't help it, queasy and shivering on the cot, clammy-skinned with the memory. Some part of my brain would still be screaming, still in that maw-mouth, the rest of my life.

And that was why I'd told Orion we couldn't fight Patience, why I hadn't been able to imagine trying. So—maybe that was why he'd shoved me out. Because I'd told him we couldn't do it, that *I* couldn't do it, and so he'd thought he had to save me from it, too. From the horror he'd known I couldn't bear to face. Maybe that meant *he'd* been part of the price, too.

I looked down at the sutras in my lap, paid off in full. I'd loved them, so much. I'd been ready to build my whole life upon them. Now even that—all my plans for the future, my own dream of golden enclaves—suddenly felt like something I'd inherited instead of something I'd chosen. I wanted to be angry about it; I felt I had a right to be angry.

Mum did too. She was standing in front of me like she was waiting for me to deliver a verdict. Intent doesn't matter, she'd say, when you've really injured someone else. You need to be open to their pain and anger if you're ever to make things whole between you. Only I couldn't find any to give her. She and Dad hadn't offered me up as a sacrifice in their place—they'd both paid worse than I had, and they hadn't even known I was there to be offered in the first place.

But if I couldn't be angry, I didn't know what to be. I didn't even quite believe it yet really, not in my gut. I don't mean I thought she was lying or making it up; it just wasn't something that I could fully believe that Mum had done. She could hurt me, could make me angry. I'd harangued her for half my childhood to take me to an enclave, and she'd refused: she hadn't been willing to make that bargain even to save my life, although she'd have died to protect me. But she couldn't have done *this*. She couldn't have put me on the hook for a summoning without my full knowledge and consent. She'd have cut her own heart out first.

Which of course was still true, and she more or less had, but that didn't help me organize my own feelings. Just because the brakes failed instead of the driver doesn't mean the lorry hasn't hit you, only in this case it felt more like a star had broken the laws of physics to collapse and destroy my planet.

"I need to think," I said. I meant it literally. I couldn't think. I couldn't make sense of it in any way that would let me do or say or even feel anything. Precious crept up from the small nest she'd made herself next to my pillow and curled up on my shoulder, a tiny lump of comfort, but that wasn't any use. I didn't need comforting. I wasn't unhappy. I was lost in the mountains without a compass.

Mum took it as instructions. She said, "I'll go to the bath-house," and went at once. I didn't know if I wanted her to go, but I also couldn't decide to call after her to stay. So she went and left me in the yurt alone.

It was still raining. The roof hole cover needed mending; one of the seams was leaking a little bit. Mum usually kept things in good trim, but after all, she'd spent the last four years waiting to find out if her only child was going to live. I watched each fat drop slowly accumulating until it finally plinked down softly. Mum had spent roughly half my childhood trying to teach me to meditate, how to find peace. I'd never been very good at it. Now I managed a full half hour just blank and staring at the leaking rain, although I didn't find any peace in the process; my head was full of white noise, not stillness.

The power of inertia would probably have kept me sitting there another month, trying to find some way to feel something. Only inertia wasn't given the chance. "So you really are just sitting here in the middle of nowhere," a voice said. "I almost didn't believe her."

It took me a moment even to register that someone was talking to me. No one ever came to the yurt to talk to me; if they looked in and Mum wasn't here, they went away again without saying anything to me, unless they really wanted her urgently, and in that case, sometimes they asked me where she was, and I ignored them belligerently until they went away. It took me another moment to realize that I recognized the voice talking to me, and that it was Liesel, and another one after that to turn my head so I could stare at her blankly.

She was standing in the doorway of the yurt, looking in at me. The last time I'd seen her had been less than a week ago, at the Scholomance gates, in the same outgrown rags we'd all been wearing by graduation. Now she was wearing a slim knee-length dress that looked like she was on her way to a party, with sections curved in on the sides that were made of some scaled fabric that gleamed like pearl—amphisbaena scales, I realized distantly; the ones Orion had got her, in exchange for her doing all his remedial homework. They were edged in a thin crust of silver and malachite beads: almost certainly some kind of protective artifice. Her blond hair shone like polished metal, grown out by half a foot and sculpted into unnaturally perfect curves that spilled over her shoulders like a glamourous image from the 1940s. She'd earnt herself a spot in London enclave—you can do that when you're the valedictorian—and they'd evidently given her enough power that she'd kitted herself out properly.

She grimaced as she knocked off the rim of mud valiantly trying to climb onto her pristine white shoes and came inside the yurt. She looked around with a faintly incredulous expression, which got substantially less faint when it reached the leak in the roof that was still dripping in rain. "This is where you live?" she demanded.

"What are you doing here?" I said, instead of responding to that. Over the last week, even in the depths of grief and confusion, I'd been rapidly remembering the many reasons why I hated the yurt. However, I didn't feel like confiding them to Liesel. It's not that I disliked her, exactly. You don't *dislike* a steamroller, and in fact it's fantastically useful in many circumstances, such as when you're trying to organize the collective exodus of five thousand kids against an even larger incoming tide of maleficaria, which she'd taken charge of for us all. You just don't particularly want to have an intimate heartfelt conversation with the steamroller, especially if you think it might turn round and come right over you.

"What do you think?" She sounded testy. "London is in trouble. We need you."

I didn't actually respond, but I suppose my expression conveyed several of my thoughts, primary among them the strong feeling that she should fuck right off, but also wondering how London was in trouble and what they needed *me* for—I'm powerful, but I'm not more powerful than one of the most powerful enclaves in the world—and why she imagined that I cared.

Liesel scowled a bit and deigned to explain. "Whoever took out Bangkok, they did it again. They hit both Salta and London, on graduation day, while we were in the middle of coming out. Salta's been completely destroyed—two hundred wizards dead. And half the wards on London have come down. And here you sit in the rain," she added, in deep disgust.

She really did an excellent job of making it seem perfectly ludicrous for me to be living quietly in my own home instead of keeping close tabs on the latest news from international wizarding circles. In case you were wondering if you'd missed something of significance yourself, the actual cities of Bangkok and Salta were both perfectly fine, and if I'd had a telly to turn on, there wouldn't have been a word about any disaster in London. Enclaves generally go up and down without mundanes being any the wiser. Separating yourself from the mundane world is the point of building an enclave in the first place: opening up a nice safe sheltered space into the void makes it harder for reality to get at you, which means it's easier to build artifice like spectacular armor-gowns and to avoid unpleasant things like mals that want to eat your children.

In justice to Liesel, however, enclaves getting attacked and destroyed left and right *was* highly significant news from the perspective of most wizards, even me. I had substantial objections to the whole enclave system, and I'd opted firmly out of joining one myself, but that didn't mean I approved of some psychotic maleficer deliberately ripping them open all over the world and dumping a lot of otherwise innocent people into flaming ruin or out into the void.

However, that was some distance from trying to *do* something about it. Staying here in a nice quiet yurt in the woods seemed like a much better option than getting involved, even with the leaky roof. "Sorry, but London will have to look after itself," I said.

"Why, so you can grow moss along with your house?" Liesel said, cuttingly. "This is no place for you."

"Who asked you, exactly?" I said.

"Liu did, of course," Liesel said, taking the question literally, and then waved her hand over me and my patently absurd existence. "How would I know, otherwise? We all thought you were dead along with Lake."

I stared at her, feeling mildly betrayed; although to be fair, if Liu's goal had been to find someone to forcibly drag me out of a hole who wasn't a continent away, Liesel wasn't a bad choice. "She didn't tell you to recruit me to help *London*."

"No," she said. "She told me you were alive and sitting in a commune with no electricity and no plumbing. I didn't need to be told this was stupid."

"Does this sort of thing usually work for you, insulting people you're asking for favors?" I said, although it wasn't very heated; it came out more as a fascinated inquiry. She'd got lucky with the timing of her approach: I still wasn't able to generate anger, so what I felt mostly was impressed by her chutzpah. I couldn't even imagine what Liesel had in mind for me to do, unless it was along the lines of set a thief to catch a thief.

"I am not asking you for a *favor*," Liesel said. "A mawmouth broke through the wards this morning. A big one. They're holding it off from the council room, but not for much longer. Once it gets in there, that will be the end of London. No one's willing to send help. They're all afraid for themselves. Well?" She finished on a belligerent note, while my whole stomach turned over and wrapped itself into a small lump like bread dough being punched down.

That *would* be a true disaster, no matter your feelings on enclaves: London enclave, one of the biggest and most powerful in the world, and all its vast stockpile of mana, going into the belly of a maw-mouth. The thing might get nearly as big as Patience in that one gigantic meal. And in the meantime whoever this maleficer was, ripping apart enclave wards, they would be out there, too, presumably getting ready to have another go. What a spectacular team they could become. It wouldn't much matter if I refused to fulfill my own prophesied destiny of spreading death and disaster if instead I stood back and let the two of them sort it out for me.

That still wasn't anything like an inducement, of course. I very much didn't want to fight a maw-mouth. I'd have done it to save Orion, but that didn't mean I was ready to make a regular job of it. Everyone's afraid of being devoured by a maw-mouth, but I'm afraid of it on a much more intimate and specific level. As far as I know, I'm only the second wizard alive who's ever survived the experience, and the other one's the Dominus of Shanghai.

But—I had in fact *survived*, and the maw-mouth hadn't. I'm completely alone in the distinction of having killed one of them all by myself. Even the legendary Krakow incident of dubious historicity involved a circle of seven, and the purge of Shanghai had required more than forty wizards all told, building mana together for the attempt. And in fact, I'd killed *two* maw-mouths. A second very small one had come into the school during graduation, lured in by our honeypot trap—and Liesel had seen me destroy it. And that was why she was here to recruit me to come and help.

So it wasn't an inducement, but it was *movement:* a hard shove out of the rut I was sitting in. "Well, that's a magnificent offer," I said, trying to fend her off. "It's just what I've wanted, to risk my life fighting a maw-mouth for the London enclave. Why exactly did the council think I'd agree?"

"We didn't ask their opinion. You think there was time to talk it over?" Liesel said. "We came for you ourselves."

"Who's *we*?"

"Alfie and Sarah are down there. I told them to wait." Liesel waved a hand irritably in the direction of the rest of the commune. "What difference does it make? Do you want a signed contract for payment? You wouldn't take anything before. Are you going to be a hermit your whole life just because Lake is dead? Grow up! Someone's tearing down the enclaves of the world, there's a maw-mouth about to devour London. This is no time for you to sit around crying. *He* wouldn't."

I stood up in outrage—I didn't whack myself on the roof struts again, but it was a near thing—but Liesel just folded her arms and stared me in the face and didn't give an inch. Vicious and brilliant as usual, because I couldn't even argue. Orion would absolutely have sailed off to help, if he'd been alive to do it. And he might have been—if I'd done something different, if I hadn't panicked and tried to get him just to run away, the last time a maw-mouth had shown up for me to fight.

I didn't actually say anything to Liesel. She was right, but I could still with great pleasure have slapped her. Anyway, she recognized that she'd won; she gave a short nod and turned and went out of the yurt to wait for me.

I stood there for a moment alone with the irregular dripping. I turned and stared down at the sutras on the bed, the cover a satiny gleaming in the dim light. I bent down and picked them up and carefully packed them into their book chest and stood with it a moment, holding it in my hands.

They had ridden me all the way here, back to the summoner, only Mum wasn't going to be able to do anything with them. They weren't healing spells. The final incantation needed so much mana capacity I didn't actually see how it could even be cast by anyone who wasn't me.

Was *I* going to do anything with them? I didn't know anymore, but it clearly didn't make sense for me to take them to London for a fight. In fact, that was a selfish incentive to go. At least it saved me having to decide right away.

"I'm going to leave you with Mum," I said. I'd got used to talking to them. "I know she'll look after you for me until I get back."

Ordinarily I'd have said a lot more—I'd have fretted and told them how sorry I was to leave them for even a minute, rambled out some plans for them, anything to encourage them to stay. I couldn't do it this time. If they vanished on me, that would save me the trouble of deciding. I didn't want that to happen, but only just enough to do what I was doing. I touched the cover once more, then I closed the lid on them, and carried them over to the table and left them there, safely out of the rain.

Then I wrote Mum a note on a scrap of paper: *London enclave's in trouble, I've gone to help.* I almost left it at that. I couldn't help thinking that it would have been a decent revenge for *Keep far away from Orion Lake.* It still hurt like knives to think of him gone with no one missing him, the person and not the power, except me alone. What I really wanted even more was to write her a long juvenile screed telling her off for having judged Orion after what she'd done herself: I could bundle all my miseries up together and heave them out onto the page in one steaming mess.

But I couldn't bear to do that to her, even if I almost felt I owed it to him. I stood over my scribble for a single lingering moment of sour resentment, wallowing in the fantasy of meanness, and then I added, *Home soon. Love, El.*

When I turned to the doorway, Precious was sitting up right in the middle of it, glowing white against the overcast sky outside and glaring up at me meaningfully. *"You* don't make any sense to take to a fight, either," I told her, but she ran at me and came up my leg and jumped for the lower hem of my dress, then scampered up and crawled into my pocket. I put my hand inside it and she curled up warm and small and determined within it. "All right," I said. I couldn't make myself take her out and put her down.

Liesel was standing impatiently on the muddy footpath, under what was pretending for the benefit of mundanes to be an umbrella but was actually some kind of artifice keeping her dry. It bobbed over between us, and we went down the hill without a single drop making it through.

Alfie and Sarah were all the way down by the main buildings of the commune, doing their best to charm the locals. It was really odd to see them, in their own impractically glamourous outfits which should've got dirty just walking in from the caravan pitch. They were even standing wrong, holding themselves unnaturally straight with their faces in stiff smiles. I thought at first they were simply overdoing it, trying to put their best foot forward for the mundanes; Alfie and Sarah had probably barely ever come out into the real world in their whole childhood. Being around mundanes made it hard to cast spells and use artifice, and I imagine that was especially uncomfortable for enclavers, since they had so much mana to spare that they used magic to keep off the rain when an umbrella would really do perfectly well if you even needed one.

But when we came into view, Alfie's head jerked round towards me so hard that I realized he was just desperately holding the line and actually he was all but vibrating with tension. "El, so good to see you," he said, with what could have passed for an air of experiencing a mildly pleasant surprise, unless you knew him, and then by his standards, he sounded two steps short of complete hysteria, too loud and frayed at the edges. "Liesel's told you? Sorry to poach her like this," he said smilingly to Philippa, who was one of the mundanes being charmed, exactly as if he were swooping past a lunch table at the Scholomance full of loser kids to carry me off to his own. Which he'd tried to do with me in the past without success, but it's a fairly reliable method for enclavers usually, so he hadn't lost the habit of trying.

And in this case, Philippa was there and ready to help him. She darted a look at me that was faintly incredulous—what were these ludicrously posh people after *me* for?—and said only, "I'm sure it's nothing to us," a bit disdainfully, as if she didn't think much of his taste. I imagine she would have been perfectly happy for him to drop me in an unmarked ditch when he was done.

Alfie didn't want any more permission, and not inaccurately assumed I couldn't much want to stay anywhere in Philippa's vicinity. He was instantly turning towards me with his arm outstretched to gather me up. I eyed him resentfully, but inertia was on his side, now. I'd come down the hill, after all. Why had I bothered, if I wasn't going? So I went.

Their transport was waiting on the hardstanding, looking exactly as weird as they did. Actual posh mundanes—who do visit fairly regularly—would've come with a Land Rover or a massive camper van, wearing raw denim and clean trainers. Their car was pretending really hard to be something between an Edwardian racing car and a 1930s American gangster car, with a ridiculously long bulbous nose and a cab that looked exactly big enough for one person to sit in comfortably.

But the racing car opened a door and let us inside, with no

difficulty about room, even though there were now four of us to cram into it. I don't mean we were suddenly in Narnia or the TARDIS or anything. You can't actually create real space, no matter how much mana you have, and even if you've got some way into the void—limitless as far as anyone's ever found out—that's very much not a pleasant place to try to exist as a real person. Enclaves generally resort to buying up large luxury apartments in the vicinity anytime they want to expand, and borrowing that space to use internally, but the further away the real space is, the more expensive the borrowing gets. Not even London enclave would waste the gobs of mana it would take to build and use a car that would hop you into some massive physical space regardless of how far away you were from it.

The car had to make do with space borrowed from its own oversized bonnet, which wasn't actually housing an engine, and a bit of psychic misdirection. When I got in, I was still just in a car, if an especially tidy one with polished brass fixtures and unnaturally pristine white leather seats: one of which was wide open for me, and came with the vague impression that everyone else was fairly crammed in. Likely we were *all* fairly crammed in, and just being given the space in turn, whenever our brains started to notice.

Alfie got in last and pulled the door shut after him, and instantly we roared off like a cavalcade of jets. Clearly the equivalent of the car yelling, "Yes, here's my *engine,* you can tell I've got *a real engine* driving me along," at anyone who cared enough to notice. As soon as we had gone into the trees and out of sight, the sound died completely, and then we were zipping along in perfect quiet, the countryside smearing past in my peripheral vision. I glanced out the window once, not a minute after we'd left, and we were already on a road I didn't know; the car was clearly sneaking through the world at unreasonable speeds. Probably that was why the antique design: the windows were minuscule and you couldn't see in or out very easily.

"Is there enough time for you to tell me what's going on?" I said, looking away to let the car get on with it.

"If we *knew*," Sarah muttered. She'd also upgraded since school, her hair in a mass of coiled braids woven through with a golden chain, and a dress of woven gold straps and flowing green chiffon embroidered with subtly disguised gold runes; it had resolutely refused to tangle up her legs or get muddy or wet in the least. She was almost as tense as Alfie, although she was eyeing me in a way that suggested she wasn't convinced they hadn't just graduated from the frying pan to the fire.

But Alfie had jumped ahead and was already taking out one of my least or rather most favorite things: a power-sharer. It was notably nicer than any of the ones I'd seen at school: the band was woven silk bound every few centimeters with thin strips of platinum that had been coated with some kind of iridescent layer, with tiny raw opal chunks embedded in the center of each one. It was designed like most of them to pass for a watch in public; this one even had a round inky glass plate for a face, like some sleek digital thing set into an elaborate antique frame, only Apple hasn't managed the trick of accessing the void yet, and that's what was under the glass. I wasn't sure what I thought of carrying a nice little hole in reality around with me, but I took it anyway, trying not to *want* it. Without much success. My fingers curled round it like claws the instant Alfie handed it over to me. I could feel the power on the other side: all the power in London's vast and ancient mana store, without a single barrier in the way.

"And they give new graduates unlimited lines now?" I said, with a façade of coolness, while I put it round my wrist and let it fasten itself up. It made the torrent of power I'd had in the Scholomance feel like a narrow creek.

Alfie was still staring at it himself, even as I put it on. "My father gave it to me," he said, low and tight. Usually the first thing you do when you get out of school is to start eating like a team of horses, but his face hadn't had time to fill in yet; his cheekbones were thin sharp lines under his skin. "It's a family heirloom . . ." He stopped and looked up at me desperately. "Liesel told you there's a maw-mouth?"

"What I'm not clear on is why your council's not taken care of it themselves," I said. "There *have* been maw-mouths killed by a circle before. London must be able to do it if anyone can." All right, so the only recorded case in modern history was the one in Shanghai, and several wizards died in the process, but given the alternatives, you'd think it would have been worth a try.

"They're trying! Do you think we're stupid?" Sarah said to me angrily. "We aren't looking to be told what any idiot can look up in the *Journal of Maleficaria Studies*."

I think she'd have liked to pick a fight, and I'd have been happy to oblige her, but Liesel was already jumping in to lecture me instead. "This isn't a maw-mouth coming out of nowhere. You think maw-mouths come after big enclaves, full of wizards, warded, all strong? They know better. I told you already, the enclave was hit by something *else* first. If London wasn't so old, so strong, the whole place would have gone, just like Salta and Bangkok. Salta didn't just lose wards; the whole enclave collapsed. London is stronger, it didn't come down, but the damage is still terrible. All the established thaumaturgical channels for the flow of mana have been disrupted! Do you not understand what that means?"

I did not, as it happens, understand what that meant, and judging by Alfie and Sarah's faces, they weren't completely clear on it themselves. None of us were thick or anything; it's just that kids who go for valedictorian in the Scholomance aren't on the same bell curve with the rest of us. I do strongly suspect that I know at least a dozen incantations that would disrupt established thaumaturgical channels very thoroughly, but those are the kind of spells I avoid thinking about as much as possible. "Well, it sounds bad," I said dryly. "Could you spare a detail or two?"

"No, and I shouldn't have to," Liesel said. "You can feel it anywhere in the place. You can feel it there!" She pointed at the power-sharer on my wrist. The only thing I'd noticed myself was the hideously alluring promise of infinite power, but I put my fingertips on the blank face and shut my eyes, trying a small pull—I would've quite liked to pull a *lot*—and instantly I did feel it. The power was there, endless oceans, but the oceans were churning, ninety-foot swells rising and crashing down again, whirling into maelstroms.

"You see?" Liesel said as I opened my eyes again. "I have not seen myself, but the damage must be somewhere in the enclave foundations. This maleficer has found some way to damage them, so they can get at the mana store."

Which did make perfect sense. Even the most vile maleficer in the world wouldn't go around picking fights with an entire enclave for no reason. But if they had worked out a way to get at the mana store of an enclave—absolutely. The bigger the better.

"Most likely they are staging an attack on the foundation point—the place in the void where the enclave is established. Such an attack would resonate throughout the enclave, throw everything off at once, the people and the artifice, all the wards." Liesel moved her hands together back and forth, like sloshing a bucket around. "And then the maleficer can strike at the mana store and steal as much as they can while the rest of the enclave is disrupted. So London did not collapse, because it is old enough and large enough that it has more than one foundation point, but it will still be months settling. And in the meantime—"

"The maw-mouth hit you," I finished.

Sarah had managed to cool off a bit in the interval. "Three wizards have already gone in, one after another, with a circle backing them," she said to me, more controlled. "They're all dead. All three, and a lot of the circles, too. More than a dozen senior wizards, we think."

"You *think?*"

"They're not exactly holding normal council sessions in the middle of this!" Alfie said. "All that we know for certain is that the first three tries didn't work, and—and there's only time for one more attempt." His voice wobbled around it. "Tonight. With three full circles, reinforcing each other. They'll all draw down as much mana as they can hold beforehand to try to avoid the disruptions. But . . . but Liesel thinks . . ."

"It's not going to work," Liesel said brutally. "Of course it's not going to work. Three times they've tried already, and each one failed in less than a day. In Shanghai, it took weeks to get at the core of the maw-mouth, and it only takes one bad moment for everything to go wrong. His shield flickers for a moment, the maw-mouth takes him, and then it will drain the circles until the others break. With three circles, he will last a little longer, but he still won't get to the core in time."

Alfie swallowed hard and said without looking at me, "It's—my father is—he'll be going in. He's volunteered."

"It's a stupid waste," Liesel said.

"But it's all right for me, is it?" I said, sourly. I didn't feel like being sorry for Alfie or his dad.

Liesel snorted. "You killed that maw-mouth at graduation in five minutes, with mana you were pulling from a crowd of stupid frightened children!"

"It was barely the size of a Shetland pony! Oddly I have the feeling that the maw-mouth that's killed a dozen senior wizards in London is a tiny bit bigger."

"So what?" Liesel said contemptuously. "Your chances are still better. You're not going to try?"

I scowled at her with enormous violence, because of course I had to try, but my expression was obviously open to misinterpretation; Alfie leaned forward and grabbed my hand in both of his and said, in ragged desperation, "El— I don't know what you'd want, I don't know what I can do, what anyone could do, to pay you back, but—I'll find a way. Anything. If the council won't make it good somehow, I'll do it myself. My word and my mana on it."

Which might sound stupid and old-fashioned, but wasn't in the least. *My word and my mana on it* is a perfectly valid incantation, when you do it properly and mean it. It's as valid as, for instance, an open-ended summoning, where you put everything you possibly have on the line to get what you want, only in this case what Alfie wanted was me, helping him, and to get it, he'd just offered to meet whatever the market rate for killing a maw-mouth would be.

I eyed him in enormous irritation. If London enclave *didn't* pay me back adequately—which was going to be hard since I couldn't actually think of anything I wanted on that scale, apart from things I couldn't get, such as bringing Orion back to life—it was entirely possible he'd have to literally follow me around trying to pay me back for the rest of his life. It's a very bad idea to promise an evil witch that you'll do *anything* in exchange for her help: that's how some maleficers end up with loyal Igor-like minions slavishly in their train. It'd look

THE GOLDEN ENCLAVES ✦ 49

really marvelous, Alfie of London trailing around behind me on a string. Whether I wanted him to or not.

"Don't make idiotic promises," I said cuttingly. "I'll see what I think of when I have a look at the thing. It can't be much further, can it?" I folded my arms and sulked back into my seat with furious determination to just get this over with.

"It'll be another—" Sarah began, but my intent won out: the car lurched to a halt and was standing in the vast circular drive of a crumbling monstrosity of a house. We climbed out. It was a giant ugly box of a mansion that wouldn't have looked out of place as an Asda, if one of the builders involved had stuck a portico of faux Greek columns on the front under the impression that actually they were rebuilding the Parthenon.

Another different builder, without communicating with the first, had been badly misinformed that there was a nice house here and had built an imposing outer wall around the property to safeguard it, festooned with spikes and topped off with a charming froth of barbed wire and security cameras. There was a choked fountain, and the drive was overgrown with moss and weeds gone everywhere, scattered broken bottles and crumpled plastic, with a thick pungent stink of rot and urine lying over everything as if an army of rats inhabited the place.

Absolutely magnificent, by enclave standards. London enclave probably owned six or seven like this in just this postcode, not to mention hundreds of massive flats throughout the city, perhaps whole condemned buildings and crumbling warehouses, all buried beneath layers of bureaucracy and paperwork. No one would ever come near, except the kind of person that the neighbors would call the mundane police to chase off on your behalf.

Meaning they could *use* all this space, the wasteland of

empty rooms and abandoned grounds. They could slip it inside the enclave, and thanks to the flexibility of the void around them, reorganize it there to suit themselves, as if you could look over your flat and decide you'd like thirty square meters moved from the living room to the kitchen that afternoon while you made dinner.

If a mundane ever did poke their nose into the dilapidated wreck of the place, they'd be given just enough of that space back to keep them from noticing while they were here, and if they were mad enough to want to linger for any length of time, with the whine and creak of a rotting house and the mysterious whooshes of air as space moved in and out of reality around them, it was entirely likely that one of the hungry mals lurking round the fringes of the enclave would manage to get them during the witching hours of the night, when mundanes do, briefly, believe in magic.

Alfie led us round the house to the back, and then through the garden along a path of hexagonal stepping-stones. I didn't take the time to inspect them closely, but they had some sort of runes etched into them. A tiny stone building, rather like a mausoleum for a single occupant, sat far back in the corner of the property, deep in shadow. As we got close, the paving stones started to give a bit underfoot, as if the ground had gone soft and boggy beneath them: the same queasy sensation I'd felt through the power-sharer, something gone wrong. Alfie hesitated a moment with his foot on the next one, feeling it too, then doggedly kept onward.

The doorway of the stone building was empty, with dangling hinges, exposing an empty narrow room beyond with a single broken window and more smashed bottles all over the floor, an invitation to slice your feet to ribbons. "Look away," he said, and after we turned away and then looked back, the door was in place waiting for us: made of thick planks of stained and dark ancient wood, with a boar-faced knocker holding a ring in its snout and a massive doorknob in the middle, both cast in solid bronze.

I could pick out runes scratched into the old wood, hidden among the other scars and lines: Old English incantations for warding and protection. I'd read Old English for three years solid at school; I'd rarely ever turned up any really useful spells, but I did recognize the extremely *useless* one I'd been assigned in sophomore year: a protection ward against storms at sea. Most probably the planks had been reclaimed from some ancient enchanted ship. Artifice wears out over time like anything, but if you start with something incredibly sound that's been well maintained, put a lot of effort into restoring it, and then build on the original magic with new layers of incantations going in roughly the same direction, you can end up with something far more powerful than if you started from scratch. Almost certainly no one with hostile intentions towards the enclave could even make it through this door.

The lock clicked at the first touch of Alfie's fingers, but the door didn't want to open; he had to put his shoulder to it and push, and then it gave way all at once—too quickly, which meant it was being helped along from the other side—and as he stumbled forward, Liesel instantly fired off one of her snappy lancing spells over his head, which sliced the lurking grom on the other side into two neat halves, top and bottom.

"Your wards really have gone down," I said, contemplating the perfect cross section through the middle of the grom. It had already done some successful hunting. There were several unfortunately identifiable remains still in the process of digestion, including a few fingers with the nails still on. Sarah was making retching noises. I'd like to say I became inured by being on my own in the Scholomance, but I was born inured, at least to ordinary levels of death and slaughter.

Then I looked up from the still-twitching body. While we'd all been so usefully distracted, the artifice of the doorway had seized the opportunity to work its way around us. Without any warning or even having taken a final step, I was suddenly *inside* London enclave, and I wasn't inured to that at all.

I've read about London enclave; I've even seen pictures in a few of the Scholomance library books, over the years. But that's like seeing a picture of a tree, and then actually climbing up in the tree with the branches going every way, the rustle of leaves and the smell and the bark under your fingers scraping and the wind going, and a thousand trees all round your tree, none of them being special and dramatic, just trees, and your tree was also just a tree being a tree, and the picture you'd looked at might be perfectly nice as its own flat thing, interesting and pretty and well composed, but it didn't have much to do with the reality of the tree.

We—and what was left of the grom—were on a rocky outcrop jutting from the face of a cliff like a terrace, looking down over a vast undulating garden. We were within some sort of huge greenhouse structure, but I barely noticed the shell. It didn't feel like being in a greenhouse or a garden, and it also didn't feel like being out in the woods. It was like old fairy-tale illustrations of gardens, where the flowers and vines and trees just pile up improbably on top of one another, everything blooming at once and forever in blithe disregard of the laws of nature.

A small gurgling waterfall was coming down the rock face beside us, continuing on underneath our outcrop and coming out the other side to go leaping down towards another landing, a bit bigger, just visible through nodding branches. I caught a glimpse of a table there, holding an empty silver carafe and narrow glasses and a domed serving tray: the suggestion that you could just turn a corner and be there, and anything you wanted would be waiting for you to eat or drink. We might have been completely alone, or in a small nook with a party in full swing round the corner; you could hear a bit of music over the waterfall if you made an effort.

Our landing had a lacy canopy of white-painted ironwork, overgrown with vines dangling yellow flowers and lamps of stained glass shaped like gramophones sprouting from the columns that held up the corners. There were two stairways going down in different directions: a narrow one of worn-down limestone going between two large boulders and another spiral one of iron descending out of the middle of the landing, along with two paths curving away to either side, each of them a promise of other spaces just out of sight, hidden away behind a curtain of willow and vines and the undulating hillside. Overhead the cliff cantilevered itself out, and vines and trees hung green, and far beyond them glimpses of the glasshouse roof, clearly designed by someone who'd visited Kew and thought *how small:* millions of triangles of stained glass set in thin iron, lightly frosted, giving the illusion of an open sky somewhere on the other side.

An open sky, just starting to go on towards night, even though it was full day outside. There must have been massive sunlamps above there to grow all the plants, but they were all turned down to twilight, or off completely. A couple of the nearby smaller lanterns had come on, evidently for our benefit, but even they were dim and struggling. It felt late. Not just the light, but the hour: the longer I stood there, the more I felt, palpable and certain, that the whole place was starting to fail. Liesel was right, you could feel it; something had gone wrong deep underneath. Whatever anchored this place in the void, it was crumbling like that hideous wreck of a mansion out on the other side.

And I did want to save it. I couldn't help that, even though I looked over the whole gorgeous sprawling wonder of it and knew instantly that Mum was right. I couldn't feel it right now, the malia she'd said was part of every enclave; the seasick crumbling sensation was too strong, overpowering everything else. But I didn't need to feel it myself to be certain that it was there. I had my sutras, and I already had some idea what I could build with them, my own magical doorway to a place of shelter. It wouldn't be anything like this. You could do a lot with a group of determined wizards working together and the greater-than-magic power of the assembly line, but you couldn't build a fairy city into the void, a stately pleasure-dome decree, and light up a new sun just for you and yours. There were a few thousand wizards in London enclave, but it would have taken ten times as many to build this place and keep it together. Of course they'd needed malia.

And they kept it running with malia, too, surely; the kind of malia that wouldn't look like malia. Most of the wizards who worked on this enclave probably lived an hour from the nearest entrance, to avoid the maleficaria that would constantly be hanging round to get at all this bounty of mana. They spent their days and strength to build mana and beauty for the enclave, and slogged home afterwards, and got paid cheap in mundane money and magical supplies and the hope, the tantalizing dangled hope, that one day, they'd get to stay. That their *kids* would get to stay. That wasn't the kind of malia that would make you sick; the enclavers weren't forcibly sucking mana out of those wizards and being fought off violently. They'd found a much safer way of extracting what they needed. Just like their kids did inside the Scholomance, leeching off the strength and work of all the loser kids, so they could make it out again to come home.

I wanted to punch Alfie in his sad anxious face for being part of it, him and Sarah and Liesel—who'd been a loser once herself and had chosen to jump on board with it anyway, as though it became all right, what they were doing to all the rest of us, because *she'd* been able to fight her way inside the garden walls.

And also I wanted to wander around these magical gardens for a month, a year; I wanted to go down every single path and find every hidden perfect nook. I wanted to go and taste whatever was in that silver jug, surely something indescribably wonderful. I wanted to climb to the top of this overgrown cliff and follow the path of that jumping waterfall stream all the way through this hidden world.

It wasn't anything like being inside the Scholomance gym. That place had been a lie: an imitation of the real world we couldn't get to and most likely would never see again. This wasn't a lie. This was a *story*, a fairy tale: it wasn't pretending to be real, it was just a place that couldn't be and hadn't been, a place of perfect beauty. And I could tell that if it sank beneath the wave, I'd lie down by the waters of Babylon and weep as much as any of the enclavers who lived here. I'd never quite be able to remember it properly. It would just be stuck in my head forever as a blurry image, something I kept trying to make come clear and couldn't.

I was angry at them for everything they'd done to build it, and I also couldn't stand to just turn my back and let it all come tumbling down. It wouldn't have fixed anything they'd done. It would only have made an even worse waste of it all. Or maybe that was just an excuse I was giving myself for wanting to save the place; maybe it was just my own greed talking. After all, they weren't going to tell *me* I couldn't come back for a pleasure stroll after I'd saved it. They'd be afraid to.

Alfie and Sarah and Liesel were all standing there watching me: hopefully, I thought. Like they'd seen me caught by the place. It had to be one of their most powerful recruiting tools, after all. It was only more irritating because it had worked. "Which way?" I said shortly.

"The maw-mouth is at the council room," Alfie said.

Chapter 3

THE OLD WALLS

ALFIE LED US DOWN THE NARROW STAIRCASE between the boulders. It ended in a strange small stony hollow, encircled by boulders taller than our heads, and one wall built of stone and marble, with an old Roman-temple-looking doorway. The pediment was held up by two statues of hooded figures, their heads bowed to hide their faces: a man holding an open book and a woman with a goblet in her hands. It was another piece of watchful artifice, just like the enchanted door we'd come through. As I went past them, I felt the strong sense that the man looked up from his book at me. But with Alfie in the lead, they let us through, into a dim hollow atrium.

I expect ordinarily it was a grand, dramatic space. There was a tiled mosaic floor beneath our feet, and statues lining up alongside a pool running the length of the room with a fountain at one end and a skylight overhead. There should have been an illusion of sky up there, made more believable by looking at it in the rippling water, but instead it was only the blank empty void, and the pool was still and pitch-dark, with nothing to reflect. The fountain spout was still letting a few drops fall occasionally like a leaking faucet, every unpredictable drop too-loud and echoing. This had to be the oldest part of the enclave, the one that had been built when London itself was just lurching its way towards becoming a city, and it was clearly meant to make you think of the glory that was Rome. Instead it felt like Pompeii just before the flames, a thin blanket of ash already laid down and more coming.

There was a single raised platform at the far end, with a table and chairs behind it that had the feeling of a bench in a courtroom: it was so clearly meant for a panel of grand superior enclavers to look down on someone come for an audience. This was surely where they welcomed the little people, the desperate supplicants come to be interviewed for the chance of an enclave space. I glared at the empty dais; I was ready to be angry at them even if I *was* here to help them. If the garden above was a fairy tale, there was another story being told in this place, one where the children never came home, and smiling wizards drank a soup of bones.

All the doorways off the room were leading to dark, just barely managing to suggest the slightest hint that there was something on the other side. Alfie stood for a moment uncertainly before he swallowed and set off through one to the left, with what I could only hope was confidence and not just blind hope. I followed after him, still seething, into an endless columned corridor, with more dark passages branching off to either side, and occasionally a tiny cell-like room: the height of enclave luxury in the days of yore, surely, but smaller than our Scholomance dorm rooms now. Standards had changed since the year 200.

I could barely see where we were going. There were sconces on the wall, but they were almost all dark, with only a handful still flickering with the tail ends of candlelight: just enough for us to barely see where we were putting our feet, and to make our shadows go dancing crazily over the walls around us, looming and wavering. The corridor went on for much longer than it possibly could have, even if the building was the size of a rugby pitch, stretching itself out with our unease. The sound of distant voices drifted out towards us from the side passageways, too muffled to make out words, clear enough to carry anxiety and fear. The nauseating heave of the mana ocean was still moving beneath my feet, and the anger leaked out of me little by little until it was all gone, and the only thing left was heavy cold dread.

All my Scholomance-honed instincts told me maleficaria were lurking on the other side of every dark doorway. The feeling only got stronger the further we went without being pounced on, because that always means one thing: there's something *worse* up ahead, the kind of mal that eats the other mals, and it's time to skive off from class and go to work in the library. Which was quite correct in this case, and we knew exactly what was up ahead. The very worst of the worse, and we were heading straight on towards it, and getting closer with every minute. The others knew it too; I could hear them all breathing raspily, loud in the narrow corridor. And then I realized it wasn't only *our* breathing I was hearing.

They all realized it a moment later. Alfie stopped short. The murmuring through the network of passageways was resolving into clearer sounds: gasps, whimpers, sobbing breaths. A woman screamed, "Help, oh god, help me," very briefly—a shrill exhausted cry that lasted only a moment, but echoed horribly down to us through half a dozen doorways. Someone who'd been eaten recently, if they still had the energy to be screaming. Probably someone Sarah had known: she'd drawn in a stuttering breath behind me, and when I glanced back, in the dim light I could see she had the back of her hand pressed over her mouth, tears gathered like a glaze over her dark eyes.

She looked back at me. "At graduation, you got that boy out of the maw-mouth," she said, barely above a whisper, a miserable kind of begging in her voice. I'd preferred the hostility.

"He hadn't properly gone down yet."

"But—"

"No," I said flatly, but Sarah kept staring at me, her face wobbling like jelly, as if she wasn't ready to trust me for it. "It would be like trying to put a single cow back together out of a butcher's case."

She jerked her head round away from me, as if she didn't want to have heard it; but what was she doing asking me for it, then? "Let's go," I said to Alfie. He had a white, nauseated look, but after a moment, he steeled himself and went square-shouldered and marched onward down the corridor.

The voices got louder and louder. Alfie kept walking steadily, resolute, just when I wouldn't have minded slowing down a little myself. I'd been spot-on about this maw-mouth being bigger than the small one I'd killed at graduation; how pleased I didn't feel to be proved right. It was going to be worse than the one in the library, too. I remembered the sound of that one much too well, the soft heavy breathing in the dark stacks amid the silenced books. That one had been small enough to squeeze its way up through the Scholomance air vents, and even so it had been unbearably, hideously large.

I couldn't have been inside it for long. It had only burned through nine of my mana crystals: a fortune to me, but even in the Scholomance, Alfie would have glanced at my box full of them and smiled politely and said, "Really nice, El; have you filled them all yourself?" Out here Sarah would have worn a handful of them as trinkety jewelry. I'd been pulling from them so hard they must have gone in a minute each. It hadn't felt like nine minutes; it hadn't felt like anything. Time hadn't really existed. There had only been the maw-mouth, endless, and the only way out had been to kill it and kill it and kill it, one death for every life it had swallowed, as fast as I could go. And I'd survived only because I could kill very, very fast indeed.

We came to the end of the corridor abruptly. It ended in a staircase, forked in half and twisted round itself like a double helix, both sides going down. The maw-mouth voices were whispering upwards out of both. The hooded stone figures from the entrance were here, too, standing together at the top of the stairs. Alfie went to the one with the cup, took a pin from his pocket and pricked his finger to let a few drops fall in, then turned and rubbed a smear from his bloody finger across the pages of the open book. The smudge looked black in the dim light, and then it was gone, soaking away into the stone. Alfie glanced away for a moment, to make it easier for the magic to work; we all did the same. But nothing had happened; he darted a look back towards us with alarm starting in his face, but when he turned back the second time, the woman's statue on the left had turned and was facing towards the passage on her side.

He heaved a shuddery breath and led us down again, but creeping now, step by slow step around the tight corkscrew curve until abruptly it yawned open again into a huge cistern chamber wide enough to drive a lorry through, full of deep water, with a stone walkway running all the way down the middle to an enormous doorway at the far end. The same two carved figures stood there atop a flight of stairs, holding up mana-lamps on either side of a massive red-painted door. The maw-mouth was enveloping the entire doorway, including the statues. It had poured itself up the stairs over the whole gateway, and the two lamps, the only light, were struggling to shine in an underwater way through its body, making it too visible: something between liquid and jelly and cloud, horrible deconstructed parts seething throughout.

It was pawing around the edges of the doorway plaintively, like a cat asking to come inside, grunts and complaining noises mixed in with the moans and weeping coming from its many mouths. Tendrils were trying to squirm under the door, feeling over all the edges, poking into the hoods of the figures: looking for any kind of vulnerable spot to start prying open the delicious treat. The same way the other one had tried to pry *me* open.

We had all stopped in the narrow bottleneck of the stairwell, frozen. The maw-mouth rolled half a dozen eyes over its surface to peer at us. Some of them were fresh enough to be weeping, or staring at us in desperate recognition. The maw-mouth could still use them, either way. I wanted to vomit; I wanted to scream and run away. Sarah was panting in short terrified breaths behind me, and Alfie's whole body was a rigid line, held against trembling.

"There is no sense standing here," Liesel said, brusque and too loud. "What do we do?"

That was a charmingly inclusive question, except none of them could do a thing, so really she was saying *get on with it, El,* which would have annoyed me more helpfully if I weren't also terrified out of my skin. The only useful thing she was doing was blocking the way out, which meant I couldn't actually run away.

"We'll make a circle and keep it off you, as long as we can," Alfie said, without looking back at me: that would have required taking his eyes off the maw-mouth. "You know the spell, Liesel." They'd been allies before we'd turned graduation inside out, and I'm sure they'd worked really hard together on perfecting his best defensive casting: a refusal spell, one you could use to keep out essentially anything you didn't like, which would certainly include any part of a maw-mouth.

He'd shared it with me, too, but it wasn't an ordinary shield spell that you could set and forget; it was an evocation, and I couldn't hold it up while also going on a slaughtering rampage of killing spells. But if they sent me in there under a protective spell they were holding up, and the spell failed or slipped away from them—the maw-mouth would be able to get at them through it. Even if they jettisoned the spell right away, as fast as they could, it might get a hold on their mana through the connection, and then that would be that for all of them. According to the *Journal of Maleficaria Studies,* that was how the three wizards in the Shanghai circle died, and presumably the victims of the last two attempts London had made. None of them had been fresh graduates, either.

So it was a genuine offer of real help, and I hadn't even had to demand it from them. That wasn't the way enclavers usually did things. Sarah made a small hitch of breath, not quite on board with Alfie's generosity, but even she didn't say no, and Liesel, to give her credit, immediately said, "Yes. I'll anchor the circle. You lead us in the casting."

I did appreciate it, except for the significant point that once they'd cast it on me, I'd need to go out there. But Liesel was right as usual. Standing here wasn't going to improve my lot any, and might make it considerably worse, if for instance the maw-mouth managed to poke through and get a hold on London's mana store or a few dozen senior wizards to digest.

"Get ready to cast it," I said, harshly. I took a deep breath and stepped out past Alfie, just onto the walkway, and the maw-mouth—*charged us.*

I'd seen them move before. They're ordinarily very unhurried; they like to park themselves in a good fishing spot and linger. But when they do decide to move, they go at shocking speed. It pulled all its tendrils back from the door and came rolling towards us like a hideous churning wave of death, the voices bursting into a fresh anguished noise of sobbing and wailing like it was ripping them apart all over again, extracting more agony from people already shredded, the eyes staring and the mouths contorted in howling. Sarah screamed, and Alfie jerked back half a step—but we were all graduates of the Scholomance, and even as he flinched his hands were coming up.

He had the evocation up over us half a second before the maw-mouth hit. And then it was crashing over us, a terrible churning mass of flesh enveloping Alfie's small dome entirely, squeezing the surface in so close around us that the horrible crushed intestinal folds of the thing were rolling inches past my face. I did let out a scream myself then, acid bile climbing up my throat, even though I was thinking too, cold clear tactical data points ticking away inside my head. There hadn't been time to form a circle; Alfie had cast the evocation alone. He couldn't hold it for more than forty-nine seconds, each one running out from under us like sandy ground giving way, and if I took the evocation over myself, I couldn't actually kill the maw-mouth. And sooner or later, it would get through.

So my choices were to let it have Alfie and Liesel and Sarah, or let it have us all, and since neither of those were acceptable, that meant I had to somehow kill this vast monstrous thing right now, in however many seconds Alfie had left to hold it off, and that wasn't enough time, but I didn't care: I wasn't going to let it have them, and if that meant it had to die unreasonably fast, it just had to die, that's all. I fixed that perfect certainty in my head and drew a breath to tell it so in clear small words—and then it rolled the rest of the way over us and was gone, the howling mass already disappearing up the narrow stairs without even slowing down long enough for a single nibble.

I just stood there shocked and still shaking with adrenaline. The dome of refusal burst and came down in a brief cloud of glitter, and Alfie said, quavery, "What—why did it—" only he didn't finish, because I understood, we all understood at the same time: It was *running away*. From me.

"Fuck," I said succinctly, and ran after it.

The maw-mouth kept rolling away at top speed. By the time I reached the top of the narrow spiral, it was completely out of sight somewhere along that endless corridor, the columns vanishing into the dark like an illusion of infinity, as if someone had set up two mirrors facing one another. I stood panting for a moment. No one else had followed me back up—I couldn't blame them—and I did have a moment of wondering what the hell I was doing, only someone screamed again from inside the maw-mouth, a cracked-glass shriek, and they were inside it, they were trapped inside, like my father, like Orion, and I couldn't let it have them, either. I ran after it.

The only reason the maw-mouth didn't manage to completely shake me was the crying of the voices, but in the corridor I couldn't tell exactly which doorway the sound was coming from, and the cries slowly started to fade out. They gave way to exhausted labored breathing that was somehow even worse, the thick struggling desperate sound coming at me like the maw-mouth itself, all around, rasping out of the corridors and echoing dully against the stone walls.

I kept going down one side passage and back, and another, and another after that. They all ended in dead ends that almost certainly weren't dead ends if you knew what you were doing. It was possible that the maw-mouth did know what it was doing—it had London wizards in its belly—and had got to the other side of one of them, but I couldn't stop long enough to go find Alfie and make him help me. If I'd stopped that long, I'd have had to think about what I was doing. Instead I just kept trying doggedly, over and over.

The only thing that helped me was that it all began to remind me forcibly of the wretched games of hide-and-seek I'd played as a kid in the commune, where none of the other kids really wanted me to play, but their parents, who loved Mum or had come to the commune to see her, would make them let me. So what they did was make it a game of *keep away from El* instead. All of them running and hiding in whispering small groups while I ran desperately from one place to another trying to find someone, anyone, and I knew what they were doing, but I pretended not to and kept trying to play anyway because it was the only playtime I could get; if I ever tried hiding myself, no one would ever come to find me, and they'd all just go play something else without telling me.

It felt insistently like that, with the maw-mouth's voices sunk back into whispering and mutters and gasping breaths, just on the edge of my hearing and scraping at my brain. It made me so *angry,* more and more angry as I went, the grating miserable *irritation* of it building on layers and layers, just like it had back then, until Mum would have to come and get me and take me away because she felt me reaching incoherent rage from all the way across the commune. Only Mum wasn't here. No one was here. It was only me hunting the sly whispering through the endless horrible murky corridors of this place, and they were deliberately making it go on and on, weren't letting me find them; in a moment they'd be sniggering at me, at how pathetic I was for submitting to this, enjoying their game at my expense.

Then I rounded a corner and there they were—there *it* was, the hideous mass of the maw-mouth completely filling one of those stumpy dead ends, pulsing and seething and moaning, and for just that one instant, I was *glad* I'd found it.

In that same instant, cornered, the whole thing came surging at me, attacking me openly—the way the other kids never had, because they'd all known, the way the maw-mouth had known, that if they ever gave me that chance, that excuse, I could hurt them in some terrible inhuman way. That there was something in me they didn't dare to face head-on. But the maw-mouth gave me the excuse because it knew I didn't need one, and for that one heartbeat, that one breath, too crammed full of rage for fear to really grab me again, I screamed at it, "Come on then! Come at me! You're *dead*, you sack of putrescence, you're *already dead*," pumping myself up like some drunk in a bar. I was going to slaughter and destroy this whole bloated monstrosity—

The whole thing disintegrated. I hadn't even used any mana, really, but it came apart before it even reached me, the skin of it giving way like holes opening up in a shirt that had been mended with magic for two years too many and now had finally lost too much of itself to keep together, fraying completely apart in an instant. Eyes and mouths and limbs and organs spilled out horribly everywhere, a rotting wave of flesh pouring out like a torrent over the floor of the corridor and *sloshing* over my feet and my legs like a wave while I screamed again, in pure unadulterated horror this time. A single grotesque contorted body at the center bubbled up to the surface for a moment, in a fetal curl—just like the one I'd seen in the maw-mouth that I'd killed in the library. And then even that was coming apart too, disintegrating and sinking into the mass of corpse matter.

But one exhausted bloodshot eye and mouth, still just

barely linked together by a thin scrap of skin—enough to get a vague idea of the face they'd once been a part of together—floated by at knee height and looked up at me and said, "Please, please, let me out, please," begging frantically, the way you would if you thought suddenly there was a chance, suddenly you might be able to escape from hell, there was a jailor at the door with a key who could be asked for mercy.

I covered my face with my hands and sobbed out a sickened breath and said it again, half choking, "You're dead, you're already dead." The mouth opened in a round O of protest, but then it sagged and went slack, the eye went unfocused and empty, and they floated away onward: dead, already dead, just like I'd told them to be. The words were a spell; they'd become a spell in my mouth and my rage, and now they would live in me forever, this brutal killing spell I'd made myself—so much more suited to me, really, than the cool superior elegance of La Main de la Mort. Surely some much more refined maleficer had come up with that one, some man with a narrow black beard and a small mouth and a black velvet doublet embroidered with silver, looking with contempt down at his enemy. Someone who had never stood in the dead end of a corridor drenched in buckets of viscera, having to clean up after herself, killing the last few torture victims she hadn't managed to get the first time round.

Chapter 4
THE UPPER TIER

I CAME OUT OF THE CORRIDOR still dripping and sick. I'd thrown up three times, wading out of the horrible remains. I'd always hated, hated the Scholomance drains, the sprayers, the loud roaring bursts when the vacuums went on: all the machinery designed to clean up the messy bits the maleficaria left behind when they killed us. Now I longed for them. The ocean of rot the maw-mouth had left behind might go on sloshing in that empty corridor forever. It didn't have anywhere to go, at least once it had reached its level. Rivulets of gore were draining away back to the main corridor, making thin sticky trails that ran down it.

I trudged down alongside them for a really long time, dull and plodding, before poor Precious, who'd been dragged along for all this, quivering inside my pocket, put her own nose out and squeaked at me, and it dawned on me that I wasn't getting anywhere: I'd been going down at least twice as long as it had taken to walk the entire corridor the first time with Alfie.

I stopped and tried to think what to do. I still had the

power-sharer; I hadn't even had to pull a drop of mana so far. My new murder spell was really efficient. I could've killed any number of maw-mouths! What I couldn't manage was to re-member a single bloody *find me a way out* spell, at least not better than the little-kiddie one Mum taught me when I was five: "Up from the hollow, down from the tree; out of the woods, it's time for tea." That refined work of high poetry had worked all right for getting me back to the yurt before dinner, but sadly couldn't quite do the trick of finding me a way out of a top working of misdirection and confusion. Probably part of the enchantment was making it even harder for me to think of anything that *would* help.

Fortunately, I did have one option simple enough to re-member: I'd killed the maw-mouth, and payment was due.

"Alfie, I'm lost, get me the hell out of here," I said out loud, with a tug on the line of obligation he'd handed me, and not a minute later I heard him somewhere up ahead, calling, "El?" uncertainly. He came out of the dark just a few sconces onward, warily picking his way along the corridor and over the still-running trails of effluvia. Liesel had come with him; they both stared at me when I came into sight, and his face turned almost comically dismayed. I hadn't any idea what I looked like, and didn't want one; I just wanted to *stop* looking like it, right now. Thank goodness Liesel didn't even bother to ask permission; she just threw a spell at me, something extremely imperative in German that I imagine must have meant something like *my god, get yourself straightened up at once,* and it grabbed me and shook me briskly head to toe. I felt a bit like a beaten rug afterwards, but I didn't mind at all: I was clean, I was clean. On the outside at least.

"What did you—" Alfie started asking, automatically, be-fore he recognized halfway into the sentence that he didn't want to know, and then just said, "Is it—did you—"

"It's dead," I said shortly, which was more than enough discussion about it for anyone, including me. "You'll have to clean up the mess yourselves."

He stared at me a moment longer and then grasped that the maw-mouth was gone, and he got to keep being an enclaver and, all right, that his father got to keep living instead of going into a maw-mouth forever, and then he heaved a deep shocked gasp of relief and put a hand over his mouth and looked away, struggling violently to avoid bursting into tears the way he clearly wanted to. He didn't manage to keep them all from running down his face.

Liesel visibly restrained herself from telling him to pull himself together, a tremendous effort on her part. I had no idea why Alfie had submitted to being acquired by someone who so clearly viewed him as barely suitable raw metal to be hammered forcefully into shape, and still less why Liesel had so determinedly gone after him. She was the *valedictorian;* she hadn't needed to sleep with him to get a place in London, and sleeping with him wouldn't have got her a place if she *hadn't* been the valedictorian, so it had been entirely optional. She said to me, "Come. The council will want to see you and thank you."

What she meant was, she wanted to take me down and display me to the council in triumph, more or less like her own brilliant achievement. Fortunately for me, I didn't have to submit to it. "Thanks, but no. I don't want to be in this place another moment. Get me out of here."

Alfie twitched a little, my insistence like a yank on a leash, and said immediately, "Of course, El—let's get you out into the gardens, I'm sure you need some air." He sounded sincere, but he'd shortly be regretting that vow to repay me no matter the cost. From Liesel's scowling, *she* was regretting it already. I suppose it felt to her like being a hawk who's just hooked a fish, only to have a monstrous eagle swoop down and snatch it right out of your talons. Hard luck for her. I wasn't in the least sorry. I'd become sorry in a few days if I couldn't get *rid* of Alfie, but not right now.

Liesel wasn't the sort to bang her head against a wall; she turned to Alfie and said, if a bit ungraciously, "Go, take her out. I'll tell the others," making the best of it, and sailed off down the passage.

Alfie took me back the other way and turned in to the very next side corridor—thankfully no sight of the one where the remnants of maw-mouth were presumably still putrefying—and then almost immediately opened a door out into the gardens, like golden Beatrice guiding Dante towards Paradise, leaving poor damned Virgil behind.

Alfie wasn't grudging about it at all, either, even though I'd done the equivalent of putting spurs to his side. He took me to a place where the waterfall jumped in a solid silver stream just past the edge of another terrace, so I could put my hands into it and cup the water and splash my face and press my hands cool against my cheeks and the back of my neck until I stopped feeling sick. I took Precious out of my pocket and put her on the edge of a small hollow in the rock, filled with clear water, and she rolled her whole body around in it; I would've liked to do the same.

Killing the maw-mouth hadn't fixed whatever damage had been done to the enclave; I could still feel the sloshing tides of mana underneath, and through the power-sharer on my wrist. But my getting rid of it had freed up all the power and all the wizards who'd desperately been trying to hold the thing off, and they were going back to work straightaway. Even while I was standing there, the sunlamps began to brighten—in a few lurching stages, like someone turning a dimmer switch up and down a few times on their way to getting it fully turned on—and the platform itself began to feel a little more *solid*, somehow. It didn't feel anymore like the gardens were about to sink under the wave; now the sensation was more like sitting at a table with one leg a bit short: you couldn't put any weight on it or it would tip, but it was still standing, with a whole team of people working at top speed to prop it up again.

When I turned back around, Alfie had poured a drink for me out of a silver carafe like the one I'd glimpsed earlier, through the jungle of growth, so those were working again, too. Even though I didn't want to put anything in my mouth, just the faint sweet smell of the drink made me feel better. So I did cautiously try a single sip, which washed all the sour nausea out of the back of my throat and let me take a clean, deep breath that I hadn't quite realized I needed.

I drank the rest of it in small swallows, letting each one linger on my tongue, giving Precious drops on my fingertip to suck up, and as I neared the end, I started to feel almost calm. I don't mean just calmed down, but *calm*. In a vaguely intoxicated way, but so what? I hadn't been really properly calm in more than four years. Not even Mum's spell had hushed me this way. Of course, Mum would have said that a month in the woods would be a better path to finding this quiet, but as I was instead here, killing maw-mouths, I welcomed this feeling, rolling down through me, tranquil and cool. The horror receded.

Alfie had sat down across from me on one of the smooth polished ordinary-looking stools, which were somehow as comfortable as armchairs, and was studying me with his long face furrowed and anxious. I assumed he was worrying about what I was going to do with this leash he'd shoved into my hands, so when he said, low, "El—I'm so sorry. It's been so mad, we just tumbled out into the middle of . . . all this," with a wave, I just waited a bit cynically for him to get around to asking me to let him out of his oath, and it took me completely by surprise when he went on, "I didn't even ask you about Orion."

It was like walking into a door someone had just opened into my face. "I know how close you were," he kept on, while I sat there trying to cling to the beautiful calm instead of going into squawking sobs or yelling at him in a fury—how dare *he* be sorry about Orion, how dare he be the first and only person who'd said anything nice or even ordinarily polite to me about Orion? "It's such a loss. It doesn't seem right, after everything he did, both of you did."

And it was all stupid and transparently obvious, and hearing him say it shouldn't have made the slightest difference, but I jerked a short clumsy nod and put down the glass and then looked away trying not to cry, half angry and half grateful. It didn't really mean anything, and at the same time it meant everything. I knew he hadn't really cared about Orion, he hadn't really known Orion, and it didn't cost him anything to say a few nice words. But it was still the few nice words you did say, the ordinary unprofound bit of decency you felt obliged to offer another human being when death knocked on the door, and he'd given it, to me and to Orion, as if we *were* people. Not his nearest and dearest, perhaps, but people he was willing to feel a little bit sorry for. And he also didn't *keep* talking; he stopped there and just sat with me, in the unending peace and beauty, with the water gurgling past us.

Delicate flowers like deep bells slowly began to bloom on the vines, petals popping back open, and after a little longer, tiny clockwork bees started coming out to poke among them. I could hear the sound of people coming for a good bit before they appeared: another carefully engineered politeness, since surely the passageway wasn't making their notables take a long winding path through the gardens. Probably there was some artifice slowing down our experience of time, so it seemed longer to us than to them. I reached out for Precious and tucked her away in my pocket again. The terrace itself was surreptitiously growing to make room for the oncoming crowd, and more stools and chairs wandered in on all sides with the casual air of pretending they'd been there the whole time.

Alfie got progressively straighter in his chair on roughly the same timeframe, and stood up as they came. I didn't need him to point out his father; there was substantial overlap, although his father was older, darker, and more staid, and looked weirdly familiar, as though I'd seen him somewhere before. I wondered if he'd ever shown up at the commune, when I'd been younger. Some of the enclavers do; Mum won't actually turn someone away who's coming to look for healing, although she's perfectly willing to speak sharply to them about their lifestyle, so they prefer not to. He had a really lovely suit on, pale cream with creases crisp as knives, a deep-green shirt, and a cravat pinned with a massive robin's-egg-sized chunk of opal: dressed up for his own demise.

Liesel was with him, along with several other highly polished figures, including the Dominus of London himself, Christopher Martel: a white-haired man leaning heavily on a bronze walking stick, his left eye and a chunk of face down to his cheekbone entirely covered with an elaborate piece of artifice like a monocle. I was reasonably sure the eye underneath, although extremely well done, was artifice itself, or an illusion; he'd probably lost the real one somehow, either directly or by trading it. Healing gets harder for wizards the older you get, but even in your twilight years, you can generally shove off even the most aggressive forms of cancer or dementia for a decade or two by giving up something important like an eye, if you also have several enormous buckets of mana to spend on the process.

The ankle might have gone to the same cause, at that; he'd been in office for at least sixty years. There's not much democracy in enclaves; they're run like a cross between a vicious international corporation and a village full of vexatious eccentrics. Most of the denizens don't care what the council are doing as long as everything keeps running smoothly from their own perspective, and the only people who get a significant vote anyway are the people who've earned a council seat, either by doing something dramatic or because they've cleverly arranged to be descended from a founding member. Generally a Dominus stays in the job until they retire or die or their enclave suffers some sort of major disaster.

Just like this one, and I'm sure Martel's hours in office were now numbered—in favor of Alfie's father, in fact, given that he'd been the one volunteering to go into the mawmouth; that's the sort of thing that people understand comes with a price tag attached. But it was going to take some time for the new situation to become official—especially with the enclave still more than a bit wobbly—and everyone was going to be excruciatingly polite about it in the meantime, obviously. Alfie's dad made quite a large production of bringing the largest chair over for Martel and setting it opposite me, before taking the one that had quietly edged up for him.

Martel let himself down into it with a sigh and crinkled a gentle, faintly rueful smile at me, an apology for being so creaky, and looked up at Alfie, who bowed a bit and said, "Sir, this is Galadriel Higgins, a friend from school. El, this is Dominus Martel . . ." He paused, darting a quick look at his dad, who in some way too subtle for me to notice signaled back *yes, go on, I merit an introduction now too,* and then added, "And this is my father, Sir Richard Cooper Browning."

"My dear Galadriel, I understand we owe you quite an extraordinary debt," Martel said, in avuncular tones I'd have been annoyed by, if I weren't too busy being annoyed at Alfie. I'd noticed the mild oddness of his going by *Alfie* at school, like a kid in primary; his mates ought to have used his last name instead. But I hadn't realized it was a deliberate avoidance he must have worked at. And his dad looked familiar because I'd seen that face, with relatively minor edits, staring out at me from all the articles about the founding of the Scholomance that had been plastered over the walls of the school.

I didn't blame Alfie for not wanting to be known as whatever iteration of Sir Alfred Cooper Browning he was apparently destined to be; I'd gone to some lengths myself to avoid becoming known as the incongruous child of the great healer in the eyes of my classmates. I *did* blame him, even more, for making that stupid oath. My dragging him around as my personal helper, after literally wrecking the Scholomance his namesake had built, that would be really marvelous. There clearly *was* a family tradition of making dramatic and potentially fatal gestures in the service of your enclave, though.

"Glad to help," I said, a bit shortly. All right, I could still muster up some annoyance for the avuncular tones, too.

"It ought to go without saying, and yet merits being said, that should you ever choose to make your home here with us, we would be delighted to have you," Martel said, that bright-blue artifice eye fixed on my face intently, as if he were hoping to peer inside and get a look at my intentions and deepest desires. I wouldn't have minded a peek myself, since now that I had finished with killing the maw-mouth, I was back to not knowing what to do with myself. But I did know that I very much didn't want to move myself into London enclave.

"Thanks, but no," I said, and several of the wizards behind him traded glances, like they couldn't quite believe it. Why else would I have taken out a maw-mouth for them, after all?

"I understand from Alfred that you are quite committed to your independence," Sir Richard said. "I hope there is some other way you'll permit us to repay you." What he meant was that he really hoped I'd let him ransom his son back—which I didn't have any objections to, lucky for him, and I *had* thought of something to demand, something big enough to be worth taking on a maw-mouth.

"Yes," I said. "The gardens." Sir Richard frowned at me a little; everyone else was glancing round themselves a little confused, as if they thought I meant packing up the gardens and handing them to me. "I want you to open them up, so any wizard who wants can come and spend the day, if they like. The library, too," I added, because why not? The maw-mouth wouldn't have left any of it standing. "Not the parts of this place you actually live in; you can keep your mana store to yourselves, your council chambers, all of that place." I waved my hand towards that awful subterranean complex. "But the rest—share it. That's my price, if you want one."

They were all staring at me with an odd mix of expressions. Liesel mostly looked irritated, as if it wasn't anything she hadn't expected from idiot me; Alfie's had a faintly anxious edge, although seeing how his dad was likely to be Dominus soon, I thought his odds of being bought out of his debt to me were considerably better than they might have been. The others were mostly frowning in the intent way you do when you're trying to understand what the game is, why someone's asked for something really weird and unexpected that doesn't make any obvious sense, and some of them were glancing back and forth to see if anyone else had worked it out.

Martel was keeping his pleasant smile lodged firmly in its noncommittal curve. "That . . . would be quite an undertaking," he said cautiously, but what he really meant was *please explain your bizarre request some more.*

"The National Trust manage it all right," I said. "I don't mind your throwing people out if they piss in the waterfall."

A woman brayed a laugh, a real jeering goose-honk of one, making everyone jump. I hadn't noticed her before. She was standing off to one side apart from everyone else, leaning against the railing, but that wasn't why I hadn't spotted her: she was in a coat of tattered scraps of mismatched fabric, sewn together with ragged ends fluttering off here and there. All of the scraps were carrying a small bit of minor artifice that insisted they were absolutely fascinating and the most amazing thing you'd ever seen—a typical cheap glamour, except by putting it on a bundle of not-at-all-amazing rags and heaping them all in together, the conglomeration produced a brilliant misdirection effect where you stopped noticing them at all. Even now that she'd deliberately drawn attention, I was having a hard time looking at her properly.

She pushed off the railing. "Little El, all grown up," she said. "D'you remember me? I don't think you would. Last time I saw you, Gwen was toting you away slung over her shoulder, howling, after you tried to use a compulsion on me. I kept wobbling and should stop, you said. You were all of four, I think."

I didn't remember her at all, but it certainly sounded like a thing that might have happened. I had in fact invented a compulsion spell round that age, all my own; Mum had been years training me out of flinging it at people.

And then I knew who she was. Yancy was the only name she used, and whenever a scruffier sort of wizard came to the commune looking for help, more often than not they said she'd sent them, with her respects. Once, I'd asked why, and Mum told me she'd helped her resolve a corruption of perception that had lodged itself too deep into her imagination. If that doesn't tell you much, just avoid consuming too many alchemical substances in unreal spaces and it won't happen to you.

I had no idea why Yancy was *here*, though; she wasn't a London enclaver herself. The opposite, if anything. London enclave had managed to survive the Blitz by opening up loads of entrances all over the city, so even if more than one got bombed in a night, it wouldn't mean the whole enclave went. After the war, they'd closed most of them up again, but Yancy and her crew had worked out various clever ways of prying and wedging them back open a bit, to get into those unreal spaces I'd mentioned: some sort of vague undefined pockets between the real world and the enclave. They'd camp out in one for months or even years at a time, enjoying the shelter from maleficaria and the convenience of access to the void, until the enclavers managed to find and boot them out, and then they'd scurry away and find another spot to wriggle in through.

So I suppose she did have an incentive to save London from being devoured by a maw-mouth, only why they'd have looked to *her*, I didn't quite get. But they clearly had. She said to Sir Richard, "Right, that's us sorted, too, then. I assume we're allowed to throw the occasional party on the green, in your charming scheme?" she asked me, in high pleasure, and didn't wait for an answer before giving another bray. "Nice to meet you, *Galadriel Higgins*." She made it sound like a sly joke between us. "Let's have a chat sometime." With that, she gave a wriggle that shook all the rags and tatters, and by the time my eyes would focus again, she'd disappeared down one of the paths, although singing loudly enough—just a nonsense *ro ma ro ma ma, gaga ooh la la* bit from an old pop song over and over—that the waterfall had to get energetic to drown her out.

There was a lot of visible irritation in her wake, with sour looks at Sir Richard. I imagined he'd been the one who'd brought her into the mix, for whatever reason. He managed his own face better, or else he sincerely didn't mind Yancy. He just gave a bit of a sigh and said to me, in wry tones, "You don't object to reasonable visiting hours, I hope, or it'll be nightly raves until seven o'clock in the morning." He hadn't been swapping looks with everyone else; he'd just shot a questioning one straight at Alfie, and evidently he'd got enough from that direction to reach the astonishing conclusion that what I wanted was what I'd asked for.

Martel was apparently having more difficulty swallowing the idea. He had gone from polite staring to flat-out staring, and the smile had gone. I didn't care. I wasn't going to sit here and haggle over details with them; Alfie's oath would do a better job of negotiating for me. "You asked, so I've told you," I said shortly. "Do it or don't."

I took off the power-sharer—I'd like to say it wasn't a wrench to give it up, but I'd be lying—and held it out to Alfie. He took it from me with another speaking look at his father that was loud enough for me to hear too: *see, I told you so.* Sir Richard watched the handover with his long face furrowing a bit. I assume his grandfather had negotiated his own deal with London's council to get it, back in the 1890s, in exchange for the keys to the Scholomance. Probably a permanent council seat for the head of the family, too. Manchester enclave had poured the best part of their strength into getting the place built; London had still got a bargain.

And they'd got a bargain this time, too. They had their enclave; their vast oceans of power, storm-tossed or not; even their secret garden was still theirs. They'd only have to endure letting other people tramp through it once in a while, and even that would only help them settle their frothing mana stores at first: getting in a bunch of wizards to stare at and believe in all of the wondrous artifice would probably be just the thing to help stabilize the place. I stood up. "You won't mind me having a walk before I go."

"Not at all," Martel said. He'd pasted the smile back on at last, although it was looking thin. "Please make yourself at home."

I didn't go very far. All I wanted was to be somewhere alone and away from everything, and the gardens obligingly took me straight to a small nook draped with vines half hidden from the outside, green and quiet, with the pattering of a side waterfall going past the leaves. It was exactly what I wanted, only once I was in it, I didn't want it after all. There was nothing to do in the nook but think or feel or be, and I didn't want any of those things. I couldn't rest; I wasn't tired. I would have liked to be, but I wasn't. Killing a maw-mouth in a single breath, a maw-mouth big enough to eat London, nothing to it. As long as I made up my mind to do it instead of insisting it couldn't be done, so Orion decided to face it without me.

That was a very bad thought. I didn't want it. I didn't want to sit here thinking it, in this garden that I'd saved instead of Orion, but it was the only thing my brain could find to think. Precious climbed out of my pocket and roamed over the beautiful twining ironwork railings and the branches, and I tried to just follow her movement with my eyes and breathe in steady waves, in and hold and a long sighing-out, but it wasn't any use. The lovely soft drugged calm of the drink

Alfie had given me had been completely crushed beneath my irritation and anger, and the more I tried to be inside my head, the more I was aware of the queasy rush of the roiling mana beneath my feet, horribly similar to the grotesque gushing wave of the maw-mouth coming apart around my legs. My stomach turned and I gave up.

What would have helped was *work,* but I hadn't any to do, and if it had been the kind of work I was made for, I couldn't have done it anyway. I'd handed back the power-sharer, and the tank was empty. So instead I got up and started doing push-ups to build mana. I was still in the very best shape of my life, having trained for the graduation five-hundred-meter dash as though my life depended on it, which it had, and my conditioning was only improved for having spent most of a week being fed and watered and loved in Wales. I did the push-ups properly, all the way down and up again, counting them off.

The poor confused garden slowly opened up the nook to either side to make slightly more graceful room around me, and when I came up from number seventeen, it tentatively offered me a tidy basket of yoga mats in the corner of the space. That would have been within normal operating parameters: surely eight or nine London wizards in expensive athletic wear got together in the early mornings on the regular for a charming group session overlooking the waterfall. They wouldn't be building mana, though; it would just be for the pleasure of moving their bodies. They ought to come out and spend a weekend in Wales on a retreat. I ignored the basket and made my hands into fists and kept going on the bare stone, counting off my driblets of painfully built mana as they went into the spent crystal still hanging round my throat, the faintest glow starting as I hit thirty.

Round then I noticed that Liesel was standing there watching me, her arms crossed over her chest and frowning. I loathe push-ups; I'd been half wishing someone would come and give me something else to do, or at least a good shove, and Liesel was certainly the woman for that. But I went all the way to fifty before I let myself get up again, defiantly dripping sweat all over the towering iridescent gladiolas in the nearest planter. I expected her to call me a numpty; I felt like one myself, to be honest. It was too much like lugging a jug ten miles from a weak muddy stream just to water a plant that was standing next to a massive lake.

But she didn't; she just went on studying me in an odd narrow way. I had the sensation I was on the wrong side of a pane of one-way glass, and on the other side, taking me in, was some vast clockwork machinery full of peering lenses and vibrating with the force of thirty thousand gears churning away. I didn't enjoy it. "Did you want something *else*?" I said coldly. "Track down any other maw-mouths?"

She made a rude sniffing noise, then said, "Don't start crying." I gawked at her indignantly, drawing breath, and then she hit me with it: "Everything else worked. It was only you and Lake left. What went wrong?"

I didn't especially want to cry; I'd quite have liked to punch her, though. "Why? Keeping it in mind for *next* time we need to trap all the maleficaria in the world?" I snarled at her.

"Is he *dead*?" Liesel said, as if she were speaking to a small child, albeit presumably one whose feelings she didn't care about brutalizing.

"I hope so," I said flatly. She could make anything she liked of that. I half wanted her to think I'd murdered Orion and left him on the floor of the Scholomance before flouncing away in triumph myself.

Only it was Liesel, so that didn't work. "Because there was

another maw-mouth," she said, a statement more than a question. I've spent my whole life alarming people when I would have preferred to make a friend of them, or at least trade with them for a hammer or a pen, so of course now, when I'd have been glad to do a little intimidating, my target was impervious instead.

Also implacable. I gave up; I didn't want to keep fighting her off, parrying her questions one after another while she went on jabbing me in every tender place. "It was Patience," I said. "It had eaten Fortitude and was hiding somewhere in the school. It caught us at the gates just before the school broke away. And before you ask," I added, savagely, "I *tried* to just leave. He wouldn't come. He shoved me out, and then it got him, and he wouldn't let me pull him out. That's all the story there is, so I hope it satisfies you. I'm going now."

Liesel opened her arms out in a grand sweep. "Are you? Where? To sit in a tent and be rained on some more?"

"I suppose you think you've a better idea."

"Yes," Liesel said. "Come and have dinner."

As soon as she said it, I couldn't help but recognize that dinner was, in fact, inescapably a better idea than blundering out of the enclave into some unknown bit of London, with no way home and nothing in my pockets but a mouse. Mum never bothers about anything like that. If she needs to go somewhere, she thumbs a ride, and someone stops for her. If she's hungry, she just asks the universe if there's anything to spare, and more often than not, someone going by will pause and offer her something to eat or invite her to their house for dinner. I'm more likely to be required to hand over exact change before the universe grudgingly allows me to buy a bus ticket and a stale bun. And I can never tell how much of it is *me*, scowling in resentment, and how much of it is *other people,* looking at a dark-skinned girl instead of my pink-and-gold mum smiling at them, and not being able to tell only makes me scowl the more.

Speaking of which, I would almost certainly have gone blundering out of the enclave nevertheless, just to spite Liesel and then myself, only she added, "Don't be foolish. Alfie will drive you back afterwards," and gestured to a small spiral stair that was now going up from the corner of the nook to a terrace overhead, and the smell of something indescribably good came wafting down. My best attempt would be telling you that it was like rice pudding I wanted to eat. It didn't actually smell like rice pudding at all; the point is that I've never much liked rice pudding, but at school I ate it whenever I had the chance, because it was one of the best things you could get there. So now I could gladly go the rest of my life without ever eating it again, only I desperately wanted to eat whatever I was smelling up there, even if it *was* rice pudding.

So I grudgingly trailed Liesel up the stairs. They went a long way, enough for my legs to start to get tired, and we came out onto a little terrace in front of a small hobbit-hole chamber set high up on the enclave walls. The setting wasn't up to the standards of the gardens below. The archway ought to have had a door, but instead only had a curtain hung across it, and the room on the other side wasn't much bigger than the bed it contained. The only other furnishing was a small half-moon stand jutting from the wall, barely enough to hold a night's glass of water. There wasn't even a lamp. The terrace itself had one slightly dim globe hanging over a small table and two chairs. The main cascade of the stream and the waterfalls were far away below on the other side of the low iron railing, and we were so close to the ceiling that there was a faint sideways glitter visible through the frosted glass, betraying the sunlamp spells for artifice.

For all Liesel's sneers at my dripping yurt, her own quarters had a distinctly shabby flavor. They didn't even come up to the standards of her clothing. But of course, even if you're the valedictorian with a guaranteed enclave spot—the winner of the Scholomance grand prix if there was one—as soon as you get out you're just a brand-new graduate, with no connections in your new enclave except for the one or two other brand-new graduates who largely made it out thanks to your help and would generally rather forget that fact. You're as low on the enclave hierarchy as it gets.

I imagine it must have been disheartening for a lot of kids who'd spent their last four years working savagely to claim the one visible prize in our shared existence, only to realize they'd won nothing more than a ticket to the standing-room section, while all those enclaver kids who'd been courting them were going down to the box seats, or taking their places on the stage. You did hear about valedictorians who flamed out entirely afterwards, like they'd spent the fuel of their lives on that one burst; who stayed in the small room at the top of the stairs and never amounted to anything more.

Liesel clearly didn't mean to be one of them. She'd already got up a delicate awning that blocked the worst of the glare, and her bed was canopied with twining white branches draped with glimmering netting. She'd coaxed or more likely bullied some of the glowing blossoms into vining up over her railing for extra illumination. She waved me to a chair at her little table, and there was another of the silver jugs waiting beside a bowl of couscous and a small blue-glazed tagine that wafted out the fantastic smell when she took off the lid. No rice pud in sight, thankfully.

Every single bite was perfect: if one was spicy, the next one was sweet, the next one salty, whatever my mouth most wanted, the dried fruits glowing like translucent jewels and the almonds crunchy, each different vegetable bursting with flavor and perfectly done, tender without having gone to mush, and each piece as smooth as if they'd been cooked one at a time with brooding care before being precisely put down, even though it was one whole thing at the same time. Despite the ongoing faint nauseating churn of the wobbly mana below, I ate three platefuls and drank two glasses of whatever was in the jug, and Liesel shoveled in her fair share, and afterwards the dirty dishes vanished themselves away, presumably to some efficient set of cleaning spells.

By the time we'd finished, there was already a bustle of activity under way in the gardens below: a set of looping paths being reshaped to wider spans, with brighter lamps and seating areas being coaxed out along their length. Sir Richard was evidently wasting no time in clearing Alfie's debt. The first guests even appeared at twilight: a handful of slightly wary outside wizards, instantly distinguishable even from high above, because they looked exactly like mundanes, whether in good suits or dresses or jeans. They were commuters: even at a distance I could see the grey bands round their upper arms, which had undoubtedly before now been good only for getting through the service entrance, and into the workshops and laboratories where they did gobs of work in the faint distant hope of being allowed into this inner sanctum someday. Their faces, upturned to the waterfall's spray, caught the light of the globes in their dazzled eyes, and I wondered with a sour taste in my mouth if I'd really done them any favors, or if I'd only made them want it more.

"How determined are you to be stupid?" Liesel said abruptly.

"And I suppose you think you're being clever," I said, waving a hand round vaguely. I don't know if what was in the jug was actually wine, but it was willing to behave like wine once it got in me. "Signing your whole life over to get into this place, just so you can suck your blood and mana back with interest out of a hundred other wizards."

"Very determined, I see," Liesel said. "I am not sorry to have got an enclave place, since I am not stupid. My mother had to smile at enclavers her whole life just to keep me alive."

"And what are you doing with Alfie, then?" I said, mean, and unjust to boot; I really couldn't accuse her of *smiling* at him, as far as I'd seen. "You can't like him."

"Certainly I like him. He wants to make something of himself, he wants to be someone of importance."

"And you're going to make something of him, is that the idea?"

Liesel shrugged, matter-of-fact; so it *was* the idea. "He has what I need, and I have what he needs. Would it be better if I insisted on being with someone who had nothing to offer?"

"It would be *better* if you found someone you wanted to be with whether they fit into your spreadsheets or not," I said tartly.

Liesel flicked this nonsensical suggestion away. "Most people are stupid, or tiresome, or they don't know how to work. Why would I want to be with them? I only get impatient. But I don't have to get impatient with Alfie, because he is worth being with regardless." I screwed my mouth up at that, a bit disgruntled; it made Mum's sort of sense, the kind where she's always telling me that the most important thing is for a person to work out what's good for them, even if it's not what's good for most people. "He does not insist on being useless, and even if he were, still it would be a good bargain, because he has everything, and I have only myself."

"What about your mum?" I interrupted.

Liesel paused, and said a little stiffly, "She died when I was inducted."

That clearly wasn't coincidental; it meant her mum's death had been scheduled. You can't always make a grand bargain like Martel for an unearned decade more of life, if you're not an enclaver with heaps of mana to spend. But there's another deal you can almost always make. If, for instance, you know you've got fifty–fifty odds of making it past your child's induction day, there're some shady sorts of healers who'll help you trade your chance of survival for the chance of dying, and then at least you know when it's going to be.

I said, a bit incredulous, "And your dad's gone, too?" I was still tipsy enough to be indelicate, or else maybe I just had waived any tact for dealings with Liesel. In my defense, that would have made for a fairly extreme form of bad luck. *I'm* unlucky, as wizard kids go. If your parents have survived long enough to produce you, they're generally grown wizards in the prime of life, and there really isn't that much that can take out a grown wizard. We're the worst monsters there are. Even her mum must have been unlucky, to get taken out young enough to have a school-aged kid: whatever had got her had likely involved a spell going wrong, or some curse going right. Losing both parents is fairly improbable.

And in fact it hadn't happened. Liesel said, even more flatly, "He's a council member in Munich."

"What?" I stared at her. "But—"

"Do you need me to spell it out in small words?" Liesel said coldly. "His wife is the daughter of the Domina. That is how he has his seat. So he told my mother if she wanted me to have a place in the Scholomance, she would keep hush and never contact him again. I have never met him. He sent money sometimes." The words dripped with contempt, as well they might. Money's fairly trivial for an enclaver to produce. Even most indie wizards can magic themselves up a fifty-pound note; the real limit is that the local enclave will come down on you if you start counterfeiting on a large enough scale to make things awkward for *them*. But there's not an enclave in the world that doesn't have a more or less unlimited supply.

I grimaced; I didn't like being sympathetic towards Liesel. But leaving your kid outside for mals to hunt while you live cushy in your enclave . . . He wouldn't even have suffered any horrible consequences for bringing her inside. No one ever gets kicked out of an enclave for a thing like cheating on your wife, even if the Dominus might want to. That's the sort of thing that would make a Dominus lose their job. Enclavers— with reason—expect to get away with almost anything, in- cluding reasonably concealed use of malia, as long as it doesn't actually threaten the enclave as a whole. That's the only bright line none of them are allowed to cross; the rest are very pliable. But Liesel's dad certainly *could* have lost his council seat over it. That was what he'd valued, more than her life. "That's why you didn't go to Munich," I said. "Why not one of the other German enclaves?"

"What good would that do?" she said. "Munich is the most powerful of them. I need a *more* powerful enclave, not less."

"To do what?" I said, because I couldn't help myself, al- though I wasn't entirely sure I wanted to know.

"The exact details will suggest themselves," Liesel said, a bit dismissively. "But I mean to acquire a position where I am *more* powerful than his wife, and then I will be able to make her sorry."

"For—"

"Killing my mother," Liesel said. "It wasn't an *accident*."

She had a right to the irritated tone; as soon as she said it, the whole thing became obvious. Her dad had done his best to hide his dirty little secret, but his wife had found out anyway—presumably when he'd finally grudgingly pulled a string or two to get Liesel that promised Scholomance seat— and instead of binning her useless husband, she'd gone after Liesel's mum, and she'd *got* her. And then Liesel had been forced to watch her mum sell off what was left of her life, just to get her over the finish line into the Scholomance.

It made sense to me of what Liesel was doing in ways I wasn't entirely sure I wanted. It had been a lot easier to think she was just a bit of a shit person, ready to do anything to get into an enclave and have a cushy life of ease and power. But instead she'd just done the maths and reached the completely correct conclusion that the only way she was ever going to be able to make the daughter of Munich's Domina feel so much as an instant's regret was if *she* was the Domina of an even bigger enclave, or next to it. And unlike an ordinary sane person, she hadn't looked at that solved equation and decided right, I'll settle for the revenge of just living as well as I can; instead she'd made herself a thirty-year plan that started with *step one: become valedictorian of the Scholomance,* and marched off on it.

And she was still on it right now. Alfie was step two. I'd wondered why she'd been so determined to hook herself a powerful enclaver boyfriend at school, after she'd *already* made valedictorian, but of course now I understood. It wasn't *good enough* to get into an enclave. She'd recognized that when she did, she'd be starting here, in the cheap seats, and she wanted a partner with a better position on the *inside.* It was actually a perfectly sensible and also a really good plan, as I should have expected.

"Sorry," I said, very grudgingly. Mum would probably have tried to sit her down for a few months of conversation, but personally I didn't blame her for wanting revenge. I still had vivid revenge fantasies about that twat who'd shoved me in the corridor in freshman year. But I'd got this far not liking

Liesel and I wanted to keep on; it felt vaguely dangerous to stop.

Liesel only shrugged. "They had power, and my mother had none. The one with power decides what is going to happen," she said, matter-of-fact. "So it's better to have power, and it's stupid not to take it when you have the chance. You come in here and save the whole enclave, and you take nothing. What a grand gesture! What will you do now if a mawmouth comes to someplace else, not an enclave, and they don't have mana to give you to fight it?"

"I'm not going in for a career of hunting maw-mouths!" I said.

"Aren't you?" Liesel said, contemptuously. "What else are you going to do?"

I could have done with a year of crying in the woods to answer that question, but under the circumstances, I had to say something or else get squashed flat, and I didn't want to be squashed flat. So I said, "I'm going to *build* enclaves," as if I'd decided, after all, that I *was* going to do that. "I'm going to build Golden Stone enclaves. Not fairyland castles and skyscrapers, just a few solid bunkrooms for kids to sleep in and a workroom or two, and it won't take malia and generations of scheming to put them up."

And I ought to have been grateful to Liesel, because it became the truth as I told it to her, the answer that I might easily have spent a year digging out of myself: yes, that was what I wanted to do. It was still my dream, even if it had been someone else's dream before mine. It felt right in my own mouth and mind as I said it out loud: a dream worth chasing, a good life's work.

"So," Liesel said. "How many years will it take people to save the mana to put up one of your golden enclaves, and how many of their children will be eaten before they have enough? Why not tell London to give you ten years of mana, and go put up ten enclaves for children whose parents can't afford it?"

That was nearly the exact question I'd spent my entire childhood yelling at Mum in a frothing rage, so fortunately I had an answer for it handy. "Because as soon as I start doing that, I'm not putting up enclaves anymore," I said. "I'm doing work for London, or New York, or whoever's got the most mana, and doing a bit of charity on the side. They've been trying to get my mum to turn into their private healer for years and years."

"That is not true," Liesel said. "Maybe for your mother, but this is not the same thing. How often will an enclave need your help? For what? If they are begging you to help because there is a monster about to eat their home and all their children, you will go anyway! You came *here*. That is not why you will not take their payment. You don't take it because you think you are better than them, because you want to make them be ashamed of themselves, and so what if you could do so much more good for everyone else with their help."

If only that hadn't sounded quite so plausible. I glared at Liesel. "And it's loads of good *you'll* be doing for all the little people, is it? Anyway, why are you trying to talk me into bullying London for mana? You're *in* London, now, in case you hadn't noticed, and you've got Alfie to ride piggyback all the way to Dominus. Don't tell me it's because you like me."

She glared back. "You're not a useless person! *You* could make something of yourself, if you were willing to try. But not if you insist on behaving in this unreasonable way, as if you think everything must become terrible and evil the moment you make any sort of compromise."

That took me aback; it was obviously as high a compliment as she had to pay, so apparently she *did* like me. In fact,

I realized very belatedly, before asking me to dinner, she'd fixed her hair and her clothes again, and the curtain had been tied up on purpose to *display* the rigged-out bed. There was obviously a checklist somewhere labeled *getting Galadriel on board* and she'd jotted down *thinks I'm well fit* because she'd noticed me noticing her, back at school. She was letting me know she'd be happy to swap her enclaver boyfriend for *me*.

Or, well, why *swap;* she'd love to collect the set if we'd cooperate. Her and Alfie and me, that was a recipe for world domination, much less for squashing her enemies in Munich like the cockroaches they were. I was only surprised she hadn't yet asked me outright. Probably she was making a massive effort to be tactful because Orion had just died and maybe I wanted to waste some of my time being sad instead of following her own highly superior therapy program of meticulously planning out a campaign for victory.

And I'd been absolutely right: she *was* dangerous, because as soon as I realized that offer was on the table along with the tagine, I discovered I could understand why Alfie had taken her *up* on it. If you had *everything,* if you had *power,* and you wanted to use it—and yet you had sense enough to doubt yourself, whether you were really going to do a brilliant job of it, and also perhaps had a bit too much caution, then what more magnificent offer could anyone make you: all the brains in the world and all the drive along with them, to tell you exactly what to do and calculate out to the nth degree the best way to do it and then give you a good hard shove on top of it.

Liesel *would* make something of Alfie, and he really did want something made of himself. Even at school, he'd helped with the plan more wholeheartedly than almost any of the other enclavers. He'd wanted to believe, almost as much as the Scholomance itself wanted to believe, in its nonsense motto: *to protect all the wise-gifted children of the world.* Which made more sense now, because it had been his family's great triumph. He wanted to *live up* to it. I couldn't even look down on that ambition, although I was fairly certain that he was going the wrong way, and his actual ancestor had mostly been a scheming mastermind looking to cement the power of his own enclave.

And if what *I* wanted was to build as many golden enclaves as I could—Liesel was telling me she'd be willing to sign on to the project, and with all her brains and drive and ruthlessness, she'd make something of *that,* too. Give her ten years, and every enclave of the world would end up signed on to donate mana, presumably as some sort of insurance policy— just chip in a bit, not more than you can spare, and if a mawmouth or an argonet shows up at your enclave gates, Galadriel will swoop in and save you. Or she'd sell them on the benefits of having satellite enclaves nearby for their commuters, dangling a taste of the better life. I could envision the shape of her whole program, even if I couldn't have executed it myself in a century. And when it was done, there would be loads more children sleeping safe, all over the world, than I'd ever manage by plodding around to one small group of wizards at a time. And I wouldn't have to give anything that I wouldn't give anyway.

It wasn't a trick, was the really seductive thing about it. Liesel wasn't a liar; she wasn't promising anything she didn't mean to deliver, and she wasn't even hiding the cost of it either. She was laying it out for me plainly: the price was *compromise.* To smile at enclavers once in a while when I didn't mean it and go to their parties and make it just that bit easier for them to give me what I wanted; and why the bloody hell *not,* if it got me what I wanted, and what I wanted was good?

I didn't even disagree. I thought she was right, in the general case. Only I'm not the general case, and I've known that ever since I was five years old with my great-grandmother, the world-famous seer, reciting my doom over my head, my glorious destiny to sow death and destruction among the wizards of the earth, shatter enclaves and murder thousands, and I know without a doubt that the first step towards fulfilling her prophecy would be made with all the good intentions in the world.

But I couldn't help feeling the pull of it. Liesel meant it from her side; it was as fair an offer as anyone could make. We weren't in the Scholomance anymore, but it was an alliance offer all the same, putting herself on the table, all-in, and *she* wasn't a useless person either. So I couldn't be angry at her for making it, even though I'd have liked to be angry. Instead it was only the familiar bitter taste of wanting things other people had, my face pressed up to the window of the cake shop full of easy sweetness I couldn't buy. Alfie had said yes in a heartbeat, surely. But I couldn't.

That wasn't her fault, though. I put down my glass; the faint heady buzz of the wine had faded out of me completely. "I don't think it would go all wrong the first moment that I ever compromised on anything," I said, not rude, only final. "Not the second time, either. But I'm not going to risk doing it until I find out how many times it would take. And you'd be sorry if I did, too, even if you don't think so now. The only tactics I've got are scorched-earth, so that's what I'll end up with, if I ever start a war. You'll have to get your vengeance on your own."

Liesel could tell I wasn't just batting it back to her. She didn't keep going, but only studied me narrowly, and then gave a faintly irritated shrug and poured out another glass from the jug, consoling herself for my intransigence, and sat back into scowling thought. The sunlamps overhead were gently descending into night now, but not the way they had been before; the artifice wasn't running out of power, it was just creating a different illusion. Pale delicate streetlamps began coming alight along all the paths, and new glowing bell-like flowers opening on all the vines twined round the railings. A dim green-blue twinkling had started inside the waterfall itself. More people were walking through the gardens, their low voices rising up to reach us but only in a wordless murmur that mingled with the tumbling water, and then a burst of raucous music erupted from somewhere I couldn't see, along with a few shrieks of laughter: a discordance that managed to override the tranquility. I was willing to bet that was Yancy and her crew. It probably *would* be nightly raves until the official rules descended.

I thought I should get up and go, but I didn't want to. My legs felt leaden, and my belly a solid immovable mass weighing me down in the chair, a drowsy stupor settling in. I didn't have anywhere to go; there wasn't any hurry for me to leave. I could just doze in the chair for a little while, or lie down on the bed and sleep until morning, or perhaps for a week, and then Precious poked her head out of the pocket and gave my thumb a hard bite, just short of breaking the skin, and I jolted loose from the compulsion and was standing up, blinking hard and breathing hard, my heart thumping aggressively. I looked down at the silver jug and shot Liesel a hard look, but she hadn't jolted herself, the way you would if someone broke out of an enchantment you were weaving; she was just eyeing me with a frown that went to sudden hard alertness as she realized someone else was having a go at me.

She stood up. I was just wondering whether I was going to have to fight past her—even if she hadn't been trying to trap me, the only other real candidates were London council, and presumably she would have liked to impress them—when

Alfie came running up the stairs two at a time, a small carafe clutched in his hand, so cold it was dripping condensation over his fingers. He stopped, still panting, when he saw me standing, and darted a quick look over at the still-made bed—right, that answered *one* question; he *was* ready to be part of the collected set—before he looked at Liesel. "You broke the compulsion?"

"No! She got out of it herself without even trying; what fool thought it was a good idea to try to enchant a tertiary-order entity?" Liesel snapped. "Your father?"

"A what?" I said.

"No," Alfie said, gulping air. "Martel's behind it, and some of the others—"

"Gilbert? And Sidney? To keep him in as Dominus, so they'll have a chance at it themselves, after all." Liesel was nodding.

"I'm not an *entity*!" I said loudly, breaking into this extremely important conversation, and Liesel had the gall to look annoyed at me.

"You know you don't cast on the baseline scale!" she said, lecturing, as if that were perfectly obvious. "You're at least two orders of magnitude up, maybe even more. Do you want to get away, or to stand here arguing about terminology until these idiots try something else and you end up killing them when you swat them like a fly? Probably one of them is already bleeding from their brain."

Oh, I wanted to stand here arguing about terminology violently, actually, but Alfie said, "Liesel—I don't know where we can get her out. The garden gates are all backed up. Father's people are trying to sort them out, and Gilbert offered to put *his* people on all the other gates—"

"And your father was not suspicious that he was being helpful?" Liesel said caustically.

"He hadn't much choice," Alfie said. "Some kind of completely jumbled word has got out about the gardens opening. People think we've issued an open call for enclave seats, to replace the wizards who died in the attack. We've got people coming over from France hoping to get in for an interview. The artifice was only just barely convinced to let outsiders in at all, and now the works are completely jammed. We've got wizards *queued* outside all the entrances. Mundanes are going to notice soon, and if that happens—"

I looked more closely down below: apart from the ongoing noise of revelry, the background murmuring had picked up considerably too, and despite the best efforts of the hanging greenery and branches to obscure the view and preserve some sense of solitude, I could catch glimpses of people everywhere I looked, in every gleam of light, on every narrow side path. The gardens were valiantly trying to accommodate everyone, but they were clearly at their limits.

And if mundanes spotted a bunch of people queuing for entry to some bizarre obscure bit of urban decay, of course they'd join the queue, because they'd be curious, and as soon as *they* got up to the gates—expecting a dance party in a badly decorated basement and at most some minor sleight-of-hand—and slammed into the already wobbly artifice with all their rock-solid confidence in the laws of physics, down those gates would go.

"Right, because your father's still trying to get me *paid off*," I said. "Alfie, do me a solid and next time, keep the bloody dramatic oaths to yourself."

He flushed. "The compulsion's off. It lifted after the first visitors came in."

So he'd come up to help me just to help me, and not because he'd had to. "Oh," I muttered ungraciously.

"Ah, *that* is what Martel's side are after," Liesel said. "The compulsion has gone because your father truly intends to fulfill the request and has begun doing so, but El did not ask for the gardens to be opened only for an hour or two. If they force the garden gates to close again, the obligation would be restored. And if they get El into their power in the meantime, your father would have to negotiate with them to get it lifted again. Martel must have sent the word out himself. Of course everyone would believe it, coming from him."

She almost sounded approving: yes, such a clever plan, what perfect sense it made, and so what if it meant turning Alfie into a weapon against his own dad, and ensorcelling me. All to claw back a bit more selfish control over the enclave that none of them would have anymore if it hadn't been for my help, and Alfie putting himself on the line to make it happen. "And you wanted me to work with these people," I said to Liesel. "Do you know where Yancy's party is going?" I asked Alfie.

He looked out over the gardens, squinting, and then said, "Oh, those wankers, they're at Memorial Green."

Chapter 5
UNFORGOTTEN PLACES

ALFIE THREADED OUR WAY through a creaky maze of winding stairs up and down the garden, and along narrow inconvenient paths that hadn't been trimmed lately and were clearly slated for renovation, presumably because all the rest of the paths were crammed with tourists. For the last bit, he had to take us into a residential section of the enclave, an odd stretch that was something halfway between a street full of listed buildings and a school diorama of Tudor architecture made by a thirteen-year-old kid who hadn't done much research.

There was a narrow cobblestoned pavement just wide enough for the three of us to walk abreast, with half-timbered buildings on either side, each one only the width of its front doorway, with a single leaded window on each of four stories above, and a dormer at the very top. The roofs across the pavement from one another were connected with more timbers, and loose fabric like sailcloth was hung over them, with sunlamps on the other side: not nearly as extravagant as in the gardens, but if you were inside one of those rooms, you could probably convince yourself that the light coming in was daylight. But from the outside, it was dim and precarious, all those too-thin, too-tall buildings looming unpleasantly, and I was glad to hurry past them and towards the patch of green meadow I could just glimpse at the end of the lane.

I drew a deep breath as soon as we escaped into the open air, and got a faceful of the pungent stink of urine coming out of someone who'd been sucking down phantasmal vapors. A fellow in a tatty neon-blue dressing gown was pissing on a corner of the green, and the wafting smell of the vapors themselves was drifting our way, too. They probably weren't unpleasant alone, but mixed with the other stench it took on the absolute foulness of someone trying to cover up cat piss by pouring on a bottle of cheap floral perfume.

Alfie sucked in a sharp breath. "That's *not on*." He snapped off a repelling-liquid incantation that he'd probably practiced backwards and forwards to deal with the fairly common category of acid- and poison-spitting mals. It made all the wee, including the healthy amount that had already soaked into the ground, leap up and spray right back all over the blue-robed wizard, who gave a howl of indignation and ripped off the soaked dressing gown and was improbably in a suit of scale armor underneath it.

"I'll have your fucking bollocks on toast, you bloodless fuck," the man yelled, fumbling after some kind of weapon he was expecting to be at his side. He was obviously two or three planes of reality off from this one, but in a moment he'd probably have persuaded it to show up, only Liesel heaved an annoyed breath and waved him clean—same spell she'd used on me, perfectly up to the much smaller job at hand—and then told him in the cutting tones of a tea lady on the train after pub day, "Go lie down and go to sleep, you are drunk," with a quick twist and flick of her fingers by her side to throw just the least hint of compulsion behind it. He paused, registered that he wasn't covered in stinking pee, then amiably agreed, "Right, yeah," and rolled off a few steps to an empty plot of grass and fell over on the ground.

But Alfie looked fully prepared to pick another fight as we approached the festivities. I hadn't been automatically inclined to care how irreverent Yancy and her people were towards any of the sacred hobgoblins of London enclave, but I have to admit, I didn't really approve once I got a better look at this Memorial Green of theirs. It wasn't a political monument, with self-important statues and engraved plaques. It also wasn't a cemetery, because you don't get bodies back out of the Scholomance. But here at the far side of the gardens, London had deliberately set aside a wide green meadow, at least a hundred meters across without so much as a single tree to break up the view, and a massive labyrinth of stones had been laid out on the perfectly green grass. Each stone was more or less the size to fit comfortably into a palm, flat and round, made of faintly translucent quartzlike stuff that reminded me immediately of Mum's crystals. But not like the one I was wearing round my neck, with a faint sheen of mana against my skin. They were like the crystals that I'd burned out completely, fighting the maw-mouth in the Scholomance library; the ones that had slowly gone dull and dead.

I didn't need to see the names carved into them, stained dark brown, to understand. You couldn't send messages in or out of the Scholomance, not on paper and not in dreams; you couldn't even get a heartbeat spell inside. If you were lucky, you got a note from your kid once a year, if they'd given one to a senior who'd survived their own graduation. But London had worked out this solution.

Alfie had surely put his name on a stone like this, and filled it up with mana he'd built himself, and then he'd cut his finger and rubbed blood into the carving until it was full. And his mum and dad had kept it with them, all four years he was away, looking at it every morning and every night. If one day it had started to go dim, they'd have told themselves it was a trick of the light. Maybe after a week they'd have started picking it up and taking it into dark corners, to reassure themselves that really it was still shining. And after two, or three, their friends would have started to be very kind to them, and one day they would have picked up the dull grey empty stone and brought it here and found an open place—there weren't many, and in some places, the lines had been doubled up—and they'd have put down the only remains of the child they'd sent away to die in the dark.

This simple unbroken green was more expensive than ten palaces. The one thing that's really limited inside an enclave is *space*. The winding paths of the fairy gardens weren't just a lovely aesthetic choice: they *had* to be winding, so that the artifice could shuffle them in and out of existence as easily as possible. Having a clear view from one end to the other made that impossible.

Yancy was there with about twenty other wizards between the ages of fourteen and eighty, all sprawled out comfortably over the green and the stones, some of them drinking but most of them gathered round a big cast-iron pot set up in one of the lanes with a balefire going underneath it. It had a lid with two big stovepipe openings that were belching irregular gouts of a heavy, iridescent smoke; they caught it in big carved-bone drinking horns and put their faces inside to breathe it in. There was a massive speaker pumping out a deep bass rhythm, and a musician sitting on top playing an electric violin along with it. There wasn't a socket anywhere

I could see, but he wasn't letting that stop him. Some others were dancing, a couple of them doing balance-beam walking on top of the lines of stones.

"Galadriel Higgins!" Yancy sang out as we came into view, and waved a silver flask in my direction, a lizard sculpted clinging round the surface and glaring at me with a yellow gimlet eye. "Hero of the hour, slayer of the foul beast, opener of the enclave gates. Come and have a drink!"

"It's El, thanks," I said, and was about to explain why I couldn't, but Alfie took two steps in at them with clenched fists and broke in, "Out of curiosity, do you not know that you're trampling over dead children, or do you not care?"

I have to admit, I didn't entirely disagree with him. Although partly that was because the whole arrangement reminded me forcibly of parties at the commune, which no one ever told me about, and at which if I showed up started to leak people very quickly until suddenly someone was saying, "You'll see the bonfire goes out all the way, won't you, El?" and then it was just me alone getting cold in the dark and shoveling dirt onto the embers in a frantic hurry so I could leave before a mal popped up to eat me.

And meanwhile all the teachers at school would glare at *me* in particular whenever they read us the disapproving lectures about drugs: the half-Indian commune kid, obviously I was a yogurt weaving tofu welding friend of Henry the Eighth. Ha. I couldn't actually have risked any drugs even if anyone had been willing to offer me some, except the boring kind that just make you better at homework and drudgery. It's hard enough fending off every mal within a hundred miles *without* being in an altered state of mind that odds-on would make me believe they were even more powerful, which would cause them to in fact be so.

That said, I would actually have been quite prepared to try

some interesting magical drugs at a party full of grown wizards who could probably kill mals even while drunk and high as Valhalla, and do some dancing along with them. It's something I wasn't likely to have many opportunities to try. But I didn't particularly like the idea of doing it on the actual graves of children who'd died in the Scholomance. I'd been expecting to be one of those for the better part of my own Scholomance career, only without even a stone for Mum to remember me by.

Alfie only got back a round of tittering. "Oh, Lord," Yancy said, unperturbed. "You'll be as bad as your father in five minutes, won't you. Your whole enclave's built on dead children, love. Is this nice lawn to be off-limits just because here's where you keep a few of them on display? Don't fuss. You'll have it barred in the rules by next week along with any other real fun anyone might have, and surely we'll all have landed on the persons-not-welcome list before the year's out. So we'll take advantage while we can. Come on, then, sit down. We'll drink to their memory, if you like. Gaudry! Play us some lamentation."

The violin player immediately went into *Danse Macabre,* and the dancers obligingly turned themselves into skeletons—metaphorically, which I suppose needs saying given that we're all wizards—and started capering round like they hadn't any muscles anymore and could only swing their bones awkwardly from the joints. Alfie only got angrier, of course, but Liesel snapped at him, "We have no time for this."

Yancy gave her a squint. "Haven't you?"

"Not all the council's feeling as grateful as you," I said.

"Martel doesn't fancy Sir Richard being crowned in his place?" Yancy said, obviously both well informed and unsurprised. "Well, it's no skin off our noses, whichever way it ends. Martel is a sack full of ferrets, but he's been one forever, and still the sun rises. It's not as though Richie will be any better once he gets in. The job devours the man."

"I don't care who wins either," I said. "But Martel's decided I'm a handy lever, and he's got people on all the doors. I was hoping you might have a quick exit somewhere else."

"*Quick* exit? No, love, sorry," Yancy said. "I can get you out, but it won't be quick. Half a day at the least, and you might be seeing music for a bit afterwards, if we get out at all. Our little secret ins and outs are halfway in the void anyway; loads of them fell off the rest of the way when the mana store blew, and the ones that didn't are still all wibbly-wobbly. Still want to go?"

"I'll have to take my chances," I said, without enthusiasm. It didn't sound very appealing, except by comparison to getting into a violent altercation with the kind of people who *did* passionately care who ran London enclave and didn't know that I was a tertiary-order whatsit who could utterly drain their enclave and smash them into jelly, and therefore would do their best to provoke me into doing just that.

Yancy shrugged and heaved herself up, swigged from her flask generously, and held it out to me. I could tell the offer was practical; presumably I was going to have to be a bit more disconnected from reality to make it into whatever this unreal space of theirs was. I took it gingerly—especially after the lizard lifted its head up and gave me a pointed hiss, and wasn't actually sculpted at all but just playing chameleon. Precious stuck her own head out and squeaked back imperiously. She was roughly a quarter of the lizard's size, but it gave her a wary sidelong look and crawled round to the other side and peered out at her with the flask between them. "It's all right, I'm not going to knock you off," I told it, and then carefully had myself a healthy gulp.

It tasted like a light sea-green with streaks of polished

brass and autumn leaves falling. If that doesn't sound drink-
able to you, my digestive system vigorously agreed. Yancy
reached out and put her hand over my mouth, or I'd immediately have spewed it back out, and vomited up whatever had
already gone down. "No, you've got to keep it down. Have
another," she said. With an effort I managed to take a second
swallow, and by the time it finished forcing the first one down
into my belly, I was already seeing the swaying bones of the
music going around us, weaving in and out of the dancing
wizards, and the stones of the labyrinth were all but invisible,
weirdly vanishing into the grass and laughter, which were
making quiltlike billows around us.

"Oh, I don't like it," I said involuntarily. In retrospect, having a pint with a pub lunch would probably have been a better first foray into the world of recreational substances.

"Gets worse from here on in," Yancy said cheerfully. "A
third dose, I think, and then we'll be on our way."

"Where are we going?" I asked, mostly to delay the last
swallow.

"A hundred years ago, give or take," Yancy said. "That's
when they demolished the old riding ring and laid out the
meadow instead. We'll have to see where we can hop from
there."

I needed a few deep breaths to make myself take the last
choking gulp, but down it went in an explosion of trumpets.
"Be seeing you," I told Alfie and Liesel, the words coming out
of my mouth in blue-green sparkles, just as if I'd drunk
something smoking-hot on a cold day, and my breath was
billowing out in fog.

Alfie nodded, a bit furrowed, and said in an undertone,
"You're sure you're all right to go with her? Yancy may think
she knows a way, but her ways *lose* people. Most of her lot
don't last twenty years, once they join up."

"There is no reasonable alternative," Liesel said impatiently, and then she reached out and intercepted the flask
when I'd have handed it back to Yancy. "I will go with you."

"What?" I said, sufficiently baffled that I wondered if I'd
just started hearing things. What reason did she have for
coming after me now?

But Liesel was already swigging from the flask—Alfie
looked nearly as surprised and dismayed as I was myself—
and squeezing her eyes shut against the effects for a moment
before forcing herself to open them. She got through the
three swallows with grim determination and quicker than I
had, then passed the flask back to Yancy and told Alfie, "We
must get El home safely, or they will keep making attempts."

"I'll be all right on my own, thanks," I said, which worked
exactly as well as protesting any of Liesel's plans ever worked.
Less, really: the attempt came out in wafts of sunset gold and
orange, and I trailed off staring in dazzlement at the swoosh
of it floating away from me.

"Don't start any more quarrels with the ravers," she went
on lecturing Alfie, paying no attention to me. "So long as
they are here, that means the gardens are open to visitors.
You had better go guard your father's back instead. Martel
will try that, next, when this plan has failed."

"Right," Alfie said, a little dismally. "Watch your own back,
will you? And don't trust Yancy," he added, soft enough not
to be overheard, but with even more urgency. "She and hers
have always had it in for us."

That seemed uncharitable to me, since it was fairly clear to
me that Yancy had been on the verge of helping his dad try to
save London. She and the rest of her crew were used to han-
dling unstable sources of mana; I imagine Sir Richard had
recruited *them* to channel the power out of the wobbly mana
store to him.

Also Alfie threw in an earnest look at me as he spoke, and I wasn't going to be any part of that *us*. Just because I hadn't wanted the entire enclave to be destroyed with every living person in it dying horribly wasn't the same as adding myself to the roster. "Yes, who can imagine why, it's not like you've been chasing them into the streets on the regular," I said, with a sniff that went into roller-coaster loops of deep snide green. Liesel only sighed a starburst of exasperation and told Alfie, "I will be back soon."

"Ready, then?" Yancy said, having a final swig herself. She beckoned us along after her into the labyrinth path, doing a hopping sort of dance between the stones as if it mattered tremendously which particular spot of grass she put her feet on. Liesel started to copy her almost immediately, and in a moment or three—I was having trouble making my brain work—I caught up and realized that it *did* matter. Each time our footsteps came down, little sparkly bursts came out, and the bursts were in different colors depending on where you landed. Yancy was very deliberately going for pale-blue bursts. I couldn't tell how she knew which way to go, so all I could do was try my hardest to land wherever she'd stepped, which wasn't easy when the grass sprang back up at once. Liesel and I only managed to land the right color one in two.

But even Yancy sometimes got a dark blue or a white instead, so presumably it was a bit flexible. And after capering around through maybe two labyrinth branches, I became increasingly certain that we were going somewhere, and not just to the center of the maze but somehow past it and on to a completely different destination—the same feeling as walking a long route to class inside the Scholomance, a familiar one, where you can't be sure exactly how long it's going to take, but you know you're getting close, the classroom door will be on your right after the next turn, or maybe the one after that; and when Yancy said, "All right, here we go, watch your step going down," I was perfectly ready to follow her, and did, not only down but out of the world as well.

When I'd just been swanning around a massive enclave built inside the void and out of borrowed space—not to mention having spent four years inside the even-bigger Scholomance— it might seem like nitpicking to complain about being in unreal spaces, but it very much wasn't. Yancy had mentioned that the enclave had traded in a riding ring for the memorial plaza. When we stepped out of the meadow, we landed inside it: an elaborate pavilion where people would have sat with cool drinks to watch the riders show off on enchanted horses. Out the front I could see the ring, or rather where the ring *had been*. It wasn't quite the brutal emptiness of staring into the void itself: more like looking at the void through a sheet of transparent film that someone had printed with a faint black-and-white photo of an old riding ring, and on the far side of it, there was an even fainter outline of a stable, like a set designer had done a faint pencil sketch on a black backdrop to show the painters where to work.

The pavilion itself just barely qualified as a solid surface. We were walking on old pitted wood planks, and they did look like wood, but they didn't *sound* like wood. Our footsteps sounded odd and muffled instead, like we were walking across a carpet laid over a wooden floor. That kind of mismatch with reality is a blaring warning sign that you're in a space that's about to come apart and drop you into the void, and *get out now.* It reminded me forcibly of the time at school when I'd aggressively disbelieved in one of the walls—I was eldritched at the time—and the walls had obligingly started to buckle.

But Yancy didn't seem especially concerned. She looked all around with satisfaction and even gave the front railing a pat as she went. "There, you're holding up nicely, aren't you?" she said conversationally, to the place. "The whole enclave might have gone into the sea, it wouldn't drag you down. This old ruin will outlast the rest of the place," she added over her shoulder to us. "They had Queen Elizabeth out here once, you know."

"I thought you said they tore the place down a hundred years ago," I blurted.

"Good Queen Bess," Yancy said. It was absolute nonsense either way, of course. Wizards were never inviting mundanes into their enclaves, because the enclaves would've caved in on themselves under the burden of disbelief. Even when mundanes didn't have science to helpfully explain the world and happily burned witches at the stake, they didn't really believe in magic. If you believed in magic, you wouldn't drag a witch to the stake; you'd have her lob fireballs at your enemies instead. But they didn't believe in magic, so even if you *were* a witch, when they dragged you to the stake and burned you in front of an audience, you'd have a bloody hard time getting yourself out of it. In fact most witches who got caught up in the net didn't.

But I didn't contradict Yancy again. Liesel had poked me sharply in the back of the shoulder, and anyway I'd had enough time for my glazed-over brain to work out that the last thing I should be doing was encouraging the place to think of itself as nonexistent. But I couldn't understand how it *did* exist.

Obviously Yancy and her people were propping it up as much as they could—encouraging it to keep on taking up space where they could squirrel themselves away from the prowling hordes of London's maleficaria, even if they had to be doped to the gills to stand it. Which they absolutely did. If it hadn't been for Yancy's potion, I'd have been clawing at the walls for a way out. But the pavilion felt just as solid as the rest of the universe around me—in other words, not very. I was seeing whispers and wind chimes—not solid wind chimes dangling, which would have been all right; I was seeing the *sound* of wind chimes, and don't ask me to describe it. My mouth tasted like having forgotten something important, and my skin was prickling with colors in harlequin patches all over.

So the stands seemed at least as likely to be real as the heat of the sun that insisted on roaring in my ears. I could imagine that it was *all* just the drugs, and as soon as they wore off, I'd be standing in a perfectly reasonable, perfectly real place. That let my brain believe in the place just enough to endure being here. And yes, on some deeper level I knew too well that it wasn't real, but anyone who's made it out of the Scholomance knows how to keep their screaming on the inside.

It was awful, but I could still understand why Yancy and her people chose to live here. The reason wizards live in enclaves—well, the reason wizards live in enclaves is because it keeps their kids from being eaten by maleficaria, but the *other* reason wizards live in enclaves is because it makes magic *easier*. All of magic essentially involves sneaking something you want past reality while it's distracted and looking the other way. That becomes loads easier once you've pushed yourself a tidy little nook into the void, but one of those only opens up naturally if your family spend, oh, ten generations or so puttering around, constantly doing as much magic as you can in the same place. It doesn't happen very often.

Or you and yours can go to enormous amounts of effort and time and build yourselves an enclave—the way my friend Liu's family in Xi'an were trying to—or much more likely, find some way to get into an existing one. And then the same mana and time that used to grow you a single fireflower can grow you a garden full of them, under massive sunlamps that some artificer has been able to make for the same reason, and you can wander the paths in the shelter of privacy incantations and watch the flights of magical birds that some other alchemist has bred, et cetera. All very nice and wondrous, and then also you can go to bed in a sheltered, shielded alcove somewhere and even if you have to sleep in the attic or a cramped Tudor-era bedroom the width of a sofa, at least nothing's going to try to eat you in your sleep.

So every wizard—aside from the exceedingly odd exception—wants to be in an enclave, and if you aren't born into one, and you aren't brilliant enough to win your way in, the only way you get into one is by signing up to work for them. That's life for most indie wizards: graduate from the Scholomance, choose an enclave that needs someone with your skills, apply to work for them, and then spend the rest of your days handing over eighty percent of your effort to the enclave, because the twenty percent that's left over is still twice as much as what you could manage living on your own outside.

Oh, and sorry, it's not nearly as good a bargain as that in practice. Because mals want to be inside enclaves too. It's easier for them to exist in an enclave, just like it's easier for any other magic to happen there, and anyway enclaves are just bursting with delicious mana. So there's not a single major enclave in the world that isn't surrounded by mals, all the time. If you work inside an enclave, but you don't get to *stay* inside—well, your commute home won't be as bad as graduation day in the Scholomance, but it's still not going to be pleasant, and it's going to happen every single day.

Most wizards who work for London enclave live an hour outside the city or more. They commute along with mundanes for the protection, just like most indie kids go to mundane schools, and your first month of work buys you a professional-quality shield holder, and half of each month after that gets you the mana to keep it charged, so by the time all is said and done, if you're lucky, you do a bit better than you'd have done on your own, and if you're unlucky, you do a bit worse, and if you're really unlucky you get eaten on your way home when you nod off on a bus that clears out before your stop.

And you keep at it anyway, because there's a dangling carrot up ahead, the enclave seat that's waiting for anyone who provides roughly thirty years of service. At some newer enclaves, they make it twenty; New York probably demands forty. Most people run out of steam halfway and take a lump sum to retire somewhere a bit further away and less infested with maleficaria, generally a village somewhere that's got a few wizards who get together to do more modest circle magic and guard each other's backs. Others—the more realistic sort—aren't even trying to go the distance; they just do the work in exchange for their kids getting to go to the enclave school and get Scholomance seats.

And the few of us who are quixotic enough to object to the whole grotesque system of squeezing, well, we live in the back of beyond, as far as possible from the crowds of mals around the major enclaves, which not coincidentally is also as far as possible from any other wizards, and struggle to raise enough mana on our own just to put up slightly wobbly shields at night, and normally we get eaten when one of the more dangerous mals drifts out into the wilds and stumbles across us and we don't have the mana to fight it off.

So I absolutely understood why Yancy and her crew would rather give up on the whole rat race and brew themselves a batch of exotic mind-altering drugs and pry open the hollow underbelly of London to climb inside for twenty years, a massive *up yours* to the enclave. Pour the champagne and turn over the tables and fuck it all. Why not? Their odds were bad, but their odds had been bad anyway, and at least they'd have a good time before they went. They could probably do absolutely amazing magic in here, fever dream spells that would topple over or go wrong half the time, and none of it would be permanent, but it would be theirs as long as it lasted.

What I didn't understand was why *London* had left enough of the place for them to ever get into at all. Mum had told me that Yancy and her people used old entrances to sneak into the enclave; that had made sense to me, but I'd imagined them hiding in empty rooms or pushing a temporary bubble of space out from the existing parts of the enclave—space that they themselves had borrowed out of the real world. That would have been loads more work and mana for them, so this was better from their perspective, but not as far as the enclave was concerned. London had torn the riding ring down to reclaim the space, which meant the rest of the enclave expected every cubic centimeter of air we were occupying to be *somewhere else.* The enclave spells were presumably having to do substantial extra work to juggle it round: like in Alfie's race car, stealing a pocket of space out of the corner of some enclaver's eye and pretending it was still there until they looked back.

It must have been a massive mana drain. Alfie might claim that Yancy's people had it in for the enclavers; it seemed much more likely to me that it was the other way round. I could just imagine Martel and the rest of that council totting up the mana that was being siphoned off for these disreputable revels and gnashing their teeth. London wouldn't have *deliberately* kept this ghostly place hanging round for anyone to crawl into; they'd have carefully and thoroughly shoved this bit off into the void.

Just like we'd done, with the Scholomance.

I've laid it out tidily here, but at the time it took my muddled brain a good ten minutes to gnaw through the confusion to that point. We weren't walking the whole time: Yancy took us to the most central part of the stands, festooned with massive swoops of glittery bunting that were clearly a more recent addition, which mostly hid away the translucent world outside. Her crew had heaped up glorious mountains of cushions around a scattering of low tables, piles of blankets and soft rugs woven out of things like the flavor of freshly picked strawberries and poems and golden-green—not me being poetic; someone doped on this potion had evidently figured out a way to actually do artifice with what they could perceive. I have no idea what the stuff would have looked like in the real world. Probably it couldn't exist in the real world; it would just have fallen apart instantly as soon as you got it too close to physics or even a sober pair of eyes.

Once we were inside and we'd sunk down into the impossible nest, I didn't have to keep pretending the void wasn't *right there, right over there, and we're about to fall into it.* Yancy's crew had done it up in a really clever way—the drapes didn't *completely* hide the outside, which would have made you think about it more and implied that there was something outside that needed hiding, but enough of it that you'd have had to make an effort to look. And even if the cushions and rugs weren't very real, they were still artifice, and their purpose was to make you *comfortable.* If you've ever imagined lying down on a cloud and having it hold you up, that's more or less what it was like. It didn't make any sense and you knew better, but at the same time, you also secretly really believed that it would work, and were delighted to go along with it when improbably it did.

The section of the stands immediately around us was more solid, and under the layers of cushioning they felt more plausibly like wood. There were gilt and paint and carvings everywhere, some of them magical runes. This surely *had* been an old and well-loved part of the enclave, the site of parties and ceremonial events back when wizards still rode things that looked like horses instead of cars. Maybe Yancy's story was part of an old tradition; maybe the enclavers had told their own children stories about royal visits, and Queen Bess was a bit more plausible than King Arthur, at least. Enough belief and memory poured into this space so that even after the enclave had more or less given it the boot, this one part had lingered on?

"How did you get into this place?" I demanded urgently, when my brain had finally lurched that far. I knew it wasn't safe to ask the more accurate question—*they must have shoved this place off into the void, how did you get it back?*—but I thought I could get away with asking that much.

Yancy had sprawled out over a heap of pillows and got hold of a silver jug so much like the ones in the garden above that I was sure it had been pilfered. She was pouring herself a drink into an old-fashioned champagne cup made of elaborate green glass, and the liquid foamed and bubbled and settled down into a froth of pink mousse.

"Give us a spoon, love," she said, in answer. I looked down at the table: at my place I had a gilt-edged teacup, slightly faded, on a glass plate, and something like a sugar bowl which had been crammed with a tiny forest of tarnished silver spoons, with delicate handles made to look like narrow branches. I slid one over to her, and she passed me the jug in return.

When I poured the liquid into my teacup, I got what looked like a crème brûlée, only when I broke the crust, underneath there wasn't custard but the blue-violet flames you get from setting brandy on fire. I spooned a bit of them into my mouth gingerly, and then the cup and spoon tumbled down in a smash from my hands while I covered my face, trying to breathe, moans breaking out of me.

It was the taste of summer rain mixed with faint hisses: the taste of being in the gym with Orion, that last day, the very last day before graduation, stupidly kissing him in the pavilion with the amphisbaena falling from the ceiling pipes all around us. It was the taste of everything I'd been thinking in that passionate, greedy moment: that it would be better to have had him just the once, in case we died, only I'd really been thinking about in case *I* died, and how stupid I'd feel to have refused myself this one-last-only-real pleasure I could dig out of the Scholomance.

And I couldn't be sorry even now, but the swallow was burning in my gut, a memory that would be in me forever, and what if maybe Orion hadn't shoved me through the gates after all, if I hadn't more or less traded him the promise of something he'd wanted more than his own life? If I hadn't told him, *Yes you can come to Wales, you can come to me*—the promise that would only have been good if I'd lived to get to Wales in the first place—and so when a maw-mouth the size of a city had come roaring towards us, he hadn't been willing to take the chance that he'd be the only one to make it out alive. It was the taste of that, too. The taste of Orion going into the belly of a maw-mouth, a maw-mouth that apparently I *could*, after all, have killed.

Yancy didn't bat an eyelash at me whimpering agony into my hands. I suppose it was a fairly common reaction. It would have taken some bad luck for people to land in her crew, surely. They weren't raising their own kids in here; the kids that came to them were the ones that had fallen or been kicked out of the rest of the world before they'd ever slipped through the back doors of the enclave.

When I surfaced, still shaking, Liesel was grimly eyeing her own mug without enthusiasm—a big clay cup with an octopus sculpted round it and tentacles to make the handle, with a round orange glass eye peering back at her. She took the jug and poured until it was full, though, and took a spoonful of the absinthe-green jelly she got, shutting her eyes as she did. She didn't whimper, but she sat there absolutely rigid, her mouth and her body and her hands clasped tight around the cup in her lap, all straight hard lines as if she was caging up whatever she was feeling. Then she opened her eyes and put the cup down with a hard click on the table. The octopus unwound itself and climbed inside and started eating the rest of the jelly.

Yancy smiled at us, mirthlessly, and tipped the remnants of her own glass down her throat in a single swallow. She didn't look as though she'd enjoyed hers, either. A toll of sorts, maybe; this place would still need mana to keep going, and London would be trying to keep it from getting any, so anyone who stopped in had to pay up?

That made sense also, except for the part about it not having fallen off into the void completely in the first place. But Yancy still wasn't taking questions; instead she said to Liesel in the bright impersonal small-talk of sharing a lunch table with a stranger you didn't much want to know, "So you're the new arrival, are you? Hard luck for you, the whole place getting knocked sideways just as you get in."

"Bad luck would be if the enclave had gone down," Liesel said, with the severity of correcting someone who'd made a mistake in a group presentation. Her face was still rigid and remote, and she sounded mechanical more than anything else, although I could see a thin gleaming-steel thread of irritated *why must I explain something so obvious* surfacing out of her voice and twining away into the air to go in a ring around her head, a bit like those fairy stories where the girl gets cursed and frogs and beetles come out of her mouth when she speaks. "Now there will soon be council vacancies, and Sir Richard will need reliable allies. He cannot give Alfie a position immediately, but he can make me secretary. I am too young to have been given a position of any kind otherwise for five years at least . . ."

Excellent planning, but it wasn't a match for Yancy's tone at all. Liesel had been knocked for a loop, or else she'd never have said it all out loud anyway. Or perhaps she would have; she'd probably jettisoned all her spreadsheets of carefully planned niceties with enormous relief once she'd made valedictorian.

Yancy only said vaguely, "Oh, how nice," very *your slip is showing, darling.* "So how's your mum, El? Still gathering moss out there in the woods?"

I wasn't ready to talk, and in fact had been giving real thought to some more howling, but the automatic programming kicked in. "She's fine," I said, which was a hilarious lie both in my speaking in coherent tones at all, and also about Mum, who was probably lying on her face in the mud somewhere right now, thinking about Dad gone into a maw-mouth and wondering if I was ever coming home again. "Any more trouble with—?" I left it there; I had to say something, but at the moment I couldn't have remembered for my life what it was Mum had helped her with.

"Nothing to fuss about," Yancy said, keeping the conversation empty of information. "Lovely weather we've been having lately."

With every line, it felt more and more like an odd playacting, carrying out some sort of ritual exchange—mimicking
what ought to have been happening here, what *had* happened
here, over and over, enclavers politely smiling at each other
with their teeth hidden while they jockeyed for power, for
standing. I ought to have said something back, kept playing
the part. But I couldn't. I understood the idea: I was meant to
want to be screaming and still keeping up the side, all to build
more mana, only it was too hard. I just managed to sit there
woodenly.

But Liesel had got the idea and said, "Yes, very nice," so
Yancy could say, "Shall we go for a stroll?" and I got up and
followed them out.

The one positive aspect of the experience was that I'd
completely stopped thinking about the place being halfway
into the void. Likely that's why Yancy was able to take us
onward. She took us out through the back of the canopy, lifting apart two massive brocade drapes, and we ducked
through behind her and were at the top of a narrow concrete
stairway going down to a cramped tunnel made of bricks.

We had to go single file. Dim caged lamps on the ceiling
flickered to life only as Yancy stepped beneath them, and
went out again right on my heels, so we were traveling in a
small island of mud-yellow light that left everything stained
the color of old sepia photographs, matte and papery, and all
around us a pitch dark that was just *barely* not the void. As if
we were somehow calling each chunk of the space into existence only long enough to get through it, like getting a reference text out of the void that you only needed for a single
essay and throwing it back afterwards. It didn't make any
sense even with magic; it was the idea that you could climb
up into the sky by taking a ladder rung from below you and
putting it above you, stepping onto it, and then grabbing the

rung you'd just left, putting it up above the other one, with the ground getting left further and further behind—it was just silly, a cartoon joke to laugh at, not something to believe in. It was almost impossible to think of it as a space that really existed outside of us, and under normal circumstances, probably I'd have thought about that too much, and then I'd have been one of those people who never came back out again.

But I wasn't thinking about how the passage was one step up from the void and how likely it was to tip off. I wasn't even carefully trying to *not* think that. Instead I was thinking the opposite: how it was so much more real than it ought to have been, how it *did* exist, and about how I needed Yancy to stop long enough that I could grab her by the arms and shake her until the answers came out that I needed, the answers that I knew I didn't want, and I didn't want them with so much sickening intensity that the passage actually started to get longer around us, lights flickering on further up ahead, a *plink-plink* dripping sound starting, and a breath of musty air moved in our faces.

An unreadable poster loomed out of the dark, smeared by damp, and Yancy abruptly turned, opened a door I hadn't noticed in the wall, and swung out through it very quick, almost a dancing movement; the instant Liesel and I were out, she shut the door hard behind us and wheeled round with her arms spread to gather the two of us up on either side, and she hustled us away as fast as she possibly could, through another short narrow unlit tunnel and up three steps in a rush. I expect she was trying to keep us from noticing that the door—possibly the tunnel itself—wasn't really there anymore behind us. She had us out of the space before we even had a chance to register where we were, squinting painfully against fluorescent lights that had come on in an unpleasant buzzing glare: a wide tunnel with a roof like someone had made a waffle out of steel girders, one of the old air-raid shelters in the Underground.

This must have been one of the emergency back doors the enclave had opened during the Blitz: sensible of them to have one leading to the deep underground shelters. They'd probably quietly dug themselves that small narrow side tunnel when the authorities weren't looking, and then blocked it up again after the war. There was still just a hint of something vaguely *soft* about the place, just like that crumbling ruin of a mansion that Alfie had taken us through. The enclave had closed up the old exit, to save themselves the trouble of guarding it, but I would have laid money they had somehow bought or rented out this place and were now using most of the room inside the enclave. It would certainly have cost less than expensive architectural monstrosities in primo London postcodes.

But the shelter itself was still a real place in the world, inexpressibly comforting. The sickening quivery feeling beneath my feet was gone so completely I only just now managed to register how horrible it had been, feeling it all this time. The tunnel was filled with identical old bunk bed frames stretching the whole length, stacked with handwritten-labeled boxes full of aggressively boring things like ancient videotapes and sewer planning surveys from the 1980s and proceedings of subcommittees with long acronyms. I went straight for the nearest one and put my hands on the cold clammy metal and then put my cheek against it too, taking deep gulping breaths full of rust and mildew and mold and dust and tar and oil and paint and dirt, a cocktail of underground stinks, and when the walls and floor shuddered with a train going by somewhere on the other side, noisy and cranky and tooth-rattling, I shuddered with almost delirious relief. My whole brain devoured every wonderful reasonable

predictable sensation. I could with pleasure have spread myself out over the dirty concrete floor and possibly licked it.

"Here, have one," Yancy said. I lifted my head. Liesel had
sat down on the floor herself and was leaning back against
the opposite wall with her eyes shut. Yancy was unwrapping
a packet of small square wafer biscuits. She pulled one out and
crunched into it, and handed the packet to me: they smelled
of lemon and vanilla.

"What's this?" I said, feeling what I think was reasonably
wary.

"A biscuit," Yancy said, with a snort of laughter. "Go on.
It'll settle your stomach." Liesel lurched up to get one herself.
They were real too, plain ordinary sugar and flour and artifi-
cial flavorings that were absolutely natural by comparison;
we reduced the whole packet to crumbs in a few minutes.
Better than licking rusty cabinets.

Yancy watched us devour the biscuits. I hadn't quite finished gobbling when she said, a little airy, "Well, that was interesting. That tunnel's usually an hour's walk with people
who all know the way. Mind telling me how you did it?"

The sweet powdery wafer dust on my tongue had a faint
aftertaste. I was a Scholomance graduate, so my brain had
both noticed it and already classified it as *not going to kill you*,
which meant it was safe enough to eat in desperation, and I
had been as desperate for it as I'd ever been for a slice of stale
toast with only one spot of mold or a brown apple slice or a
bowl of noodles fished out from one end of a pan with a mi-
asmic wriggler on the other. So I hadn't stopped eating, but
now that the biscuits were down, I knew there had been
something on them, nothing really nasty but a quiet little
nudge that would only last a few minutes at most: *go on, tell
old Yancy what she wants to know.*

Knowing that you've been enchanted doesn't stop it working, necessarily, but in this case Yancy had asked me a really unfortunate question, because it dragged me straight out of the overwhelming physical relief of being in the real world and smashed me back into the reason why I'd been able to get out: the questions I didn't want to ask and had to ask. "It was *there!*" I said, my voice fraying like rotting cloth. "The enclave shoved those places off into the void, but they were *there.* Why aren't they *gone?*"

Yancy spread her arms, smiling. She wasn't even lying, really; she was just saying *sorry, not telling you my most valuable secrets.* "How should I know? I know they're there, that's good enough for me."

"Not for *me,*" I snarled, taking a step towards her, and the whole tunnel washed over with green underwater light, the air clenching into a cold fist around us.

I didn't have any coherent intention in mind. What I did have in my mind was the visceral sickening pressure of a maw-mouth trying to get in at me, the pulsing wet hunger all around me, something that wouldn't ever be satisfied, couldn't be satisfied, that wanted to crush me into living putrescence and feed on my agony forever. Only it wasn't me, it was Orion. If the Scholomance *wasn't gone,* if the Scholomance was *there,* then I was going to have to go back into it. Not to save him; I'd missed my chance to do that. Instead I was going to have to find Patience, and I was going to have to look at Orion's eyes looking back out at me from that horrible endless crushing mass, hear his mouth say, *Please, El, please let me out,* and then I'd have to tell him that he was *already dead,* so I could make that true, because there wasn't anything else you could do for someone who'd gone into the belly of a maw-mouth.

Yancy took a step back from me and lost her smile, the bland mocking smile that had been meant for the four-year-old kid she'd remembered from the commune, easy to transfer to the teenage witch with her little enclaver buddies, coming to ask her for a way out. It hadn't annoyed me before. She'd mocked the Dominus of London to his face in the middle of his enclave; I imagine she'd have smiled at anything less than a maw-mouth.

But I wasn't *anything less*. I was the thing that maw-mouths ran away from in the dark, and I suppose whoever the maleficer was, destroying enclaves left and right, *they* might be hiding from me, too, or trying to suck up power to fight me with, as if they'd caught a hint of me coming out of the Scholomance before I'd even made it out the gates.

And Yancy would have tweaked Sir Richard's nose for him, but she wasn't stupid. She stopped smiling at me and pulled her hands up into a defensive casting position that wouldn't have done her any good, because the ground beneath my feet was real, but it was also a little bit part of London enclave, and I'd given back the power-sharer, but I didn't *need* a power-sharer. The power-sharer had made the mana a gift, freely offered, but I could have reached out to the still-sloshing oceans of power and grabbed away as much as I wanted, and tipped over the whole reeling enclave most likely and smashed the whole shelter into pieces while I was at it.

I'd like to think I wouldn't have done any of that, but I'd have done *something*, even if it was only to grab Yancy by the shoulders and scream into her face to tell me, tell me, tell me. What I wanted more than anything was for her to say that they'd *done* something, someone before her had done something all the way back then to save those old places from falling off into the void, and otherwise they would have been gone, only I don't think I'd really have believed her if she'd told me that.

But Liesel said to me, "Stop that!" in a crisp peremptory

tone, and snapped at Yancy, "We broke the Scholomance away into the void. You've heard this, yes?"

Yancy didn't take her eyes off me. There was a flush of purple-pink color standing in her cheeks and glowing through the skin a bit, something coming to the surface. "I've heard a lot of things, the last week. Wasn't sure what to believe."

"You haven't noticed that more than half the maleficaria are gone?" Liesel said tartly.

Yancy shrugged a bit. "We hole up underneath the enclave so we *don't* see mals, love. It's been better, yeah. Doesn't mean I was ready to swallow the idea that the Scholomance got booted off the world. We get a lot of backwards stories, listening to whispers, and the ones that come straight out of the enclave are mostly just better lies. We couldn't work out any reason why New York and London would've done it. But they didn't, did they," she finished softly, still looking at me. "*You* did it."

Liesel scowled in irritation, and to be fair, I certainly wouldn't have got far on my own. But I wasn't giving a bloody speech, was I, so I didn't care about correcting Yancy and sharing the credit. I just stared at her, waiting, and Yancy gave a small huff. "Your mum must be proud." I could've slapped her, only I couldn't; if I'd let myself act with that much violent intention, probably I'd have set her on fire. She saw my expression, I suppose, and rolled her eyes and spread her hands as if to ward me off. "I'm serious! Bloody hell."

Maybe Yancy had been serious, but I couldn't help but think of Mum seeing me like this: down in London's underbelly with a cold malicious green wave gathered round me, threatening someone who'd only helped me, trying to bully her into telling me the secrets she and her people used to survive. So I shut my eyes and did my best to stop wanting to set Yancy on fire, and Liesel, forcing me to be grateful she'd come along, said, "We did it, yes. But one boy was left behind. Can you tell us how to get back in?"

Yancy didn't say anything at first. I opened my eyes again. The mirk had faded away from around us, and the tunnel lights were basting us in their gloriously mundane fluorescence again. She was studying me like puzzling out a book in a new language. "Is the door still there?" she asked after a moment. "The outside one, I mean—the way in."

"I don't know," I said, calming a bit; she was telling me something, at least. "I was standing at the gates when I cast the spell to break it off. I don't know if it would have hit—"

"Did you go to the door in the real world, smash it up completely, brick up the hole, build a wall over it, brick up the nearest passage too, and then cast four curses of forgetting over the place?" Yancy interrupted, prosaic.

"Right, no," I said.

She nodded. "Then there's not much trick to it. If the door's still there, you just open it and go through the usual way, whatever that is. And if you remember the place on the other side well enough, and it's got enough mana left in it and you give it a bit more, and you're lucky, then you might be able to convince it to be there, long enough for you to be in it. Or you might not. When it's the Scholomance—I don't know, actually. Could go either way. Either it was so bloody big that it burned up all the mana left in the place in a flash, and the whole thing just went, or it was so bloody big that it'll be centuries crumbling away. If I had to guess—it'll linger a while, in bits and pieces at least. There're a lot of wizards out there with the place burned into their brains. But as for going round inside the place—" She shrugged. "You'd just have to try it and see."

She hesitated a moment, and then added, "And you'd better think about whether you want to. How long has it been, more than a week? We try to poke our heads out every few days. Longer than that, and you start sliding off yourself. And that's *with* our little helpers." Yancy opened a flap of her coat to show the flask sitting in an inner pocket, the lizard peeking out around it. She let the coat fall shut again. "We run into the others sometimes—people who've gone too long, or fallen off somewhere. It's not pretty."

"It doesn't matter," I said. I already knew what I found wasn't going to be pretty. "Thanks, Yancy. Sorry for . . ."

Yancy eyed me, then shook her head. "I won't say sorry myself. I poke bears: it's how we live down here, and if I could stand to do it any other way, I wouldn't be here in the first place. But every once in a while you have to expect to see some claws and teeth. Just do me a flavor and don't come back through our doors. It's not the place for you."

"Where is?" I said, sour as turned milk, and I turned my back on her and headed down the tunnel, past the sign with the arrow pointing EXIT.

Chapter 6
HEATHROW

IT WAS A GOOD TEN MINUTES' WALK through the tunnels and round and round and round the stairs until the building finally spat me and Liesel out near Belsize Park station. We weren't heaving for breath or anything, as we were still in sprinting-for-the-graduation-gates trim, but it wasn't a delightful stroll either. At last we were out in the July night air, late enough now that all the posh cafés and restaurants around us were closed, a few very faint stars or satellites glittering overhead.

I stood on the corner blankly. Not out of indecision: I was full of perfect certainty. I knew exactly what I had to do, bright and clear and utterly necessary. I had to get to the Scholomance doors, and I had to go in, and I had to kill Patience. Only I hadn't the faintest idea how to start on that project in any practical way. I'd spent the last four years of my life in a single building—a bloody big one, but still there hadn't been anywhere in the place I couldn't get to by walking, and the meals were terrible but they were provided for me, and I know how to set off supervolcanoes and destroy castigator demons and murder ten thousand people at a time, but I didn't have a passport or a mobile or a tenner in my pocket. And for that matter, I didn't even know where I was going. I looked at Liesel ungraciously. "Can you ask Alfie for me where the Scholomance doors are?"

"No, of course not. If I contact Alfie from here, while he is in the enclave, his father's enemies will be able to trace us, and then we will have done all this," she waved with vivid disgust at the squat round turret we'd emerged from, "for nothing. Anyway, what good would that do? Yancy said it would take mana. London is still in no position to help you with that at the moment. We must go to New York."

I had several different competing reactions to that statement, most prominently the intense desire to demand when *I* had become *we,* and also why, but unfortunately the well-honed strategic bits of my brain pointed out that Liesel was in fact perfectly right. The only people in the world who could give me the kind of mana I'd need to get back into the Scholomance and kill Patience, and who *would* do that, just to save Orion from screaming in the void for however long it took the school to really go, were in fact his mum and dad, in New York.

And I hadn't any idea how to get there on my own. There's a terribly impressive Trans-Atlantic Gateway between London and New York, but with London's mana store flobbing about like jelly, I wouldn't have bet on it being stable enough to use at the moment even if I could have gone sailing back into the enclave I'd just gone to great effort to sneak out of. That left the prosaic but reliable method of getting on a plane, and that meant I couldn't afford to ask Liesel *why,* because if she didn't help me, I'd land myself in the clink for inadequately forging a passport and stealing a plane ticket, and that was if I wasn't shoved into deep dark detention somewhere.

Of course, Mum doesn't have a passport or a mobile either. She'd have told me to just set off into the world and trust it to get me where I'm supposed to be. That always works for her, but the world has given me the strong impression that it thinks I'm supposed to be in a dark fortress on top of a mountain somewhere, wreathed with storms and lightning cracking down as I laugh maniacally, so I didn't really trust that approach myself.

But I was still wary about taking Liesel's help. I'd already turned down her offer, so now I didn't have any idea what she thought she was going to get out of shepherding me around the world like a wayward hurricane she'd have liked to aim, and that made me uneasy since I was absolutely certain she *did* think she was going to get something out of it. What if it was something I didn't want her to have? It could have been something as simple as wanting to get herself in good graces with Orion's mum, who was in line to be the next Domina of New York, but flying across the Atlantic seemed like a fairly large outlay for the small chances of that return.

But I do a lot of things in my life warily, so this time wasn't particularly novel. I let her summon us a taxi and off we went to the airport. She radiated exasperation when I needed help turning a small notebook from Paperchase into a passport, but she also did it for me, and then had a strongly worded conversation with the ticket machine that persuaded it to meekly hand over two first-class tickets, and once we'd been ushered through security and into the concourse, she dragged me past a bunch of perfume shops that together smelled like an unfortunate alchemy lab section and found a small phone store—tucked in a nook between one shop selling handbags for five hundred pounds and another one selling iPads, because after all, what if you just desperately needed an iPad on the spur of the moment whilst passing through—where she got me a proper phone on contract.

I didn't resist the phone. The instant Liesel handed it over, I called Aadhya. Liu had written me an annoying little jingly song with her and Aadhya's numbers in it, concluding with the line *And El is going to go and get a phoooone!* so I hadn't any trouble remembering it, now that I actually had one in my hands. "It's me," I said, when she answered.

Aadhya shrieked, "Oh my God, I'm going to *kill you*! A *week*! We started calling random communes! Liu called *Liesel*!" At the sound of her voice, her voice caring about me, I had to go blindly stumbling off to the side of the corridor, nearly running into people going by in both directions, and turn myself to face the wall so I wouldn't just go into a fit of blubbing.

Aadhya managed to conference Liu in while I got myself under control. Hearing both their voices prolonged the struggle, though. If I shut my eyes, I could be back in one of our dorm rooms, sitting together eating a mishmosh of snack bar horrors several steps down from the worst fast-food options in the airport around me, and I couldn't want to be back inside the Scholomance, but I did want to be with *them* again; I wanted the circle of their arms around me, so desperately.

I couldn't even tell them exactly what had happened: it would have been a bad idea to start talking about maleficaria and enclaves and maw-mouths, or even just Orion dying, there in the corridor with mundanes going past two feet away and a pair of police constables already eyeing me with some skepticism after I'd gone careening wildly across the flow of traffic. But I told them I was going to New York. "And I—have to go back to the school," I said.

"*Can* you?" Aadhya said. "Isn't it—gone?"

"There's a way," I said. "I just need . . ."

"Mana," Liu finished for me. Of course, it's what you always need, to do anything impossible.

"Yeah," I said.

Aadhya blew out a breath and said, "Okay. I'll call Chloe and see if she can get us in to see Orion's mom and dad," without my having to say anything more, already understanding. "Text me your flight info, I'll come meet you at the airport."

"Thanks," I said, and added, "Liesel's coming with me."

"What? Why? What's she getting out of it?" Aadhya instantly demanded, in flat suspicion. It was very comforting to have someone else sharing my feelings.

"I don't *know*," I said, grimly. "But she's got us the tickets and everything."

Aadhya didn't like it, but she told me she'd be there to pick us both up and not to do anything stupid—anything *else* was strongly implied in her tone—until she'd got hold of me. "Liu, how long will it be before you can come?"

Liu was silent for a moment, and then she said, softly, miserably, "You haven't heard yet."

"Heard what?" I said, my chest clenching.

"Beijing was hit," she said. "This morning, our time; a few hours ago."

"Well, *shit*," Aadhya said.

Liesel had followed me over to the wall and was watching me talk on the phone. "Another enclave?" she demanded, just looking at my face. I nodded. "How bad?"

"It hasn't gone all the way down, yet, but it's too badly hit to stay up for long," Liu said, when I passed along the question. "And they've asked my family for help. My mother told me they think there might be a way for us to save their enclave and build ours, at the same time. My uncle and the rest of our council members are already there; the rest of us might be leaving any minute. I'm so sorry, El," she finished, low. "I can't come to New York."

"It's okay," I said, my throat tight, but it wasn't okay, because the reason she couldn't come was that by the time her plane landed, there might already be an enclave war going, and if that happened, her family and New York enclave were going to be on *opposite sides*. Probably the only reason New York and Shanghai weren't *already* at war was because London had been hit, too: it wouldn't have made any sense for New York to have attacked its own most powerful ally, not to mention Salta, which had been launched the year before we went into the Scholomance and had been carefully staying totally neutral.

But it didn't make any sense for a maleficer to hit all of those enclaves either. If you *were* trying to suck power out of enclaves, surely you'd be delighted to have them blaming one another and going to war instead of hunting for you. Instead the pattern was looking nearly random, jumping all over the world.

"Why would anyone be doing it that way?" I asked Liesel, over tea and biscuits in the first-class lounge, trying to drown out the lingering ghostly taste of trumpets that kept coming through my mouth. "Hopscotching from one continent to the other?" I was being cautious about my word choices, although the lounge was mostly empty, only us and a handful of other travelers scattered around the wide expanse of vaguely *Star Trek*–like furniture. It wasn't as though Liesel couldn't guess what I was referring to.

Liesel shrugged. "There is no obvious reason. Whoever it is, we can only say that they are not being efficient."

We had five hours left to kill before our morning flight.

We stuffed ourselves from the buffet like the until-recently-starving urchins we were—the staff looked annoyed with us after our first trip loading up our plates, as if they thought we were being greedy, and then became vaguely impressed after our third round—and then we discovered there were even private rooms with beds and showers, too.

I let Liesel shower first, because I didn't want to feel any obligation to come out. I stayed in for nearly an hour, washing over and over, trying to scrub away the lingering jangly edges of Yancy's potion and memories I didn't want: the maw-mouth exploding all over me, the agonized eye looking up at me, the mouth begging to live. The last glimpse of Orion's face as he shoved me through the gates, with Patience coming to swallow him up. Liesel's cleaning spell hadn't wiped any of those away. The shower didn't either. I kept trying until I was pruny and exhausted with the effort, but they went on rotating steadily through my head like they'd been put on a loop.

When I finally gave up and came out, the room lights were off and both Precious and Liesel were asleep, one in a nest of tissues and the other on the bed with a small glowing ball of an alarm spell hovering near her head and the faint comforting soap-slick shimmer of a good warding spell over the door. A warding spell we didn't even need, because of my brilliant scheme, which had wiped out all the maleficaria in the world and handed Orion over to Patience in return. I was still involuntarily glad to notice it there.

I didn't want to sleep; between the drugs and the horror, I was sure I'd wake up screaming, and possibly trying to alter reality around me. I only sat down on the other side of the bed with an empty magazine, but it couldn't hold me; the intoxicating sense of safety unlocked the muscles I was trying to keep clenched tight, and at some point I slid down the bed and just went under.

I'd been right, though. I didn't wake up screaming, but that was because Liesel woke me up before I got that far, holding a silencing bubble over us with one hand as she shook my shoulder with the other. The half-devoured face had been floating over the putrefaction, and it had been Orion's face, and his one eye had looked up at me and his mouth had said, "El, I love you so much," just like he'd said it at the Scholomance doors before he'd *shoved me out,* and then I sat up out of it and I was looking at Liesel instead, frowning at me in the dim light, the small room, with the soft muffling weight of the silencing spell around us, and I put my hands over my face, panting, full of agony and rage I couldn't let myself feel.

"Sorry," I said, rusty and resentful, when I'd got my breath back under control. "I won't fall asleep again."

"You will," Liesel said, not even arguing, just stating a fact. "You must calm your mind, not stay awake."

"Do you happen to have any Oblivion Water handy? Drops of Lethe, maybe?" I said, ostensibly with sarcasm, but I admit that if she'd pulled out a bottle, I'd have let her put them in my eyes without hesitating, even though I knew to the word what Mum would say about that, even aside from the stupidity of mixing anything more in with whatever concoction Yancy had given us.

"Mixing with that potion we drank?" Liesel said, and then she cupped my cheek and we were in bed together, alone here in this little room, floating in the void, and when I said, waveringly, "I'm not," meaning that I still wasn't interested in the grand alliance—which I wasn't, although I had to admit the immediate prospect made it loads more tempting—she said peevishly, "Yes, yes; *well?*" meaning she'd taken no for an answer on that and was offering me a shag anyway, without strings attached.

And of course I had no business believing that; Aadhya and Liu would have yelled at me for days. The first lesson you learn in the Scholomance is that you don't get anything you need for free, so if someone's giving it to you, there's a reason, and I didn't know what Liesel's was. But whatever her reasons, at the moment she was here, and where she was touching me it was only her hand on my skin and the faint sandalwood smell of the free soap, and there wasn't any room left over in my head to go circling back to Orion, Orion, Orion, and maybe I was looking for a way I could shove *him* away, out of the gates of my mind, for at least a few minutes, because when Liesel leaned in and kissed me, I kissed her back.

And as soon as we started, I couldn't bear to stop. It *was* a belly-deep relief, in every possible way. The last traces of the awful blurring drugs went fading away before the physical reality of our bodies moving against one another, the exotic wonder of someone this close to me, much harder to believe in than a thousand forgotten places. I let it fill my whole brain: the touching; the humid warm air still hanging in the room from my endless shower, miles away from the clammy coldness of the Scholomance bathrooms; the sound of our breath, quickening, and not because we were running away from something horrible. Her hands were brushing away a sticky layer of cobwebs that had resisted all the hot water in the world, her mouth warm and mint-cool at the same time.

And it didn't have to be hard. I didn't have to think, I could just put my arms round her and touch, and kiss, and *be* touched; I could have pleasure and give it back in turn. And that was easy too, ridiculously easy; I didn't have to wonder what she'd like, because she just told me, *here,* or *again,* or *yes,*

like so, and I didn't have to wonder what *I'd* like, either, because Liesel just tried things out on me methodically, and
asked me which was best, and anyway all of them were best.
We moved together just like we were back running the obstacle course again, a single smooth well-oiled machine, toss-
ing the lead back and forth between us, and I didn't even
mind whatever she was going to charge me for it. Of course
something this wonderful would have a price. I didn't care.

I was waiting for it afterwards, when we were lying
crammed in on the narrow bed next to each other panting
and sweaty, needing showers all over again. But Liesel didn't
say anything right away, and I couldn't help thinking about
Orion again, running the course with him, being in the gymnasium with him—a million years ago and barely more than
a week, amphisbaena raining gently down outside the pavilion and his hands on my body, hearing him say my name as if
I was the single most astounding thing in the universe.

My throat swelled up with longing and rage: he'd asked to
come to me, he'd asked me to let him make me that promise;
that had been the price *he'd* charged me, for this magical
thing, so good and healthy and simple, and I'd paid it. I'd let
him promise, and he hadn't kept his promise. Instead he'd
gone as far as he could in the other direction; he'd gone to
spend the rest of eternity unreachable and screaming in the
belly of a maw-mouth, in the back of my head, screaming
forever, and Liesel made an impatient noise and rolled over
onto me and kissed me again, and I kissed her back with desperate gratitude and let her yank me out of my head and
back into my body.

We ended up having to make a mad dash for the gate in
the end, despite all the time we'd had to wait. The corridors
of Heathrow annoyingly insisted on remaining exactly the
same length the entire time we were pelting towards the

aeroplane, but I suppose that was better than if they'd stretched themselves out twice as long. We got ourselves aboard and I turned into something of a wide-eyed naif staring out the window as the ground fell away below us. Flying is one of the things you really can't do with magic, at least not outside an enclave: only imagine how wonderful it would be to be soaring a hundred feet off the ground and then some mundane glances up and doesn't believe you're doing that, so rather abruptly you aren't anymore.

My gawping lasted for maybe ten minutes or so, and then I took a deep breath and turned to see what Liesel was going to say to me now, demand of me, and instead she was already asleep and even snoring a little, just barely loud enough to hear it over the burring whine of the engines. I stared down at her and then I spread out my pod seat and went straight to sleep myself, in the comfortable familiarity of discomfort: the cot narrow and hard and cold, the air stale and recirculating through a hundred other pairs of lungs, the wall vibrating with the low whining engines, incomprehensible machinery working somewhere out of sight, keeping us all alive, suspended out of the world.

I slept the entire way. When the attendants turned up the lights and started to make the rounds to bring us a meal we were calling lunch, Precious—she'd made her own way past security and got back in my pocket afterwards—had to creep out and bite my earlobe to wake me up properly; I'd been ready to stay down. At that, I might almost as well have done. The food wasn't *as* bad as the Scholomance cafeteria, which was as much as you could really say for it, although they presented it with the confident triumph of someone offering you marvels of the culinary art, complete with heavy white napkins and inconvenient cutlery that repeatedly threatened to fall down and disappear into the crevices of the seat or into

spots unreachable except by someone with arms like a fla-
mingo's legs.

Liesel and I ate it all anyway; we had low standards. She
kept not asking me for anything, and I continued to feel if not
well, then at least like I had a body and it existed in a function-
ing world, which had seemed questionable at times yesterday. By the time we made it out of the endless bureaucratic
airport queues and were blinking on the pavement in the
daylight of a different continent, I was entirely grounded
back in material reality. New York—or rather New Jersey;
we'd landed one state over—was oven-hot and unbearably
sticky, sun radiating off the black tarmac in waves, and cars
and taxis blaring horns and shoving in and out to the curb in
an ongoing wave that was both always the same and always
different.

Aadhya pulled up to the curb in a massive white vehicle
only slightly smaller than a campervan, and we climbed into
the blessed relief of the air-conditioning and her arms around
me, squeezing me tight: she was alive, she was here, out in
the world with the sun hammering on the car windows.
She'd made it out of the Scholomance, and if she had, and I
was here with her, then I had, too. It was a reminder of gratitude, and I couldn't help but feel some, even with everything
else.

When the honking behind us started to reach the frenzied
pitch of *no we really mean it,* Aad finally let go of me and
started driving with slightly alarming confidence: the car
wasn't as full-on magic as Alfie's London race car, but it had
clearly been told in no uncertain terms that she knew how to
drive and therefore it was going to do the right thing for her
at all times. The right thing seemed to involve a lot of honking at taxi drivers and weaving aggressively through traffic. I
sat in the front seat staring out at the passing road full of cars.

It looked as though someone had come through with a pump and inflated everything in the scene by thirty percent, highway and cars and all, before going away satisfied.

"Are you okay?" Aadhya said, glancing over at me. "Chloe said we could come straight in, but I can call her if you need to lie down for a while."

I wasn't okay, but I'd had the sleep I'd desperately needed, and I wasn't going to get any better by going to lie down for a while. Getting to New York was the only chance I had to get anywhere near a more permanent kind of okay, and I already knew it was going to be the long way round. "No," I said. "Let's go."

Chapter 7
NEW YORK,
NEW YORK

E HADN'T BEEN INVITED into the actual enclave. New York was on high alert, and in any case strangers don't normally get ushered into enclaves, unless of course the enclave is under attack by a maw-mouth and desperately needs the stranger to haul them out of a ditch. Chloe met us at a pavement café somewhere in Manhattan, I couldn't have told you where, on a side street full of townhouses. The fortress of skyscrapers mostly just loomed in the distance, although on the corner someone had knocked down a quarter of the block and put up a complicated steel-and-grey-glass tower some twenty stories high that gave the impression of having been put down by accident in the wrong place.

Chloe was dressed properly mundane in denim and a T-shirt, much more sensible than Liesel's somehow-still-pristine white dress, and there was an older man with her at the table whose clothes might have passed for the same at a quick glance. But if you looked just a smidge longer at the waistcoat he had on, there were more pockets than ought to have been able to fit, and the small gold buttons on them were inscribed with tiny runes. I was willing to bet that when he touched each one, he got out exactly what he needed.

I knew that Orion's dad was an artificer, and that Chloe was bringing him to meet us, so presumably this had to be him, but even so, I found it hard to believe. But Chloe said, "Mr. Lake, this is El—Galadriel Higgins," after we sat down, and I had to accept that yes, he was Balthasar Lake. It wasn't that he didn't look like Orion. They had more or less similar noses, and the same bony wrists, and a scattering of other details. I just couldn't see how Orion had come from him. It was like looking at a maze puzzle in a book with the beginning and the end clearly marked, and no path that made sense in between.

Most people would have said the same about me and Mum, of course, but those were only the people who didn't understand the principle of balance, like the guests at the commune who always looked mildly surprised when they first found out she was my mum, and asked if I was adopted, and then only got even more surprised if they spent any time in my company. But any wizard who *did* understand the principle of balance would have spent a day with us and then would nod wisely and say oh yes, of course.

Of course, both of those reactions enraged me so badly that I'd gone to great lengths at school to avoid telling anyone about her, so I was being a hypocrite, but I couldn't help it. I *could* easily believe Balthasar was what he was, one of the best artificers in New York enclave and therefore in the whole wide world. When we'd walked up, he'd been frowning at the building on the corner with the kind of abstract dissatisfaction that goes with fixing something inside your own head. If you'd shown me some piece of precisely balanced artifice the size of a jet and told me he'd built it, I wouldn't have questioned it for an instant. I could tell he was powerful. Only it was a normal, expected kind of power, too ordinary to have Orion on the other side of it. I *do* understand balance, and I didn't understand him.

Also, I'd stupidly not thought at all about what I was going to say to him. I hadn't prepared any of those gracious empty phrases that I'd wanted so much myself. The only sentence clear in my head was: *Can I please have some mana to go open up the school and kill your son?* The only reason I didn't just start blubbing again was I knew I hadn't the right to do it in front of his dad. Orion had been my friend, my something more, mine, for less than a year; he'd been theirs for his whole life, and they'd surely sent him to the Scholomance with more hope of getting him back out than any other parents in the world.

Back in the Scholomance, I'd put together a story about Orion's family in my head, about his enclave; about all the things they'd done to him to *make* him want to be a hero, to make him think he *had* to be one, or else be a monster and a freak; all the ways they hadn't let him be human. But now with his dad in front of me, being a human being instead of a monster himself, I couldn't help but recognize with a sharp pang of guilt how convenient that story was for *me*. It had given me the right to ask Orion to walk away from his family and his home to be with me, to abandon the people who had raised him and who had hopes for him.

And even if their hopes had all been selfish, he still hadn't died carrying out one of *their* schemes. I was the one who'd come up with the brilliant idea of saving everyone in the whole bloody school and future generations to boot, like we could do something like that without paying the price. Orion had paid for us all, and he'd paid at *their* cost—his parents and his enclave, the effort they'd put into raising him and all their wishes to see him again.

So I clamped down on the quaver in my voice and grated out, "I'm sorry," feeling even as the words left my mouth how utterly inadequate and stupid they were.

But Mr. Lake only said, remote, "Chloe tells me you and Orion worked together on this plan to lure the mals into the school." It was unbearably polite and neutral. I would have rather he'd shouted at me, demanded to know what I'd been thinking, what sort of arrogant twat had I been to think I could make the world better, how his son had ended up the only one left behind. He ought to have been angry. I *wanted* him angry.

"It was my idea," I said, which wasn't exactly true—my idea had been to *do something,* and it had taken Liu, and Yuyan from Shanghai, and Aad and Liesel and Zixuan and a lot of other people to work out the details. But I half wanted to provoke him into a reaction. "It was just the two of us at the gates, at the end. We were about to go through, and then Patience came at us. Orion—he shoved me through."

I had to stop and swallow down an entire tangle of feelings. Balthasar didn't wait for me to keep going. "I'm sure you did your best," he said. "Orion was always very brave. He would never have wanted anyone else to suffer in his place."

There was a way he could have said those same exact words that would have been someone plastering over one of the ugly miserable wrong things that happen in the world, a parent trying to build meaning out of the worst thing that had ever happened to them. People come to Mum with those stories in their mouths all the time. She had to teach me as a kid to stop telling them that their stories were nonsense, even when they obviously were. But Balthasar wasn't trying to be-

THE GOLDEN ENCLAVES ✦ 149

lieve in this story. He was just using the words as a convenient
plank to get from one step of the conversation to another, as
if this mattered to him just as much as that hollow nonsense
conversation I'd acted out with Yancy and Liesel down in
London's forgotten underbelly.

"So how can I help you, El?" he went on. "Chloe says you
were offered a guaranteed seat at school but didn't accept it.
I'm afraid I can't renew that—"

He paused on his own, possibly because Aadhya and Chloe
and Liesel were sitting at the table with us and their faces
warned him, even before I snarled, "Go to *hell*," on a surge of
rage, and everything on the table around us shook with a
wild alarmed clattering. "Patience has him. Orion's *trapped in
a maw-mouth,* and you think I'm here to beg a place from
you? You couldn't pay me to come live in your fucking enclave. The only good thing in it is *gone*." I only stopped there
because one of the water glasses fell off and shattered into
pieces on the pavement.

So obviously I'd been lying when I was going on about
being respectful of his parents' greater claim to grief. I
wanted to unhinge my jaw and bite his entire face off. It was
almost worse than Mum talking about Orion. Mum hadn't
even known him, much less been his *dad*. I had to get up and
walk away while the waiters came over with a tea towel and
a bin to get rid of the glass.

Chloe came timidly after me. "El, I'm so sorry. I didn't
have much time to—I tried to explain—"

I just waved her off without trusting myself to say words,
and then I turned round and went back to the table, once the
mundanes were gone again. "I broke the school off into the
void," I said, savagely, "but it's probably not all the way gone.
I need to know where the doors are, and I need enough mana
to get in, so I can kill Patience. That's how you can help me.

Unless you don't mind Orion screaming until everyone who remembers the Scholomance is dead. And if you *don't* mind that, say so, and I'll get it some other way."

It wasn't fair in the least, of course. Why shouldn't his dad be suspicious of some strange girl showing up, displaying her grief for Orion? In fact, I'm sure it's a routine thing whenever an enclaver kid dies: other wizards from their year turning up at the enclave gates with earnest stories of school romance and promises made. But I wasn't feeling fair. And meanwhile Balthasar was staring at me as though I'd grown a second head. He looked back at Chloe, who was only just shy of wringing her hands in anxiety, and then at me. *"That's* why you want—"

Bile climbed my throat. "That's all I can do for him now," I said. "Sorry, did you think I was offering to bring back your perfect weapon? He's gone, like the whole place is gone, and I can't fix that, and I wouldn't bring him back to you if I could, you sitting there bleating at me about how *brave* he was. No one's brave inside a maw-mouth. He was an idiot who thought he had to be a hero instead of a human being, and that's *your* fault, you sorry bastards, the whole lot of you."

I wasn't expecting him to help me after that howl, but I'd given up on him helping me anyway. I turned round and was ready to march back to Aadhya's car and go, but he got up and intercepted me, catching me by the shoulders with the first real emotion in his face: not grief, not anger, just utter bewilderment, as though I didn't make any sense to him at all, and he said, "You really," and stopped there, as if the next word didn't even matter; as if he found it impossible to believe that anyone had really *anythinged* Orion, and then he looked back at Chloe and said, *"Orion* really—?" and his voice cracked, audibly. She nodded, urgently, and he let go of me and turned away, put a clenched fist up to his mouth, which went clownishly turned-down at the corners, his whole face wrenched. As though it hadn't meant anything to him that Orion had *died,* but this—this meant everything.

I could still with absolute joy have picked up a chair and smashed it over his head, because what right did he have being so astonished about it, but at least it was *some* kind of caring, something that wasn't just grotesque and selfish, and when he turned back to me, his face was wet. "I'm sorry. El— El? I'm sorry. Please, come sit back down. Please." He tried to smile an apology at me, wavering. "I'm so sorry, I shouldn't have assumed—"

Once I had stopped blazing away, I couldn't help but recognize he'd had every sensible reason to assume the worst of me, and apparently now he might help after all, so I did grudgingly go back to the table with him. Only he didn't want to talk to me about how I was going to get back into the school. He just wanted to talk to me about Orion. How we'd become friends, every word we'd ever said to one another— most of which had been unpardonably rude—and everything we'd ever done vaguely in the vicinity of each other.

Mum would have approved tremendously. For me it was the slow hideous excruciatingness of a root canal performed with dull instruments and no anaesthesia. Unfortunately, now that his dad's feelings had actually appeared, I *did* respect them, so I couldn't refuse him. But he almost wasn't grieving. He drank up everything I told him with unbearable happiness, as if I *had* brought Orion back to him. He hung on every word of every trivial human interaction we'd ever had, and I couldn't help but remember Orion telling me earnestly how his father had given up his own work to homeschool him, trying to keep him from sneaking away to hunt mals; how his parents had longed for him to want anything else, to care about anything else.

I couldn't bear it. In desperation I even aggressively told Balthasar about my plan to take Orion *away*, how Orion had said he'd come to Wales and set off round the world with me, trying to get him to let me stop, only even that didn't make his dad sorry in the least. He just got almost glassy-eyed at the idea that Orion had been making plans for the future, which only made things worse.

I finally couldn't stand it anymore. "Look, *will* you help me get back in?" I demanded baldly, instead of giving Balthasar the next story he was asking for, and he paused and apparently only then remembered what I'd told him I was there for in the first place, or at least took it seriously for the first time; I suppose he'd mentally filed it away as nonsense when Chloe had told him about it.

In fact, he still wasn't taking it seriously, not the way I needed him to. "El," he said, instead, with all the gentle kindness of someone having to break bad news, "I'm so sorry. I can't tell you how much it means that you want to save Orion from this, that you care about him that much. But he wouldn't want you to do this." Almost certainly spot-on, but I didn't care in the least what Orion would've wanted. As far as I was concerned, he'd given up the right to an opinion after he'd shoved me out the gates without asking me for *mine*. "It's— the situation is complicated. Even if you're right about what happened . . ." He paused as if he were trying to think through what he was going to say.

"If I'm wrong," I said, "I won't do anything but waste mana. But I'm not wrong. Patience got him." I forced myself to say it. "I tried to pull him out. I felt Patience get hold of him."

Balthasar shook his head a little. "If you're right, there's nothing you can do. You can't . . . Killing a maw-mouth, any maw-mouth, not to speak of Patience—it's not like killing other mals, not even powerful ones. Ophelia, Orion's mother, she's done research into—"

"I've done it three times," I said flatly. "You can ask London if you don't believe me. I did one at their council chamber doors just yesterday."

I'm sure that Chloe had told him; I think Balthasar had simply been having so much difficulty swallowing the idea that I'd really cared in some way about Orion that he'd completely put aside the equally indigestible idea of my going in to kill Patience, much less having any chance of success in this endeavor. He didn't want to swallow it now, either. In fairness to him, it was a ludicrous thing to claim. But Liesel backed me up, and slowly it went down; he sat back in his chair staring at me, and I could see his face changing as he gathered up all the bits and pieces of information about me that he'd left scattered round while he'd been thinking of me only in conjunction with Orion, and assembled them together into an alarming picture.

Or, I suppose, a potentially useful one. I couldn't think of him as a heartless weevil anymore, but after all, it's not some revelation that enclavers love their kids; it doesn't stop them being enclavers. It's why most of them became enclavers in the first place, or their parents or someone even further removed into the past. And Orion *had* been their game-changing mal-killer. Even if Balthasar improbably seemed to care more about Orion's brief happiness than his long-term usefulness, the rest of New York certainly wouldn't. For all I knew, Orion's mum was going to have a hard time becoming Domina without him, and a replacement might have been called for.

Maybe I was being unfair. Balthasar could instead have been thinking about my chances of success, and whether it was worth sending me in, whether I could really save Orion from agony. But there was *some* kind of calculation going on behind the stilling lines of his face. And I'd just spent an hour talking about Orion with him, cutting paper-thin slices of my heart to lay out on a plate, and I'd hated every minute of it, but he'd *cared,* he'd really truly cared, and it had, after all, made me feel better to have shared it with him, to have been able to grieve Orion with someone else who'd loved him. I didn't want him to say anything that would make me despise him.

"That's the only reason I've come," I said, before he could say anything at all. "If the Scholomance is still there, if it can be reached, Patience is still in there. And everyone it's ever devoured is still screaming. It won't end for them unless I stop it. It won't end for Orion. That's why I'm asking. I don't need a circle, and I don't need help. All I need is mana and a map."

He didn't tell me any more reasons why I couldn't do it, and he didn't, thankfully, drop any hints about enclave seats. Instead, after a moment, he only said, softly, "You'd better come talk to Ophelia."

I knew that New York had its front door in Gramercy Park, a private gated garden square that was somehow—yes, *somehow;* I'm sure the enclave hadn't anything to do with it—still hanging on in the middle of Manhattan. Orion had made a point of showing it to me on a map, as if he'd wanted to be sure I could find it. The enclave owned a shifting assortment of the surrounding townhouses and flats—they sold and bought new ones every so often, following the vicissitudes of the housing market; one of the many perfectly mundane ways New York arranged to have what I gathered was a blazing amount of money even by enclave standards—and a substantial stake in an insanely expensive hotel on the corner, whose rooms were quietly borrowed whenever they were empty.

But presumably that entrance was barricaded at the moment, under the circumstances. Instead Balthasar took us uptown on the subway to Penn Station—a massive and hideous low-ceilinged place filled with noise and grime and cheap fast-food shops—and in the back of a cramped newsstand, where the woman on the cash register nodded to him, he opened up a tiny door marked EMPLOYEES ONLY, and we stepped through and went down a short dark corridor.

My whole body was still tight with misery and the remains of anger. So I didn't even notice at first, but with every step down the corridor, the sensation got stronger until my stomach was full of it: a low queasy seasick feeling just like in London, only not quite as bad, and I slowly realized that it *hadn't* been their mana store, sloshing around. I'd just felt it more strongly over there, maybe because of the damage. This *was* what Mum had meant, the feeling of the malia that enclaves were built upon, only I couldn't understand how they couldn't feel it, all the time; how they could stand it. "Do *you* feel it?" I whispered to Aadhya, low, but she only looked back at me puzzled, and when I explained it, she shut her eyes and stood for a moment, frowning, and then she said, "Maybe? It doesn't really feel like being on a boat to me. It's like driving, maybe, with the engine going."

Chloe had turned round from an open archway at the other end to wait for us anxiously. We slowly went to her, and the archway deposited us in an astonishing entrance hall on the scale of Kings Cross, a gargantuan vaulted ceiling mounted on stone pillars, full of lamps and arches. It was the exact opposite of the carefully crafted layout of London's fairy garden with all its deft concealed angles that let the space move to where it was needed. Twenty-six enormous archways led out of the hall just as if they were going to trains, only they were full of the pallid grey clouds of an overcast sky, churning with possibility: New York's famous gateways. The one going to London stood pitch black, completely shut down.

The hall was certainly imposing and dramatic, but I hadn't any idea why anyone had built it inside an enclave, with the attendant waste of space. It wasn't as though New York City had loads of room going begging. But by the time we'd got halfway across the stubborn floor, which persisted in being exactly the size it was, exactly like the endless corridors in Heathrow, I'd realized they hadn't. This was a real place. Someone had literally built this whole enormous building solidly on the *outside,* and they'd just—moved it in. It was equal parts amazing and outrageous: how had they done it without anyone noticing?

The Scholomance had been really constructed, too, but that was why the iron skeleton of the structure had been built in tidy individual sections in the factories of Manchester, each one quietly shipped to the final destination under cover of night, popped in through the doors—wherever those were, which hopefully I'd be told soon enough—and bolted on to the rest of the growing structure from inside. There had also been a lot of elaborate spells that had encouraged those sections to stretch out along the way. The largest classrooms and the cafeteria had all been built out of negative space, and the outer walls had all been at least halfway fictional.

No one had built this marble hall in sections, and it hadn't been inflated, either. Every last square inch of the ground was so perfectly solid that probably you *could* have brought a mundane into the place without so much as a ripple. "How did you get this place *in* here?" Aadhya was hissing to Chloe as we hurried after Orion's dad.

"What?" Chloe jerked to glance around: couldn't even be bothered to notice the everyday local miracle. "It's just the old Penn Station. The enclave bid on the demolition, and then brought it inside while they pretended they were knocking it down."

"What vandal would demolish this place to build that rat's-nest we just came out of?" I said, in flat disbelief. Chloe just shrugged, but as soon as I'd asked, I had the strong suspicion that the enclave had made it very much in the private interests of whatever marauder or twenty had made it possible for them to snaffle the place right out of the city. Using a building made for transport, with probably a million mundane people gone through each of those archways, going somewhere different, full of purpose and bent on journeying—that was the kind of psychic foundation you couldn't make or buy, no matter how rich an enclave you were, and undoubtedly it had made it significantly easier to build all these gateways.

The place was full of wizards rushing through at almost exactly the same pace as the mundanes in the station outside, with the same sense of urgency. There were small guard stations flanking each archway, charming brass-and-iron follies with a single seat inside, clearly intended for some bored guard to spend the day sitting in. Only at the moment, there were ten grim-faced and heavily armed wizards stationed next to each one of them instead. The gateway going to Tokyo—that was the one they reckoned Shanghai was most likely to hit, presumably—had at least thirty guards, and they'd installed a huge spiky steel wall in front of it that looked more suited to a medieval siege than its surroundings.

It was even decorated with scowling brass heads of eagles, and enormous talons protruding from the bottom edge.

Despite the elevated security, no one stopped Balthasar bringing us through. The guards were easy to pick out in their uniform of thick tufted armor—undoubtedly highly practical, meant to muffle and absorb all sorts of magical attacks, although it did make them look vaguely like angry sofas. They were all carrying the same weapons as well, long metal poles with a thin slice of an axe blade and a focusing crystal mounted on the top, again sensible; if you can jab a physical object right up close at an enemy wizard, you can often get a spell off past their defenses.

They were only the cannon fodder, though: hired wizards working for the enclave. The real powers in the room weren't wearing uniforms. I picked out half a dozen of them along the way without half trying, as if some instinct of mine was sniffing them out as potential threats. There was a really beautiful and really dangerous man in red leather pants and a long-sleeved turtleneck of iridescent black snakeskin that almost seemed to melt into his actual skin at the hard-to-see edges, who wore a single short blade at his side roughly the length of my forearm. He was standing talking quietly with a fat grey-haired woman in a flowing kaftan of embroidered silk who was slumped on one of the benches and radiating the impression of having undergone great trials just to get herself there, only when she answered him, I could literally feel her voice through the floor, wordless, as if she had the whole room under her hand, like that volcanic spell I'd used to smash the Scholomance off the world.

A tall man was leaning against one of the columns and reading a paper copy of *The New York Times*, wearing an elegant old-fashioned suit and hat and leather shoes, with a heavy antique gold watch on his wrist and a wolf-headed cane under his arm; he looked so much as though he could have been moved into the enclave along with the train station itself that he had to have been doing it on purpose. To move around through time, maybe? It's a brilliant fighting technique, although most people can't stand it any more than they can stand the unreal places. As much as I understand it, you can't go back in time and change things; what you can do is essentially haul yourself towards the past so vigorously that you stop being *here* for just long enough that you can then pop yourself back into the present moment in a different spot, without any bother about physically moving there, or inconveniences like shields that might be between your two locations.

A girl with pink-and-green-streaked white hair and bushy eyebrows was sitting on the floor in an isolated corner with her eyes closed. She only had on a paper-thin black cotton dress and not a single visible weapon. She was vaguely familiar; after a moment I recognized her as one of the top seniors during our freshman year—not the valedictorian, but she'd still bargained herself a guaranteed spot after the obstacle course had opened that year, by doing a demonstration for several senior enclavers where she'd slaughtered her way through it, all alone. I certainly hadn't been invited to the demonstration, so I didn't know exactly how she'd done it, but she had been alchemy track, and there was a small potion bottle on the floor next to her. Her hands were clenched in her lap tightly, so I suspected she wasn't looking forward to repeating the experience, whatever it was.

But that's the price for using a tidy trick like that to get yourself into an enclave. They'll expect you to use it for them again, whenever they need you to. That had been my own plan, or at least I'd thought it had been my plan, those first three years at school: to barter my power for a ticket straight to a major enclave, where they'd take me in and keep me safe the rest of my life, just to have me in reserve when something terrible happened. Something like an enclave war, and I didn't need to have it spelled out for me in small words that we were on the verge of one.

None of them stopped us. The woman on the bench just said, "Balthasar," a deep booming, as we went by, and nodded him on with a wave of her hand despite us tagging along behind him.

"Ruth, Grover," he said, nodding back to them both, without breaking stride. He led us to one of the narrow brass-and-ironwork staircases going down through the floor. Going into the dark out of the brilliant light of the hall left us blinded and blinking for an unsettling moment that cleared up only as we came off the landing below and were in the narrow plush-carpeted corridor of a Gilded Age mansion block. Elegant wooden doors with knobs in the middle took turns with dim green-shaded lamps held up by brass hands, appearing at irregular intervals going down the length.

It wasn't nearly as real a place as the transport hall above. It only took a few steps before we were at a door marked 33. Balthasar swung it open for us and let us in. I made it a few steps inside before I realized and stopped short, standing just inside the handsome sitting room—he'd brought us to his own flat. I'd assumed he was taking us to some council chamber, some garden or library or something of the sort.

Of course I couldn't turn round and say *no wait let me out*. But I wanted to, because this was where Orion had lived, this had been his home, and I was here, and he wasn't. I wanted to run away at once, and I wanted to go prowling over the whole place, looking for any last scraps and shreds of him I could gather up and squirrel away inside myself, and hold on to him like holding on to one of the lost places.

By mundane standards, it was a cozy little place, the sort that a real estate listing would call *charming,* meaning not quite as large as you'd like. By enclave standards, it was enormous, and with an almost unimaginable luxury: *windows.* The short wall of the sitting room was made entirely of panels of one-way mirrors in ironwork, and on the other side you could see a garden, a garden *outside* in the real world. It looked like the yard of a townhouse, nine feet square at most, but the brick walls were covered with ivy and rosebushes, and all the space was filled with large plants in pots. The windows surely didn't open—you wouldn't want an actual opening to the outside world in your enclave home, since dozens of mals would try to get in—but it was still real sunlight and greenery.

One long wall was entirely full of bookshelves and a fireplace, and in front of it a small sofa and two large comfortable chairs were arranged round a rug large enough for a child to sprawl upon, playing. There were photographs scattered over the bookshelves, and I wasn't close enough to see them clearly, but there was someone in them with silver-grey hair.

"Make yourselves at home," Balthasar said, an invitation to go on and stab myself in the chest, just as I liked. "I'm going to go get Ophelia. Chloe, would you mind helping the girls with the pantry, if they'd like anything?"

I didn't want anything I could get in a pantry. I left Chloe showing the others how the sleek antique cupboard in the wall opened up to reveal a bank of illuminated drawers just like the old Automat food carts we'd enjoyed every year on Field Day, if those carts had been full of beautiful food that you'd actually want to eat, and also polished to a high sheen instead of nearly blackened with a century of grime and tarnish. I went down the corridor instead, slowly, to the door at the far end of it, the door that was shut. I passed a sliding door half open, going to what looked like the inside of a garage, the workshop where Orion had told me his dad had tried to keep him busy; there was another door ajar on my right, with a mirror on the wall showing a glimpse of a large canopied bed, hangings of grey velvet and mosquito-netting glimmering faintly with light, and when I paused to look at it, the mirror clouded over uneasily and I think something inside it started to peer back at me, only Precious made an alarmed squeak of warning, and I hurried on before it managed to pull itself together.

I stood in front of the closed door for a long time. I didn't want to open it. I didn't want to open it almost as much as I hadn't wanted to open the door of the maintenance shaft in the Scholomance and go out into the graduation hall, expecting to see Patience and Fortitude waiting for me. No one was going to make me open this door; the Scholomance wasn't going to bully me through it. But I opened it anyway, because I couldn't walk away from it either, so there wasn't anything else to do.

Orion wasn't there. In any sense of the word. The room looked almost exactly like one of the pages of the glossy in-flight magazine from the seat-back pocket on the aeroplane, advertising toys for boys: bat, ball, a football, a basketball and a hoop mounted on the back of a door, an American football, a racquet and tennis balls still in the plastic tube, another ball, a fishing rod, two different cameras, a remote-controlled car, three Lego kits and five science kits, a television mounted on the wall with shelves beneath it holding at least four different video game systems, a computer on the desk with a gigantic monitor, neatly filled bookshelves, a row of stuffed animals.

And every last item was as pristine as if it were still in that advert waiting to be shipped off to some lucky happy boy who would use it, just as soon as someone had dusted it off a bit. The kits were still in cellophane.

The only thing in the room that showed any sign of use, besides the bed, was a single large cardboard box tucked away in the corner, fairly battered, and full of weapons. At first glance, they might have been toys, too: the swords sized for a child, the coiled whip, the assortment of maces and flails. But they weren't toys. Actually some of them still had vivid purple ichor stains, which is what you get when you don't properly clean the corporeal surfaces of your weapon after you've used it to kill a psychic mal, which based on my personal experience of Orion's dorm room was extremely unsurprising.

It hurt to look at it and see everything he'd ever told me, everything Chloe had ever told me, that I hadn't wanted to believe. *I never wanted anything except to hunt,* he'd insisted. Chloe and the other New York seniors had literally offered me a spot in this enclave, their single most valuable bargaining chip to recruit help and resources for graduation, just because Orion had made a friend of me for the span of two weeks. Also they'd tried to murder me, *mostly* by accident, on the suspicion that I was a maleficer who was enchanting him. But now I didn't mind that nearly as much as the looming possibility that they'd had some real reason to be worried, after all.

This had been Orion's life, this awful stale barren room full of plastic and desperation, a mass of sacrificial offerings his parents had made to try and turn him into *a normal person,* and instead had only managed to make him recognize he wasn't one. And I'd have liked to comfortably keep on hating them for that, only I couldn't hate them for that and also hate them for letting a ten-year-old hunt maleficaria. I couldn't have it both ways, and I had the sinking feeling I also couldn't have it one way or the other, either.

But if I couldn't blame them—then there was something I couldn't understand here, a gaping void between the Orion who'd lived in this room and the Orion I'd known, the boy who'd made a friend of me because I *didn't* suck up to him, who'd squabbled with me over the lunch tables when I told him to do his homework and smugly counted points for every time he'd saved my life, who'd listened to me and cared about me and *loved* me. *El, you're the first right thing I've ever wanted,* he'd told me, and I hadn't wanted to believe that, or at most I'd wanted to believe that he'd been *trained* that way. But if it was *true,* then I didn't understand how to put the two halves of his life together, the one his parents and his friends had been holding, and the one I'd held myself. It was a puzzle with an enormous missing piece, and I stared into the room as if I could somehow save him after all, if I only found it now, too late.

"El?" Balthasar said, and I looked down the corridor. He was standing at the other end. I pulled Orion's door shut—I hadn't even let go of the knob—and walked back towards the sitting room. It was oddly hard to do, my steps coming slower, one after another, elongating almost as if I were back in the stretching staircases of the Scholomance. It was only a short corridor in a small flat, so I couldn't stretch it out very far, but I took as long as I possibly could have; I didn't want to get to the other end, and I didn't even understand why, until I came into the sitting room and Orion's mum was standing there talking to my friends. She turned when I came in, and there wasn't any more difficulty seeing where Orion had come from.

She was a maleficer.

Chapter 8
THE MALEFICER'S DEN

I'VE ALWAYS HAD a really remarkable nose for picking out maleficers. I knew Jack was a mana-sucker with human blood under his fingernails even when everyone else in our year thought he was a charming lad, friendly and generous by Scholomance standards. I knew Liu was dabbling—in a much more restrained way—when everyone else only considered her a bit aloof and awkward.

Malia isn't like drugs. When you first start messing with the stuff, that's when it leaves marks—blackened fingernails and milk-white eyes, an unpleasant sticky aura, things like that; Mum calls them symptoms of lesions in the anima, which is the badly defined word we use for whatever it is in wizards that lets us build and hold on to mana, unlike mundanes. The term has as much scientific validity as aether or the four elements or humors—a fair number of wizards have gone in for medicine and neuroscience trying to find the anima, and no one's had much luck yet—but everyone hates not having a name for it, so anima it is. What we do know perfectly well is that the more you mess with malia, the more damage you do to whatever it is, and the harder it becomes for you to keep building and holding on to mana of your own. Sometimes people with damage of that sort show up at the commune, wanting Mum's help. She doesn't help them the way they really want her to; she doesn't do spirit cleanses and patch them up and send them off to do it again. All she'll do is give them a chance to spend however many months or years it takes, working off their debt in the woods with her. Mostly they go away again, but a few of them have stuck it out.

But when you commit to the maleficer lifestyle, give up making mana of your own at all and switch to using malia exclusively, that's when the path really smooths out before you. Serious maleficers don't have to worry about people getting uneasy round them, or even any outer signs, at least not until they cross the finish line far up ahead and the worn-thin outer façade peels away, years of accumulated psychic pollution exposed all in a rush, and they graduate to their final form, the ancient stringy sorcerers and hideous crones that show up in fairy stories, mashing bones in a mortar and pestle. It's a puzzle no one's going to solve: do they look that way because that's what people think of when they think of *evil mage,* or have the stories been told because at that stage the maleficers get desperate enough to even go after mundanes, having to work harder and harder and more grotesquely to extract enough malia from hapless victims to keep themselves from falling apart entirely?

Ophelia wasn't in the end stage, certainly. Oddly, she also wasn't especially beautiful, which most maleficers are until they aren't anymore. She was an ordinary, well-kept middle-aged woman, slim in a way that suggested she exercised every day and practiced portion control, with a smooth cap of short-cropped brown hair and clear grey eyes horribly like

Orion's, with posh mundane clothing and a light coating of expensive makeup. Or rather, that's the woman she looked like. At the commune, a lot of the regulars would sneer when those women turned up for the yoga weekends; I'd liked that it wasn't just me sneering for once. But Mum had always said that it was good to care for yourself, however you chose to do it.

That wasn't what Ophelia was doing. She was just wearing the skin of it on the outside, like camouflage. It was really good camouflage, too. Aadhya and Chloe and even Liesel were smiling, charmed and made welcome, until they saw my face. Aadhya immediately put her hand in her pocket, I'm guessing because she had some kind of protective artifice in there, and Liesel shifted a step back, putting herself in a position to fire off an offensive spell from behind a shield. Poor Chloe's face went almost comically horrified.

Ophelia was smiling too, until *she* came round and saw my face, and then she paused and said, "Well, I guess that makes things easier for me," in a brisk tone, the smile folding up and packing itself away like a raincoat made unnecessary by a change in the weather. "But you're probably freaked out. Do you want to go somewhere more public?"

What I wanted more exclusively with every passing second was to get as far away from her as I possibly could. She wasn't like Jack. Jack had been a tiny pathetic worm of a parasite just trying to gnaw himself a way to survival. She was a pillar of darkness in a clear sky, the promise of mushroom clouds billowing, with all the power of New York enclave behind her. She was what I'd been trying not to become, my whole life, and I couldn't imagine anything I could do against her. I desperately wanted an ocean of mana; if Alfie had offered me the London power-sharer again in that moment, at the cost of having him tag around behind me his entire life,

I'd have taken it in a heartbeat, yes, just give it to me; yes, please, hurry.

"Take a few breaths," Ophelia advised, when I didn't answer her. "I'm not looking to start a fight in my living room. In my worst-case scenario, you'd destroy my enclave. In the best case, you'd be dead. And I don't want you dead. Why don't you sit down? Would you like some tea?"

She delivered all of this with the air of a mildly beleaguered teacher in a junior school—not the slightest hitch when proposing either that I might destroy New York enclave, or that she might kill me. The tea was even offered exactly in the same way that Americans always did it, namely with the faint hint that they didn't really understand *why* I might like some tea, but they understood that this was the appropriate thing to do. It was even reassuring, in an odd way. But not enough for me to want to sit down and have a cuppa, pretending there wasn't something worse than a mawmouth across from me.

"Have *you* been destroying the enclaves?" I blurted out, a brief shade away from panic.

She tilted her head. "You mean that, don't you?" I just stared at her. "No, I haven't been." She didn't even try to say it in any kind of convincing way—not indignant or even urgent. She simply said it, and left me with the dampening impression that I was being a silly goose: what use was it to make her say anything about it? If she *had* been, and she didn't want me to know, she would just have lied without the slightest difficulty. For that matter, if she'd told me she *had* been doing it, that might have been a lie just as easily, for her own reasons. I wasn't getting any information out of her; she was just making noises to be polite.

And what if she *was* the one smashing enclaves apart? I could certainly have believed it. She wouldn't have batted an eye at ripping London open just to make it look less likely that New York was behind it when she went after Beijing. But so what? Was I going to loudly declare that I was going to stop her wicked plans? In *my* best case, if I managed to convince her that I meant it, she'd come at me immediately, of course, and I was standing in the middle of her enclave, in her very own house, with a significant fraction of all the people in the world I cared about—and bloody hell, Liesel had somehow *joined* that group, which would teach me to shag people I didn't want to like—in range. I couldn't come up with a single idea for how to get us out of here if Ophelia meant to stop us, at least not any idea that didn't include my turning *into* her, or even worse.

She waited long enough to let all of that sink in, more or less forcing me to quell my own nascent panic, then added, "Balthasar tells me that you'd like to go back into the Scholomance."

And I did still want that, but I wasn't taking anything from this woman. "I'll manage it on my own," I said. "We'll just be going."

She gave a very faint sigh. "I don't think you will. You don't have much time, and you're not getting the mana anywhere else."

I would've told her I wasn't taking a drop of anything she called mana, but Liesel broke in on us. "Why do we not have time?" she demanded, and that did stop me, because it was clearly something I needed to know.

Ophelia turned away and went to the nearest couch and sat down; she reached out a hand and a glass of water was waiting on the small table next to it for her, cold enough to dew the sides. "Keeping the Scholomance going takes about fifty lilims per day, per seat."

The number sounded like nonsense. We don't measure

mana on an individual level; it's too wobbly for that. The same thirty push-ups that build you a shield spell's worth of mana one day won't build you enough to light a candle the next. You just build as much as you can, and when you need to cast a spell, either you have enough mana or you don't. But on the major enclave level, you can start to average it out over the two thousand wizards working for you, all day every day, and then make yourself a budget, and plans. And in that kind of a budget, fifty lilims is roughly equivalent to the mana you'd let a hired wizard take home in a year—the amount that's twice what they could manage to raise on their own working outside an enclave. So she was talking about ludicrous amounts, vats of mana just pouring into the school, every single day.

"And your plan worked," Ophelia went on. "Every maleficaria survey in the world is reporting a giant drop in sightings over the last week, since graduation. The big one in Tokyo just came out this morning, showing a drop of ninety-two percent from the week before graduation. With these enclave attacks happening, a lot of people want to ditch the school permanently and keep all their mana at home. We've already got fifteen minor enclaves who haven't put in their contributions for the month." She shook her head as if it disappointed her. "Fortunately, the major enclaves can't pull out that easily. Anyone with more than five seats had to sign on to the long-term contracts, and they can't stop the flow unless the Board of Governors votes to close down the school. But the way things are going right now, about half of the school's mana supply will be gone by next week."

She didn't have to spell it out further: if the Scholomance needed that much mana to function, every single day, then I couldn't possibly raise enough mana on my own to get back inside. I wouldn't even be able to try and fail, change my mind, and come back here to ask her for it after all. Not even New York enclave could give me enough to open it up again, once everyone else pulled out.

But that didn't mean the whole thing would be *gone*, either. If it was mana *and* belief that kept places from falling away into the void, then pockets of the Scholomance would be lingering on for years if not decades. And Patience would ooze its way into one of those pockets and sit there as long as it lasted, digesting slowly away.

"I've been trying to put together a team to go inside myself," Ophelia continued. "I'm having a hard time getting one, and I'm already flat-out offering seats on the open market at this point. So I really *don't* want to have a fight with you. I want you to do exactly what you want to do anyway."

"Why?" I said. If she had the gall to tell me it was because of Orion, because she loved Orion, and wanted to save him pain—

She didn't. She only tilted her head slightly, a clear-eyed raptor examining a potential bit of prey. "Does it matter?" she asked me, and what she was asking was *Do you need me to tell you another story about it?* My gorge rose. I wished she *had* told me that it was for Orion, after all.

I might have said, *No, thanks, give me what I need and I'll be on my way,* just to get away from her, from the horrible understanding that this had been in Orion's life, the poisoned ground he'd had to grow in. I wanted to go and do something clean and simple like fight my way through a horde of maleficaria and kill the world's largest maw-mouth. But I couldn't do that.

"Yes," I said. "It matters. I'm not going to help you reattach the Scholomance and dump all the maleficaria in the world back in, just so your enclave can keep the power it represents."

She gave a snort, like I'd said something funny. "Power? It's a giant mana pit. We're carrying more than twice our fair share, we cover all the shortfalls. But it's still a massive chunk of capital infrastructure, and it's the only long-term solution we've got. Yours is just temporary. We'll be right back at the seventy-five percent child mortality rate in sixty years, and then we'll have to build another Scholomance. I don't want to throw this one away. At the very least, we should keep it going on a subsistence level until we need it again. What I'd really like is to find some way to use it to repeat your technique on a regular basis instead, but from what we've heard," she nodded towards Chloe, "it's not going to be all that easy."

"Wait," Liesel said sharply. "Why so soon? We calculated that it would be more than a hundred years to reach a mortality rate of fifty percent. That was why it was worth it, sacrificing the entire school—"

"I'm guessing you kept the maleficaria generation rate steady when you crunched your numbers," Ophelia said. "It's not steady. The more wizards there are—and you just saved a whole lot of them—the more mals there will be."

"Why would more wizards surviving mean more mals?" I said. "We'll *kill* mals."

She gave me what wasn't quite a pitying look, because she didn't have enough pity to manufacture one. "We'll make more than we kill. Did you think it was all crazy maleficers in secret labs cackling, or careless mistakes? Any cheating does it. Remember? *You must never use any mana you do not generate yourself. Any use of malia leads to the generation of maleficaria.* First page of every single textbook, the Freshman Orientation Handbook, the contract you signed to get into school?"

I did remember it, and sourly, because no one else paid any attention to it. The real reason no one used malia at school was because there weren't a lot of options for getting hold of it. Outside, almost everyone cheats at least a little; they steal from ants or beetles, wither a vine or a patch of grass, without ever seeing the damage they do. Mum didn't let me get away with that sort of thing, but most parents do it themselves.

Ophelia nodded. "Whenever somebody needs a little more mana than they've got, they steal it from somewhere, seems like no big deal—but you end up with a negative flow of mana. When that negative flow gets big enough, a mal will generate around it. It's not a secret. But people do it anyway." She lifted her hands to the heavens.

"Is that meant to be funny?" I said, with a surge of rage— her sitting there sounding exasperated about anyone *else,* about kids who were using the tiniest scrap of malia in desperation—

Ophelia paused. "Why do you think I did it?"

"Did *what?*" I snarled. "Turned *maleficer?* I expect you wanted to be Domina. Does that make you better than a loser kid who cheats a little so they can survive to the age of majority?" Out of the corner of my eye, Chloe involuntarily cringed back with a hand over her mouth, already distressed enough before I'd openly accused the most powerful wizard in her enclave of being a flat-out evil witch. Aadhya just looked grim. Liesel had unobtrusively urged them both round to the far side of the room closer to Balthasar, presumably on the theory that if it *did* come to flinging spells, better to be over there, out of Ophelia's line of fire.

And Balthasar himself—he wasn't surprised in the least, clearly; he was just looking at us both—mostly at *me,* even— with a kind of sad concern, yes, how unfortunate that I'd *noticed* his wife was a monster, it was too bad I found it so upsetting—

"You know, El, I'm going to go out on a limb here and say you didn't get half the mals in the world to come running with mana that every last kid in the school honestly built for themselves," Ophelia said, with the bite of an adult who's got tired of an unreasonable child yelling at them. "Someone in there got someone else to do their homework with a compulsion, or stole a little mana out of their best friend who fell asleep at the library table. Just because they handed it to you afterwards doesn't make a difference to the universe. It just makes a difference to *you*."

It was a sharp, accurate hit; of course that was true, and I knew it, and I didn't have an answer for it, except the wrong answers: I hadn't known for sure, I hadn't done it myself, I'd been doing something good enough to justify using it, she was worse—

Ophelia gave me a mirthless smile, a thin slice of winter. "I didn't do it for power. I'm a New Yorker. There's mana to spare around here. Everyone I work with in the lab voluntarily lets me pull from them and gets paid back twice as much."

I stared at her in horror, imagining it vividly, a collection of poor desperate bastards in her laboratory letting themselves be drained by a maleficer, crossing their fingers this wouldn't be the time she went over the line and sucked them dry. "So you jettisoned your anima on purpose, then? Too inconvenient, all those twinges of conscience?"

"Anima and conscience haven't got a thing to do with each other," she said, a strong statement that I didn't believe for a moment. "The kind of maleficer who deliberately starts murdering people doesn't have one to start with. But all the psychopathic wizards in the world put together aren't the real problem. The problem is that *everyone* cheats. And then we get more mals, and our kids die, and still everyone cheats, because the two things are too far apart. You can live your whole life without cheating once, like you're trying to do, and still your kid's just as likely to get eaten, and meanwhile someone else cheats every day and their kid sails on through. The only solution we've got so far for *that* are enclaves."

"Enclaves you've built *with malia*," I said, the malia I could feel even now, the uneasy subtle sloshing back and forth still going beneath my feet.

She didn't even bother to deny it. "It's a numbers game," she said instead. "The malia it takes to make an enclave and keep it going might look like a lot, but it's still less than what you'd get if the same wizards were all cheating on their own, trying to survive. Economies of scale work in magic too. And wizards mostly don't cheat in an enclave, because they don't have to. But enclaves . . ." She paused, looking at me, and her mouth quirked briefly, a curl of one corner. "Enclaves have their own unique costs. And the wizards in an enclave might not cheat, but they also don't want to share. There's a squabble over every new seat we add and every new person we hire, because no one wants to give up a square inch of their own space. And every year, more of us survive, and it gets worse. We need better solutions."

"Looking for more *efficient* uses of malia, is that it?" I said, nauseated. I didn't want to believe she was in earnest, but there was something hideously plausible about it all. A New Yorker really *didn't* need malia. She'd got rid of her own anima *on purpose,* probably for some sort of horrible massive working, or maybe just so she could work with malia without the distraction of getting hurt. And she surely rationed her malia usage as carefully as Liu ever had, never taking more than precisely necessary, refusing all the side benefits on offer. It explained why she didn't look like a maleficer, in either direction.

She'd more or less turned herself into the Scholomance. The school hadn't cared—hadn't been *able* to care—about

any of us one at a time. The numbers had been its only implacable concern, and so it had marched us ruthlessly through
an inhuman triage process, doing the best that it could. Only
Ophelia didn't even believe the stupid unbelievable lie that
the school had swallowed, the mad ambition written too effectively into its steel and brass, the one that had sent it grabbing for the chance that Orion and I had provided: *to protect
all the wise-gifted children of the world.* She wasn't going to try
to do that. She perfectly understood that some children had
to die.

Ophelia sighed. She put aside her glass of cool clear water
and stood up again and came towards me, my whole body
clenching at the approach, but she stopped at arm's length,
looking up into my face. "El, you're clearly a very nice girl,"
she said, possibly the first time in my entire life that anyone
had said that to me sincerely, and wasn't it delightful to find
someone speaking from a vantage point that made it possible. "I'm glad Orion met you. You won't believe me, but I do
love him. I always wanted him to be happy. If I could have
made him happy—I would have." Her face wavered oddly,
almost more bewildered than sad, as if she found it hard to
believe herself. "But that's part of the problem, of course.
We're all greedy, but children make it easier to be. We feel it's
only right to give them everything we can grab, even when
you know that anything you feed your own child still comes
out of someone else's mouth."

Then she held out a small flat square box to me, about the
size to hold a makeup compact: a box she hadn't had in her
hands a moment before, with the enclave's symbol on it, the
gates with the starburst behind them. "I can't make you go
back to the Scholomance if you won't. But I can give you the
mana, and I can give you the location. And no one else will
go. So it's up to you."

What I ought to have done, which I knew perfectly well, was shove the box back at her and run away and give up on the whole idea. But I couldn't. I couldn't get Orion away from Patience, and I couldn't get him away from Ophelia either. I couldn't rewrite his whole life, snatch him out of his cradle and carry him across the ocean to Mum, or just to some decent person. I couldn't even take back every rude and nasty thing I'd ever said to him. I would have done that, if I could have; the memory of every word stung in my brain like bees. He'd only liked me in the first place because I hadn't been trying to make up to him, but I could have simply been nice, without wanting anything of him, and surely that would have worked, too. But it was too late. The only thing I could do for him anymore was kill him, and everyone else trapped inside Patience along with him. So I had to do that. I had to do the only thing I could do for him.

Horribly, I almost had to be glad that he hadn't made it out, because he *wouldn't* have come to me. Ophelia wouldn't have kept him with love and appeals to his loyalty and conscience. She'd just have kept him by any means necessary— a compulsion or a collar or anything it took. He was one of those more efficient solutions, after all. You couldn't have asked for better. A brilliant engine of a maleficaria-killer, who dumped the power back into the enclave share after? I *didn't* believe her. I didn't believe she'd have made Orion happy if she could have. I could believe, at a stretch, that she'd have liked him to be happy on the side, and had been sorry that she couldn't find a way to make him so, with her toys and obedient friends and flash cards. But not that she'd have chosen to make him happy, if it had really been a choice between his happiness and having the use of him.

Otherwise surely she wouldn't have *got* him in the first place. A slayer of monsters who'd put himself on the line for every stranger who came into reach; who'd been, besides that, a *good boy,* who'd tried to please his mum and dad and be kind and polite to other children even when they blatantly only wanted to use him—I'd been absolutely certain that his parents and his enclave had programmed it into him, but Ophelia surely hadn't cared about anything of the sort. It had all been Orion, after all. Just like Mum, who with her infinite kindness had got herself a sullen wrathful death-sorceress child for her pains, Ophelia had got a selfless noble hero, who'd never made a single calculated move in his life, who'd saved children indiscriminately and without the slightest consideration of how he'd throw off the balance by doing it. Who'd been kind even to the girl who'd snapped his head off for daring to save her.

And if he'd made it out, and he hadn't come to Wales . . . I'd have written him off, in my selfish guarded pride, and told myself I didn't mind it, pretended that I wasn't sorry. I would have abandoned him to her, to the enclave. He couldn't have trusted me to come and save him.

Maybe he'd known, on some level, what he was going back to, if he went. Ophelia had surely put on a good show for him, and Orion hadn't been able to tell a maleficer from a doorknob. But he'd lived with her all his life. Maybe he'd guessed, by the end. *The Scholomance is the best place I've ever been,* he'd said to me. Now I knew why that was true. And so now I felt, with a horrible sharp stab, that maybe—when the moment came—he'd *chosen* not to go home. He'd chosen a final blaze of self-sacrifice, turning to fight the indestructible monster, to avoid going home to the one he couldn't bear to fight. I didn't know if that was true, but it felt nauseatingly possible, in a way that filled in the question I still couldn't answer, hadn't allowed myself to ask: *why hadn't he come out?*

But I hadn't asked that question partly because it was useless. It didn't matter why, not anymore. I hadn't got him out. I couldn't save him now. But I still had to go and do the last little thing for him that I could. And after that—I'd have to decide if I needed to come back here and try to destroy Ophelia. I was more than halfway convinced she *was* the one destroying the enclaves at this point. If her problem with enclaves was getting enclavers to share, then terrifying them all with the threat of some mysterious indiscriminate maleficer who was going to destroy their enclaves without warning would be an excellent strategy. Was that justification for killing her? If she was responsible for killing everyone in Bangkok enclave, everyone in Salta, all the people who'd died in London and Beijing? Even if I couldn't be sure, she was certainly going to do *something* absolutely horrible, sooner or later.

I could just see Mum reaching out to put her hand on my forehead to make that thought go away, to make all those thoughts go away. But Mum wasn't with me, and I couldn't even call her, because if I did, she'd tell me what I already knew, that I shouldn't take anything from Ophelia. And I couldn't bear to hear it exactly because I knew it was right. But I still couldn't make myself hand back the box that held the only chance of the last scraggly miserable thing I could do for Orion.

Ophelia had waited for a bit, I suppose to be sure I wasn't about to throw her box at her head or out through the windows, but after I didn't do that for long enough, she decided that I was keeping it, which apparently I was. She nodded politely to us all and went to give Balthasar a quick kiss, exactly like an ordinary loving spouse, and told him, "I've got to get back to the council," and then she left the flat without another word, or looking back at all.

Balthasar saw us out; he even offered to let us use one of the gateways. "No," I said flatly, without even bothering to open the box and find out where I was going. All I wanted was to get *out* of this place, at once, and if that meant a thirty-hour intercontinental flight in my future, so what?

Chloe trailed along with us, darting deeply anxious looks towards me. I imagine she had quite a lot of questions about her own future Domina to ask me. But she didn't get a chance. They saw us back to the exit, and just inside, Balthasar said, "They'll be locking down the perimeter shortly. El— thank you so much for coming. I'm very glad to have met you." He hesitated, and then added, "I know this has probably been very confusing—"

I turned and walked out on him and Chloe at that point, before he could get round to explaining to me earnestly how Ophelia meant well, and how he'd like to tell me more about her very important and excellent plans for the world. I was sure he'd have meant every word with full sincerity, too. He had to be a true believer: he'd already been an enclaver, and a powerful one, so it wasn't that he'd married Ophelia and gone along with her plans just because he'd been desperate for an enclave spot.

Liesel and Aadhya were hard on my heels, which was just as well, because I didn't slow down even though I didn't really know where I was going in the stinking dirty train station, the one that had taken the place of the marble halls the enclave had stolen. I just headed for the nearest red sign marked EXIT until I found daylight. When we finally emerged blinking from the depths, Aadhya marched us to the nearest convenient waiting point, not even a café but just a tiny frozen yogurt stand with a handful of rickety uncomfortable metal chairs scattered over the pavement vaguely in the vicinity. She told Liesel, "Don't let her go *anywhere*," as though I needed a keeper, who snapped back, "Come quickly."

Aadhya went to fetch her car from the parking space—another convenient bit of magic; she'd found one with no trouble, less than a block away—and as soon as she had us in it, she began driving without any discussion. By some sort of instinctive and unspoken agreement, none of us said anything until we'd got through the tunnel and back into New Jersey, as if we needed to get running water between us and the monster on the other side, but then we came out from under the river and Liesel immediately said, "She is a *maleficer*?" at exactly the same time as Aadhya said, "Okay, El, what the *fuck*."

"Yes," I said, which was the answer to both of them.

"Do you think they . . . know," Aadhya said, but it stopped being a question by the time she finished asking it. Of course *they* knew, where *they* was everyone who mattered: the rest of the New York council, the senior wizards of the enclave. It was a *feature* for them, surely, not a bug. A fantastically controlled dark sorceress, capable of anything and willing to do worse yet—of course any enclave would grab at her with both hands. That had been my own strategy for getting an enclave place, after all, and an excellent strategy it was; it had only broken down on my being willing to execute it. No wonder Ophelia was a shoo-in for the next Domina. In fact, it was probably her own choice not to have taken the position yet.

I had Ophelia's small box cupped in my hands—not protectively, more like making sure it didn't go off in some way—and I spent the rest of the way just staring at it, until Aadhya was pulling up in front of what I assumed at first was some sort of club or restaurant, a vast hulking mansion of pink brick that was only a tiny bit shy of London's monstrosity, only it hadn't been allowed to collapse in on itself. The plantings were absolutely stupendous, what seemed like the entire garden in bloom. But she left her car in the drive and led us to the door, so I said cautiously, "This isn't your house?" half expecting her to laugh at me, only she said, "Yeah, sorry, I'm throwing you to the wolves," before she opened the door.

The wolves were her entire family, who indeed descended on us in a pack; her mum sailed straight to me, grabbed my face in her hands and kissed me on both cheeks and then held me back a bit so she could smile at me fiercely, her eyes wet. "Aadhya told us all about you," she said, her voice thick. I swallowed hard.

It wasn't anything like the vague fragments I remembered from that one catastrophic visit to my father's family. The gigantic American house was full of slightly wrong architectural details and every imaginable mod con, aggressively mundane. That was how Aadhya's family had protected their last remaining child: they'd hidden all the magic away into small rooms upstairs, a workshop down in the basement, behind locked doors, and threw the rest of the house open to the mundane friends she made at the local middle school and turned it into a warm welcoming feast of a place for them, so mals wouldn't come anywhere near.

And they hadn't shut the doors after she'd gone away. While we were all sitting round the pool in back with tall cold glasses of iced tea full of fruit and a bowl of freshly made snack mix that I couldn't stop eating by the handful, a mundane neighbor dropped by unannounced with a whole basket of glowing ripe tomatoes; she said they were overflowing her vegetable patch, exclaimed with surprise and delight to see Aadhya all grown up and home from boarding school, was beamingly friendly to Liesel and only wobbled a little when she came to me, with a vague expression of unease crossing her face that she hurriedly papered over with an even more determined smile before making a slightly awkward excuse to leave rather than sit down and have a drink.

Her own family probably felt that sensation too, since everyone does. But they didn't let on if they did. They weren't mundanes, and I wasn't just a friend from school: I was Aadhya's ally. I had got their daughter out of the Scholomance, and she'd got me out. For most of us, the loser kids who don't have an enclave ready to take us in when we graduate, that's the most important relationship in our lives short of marriage, and sometimes beyond it. I'd needed most of last year to wrap my head round the idea that anyone had been willing to be my ally at all, my ally and my friend, and not just someone using me at arm's length, warily. I'd never thought about what it would be like having that relationship *after* getting out. And this was what it was like: I was *welcome*.

So it was, after all, like that visit to the compound outside Mumbai, only it was just the first shining moments of that visit, which had stuck with me all these years, warm and golden, *family,* and this time the beauty didn't stop. And I didn't say *I need to get going,* even though if I was going, I did need to go. It was like having cool balm applied to the searing pain of meeting Ophelia, of looking at Orion's life.

Aadhya's grandmothers kept bringing more amazing snacks out in waves. There wasn't really a break between teatime and dinner, we just migrated from our lounge chairs to sit at the large outdoor table in the yard under golden hanging lamps, and Aadhya's dad came home—he was working in Boston enclave that week; he'd literally got in the car and driven home the whole way just to have dinner with us—and he'd brought her cousin from Kolkata enclave who was train-

ing in Boston with a senior specialist in computational artifice. He was a handsome strapping lad of twenty-two that
they made a point of mentioning by the way wasn't engaged
yet, when they seated him next to me, and asked me about
my mum and hoped I would bring her for a visit sometime.

Aad rolled her eyes dramatically at me behind her mum's
back during this process and mouthed an apology, but it
didn't feel like aggressive matchmaking or anything to me.
They didn't really expect me or him to suddenly want to start
dating one another, they were just—showing me a door, telling me that if I wanted to walk through it, I'd have been *acceptable,* and that still wasn't something I expected enough to
be able to find it annoying. And he smiled at me and even
flirted a bit, in a way that would probably have stunned me
into amazement, or maybe even delight, another time. Liesel
making me her offer had been its own surprise, but at least
she'd had some sort of rational ulterior motive. I wasn't really
prepared for a complete stranger showing signs of *wanting* to
know me, for no particular reason whatsoever.

Other circumstances, I would have gone fumbling through
hardly believing it was happening, then flirting back awkwardly, perhaps giving him my squeaky-new number, maybe
even making plans to meet him for a coffee in some magnifi-
cently ordinary way. If only Orion were alive, and I could
have firmly informed him that I wasn't tying myself down
just yet, and I expected him to see other people a bit too, and
be sure it wasn't just a school romance, or anything like that,
and all those sensible things that I thought on principle were
a good idea but which hadn't really seemed like an option I
needed to bother considering. I'd imagined myself with
Orion, or alone; never anything else. And of course it was
good and healthy and wonderful for me to imagine myself
with someone else, to imagine myself with Liesel or with

Aadhya's cousin or with someone I hadn't even met, but I could do that, and Orion couldn't, because Orion was dead and screaming.

So instead of having a nice ordinary conversation, I had to excuse myself to go to the bathroom and lock myself in to breathe deeply a few times and wash my face, and after I dried it off, I finally took Ophelia's box out of my pocket and opened the lid. It unfolded and kept unfolding until it was nearly six times the size, lined with black velvet, and inside there was a power-sharer. It looked a bit like a pocket watch on a strap, the lid engraved with the enclave's symbol. Just like the one Orion had used to wear, only obviously this one would let me pull. A small scrap of heavy paper with rough edges was laid out next to it, with a set of GPS coordinates written down, and labeled underneath *Sintra, Portugal.*

Precious hauled herself out of my other pocket a bit groggily—she'd gorged herself on the puffed rice out of the snack mix, which I hoped wasn't going to give her indigestion—and jumped over to the counter, next to the box. She put a paw on the power-sharer as if to bar me from it, and looked up at me with her bright-green eyes and squeaked anxiously: she hoped I knew what I was getting into.

"You and me both," I said. She drew her paw back and watched unhappily as I put the power-sharer on, and then gave a small shiver and crawled back up and got into my pocket again.

I put the paper from Ophelia in my other pocket, like a counterweight, and went out to say goodbye.

Chapter 9
SINTRA

I FACED OBJECTIONS ALMOST IMMEDIATELY. "First of all, I'm coming with, and second of all, we're going *in the morning*," Aadhya said, as soon as I pulled her aside. "You look like someone went over you with a Zamboni a few times."

"We will look worse if there isn't enough mana in the Scholomance when we try to go inside," Liesel said, disagreeing, having come over and horned in; she was already poking at her phone. "The best flight will be in four hours. We should go to the airport at once."

After Liesel started drawing actual charts to explain all the horrible things that would happen to us if too many enclaves pulled their mana out while we were inside the school, Aadhya gave in on the departure time, but she insisted on my coming upstairs to her bedroom while she packed. "Okay, seriously, what is Liesel's deal?" Aadhya demanded, while she hurriedly threw things into a large trunk. She'd hardly been back a week, but the closet was already full of clothes, and I had to navigate a minefield of posh shopping bags to get to the bed to sit down, explosions of tissue paper scattered everywhere around, evidence of a massive spree. "Why does she want to come along? Why is she even here in the first place? Isn't she a London enclaver now?"

"If you get an answer out of her, let me know," I said. "I expect she would like to hurry things up, though; Alfie's waiting in London, and she has a plan to get herself onto the council."

"And she's running around after you anyway?" Aadhya said. "El, that makes zero sense. She's got to have something else going on, and if she's not telling you about it, you're not going to like it. Is there some reason you haven't ditched her?" I couldn't help but squirm inwardly, which delayed my answer long enough that Aadhya turned around from packing and stared at me with narrowed eyes. "*Is* there a reason?" she said, in dangerous tones.

"Well," I said feebly. I'd known it was coming, and that I didn't have an acceptable excuse.

"Okay, *no*," Aadhya said. "*Liesel?*"

I groaned and flopped backwards on the bed and covered my face with my hands. "It was a moment of weakness?" I said, muffled.

"A moment of total insanity maybe!" Aadhya said. "That's even more awesome. El, Alfie is her *ride*. He got her into London enclave, now he's going to get her on the council? No way she would risk cheating on him unless she had a *crazy* good reason!"

"She's not cheating," I muttered. "He knows about it."

"Great, because it's all part of some kind of plan to *get* at you," Aadhya said, unmercifully.

And even if I'd turned down Liesel's alliance offer, Aadhya was fundamentally right, and I knew it. I still couldn't be *sorry;* even now I felt almost pathetically grateful to Liesel for the ocean-deep relief of physical release and dreamless sleep she'd given me, not to mention *getting* me here. But I should absolutely have made her tell me what she was looking for in return *now,* instead of just letting her keep tagging along after me, being helpful, as though that was all she wanted. That wasn't what anyone wanted, and Liesel wasn't even the doormat sort of person who'd pretend it was for any length of time. She was the highly strategic sort of person who was just waiting to hit me with an appropriately large demand right when I was most vulnerable, and I should absolutely have known better. Even if the Scholomance hadn't taught me better, my entire life was an object lesson in the dangers of not getting the price tag up front.

"I'm warning you right now that if you move into London enclave and start a ménage with *Liesel and Alfie,* I'm hunting you down with chains," Aadhya said. "Also if the Scholomance wasn't literally a time bomb waiting to go, I would be chaining you up *right now.* El. It wasn't your fault." I dragged a breath in, painful in my too-tight chest, and sat up to hunch over it.

Aadhya came over and sat next to me on the bed and put her arm around me. "You didn't get Orion killed," she said. "The plan *worked.* You were at the doors. All he had to do was jump out. I don't know why he didn't, but you're acting like you left him behind, and I don't need to have been there to know for sure that is just not a thing that you did. And he wasn't stupid, so he never thought for even a second that you'd *want* to." She snorted. "Why would he shove you out if he thought you'd go? He knew you *wouldn't.*"

Aadhya was right, of course she was right, and I knew it, except if it wasn't my fault— "Then he was a fucking *wanker* who died for *no reason!*" I said through my teeth.

"People fuck up sometimes," Aadhya said bluntly. "You do something stupid, and it turns out to be something you can't fix or take back. Orion made a bad call in one second in the middle of the worst fight of your lives, with Patience coming right at you. That doesn't mean he was worthless. You're not dumb for loving him or being sad he's dead! You *are* dumb for letting Liesel bag you on the worst rebound ever," she added, with a caustic edge, giving my shoulder a shove as she got up to finish packing. "You don't even *like* her!"

I grimaced. "She grows on you. A bit."

"Like a rashling?" Aadhya said, giving zero credence.

I didn't have anything to wear except what was still on my back, Mum's baggy linen work dress, and despite Liesel's cleaning spell, it had reached the limits of what it could bear without a wash I didn't have time to do. None of Aadhya's shiny new purchases would fit me, but she gave me an un-opened packet of knickers and went for her mum, who brought down an outfit she'd been working on, a salwar kameez in satiny thin cotton, embroidered up and down the neck opening with runes of protection in golden thread; it ought to have cost a year of mana, but she pressed it on me.

Her dad insisted on driving us all to the airport, although he looked at Aadhya anxiously in the rearview mirror several times along the way. It made me feel guilty, but I didn't even try to tell Aadhya not to come. I wanted her too badly. I *didn't* want to take her into the Scholomance with me when I went in hunting Patience—I wasn't taking anyone in there for that jaunt—but I did want her to be outside the doors, with desperate selfishness. I wanted someone waiting for me that I'd feel obliged to come back out to.

The flight was late enough that the airport had an odd half-deserted quality, nowhere near empty but muffled, shops mostly closed and people with tired faces dragging their cabin bags along behind them. Aadhya flatly refused to leave me with Liesel for even a moment, to the point of making me go and fetch the coffee after we'd parked ourselves in the club again.

Liesel noticed. "What do you think *I* am going to do to *her*?" she said to Aadhya sharply, as soon as they thought I was out of earshot, which I wasn't, because I'd crept round the other side of the planter to listen in, and maybe catch Liesel out at something that would give me a push to tell her to go back to London and Alfie.

Aadhya had her arms folded across her chest, glaring. "I get that you have zero shame, but she's *freaking out*."

"Yes," Liesel said. "Are you thinking I made things worse? I promise you," she went on, with the grim tones of experience, "to feel good in your body makes things *better*, even when they are very bad, and they *are*."

"Yeah, and I think you're looking to plant a hook in El while she's messed up so you can yank on it later."

Liesel made an impatient dismissive gesture. "Yes! You have a hook in her yourself. And why will we yank on these hooks? To make her protect us, save our lives? She will do that for strangers, for nothing. What else? You are her ally. Have you asked her to do anything for you? To make someone give you an enclave place, or an artificer contract? Why not? Because you are also a great martyr, who does not want these things?" She snorted as Aadhya scowled at her. "No! You don't ask because you know she would say *no*. I tried asking myself. But she will do nothing selfish for *herself*, much less anyone else. And she is not wrong," she added, in a grudging tone of having been unwillingly persuaded. "She *is* too powerful. Once she started, there would be nowhere to stop. So there is only one use of our *hooks:* to *help* her stop. You had better be glad that I have one, and hold tight to yours, too."

I stopped eavesdropping and stalked off in total outrage. I

couldn't deny that I was in fact freaking out, and it was very clearly an excellent idea for me to have people around who *could* yank me back onto the rails if I should go off them. Only what business did Liesel have making herself one of those people, and I couldn't help but see she'd successfully done just that. Because what she wanted, the reason she was helping me, was to *stop me from going maleficer,* which is the one thing I've been desperately afraid of doing since the age of five, and I would absolutely take Liesel's help on *that* project.

I got the coffees and came back and grouchily handed them round. Aadhya was still scowling at Liesel across the table, but with the same kind of sulky annoyance I felt myself: yes, we were stuck with her, after all.

We landed in Lisbon in daylight. I hadn't really been in New York long enough to feel jet lag, and now we were back with the sun where and when my brain expected it to be, which ought to have made me feel better, but instead it made the whole interlude recede into a chaotic nightmare that melted into the other half-remembered nightmares I'd had trying to sleep on the plane, with Ophelia stretched across them like a distorted shape floating on the surface of a murky lake. I had three voicemail messages from Chloe, and half a dozen texts asking me to call when I had the chance. I stared at them and thought of calling her, only I knew what she was going to ask me about, and what was there for me to say? Grab your things and flee the enclave straightaway? Ophelia wasn't a threat to Chloe at all, unless Chloe started running round yelling to everyone that the future Domina was a maleficer. If anything, she was better off not knowing anything more.

Liesel headed us directly onto a train out to Sintra, and

from there to a lavish boutique hotel in the middle of the town. While she and Aadhya made a room appear for us—with money, not magic—I stood in the charming lobby stuffed with antiques and watched the literal army of tourists marching on past towards the old scenic bits of the town, a tide coming in from the train and flowing up either side of the mountain road with taxis and golf carts running through the middle, carrying whoever wasn't ready to huff their way up on foot.

At first I was only watching because it was there in front of me to look at, but after a bit I started to wonder why they had apparently put the Scholomance entrance in the middle of a tourist trap. There're enclave entrances in New York, in London, in most of the biggest cities of the world, but that's because people build enclaves where they already live, and mostly they live in cities, so they have to put up with all the inconvenience and difficulty and mana-expense of building entrances there, where collisions with the mundane are a constant danger.

But the Scholomance was meant to be far away from any other enclaves and hard for maleficaria to find: why hadn't they tucked it into a truly obscure corner of the world? I understood even less when we tracked down the coordinates and found they were in the middle of an actual museum: an old historical estate, and not even *very* historical; the place had been built in the 1900s, after the Scholomance had already been open for more than ten years. It had to be deliberate, but it made no sense.

Our coordinates had been rounded off to three places, so we had to hunt through the whole sprawling estate: it could have been anywhere inside the grounds. And we couldn't even skip the queue for tickets and slip in through a wall when no one was looking; there were just too many people

ambling through the picturesque nearby streets, taking selfies against the outer walls. Even if we'd found ourselves all
alone for a moment, we couldn't have counted on it lasting:
every few minutes another one of the carts came careering
around the turn.

So instead we waited on the queue and bought tickets just
like everyone else, and then went through a long droning
tour of the preserved house, hearing about the self-important
owner and his architect and their fascination with Tarot rituals and initiation rites and primitivism—by which they'd
clearly meant nature unspoilt by anyone who didn't look like
them; Aadhya rolled her eyes at me and silently mouthed
what a dickhead—and all the lavish parties he'd hosted in the
gardens. We kept trying to look for a place where someone
might conceivably slip away, a door that might lead you out
of the world, but the annoying nine-year-old boy in the group
got to literally every single one before we could do, yanking
on old brass doorknobs and opening antique cupboards while
his beleaguered mother kept asking him wearily not to touch
things.

When the tour finally spilled us out into the gardens, I was
ready to believe that Ophelia had actually sent us out here as
some sort of diversion, but when I suggested as much, Liesel
said, "She would have sent us somewhere further away and
more remote!" which was true, so we grimly set off to wander through the gardens, trying to find the entrance to the
world's most secret and hidden enclave of mystical power,
hard on the heels of an entire tour bus of people with their
guide carrying a waving flag of Hello Kitty at the head.

The grounds were dazzlingly beautiful, enormously lush,
et cetera. Also it was hot as Satan's tit, to put it in the most
colorful terms possible, and what primitivism seemed to
mean was that the paths went in loops, meandered aggres-

sively, and the whole thing was full of stairs that pretended they'd been worn naturally into the rock and were therefore uneven. We kept trying to avoid the worst crowds, and as a result managed to go in circles three times in a row, which we only realized when we kept coming past the same distinctive moss-eaten staircase. I was overheated, sleep-deprived, wretched, and when we hit the same bloody staircase a fourth time, I started giggling and couldn't make myself stop, and had to be taken to the café and revived with cold water and strong coffee.

Liesel was enraged by then herself—I reckon she didn't much care for primitivism—and she stormed back to the ticket booth, got a map of the grounds, and after I got hold of myself, she led us on a systematic exhaustive tour of the place, and even insisted on our waiting in the painfully long queue to go down into the initiation well. The pamphlet told us it was part of some trumped-up mystical initiation rite of Freemasonry that the owner and his mates had liked to perform. It sounded to me that they hadn't had enough hazing in university, and in order to justify more of it to themselves as grown men, he'd had to build himself a palace and dress it up as some ponderous mystic rite that none of them really believed in, as if they could cart themselves back in time to a pagan era they'd mostly made up.

I wasn't in a mood to be fair to them, and also on some level I'd stopped thinking of finding the gates. In my head I was just on a horrible grade school trip that was happening to me as if I couldn't stop it. I couldn't imagine the Scholomance being in this adult Disneyland sort of place, so I wasn't wondering *why* it was here, what any of it was for. I dragged myself through the queue in sullen sweaty annoyance, and into the actual well, which wasn't literally a well: it was a tower that someone had hollowed out of the ground instead of building into the air, with a long spiral stairway going down around the empty space in the middle, people leaning over the sides to take photos up and down and across.

By the third level down, I wasn't sweating anymore, and I also didn't have the slightest doubt: the Scholomance was here, somewhere, close by, and whoever had built this place had known exactly what they were doing.

The voices of all the tourists, dozens of conversations in dozens of languages, were bouncing back and forth off the walls and blurring together into a wordless clamoring, deep and insistent: a Greek chorus speaking urgently to you from the other side of a wall, trying to tell you something important. It didn't seem to matter what they were saying, whether they were laughing or leaning over the edge to take photos; the echoes took everything and mashed it into the single low reverberating message.

The world above had been swallowed up by the dark inside the walls: it had receded into a round white circle of sky, too bright to look at from down here. I didn't want to keep going, but the walkway was too narrow to pause for long, people crowding behind us and in front of us, pushing us onward. Anyway, I had to keep going. We had to keep going down. We had to go *in*.

In a city, you wanted your enclave entrance to be as hidden as you could manage, so you could slip in and out of it easily, without drawing attention. If a mundane ever caught sight of a wizard going into an enclave, disappearing impossibly through a wall—that would have cost the enclave an enormous amount of mana, if it didn't literally make the entrance collapse.

But no one went in and out of the physical doors of the Scholomance on a daily basis. As students, we were brought in through the induction spell that whisked us in an incorporeal form through the gates and wards all the way up to our freshman dormitories, at hideous expense, during the tiny window of opportunity right after the mals were gorged from graduation or had been cleansed. And at graduation, we walked back out through the doors, but we didn't pop out into Portugal; the portal spell just sent us back whence we'd come.

The only things that used the doors were the *mals,* and this packed-solid river of mundanes would only make it harder for them to get through. The builders had started with parties and elaborate ceremonies—the owner had surely been a wizard himself, or maybe just the architect; in any case they'd made the place a *destination* for mundanes from the start. And then they'd traded off the solemnity of the fake rituals for the sheer masses of tour groups.

When once in four decades the enclaves did need to send something through the doors into the graduation hall—like New York's golems installing the new cafeteria equipment after the war—they presumably just hired the whole place out, claimed to be a film crew, and perhaps put out a documentary while they were at it. A documentary that would bring even more tourists here, to go through the ritual over and over and over, each one putting in just a little bit of mana in between the selfies—a moment of delight and wonder, a hint of unease, the half a second when they shut their eyes and imagined they were here alone, put themselves willingly into the story that the guidebooks and the pamphlets told them of initiation, and willingly went *in,* going down into the pitch dark below.

The well deposited us in a misshapen tunnel with many branches that didn't go anywhere, made of weirdly soft limestone, as if they'd been chewed open by something living. The weight of the earth was palpable overhead, and the cheap LED lightstrip they had set up to keep people from tripping didn't make it less terrible, partly because it so clearly didn't belong: it was only a feeble struggling effort to hold off the dark. There were no faces even in the crowd. People talked and muttered and someone screamed with laughter somewhere up ahead. Tears were glazing my eyes, blurring the orange light, and my breath was loud in my own ears. All I wanted was to keep going towards the gleams of light that I could just glimpse every once in a while up ahead, along the streaming river of tourists. I wanted to keep going and get *out*, escape along with them. That was the other reason they'd built this elaborate passageway: to make unsuspecting mundanes walk through the same journey that they hoped for their own children to make, the journey down to the smothering awful dark and back out again on the other side.

But there was a tiny thread of cold air coming at me along the side of the wall, with a faint familiar smell of ozone and iron and machine oil, and a hint of rotting compost: the smell of the Scholomance. I breathed it in, and felt in my gut how close I was, how close we were, and I stopped going along with the river of people. None of them really knew that I was here. None of them could see me. I was just one of a thousand shadows moving with them in the dark, I didn't matter, and they wouldn't even notice, they didn't notice, when I stepped into the next dark tunnel branching and stopped being there.

My foot came down hard on a jagged broken stone. I almost went sprawling on my face before I caught my balance, clenching my abdominal muscles tight instead of using my hands, and straightened up with the evocation of refusal in my mouth and my hands held up in front of me, ready to push it out, but I didn't need to. Nothing attacked me.

I couldn't see a thing, but I had a strong impression of

space round me, and a moment later Liesel and Aadhya were there on either side of me. We all nearly went over again as they both instantly jerked into casting positions themselves. The floor under our feet was so uneven we were more or less falling down against one another. A faint light appeared a moment later: Aadhya had taken out a round glimmerball, a lacework of gilt brass over a crystal innard, with a satellite ring of brass around it and tiny little propellers like a drone. She gave it an underhand toss upwards, and it whirred to life and brightened slowly, shining over an enormous cavern, so huge it must have been almost as large as the entire gardens overhead, a hollow excavation that made everything up above belatedly feel precarious.

You could tell there had been a massive plaza down here once, with columns and fountains carved into the walls all around: possibly some sort of protective artifice. Now they were only vague suggestions of caryatids and lion's-heads beneath thick layers of dirt and sludge. There was a green wet dripping everywhere, a stink of mold and stagnant water, and of rust; old scattered relics of dead maleficaria, scorched shells and cracked bits of constructs.

Across the center slab of the stone floor, they'd carved the familiar words at the heart of the Scholomance: TO OFFER SANCTUARY AND PROTECTION TO ALL THE WISE-GIFTED CHILDREN OF THE WORLD, and around them in curving patterns were monumental versions of the same spells that had been engraved into the Scholomance doors, a litany of protection. I spotted MALICE, KEEP FAR, THIS GATE WISDOM'S SHELTER GUARDS: deep letters filled with gold that was still bright despite a glaze of algae.

But the spell was cracked right through GATE, a wide dark fissure crossing the curved shape of the words. Massive slabs of stone heaved up in every direction at sharp angles, piles of

crumbled shards. The whole plaza was shattered in a sun-
burst of jagged cracks—radiating out from the immense
bronze doors of the Scholomance, which were hanging
askew out of their frame in the cavern wall. It looked—well,
it looked like a supervolcano spell had gone off here in the
recent past.

There was nothing else moving in the whole chamber, except the dripping water coming down from some leaky place
overhead, plinking every few moments. There were gaping
cracks between the doors and the frame, big enough we
should have been able to see through them, but even in the
glimmerball's light, there was nothing but pitch dark on the
other side. It could have been a shallow niche in the cavern
wall; it could have been the unlit graduation hall; it could
have been the empty void. It could have been the side of an
enormous maw-mouth, pressed up tightly against the doors
on the other side, trying to get out.

"I'm going in," I said. My voice echoed weirdly off the
walls round me, unbalanced. "Stay here."

"And wait for Patience to come fleeing out ahead of you?"
Liesel said caustically. "No. We are safer with you than alone."

Aadhya just said, "Let's go."

I didn't argue. Maybe I'd known all along that they would
come with me, and I'd only told myself that I'd stop them
because it was horribly selfish to drag them along, and so I'd
had to pretend I wasn't going to do it. I imagine it's always
easier to do something monstrous if you can convince yourself you aren't going to, up to the last minute, until you do.

Chapter 10
THE SCHOLOMANCE

WE WENT INTO THE SCHOLOMANCE.

I don't know how to describe what that was like, going back in through the doors, knowing what was on the other side. I don't mean Patience, not just Patience. *The Scholomance* was on the other side, and that was so much worse than any one mal could have been. We'd considered a few plans, last year, in our frantic hunting for ideas, that had involved the younger kids leaving the Scholomance for a while and going back, and we'd abandoned all of them. You could only go into the Scholomance once, when you didn't understand where you were going: to the endless awful hope of getting out, a hope you could only buy with other people, who were all trying to buy the same hope with you, and the open maw of Patience and Fortitude waiting at the end so you couldn't even be sure of getting out by dying. Once you understood, once you'd been in it and got out, you couldn't go back in. But we had to.

We scrambled and slid across the shattered stone floor over

to the doors. I put my hands on the right-hand one, which was more or less still on its upper hinge and could be pushed. I didn't try it right away. I shut my eyes and told myself the school was still there, still right over there. It had been there forever, it had been there for more than a hundred years, for the lives of tens of thousands of wizards; of course it was still there. It was still there, and so was Patience, and I didn't want to go back, but I had to. So it had to be there.

Liesel put her hand on my shoulder. "The doors are here, so certainly we can get back inside," she said, with iron certainty. "It will just take mana. You get us through. I will have a recoiler spell ready. That will give you enough time to put up the evocation."

Aadhya hadn't been with us in London, but she got the idea. She called back the glimmerball, closing her hand tight around it, so the light didn't show us what was or wasn't on the other side of the cracks. She put her other hand on my shoulder, too. "I'll put the light up as soon as we're through."

I don't know if they felt as confident about getting through as they sounded, but that didn't really matter; they helped *me* be more sure about it. I took a deep breath and pushed on the door.

It should at least have creaked, but it didn't budge at all. The entire horde of mals might as well have been on the other side trying to keep it shut. I put my head down and braced my heels, pushing harder, a burn starting across my shoulder blades. I didn't consciously pull mana, but the power-sharer on my wrist began heating up, as if mana was being sucked through me so fast that I wasn't even feeling it in my own body. "Come on, let us in," I said under my breath, not really a spell; I was talking to the school, I suppose, which had occasionally answered me before, and maybe it heard me. The doors groaned and shifted, and a triangle of dark opened up between them that was just barely large enough to duck through.

I stepped through the opening with Aadhya and Liesel still clutching my shoulders, ducking right behind me. Liesel made a quick jerk with her free hand before she even straightened, and I felt the recoiler spell go flashing out from us. If it hit anything, I didn't hear it. I was ready to be attacked instantly, but nothing came at us. I couldn't feel anything moving or stirring in the air around me.

Aadhya heaved the glimmerball up and ahead of us. We were standing on the dais in the graduation hall—on the one unbroken part of the dais. I'd been standing right in this same place when I'd cast my earth-shattering supervolcano spell, which I could tell because the outline of my footprints was marked out on the surface with negative space: a crazed starburst of cracks radiated out from it in every direction, through the entire hall.

The floor around the dais was covered with a thick horrible crust of dried-up rotting ooze, still glistening in a few places. I gagged at the faint familiar smell: the detritus of a thousand corpses, those lives I'd slaughtered out of Patience or Fortitude, left in a gush on the floor. There was a thick scorched line around the bottom of the dais still visible through the dried ooze, marking the line of the shield I'd put up to hold off the horde.

Orion had been right next to me when Patience had rolled through their ranks and slammed into it, trying to get at us. Trying to get out, just like us. And behind the maw-mouth, the whole room had been packed from wall to wall with maleficaria. They'd been pouring back down into the graduation hall, cramming every available inch of air and space.

Now the hall was empty. There wasn't so much as an agglo creeping around a dark corner.

"Where did—" Aadhya said, and just stopped there; the word echoed unnaturally loud off the marble walls, before it died away just as unnaturally into stillness. Anyway she didn't need to finish the sentence. We all had the exact same question in our heads.

"They can't have got out," Liesel said, almost angrily. "All of Portugal would be swarming with mals."

I made the mistake of looking back at the smashed doors, and discovered I couldn't see out into the cavern we'd come from. The gaping holes around the doors were just featureless black, as if there were nothing outside but the void, after all. I didn't think the mals had got out. I looked back to stop thinking about it. The room here still felt solid enough; it wasn't anything as bad as Yancy's half-real pavilion. But the mals were gone, and if they hadn't got out—

"Maybe they just—fell away into the void," Aadhya said. "The school is being kept up by external mana, but there wasn't anything inside for the mals to eat, so . . ." She trailed off, dubiously, as she should have; that would have been much too nice and convenient. Liesel shook her head, rejecting the idea, but she didn't volunteer one of her own, just frowned in deep irritation that meant she didn't have any plausible enough to believe in.

I didn't either, and I didn't want them anyway. I didn't care where the other mals had gone. I couldn't care about anything except what I was here for, and I couldn't think about that because I would have started screaming. I just walked out across the hall, and Aadhya and Liesel came after me. The huge maintenance shafts were still standing wide open on either side of the hall, the ones we'd used to funnel the mals through the school. A skinny ladder ran up the inside wall, looking tiny and precarious in the vast gaping space. I got onto it and started the climb.

The glimmerball whirred and flitted around up above our heads as we went, illuminating a globe around us that faded out into solid dark above and below. I'd just have gone on climbing mindlessly, but after the floor disappeared into the dark, Aadhya said from below, "The shafts are sixty feet tall, and every twelve rungs is ten feet. It shouldn't be too long," and Liesel started counting them off loudly, one after another, fixing us in space. And when she finished counting off the last one, I reached up my fingers without looking and they found the edge of the floor. I pulled myself up the last few rungs and onto the floor of the workshop, the glimmerball bobbing out into the big space just ahead of us.

We did find signs of the horde's passage. The edge of the shaft that I'd climbed out of was gouged with claw marks, all the worktables smashed and overturned with scorch marks and dried slime trails left across the floors, scattered limbs and shells where they'd been dropped, most of them gnawed and cracked: mals would eat each other when they couldn't get delicious wizard children instead. But there still weren't any actual mals anywhere. Liesel even picked up one of the furnace pokers and jabbed at the ceiling panels overhead, which ought to have stirred up at least a few baby flingers or larval digesters, but nothing.

Aadhya took Pinky out of her pocket. "What do you think? Chance you could sniff out a maw-mouth?" she said to him.

That wasn't an act of cruelty or anything; under ordinary circumstances, mice—even magical familiar mice—were well beneath the notice of a maw-mouth. Most maw-mouths won't even stop to eat a single wizard. Their idea of a midday snack is ten of us at a minimum. But Pinky just gave a loud squeak of protest and made a leap out of her hand and onto the side of her dress and squirmed himself back down into the pocket. Precious stuck her own pink nose out just long enough to chitter in vociferous agreement.

"What about *you*?" I said aloud to the air, asking the school itself. "I'd think you'd want me to do for Patience. It would certainly protect the wise-gifted children of the world."

I was sorry that I'd done it as soon as the words finished leaving my mouth: the only thing that came back was the opposite of an answer. The sound of my raised voice died away too quickly in the air that I now couldn't help but notice felt strange and thin. Our breath was misting. It was cold, and not just cold the way the tunnels had been after the heat of the gardens outside. The workshop should have been full of noises: the grinding of gears, endless fans rotating, the gurgle of the pipes and the roaring furnaces. Instead it was silent, muffled.

The Scholomance was dying.

And yes, it was still being fed with mana, with belief. But you could tell it wasn't all there anymore, either. I had the strong sense of living in the hushed moment just before an old rotten tree falls in the forest, inside the held breath, waiting.

Waiting, in our case, directly under the creaking tree. "I think we should just start looking," Aadhya said, with sensible urgency.

"Let us follow the path the maleficaria would have taken," Liesel said, and pointed up at the speaker wires rigged to the ceiling, where the honeypot song had been piped out to all the mals, luring them along. Long pieces of wire were dangling down like caterpillar threads: it was lucky we'd had half a dozen backups for every connection.

We went along the line all through the warren of the seminar rooms and then finally up the stairs to the next floor. For a long stretch we had only the yawning void on our left, where the junior dormitories should have been; apparently they'd crumbled away and taken the outer wall of the main school with them. We crept past it clinging to the inside wall, half plastering ourselves against it, and when we didn't find a single mal anywhere in the alchemy labs, and the wires would have led us up the main staircase to the third floor, we detoured and found the interior staircase instead. It wasn't much better. The stairs and corridors had always been the thinnest and most flexible parts of the school. We were a long time getting up to the language labs, my legs burning with the acid pain of climbing. We only had Aadhya's glimmer to keep us from pitch dark: all the lights were out. It made every muscle from the top of my head to the bottom of my spine tight with well-trained anxiety: this was how you got taken out, stupidly going up a bad way. Something would always be waiting, something would leap out at you. Something *should* have leapt out at us.

Nothing did. The strange unnatural quiet was broken by occasional nerve-racking groans and creaks that sounded less like machinery working and more like something large about to break off and fall on our heads. Eventually we made it up to the language labs and all just sat down on the floor of the corridor together to catch our breath and let our legs stop whinging. We hadn't stopped *on* the stairs: possibly it would have been all right if we had, but no one who had made it through six months in the Scholomance would ever stay to find out.

"This makes no sense," Aadhya said, between panting. "Patience can't have eaten *all* the other mals. There were a *million* of them," which might have been an exaggeration, but it had certainly felt close at the time. "Some of them would have got away or hidden."

"It was not only Patience," Liesel said. "The maleficaria were lured here to hunt. When we were all gone, they would have fed on each other, and the school has been devouring as many of them as it could catch with the wards." It sounded plausible, but I could tell she didn't believe her own words. She was only selling it the way you would an essay question on an exam when you hadn't a clue of the real answer.

"It doesn't matter," I said flatly. "I'm here for Patience." I pushed myself up. "Let's go." Aadhya and Liesel weren't very enthusiastic about getting up, but they did it. I got ahead of them a little, banging open doors to the language labs, looking inside, banging back out. I was aggressive about it, letting doors slam and crash. The noise didn't travel properly, but as long as I kept on making it, I could almost fill the heavy muffling air.

Then they caught up to me, and Liesel stopped me opening the next door. "Listen!" she hissed.

We all stood holding our breath, and faintly from down the hall I heard a low murmuring sound, like voices talking on the other side of a wall. I didn't move for a moment. I'd half been hoping to be attacked, for Patience to come at me roaring and horrible and fast, so fast I could just kill it right away, kill it without hearing anything any of its mouths might have to say to me.

Finally I forced myself back into motion, and we went down the corridor. The murmuring grew louder, still unintelligible but more clearly a single voice speaking, speaking without a pause. I couldn't understand the words. I stood outside the door another thousand years before I shoved it open and went inside.

It was one of the honors language labs, the small ones with the nice private carrels and the padded headphones. I'd been languages track my entire career, but I'd never been assigned to one of them. I *ought* to have been sure of at least one course in here during my senior year, but instead I'd been

208 ♦ NAOMI NOVIK

loaded up with four interdisciplinary seminar classes and not a single straightforward language class, and yes I could still feel bitter about it, or at least I tried to still feel bitter, tried to hold on to that nice small feeling of resentment and spite as hard as I could.

The room wasn't especially large by Scholomance standards. The Patience in my memory would have filled it completely. But the back half was sunk in darkness, and the murmuring was coming from in there. I was tight all through my body as Aadhya sent the glimmerball shooting forward—but the room was still empty. There had been fighting in here at some point: a handful of carrels had been smashed apart, and a set of massive clawed gouges ran in parallel along the ceiling, through the overhead lamps, and down the far wall, like a dragon had been thrashing around wildly. But whatever had done the fighting was gone. The murmuring was coming from the headphones dangling from one of the carrels, repeating a lesson in a language I didn't know.

Aadhya let out an explosive breath that helped me let go of the one I hadn't noticed I was holding on to, and we all just stood there a little bit shakily, until Liesel reached out and took the headphones and unplugged them, to stop the endless murmuring noise.

We slogged onwards up to the cafeteria, the wreckage of our last breakfast still left on the tables: no one had bothered to bus their trays. We followed the speakers through the library stacks, a weirdly short walk: sections seemed to have entirely disappeared, and the ones that were left were mostly full of introductory textbooks in rubbishy condition. The books were all slipping off the shelves by the dozens, I suppose, going wherever books of magic hide when they don't want to be on a shelf. I had an instinctive burst of alarm about the Golden Stone sutras, back home with Mum. I wasn't paying enough attention to them, I should have cleaned the cover, I should have told them how wonderful they were—all the habits I'd built over senior year.

And I missed them, with a sharp jab of pain; I missed *Mum,* missed *home,* wanted to be there with every atom of my body again, as if coming back into the Scholomance had erased away all the confusion and misery of her revelation, and replaced them with the much larger misery of being in *here,* hunting for what was left of Orion, so I could kill him.

We followed our thread through the labyrinth of the library stacks and back down again through the other half of the school. We passed the wreckage of the Maleficaria Studies auditorium: we'd torn the loathed place apart for building supplies at the end of last year, and the damage there had only worsened, the outer walls left gaping. The new freshman dormitory level ought to have been visible on the other side and wasn't, only pitch-black void there past the handful of skeletal girders still standing. A few partial mals still peered out at us from the walls, but they stayed in the almost-destroyed instructive mural and didn't come alive the way they'd used to sometimes, in class; they were just flat paintings now.

That was the closest we got to seeing a mal or for that matter anything even moving. "The maw-mouth in London ran from you. It knew you could kill it, even before *you* knew," Liesel said as we slogged back down the stairs to the workshop floor. "Patience must be hiding."

"How can a maw-mouth the size of a barn *hide*?" Aadhya said.

"Maw-mouths are oozes," Liesel said. "It could simply spread itself out between two floors."

We all looked down at our feet with an involuntary flinch, even Liesel. "Except we already hacked up the school all over the place," Aadhya said after a moment, sounding as if she was trying to convince herself. "Half the rooms have some floor and ceiling panels missing. We'd have seen it."

I *wasn't* convinced; none of us had spotted Patience before graduation, had we? For lack of any better ideas, we went into a classroom and Aadhya took the legs off one of the old metal chairs and reshaped them into pry bars. We started lifting up floor panels as we went and sending the glimmerball inside. It slowed our progress to even more of a crawl. If we were going to do an exhaustive search, we ought to have gone back up and started at the library, but we didn't, in the same way you know perfectly well you ought to stop reading and go to bed and you'll feel hideously groggy in the morning if you don't, and yet you keep going. We couldn't possibly have done an exhaustive search of the Scholomance anyway. This place had been built to house five thousand wizards. An entire army of maleficaria could have avoided the three of us for years, much less a single mal.

But it shouldn't have made a difference. We were looking for something that none of us wanted to find. In the Scholomance, that ought to have made it bog-easy. We should have turned a corner and there Patience would be, waiting for us, with Orion's eyes and mouth staring out at me right at eye level. Half of what made the search agonizing was the certain knowledge that I was going to find exactly what I was looking for. Even if Patience was putting an enormous effort into hiding from us, even a modest effort on *our* side ought to have won out. Only we kept looking, and we kept not finding it.

"I'll have to summon it," I said finally, as we went down the last stairway, back to the workshop level.

"Well, that sounds amazing," Aadhya said. "How can we have to *summon* a maw-mouth? That literally sounds like what you'd offer if you were trying to summon something *good*. Universe, bring me a basket of soma, and in return I'll face the world's biggest maw-mouth! Maybe you should try it that way."

"It will not work *either* way," Liesel said, savagely, and threw her pry bar down with a clang. We both paused and looked at her. "It isn't here! We would have found it if it were here. It is not in the school."

"Oh, okay, so now you think it's worth considering the possibility that it *did* get out," Aadhya said, dropping hers too, and putting her hands on her hips with a glare of outrage.

"No!" Liesel said. "If Patience could get out, the others could get out, too. None of them got out. The school lingers, but the maleficaria are gone. They spent their malia to survive as long as they could, but they dwindled and faded into the void. They are gone, and Patience is gone."

She said it with the aggressive confidence of someone trying to impose their own truth on the universe, only in this case, I understood at once that she was trying to impose it on *me*. She didn't really believe that all the horde and Patience had just quietly gone into the void. She'd only decided that, to her fury, something she didn't understand in the least had happened to the mals and to Patience, and so we weren't going to find Patience no matter what we did. And she didn't want me trying to do a summoning, because she was concerned about what I *would* offer, to set Orion free. She was right to be concerned. I'd have to offer enough to break through whatever hideous thing had happened to all the mals, which was presumably even worse than all of them lumped together.

"I'm going to try," I said flatly, answering what she was really saying. "We'll go back down to the doors first, and you can both go out before I try it."

"Don't be foolish," Liesel said. "Listen to me—"

"Sorry," I said, meaning *fuck off,* and didn't. I walked away from her down the corridor to the gym, where the other maintenance shaft would be waiting to take us back down to the graduation hall. I knew Patience wouldn't be there. But I kept prying up floor tiles on the way, and when I got to the big doors, I pried them open, too, and I was right; Patience wasn't there. Even though half the school had fallen apart, and the rest was threatening to follow, the gym artifice was still running in full form: trees heavy with late-summer fruit and the horribly beautiful smell of perfectly ripe peaches on every breath, a winding stream gurgling over rocks and crossed by a charming little bridge, branches entwined to frame the pagoda building in the distance like a picture.

And Orion was sitting on the porch, looking off into the distance.

I just stood there in the doorway at first. You might think I'd have entertained at least one fantasy, one tiny little dream of finding Orion alive and well and really properly rescuing him, but I hadn't. The Scholomance trains you out of expecting miracles. The only miracles we ever received were the ones we made ourselves, and we paid for every one in advance. I hadn't hoped for it at all.

Just about when I'd have screamed my throat raw and run at him, Liesel grabbed my arm with both hands and leaned back with all her weight, which she needed to hold me. Even as I tried to wrestle loose, Aadhya was gripping my other arm to help and putting her hand over my mouth, and Liesel hissed at me, "It's not him! It's a trap for you!"

It would have been a jolly good trap, too, and I'd have gone straight into it in a second, only before I could heave them both off, Orion turned his head and saw us. He stood up and came at us through the peach trees.

Liesel and Aadhya both froze into complete stillness, like a prey animal realizing it's exposed to a hunter in full view. I felt it through their hands, still locked on my arms. I felt it in my own shriveling gut. Orion was looking right at me, and I wish it *had* been a trap, I wish I'd been able to imagine for even a moment that it *wasn't* him, but it was. It was him. The real difference was that *I* wasn't *me,* not in his head. He was looking at me with absolutely nothing but the utterly focused calculation that filled him when he was hunting mals, where the only thing in his head was what he had to do next.

I could have vomited or screamed, but I couldn't, because he was coming at us, and what I mean was, he was coming to *kill us.* Liesel scrabbled at Aadhya behind my back until she let go of my other arm, setting me loose, as if she thought I was going to have to fight Orion. And the worst part was, I thought so too. *"Orion,"* I said. "Orion, it's *me,* it's *El!"* my voice rising to a yell, but he didn't even break a single stride. Just as if he'd been locked up alone with all the mals in the universe, with the worst mals in the universe, and he'd killed and killed and killed until there was nothing left in him but killing, and the power of wanting anything, of *doing* anything, besides hunting mals, had been stripped out of him. Exactly what everyone else in the world had ever wanted out of him.

I couldn't imagine actually fighting him, but I also couldn't imagine standing here and letting him kill us. So I did the only thing I could: I shoved Alfie's evocation of refusal into Orion's face. I didn't even cast it properly; I just pushed it out and said, *"No.* No, *thank you,"* with all the absolute profound revulsion in me for the horrible killing machine he'd been turned into.

Orion ran straight into it and was halted in his tracks. He paused for a moment, stymied, but then he put both his hands on the surface of the dome and my whole stomach heaved over, because it felt like *Patience.* It was just Orion, just his two hands, but that touch felt exactly like a maw-mouth enveloping my shield, trying to get through to me, oozing over the surface and pushing on it to test for weaknesses.

There weren't any. My entire being was behind that dome, a solid unbroken wall of *no,* with the endless vat of New York's mana behind me. Except for one small opening: I was looking through the faint golden glitter of the spell at Orion's face, and I *did* want him. I wanted Orion to come straight to me and let me howl at him for being a colossal idiot before I let him pull me into his arms so I could wail against his chest for a month or so. And the Orion on the other side prodding the wall of my shield, the Orion that I didn't want even a little, paused, his gaze narrowing. And then he put both his hands on the dome again and started to push his way through on the strength of that longing, which I couldn't have helped if my life and the lives of everyone I loved depended on it.

Not that far off from the current circumstances. "El!" Liesel said through her teeth, but I didn't need a bloody reminder. I would have closed up the vulnerability if I could, but I might as easily have popped open my rib cage and taken my heart out for a bit. Mana was pouring through the New York power-sharer and out of me into the dome, holding off the grotesque sucking hunger on the other side as hard as I could, the hunger that wasn't Orion, as if he'd somehow killed Patience and then had *become* Patience.

I remembered with horror when I'd reached him through the scrying water, back in Wales, on graduation day—that moment when I'd tried to grab him and had got a handful of maw-mouth instead. Orion had never fought a maw-mouth before. I'd killed the only maw-mouth that had ever made it upstairs in the Scholomance. What if his power, his power that let him pull mana out of mals, had been overwhelmed by taking in that torrent of polluted malia? A century of torment and malice crammed down his throat all in one rush. I couldn't help wanting to reach out to him—

And he shuddered all over and pressed his entire body up against the dome and came swimming through the cold honey of the wall, one fingertip after another curling away, making it inside, and then his hands, and his face surfacing out of the gold glitter as it slid away, and then he fought his shoulders through, one after another, and thrashed the rest of the way in, falling through onto the floor. And I couldn't fight Orion, I couldn't, but as he got up and came at me, I snarled at him in rage and agony, "You *bastard,* if you come any closer, I'll beat your *skull* in," and heaved up my chair-leg pry bar to bash at him with it, because I could imagine *that,* the way I couldn't imagine dissolving him into maggots or commanding him to stop existing or melting the flesh off his bones. But I could hit him with a stick; I'd been ready for that at almost any given moment since I'd met him, and as if he'd believed me, Orion slowed, mid-stride, and stopped just barely out of range.

His face had stayed serenely untroubled all this while, inhumanly blank, but now the very faintest hint of a frown line wobbled into view on his forehead. We all stood squared off, none of us moving. I was still gulping, cramming rage and horror back down my throat together, and he said, "Galadriel," moving his mouth wrongly around the sound of my name, breaking it into too many syllables, as if he was trying to remember how to speak. "Galadriel." It was better the second time, and then he said it again, "Galadriel," and it wasn't *right,* it wasn't the way Orion had once said my name, where he'd almost made me like hearing it, but at least it sounded like a human being talking.

He stopped after that, as if satisfied he'd got it right. He didn't say anything else. He didn't come at us again, either. He just stood there, looking at me.

Chapter 11

THE ROUNDHOUSE

W E ALL STAYED frozen in place there for what in retrospect felt a silly amount of time, until Orion carried on *not* trying to kill us for long enough that we finally began to believe he wasn't going to start again. And once we did believe that, we spent another good long while whispering to one another about what the hell we were going to do with him. Liesel made a case for leaving him in the school while we went and got some sort of help, which Aadhya rolled her eyes at, and I didn't even bother vetoing out loud. The next obvious answer was to take him straight home to his mum and dad in New York, only that was even more obviously wrong.

"Anywhere else you would take him, New York will come," Liesel said. "And if not, then someone *else* will come. Orion Lake cannot be hidden quietly away anywhere in the world."

"I'll have a go at it, anyway," I said grimly. "I'm taking him to *my* mum."

I didn't have the faintest idea what Mum would do with Orion. Based on past experience, she'd want nothing to do with him, except to get me away from him. Horribly, I could even have seen her point. Orion wasn't trying to kill us at the moment, but it felt very much *at the moment*. My own skin was still crawling with a visceral terror at even being in arm's reach. It wasn't just me, either; Liesel wasn't taking her eyes off him, her hands poised out to her sides just ready to come up into casting position, and Aadhya kept putting her hand out in front of me every time I looked at him, I think out of the same instinct to stop someone leaning a bit too far out over a mortal cliff, a child or a drunk, someone you didn't quite trust to keep themselves from going over.

Aad was right not to trust me. I'd have immediately done anything, however stupid and reckless, to try to save him, except that I completely understood on a visceral level that I couldn't do anything of any use. Whatever had happened to him, whatever Patience had done to him, I hadn't a hope of fixing it. The only spell I could have cast on him that would have worked was the exact spell I'd come in here to cast: I could have looked at Orion and told him he was already dead, and he would have had to believe me, exactly the way Patience would have had to believe me. Of course Orion was dead. He'd been locked alone inside the Scholomance with half the maleficaria in the world, with the single worst mal in the world. I'd come in knowing he was dead, and I still knew it. I could have convinced him, too.

What I needed was someone to convince both of us that he was *still alive,* that he was still somewhere in there, smothering under the weight of a million maleficaria. And the only person I knew with any chance of that was Mum.

"And how are we going to *get* him there?" Liesel snapped, deeply irritated by my ongoing refusal to negotiate with reality. "Will you take his hand and lead him along? Will you be taking him on an aeroplane perhaps? How will we even remove him from this tourist park?"

I hadn't answers for any of these really excellent questions. I looked at Orion, his eyes bright and glossy and fixed on me, and I took a step away towards the doors of the gym. His head turned to follow me. I swallowed and took a few more steps, tensed throughout my body, and I barely managed to keep from letting out a whimper when he went into motion again; Liesel and Aadhya both scrambled to stay ahead of me. But he only came a few steps more and stopped again, just out of reach again. I needed a lot of deep breathing before my heart stopped thumping, and I was leaking tears while it did. It was wrong, *wrong wrong wrong* to be standing here *afraid* of Orion. No one in their right mind would ever have been rude to this thing wearing his face.

"I don't care," I said, when I could get words out. "I'm taking him to Wales even if I have to walk there."

Lucky for me and probably a lot of other people, after I made my grand pronouncement, Liesel gave up on trying to persuade me to do anything sensible and instead put her brain on solving all the problems she considered unnecessary that I was nevertheless creating for myself and by extension her. She led us back to the workshop, and Aadhya cobbled together a spell holder for her out of the bits and pieces left around. Fortunately, those included several bits of maleficaria, and Aadhya's affinity was in working with exotic materials. She put together a pendant out of the teardrop-shaped eyecase that had come off a chitter, surrounded by fragments of the shells of at least half a dozen mournlets tied on with sirenspider silk, and Liesel put a spell of obfuscation into it, and then handed it to me. "Put it on him," she said.

Orion had stayed at exactly the same distance the whole time, following me here, that precious arm's length of space between us. Having to go closer was as bad as having to go down a tunnel to a waiting maw-mouth. But when I tried, when I took a breath and took a step towards him, he stepped *back*. I paused, and then tried again, and he did it again, as if he didn't want me to come any closer either. I stopped, wanting to burst into tears all over again, and then I said, "Just put it on yourself, then!" and set it on the workbench nearest me—well, the half a workbench that was still standing—and moved back. He came by and slowly turned his head to look down at the pendant, and after a moment, he did pick it up and put it on.

I saw him under it in a way I hadn't before. The pendant was sitting incongruously glowing over the remains of his old T-shirt with the Transformers logo across the front, reduced to tatters hanging on between the bands round the neck and the arms, the edges browned with dried blood. His trousers were torn up too, gaping holes across the legs from seam to seam and both back pockets ripped open and the shredded remnants dangling. His trainers looked more like gladiator sandals, a loop round his ankles and the metal-capped toes all that were keeping them on his feet. He'd only been sitting there in the pavilion; he could have mended them. He hadn't been able to care. "You're a mess, Lake," I said, because I would have said exactly that to him under any other circumstances, only after I did, I burst into tears, and I couldn't even put my hands over my face, because I couldn't stand to take my eyes off him, in case he *came closer*.

"Do I need to put one on *you*?" Liesel said, caustically.

"Are you *serious*?" Aadhya said to her, in irritation, but I was grateful. I scrubbed my arms over my face in opposite directions and then accepted a rag from Aadhya to honk my nose and get the worst of the tears and snot off myself.

Then we left the Scholomance and went back to the hotel.

I'm going to leave it at that, because I don't remember most of it, actually. I got through it one minute at a time, and let each one go as soon as I'd got through it, because here came another one. They were all the same minute anyway, the minute where I could feel Orion alive and at my back, just a few steps behind me, and that feeling was the most horrible sensation in the entire universe, and I had to keep pushing on through crowds of people, mundane ordinary people on holiday, hot and sweaty and laughing or bored, children whinging for drinks, and I knew if I turned round and looked at Orion even once, seen him among that sticky noisy living throng, I would see that he was dead so vividly that he would have been, so I couldn't look around. I had to keep going, to let him keep following me and my wide open back.

I couldn't think at all by the time we got to the hotel. If I had, the idea of trying to take him on an aeroplane would have been laughable to the point of hysteria, unless we'd packed him in a box and checked him in as luggage. I vaguely have the sense that Liesel and Aadhya had a conversation about it in the hotel room that I didn't pay attention to at the time enough to know what they were doing, as though I had stopped being a significant character in my own life and I was only standing in the background of the scene, decorative, staring at Orion. The one saving grace was that the beautiful ornate hotel room didn't make much more sense than he did, and therefore he could exist in it and stare back at me.

They went out and got a van and put Orion in the back of it, and drove us back to Wales. We were in a ferry for a lot of it: I remember the heaving of the ocean under us, waves of nausea from the outside and not just the inside, crossing over and doubling one another. I must have gone to the loo and slept a bit, or at least passed out now and again, but I don't remember it happening. I only remember sitting there hud-

dled in the front passenger seat and staring out the wind-
shield at the blank walls of the hold with Orion's face floating
in misty reflection in the glass. Once, Precious crept out of
my pocket to come and nose at my ear, trying to give comfort, and crept back in again when it couldn't be done. And
then we were driving again, Aadhya and Liesel taking it in
turn, until suddenly the roads became too familiar for me not
to recognize them. We pulled into the car park at the commune, and Mum was standing there in the dark, her pale face
caught out by our headlights.

We'd barely stopped moving when she ran around to my
door and all but pulled me out. She clutched my face in her
hands, her whole body shaking as she went gripping my arms
up and down my whole body as if she didn't quite believe I
was all there, whole. I wasn't sure I was, either. Aadhya and
Liesel got out, too, and started trying to explain things to
Mum, which I was well beyond being able to do myself, but
before they got anywhere, Orion came out.

He'd sat quietly unmoving the entire time we'd been driving; he hadn't drunk any of the water we'd pushed over to
him, he hadn't eaten any of the food. He didn't burst out of
the van dramatically like the Hulk or anything now. He just
came out as directly as possible, which in this case meant he
peeled open the side of the van along one of the seams and
squeezed out as soon as it was wide enough for him to get
through. Mum gave a strangled moan of horror in her throat,
recoiling, and I grabbed at her in desperation to stop her saying anything, to stop her telling me anything I couldn't stand
to hear. "It's not him!" I said. "It's not Orion. It's not his
fault," trying to explain to her that he'd been trapped with all
the mals in the universe and she had to help him.

Mum didn't let me finish. "Who *did* this?" she said, her
voice a whisper, and I was going to tell her it was Patience,

he'd been locked in with Patience, but instead I said, "His mother. Ophelia Lake," and all the other words backed up in my throat and stopped there, because as soon as her name came out of my mouth, I was sure that it was the truth, even though I didn't understand what she'd done, or how.

Aadhya and Liesel stayed behind in the yurt without more than a token argument; they both looked washy and green with exhaustion after the trip. I could have slept for a week myself, but Mum wouldn't wait an instant, and I shared the same urgency. She led me and Orion straight out to the woods, in the dark, calling moonlight to light our way. If a mundane had been with us, they would only have thought it was an unusually bright night, and their eyes were well adjusted to the dark, and somehow the moon was reaching us despite the trees overhead.

Mum doesn't always go to the same place with her circle. Whenever she goes out, she listens to the place and doesn't work there if it isn't in the mood. I have no idea how trees and grass let her know they aren't in the mood, but apparently they do. But she does have regular spots she goes back to fairly often, and some that she saves for special occasions. I always knew that someone was really badly off if she took them to the one furthest away from the commune: there's a round meadow up where an old oak came down in a storm a decade ago. The jagged hollowed-out trunk is still standing, and she has the patient stand inside it with the circle all round.

I expected her to lead us straight there, and for the first part of the way we were going in that direction, but when we got to the turning, she led me straight past it instead, and onward into the woods. After half a mile or so, we came to a massive thicket of brambles that blocked the way completely like a wall. She stopped in front of them and held out her open hands and just said, "Please," softly. After a moment, the brambles creaked themselves apart, just enough for us to pass.

We were walking for another hour after that. There wasn't any kind of path or trail, but Mum kept on steadily, as if she knew where she was going, although as far as I could tell, no human being had been this way in at least a decade, and possibly not even a deer. It wasn't anywhere she'd ever brought me before. All the overgrowth curled slowly out of our way the whole time, and closed back around behind Orion, bringing up the rear, the faint pallid shimmer of Mum's light making a circle round us.

But it wasn't anything like moving through the forgotten places, halfway in the void. It was the opposite, as though we were moving deeper into the *real,* into a place that didn't want to allow any magic at all, and was only grudgingly letting us slip past while it looked the other way.

The brambles finally let us out into a small clearing with the last traces of an ancient roundhouse standing: the upper half of the wall rotted away but the round stone ring of the foundation remaining. The doorway was still there, two big stone slabs and a third across the top. The roof was long since gone, but in its place a massive old yew tree was standing next to the foundation, almost bent over the walls. Two large branches were spread out over the top of the walls, sheltering, with a third low one stretched across the doorframe blocking the way in. It was too shadowed to see inside.

I knew at once that someone had lived and died here a long time ago. Someone like Mum. Someone powerful, who'd lived here all their life, offering that power to anyone who came to their door, but who had made a choice not to use it for themselves when death had come knocking on their own door. Someone who hadn't taken the enclavers' bargain, maybe even before there had been enclavers to offer it. I knew, because it felt just like the yurt, only deeper.

"I'm sorry to ask," Mum said. I'm not sure if she was talking to the ancient yew, or to the hut, or to the spirit of that healer who'd lived here long ago. To all of them, I think; this was a place of power, of generosity, of life, and you couldn't pick it apart into one single thing. They were all a part of it. The healer had built the hut, and planted the yew, and the stone walls and branches had sheltered and shaded her and those who'd come for healing, and now they still remembered her, long after she'd gone out of the world and all human memory. "But I can't do this alone. Will you help me?"

She turned and gestured to Orion, and everything in the clearing drew back from him somehow, the same way Mum had recoiled, an instinctive flinching: twigs and leaves curling away, the yew itself going still despite the stirring wind. For a moment, nothing moved, and I felt the visceral refusal. I would have yelled, but there wasn't anyone for me to yell at. I understood what Mum had found here, how she'd connected to it, but I couldn't do it myself. If I yelled at the tree, I'd just be random noise in the forest, nothing that the tree would understand or even notice. What was here couldn't have been yelled into submission, or taken by force. Some greedy idiot might have come here and sucked the mana out of the place, and left the tree dying and the rocks crumbling away, but they couldn't have made it heal them or anyone else.

But Mum stood there looking up at the yew with her hands spread open and said, "I know. I'm afraid too. But he didn't choose it. It was done to him."

There was another unbearable endless silence, and then

the branch in front of the door slowly creaked up and out of the way. Mum turned to Orion—the first time she'd looked at him since he'd come out of the car, and her whole face flinched all over again. Her voice barely made a whisper. "You have to go inside," she said to him. "No one can make you. You have to choose to try."

Orion stood there as if he hadn't heard her. He was still only looking at me. "The hut!" I said, and pointed with both arms. He slowly turned his head to follow the gesture and looked at the mystical ruined hut as if he hadn't really noticed its existence before now, and when I went over to it and made even more exaggerated gestures of *GOING IN,* through *the doorway,* he finally took a step or two towards it. I started nodding wildly like someone encouraging a toddler or a puppy, yes, well done! He kept coming until he was just before the threshold.

I was so relieved to have got him that far that I didn't realize he was getting *near me* until he was there, right next to me, and he looked at me and wasn't Orion at all. He was only hunger, a hunger that couldn't be satisfied and that was only following me round because it wanted to swallow me up, and was hoping for a chance: was this one?

I flinched back from him, from it. I could have destroyed it. I *wanted* to destroy it, right now, before it could ever get near me or Mum or any living thing in the world. The only sane thing to do was destroy it, and that was what Liesel had really been trying to tell me to do, when she'd said to leave Orion in the Scholomance, or send him to New York, or just get away from him; she'd been telling me to destroy this thing that shouldn't exist, that should never have existed, and let it go back into the void where it really belonged. The words were in my mouth. *You're already dead.*

"Orion," I said instead, despairing, wanting to make his

name into a different spell, but he just stood there. If it would have done any good, I'd have shoved him through. It was only fair, since he'd shoved *me* through the Scholomance doors. I'd have gone inside to lure him in after me. But I didn't even need to ask Mum to know none of that would have worked. We weren't trying to physically get him into the hut so some magical power could work on him that couldn't reach outside. The power was already here, all around us. It was his choice that mattered now. He had to choose to go in there, to reach out for the healing. Because this power couldn't do anything *to* someone. Even someone who wasn't well enough to make a choice. If he couldn't, if there wasn't enough left of Orion in there, then there was only my choice left, my solitary horrible choice: to let him stay in the world until he *did* start hunting again, or send him out of it forever.

"You said you'd come to me in Wales," I said to him. "And you're not here, not really, so go in there and *come to me*. Do you hear me, Lake? You promised me. I *let* you promise me, you wanker! Will you go into the bloody hut?"

I was yelling by the end of it, and in a frenzy I grabbed a stick off the ground and whacked him across the rump. He jumped a little and then looked at me with a flash of something human in his face, of Orion, and before I could react, he looked back into the hut—and he was afraid.

I'd never seen Orion afraid of anything, even when a sane person ought to have been terrified out of their mind; not of monsters or heights or late schoolwork. But he looked into the tiny empty hut, and it *was* him, it was Orion, and he was terrified of whatever was in there. I whacked him again in my own absolute terror, only magnified by the instant of hope. "It's a pile of rocks, not the whole school crammed full of mals, stop being such a coward and *go in there!*" I howled, and maybe he heard me, because he squeezed his eyes shut, the first time he'd closed them at all, and heaved himself over the threshold.

The whole clearing went utterly silent and still. Mum gave a short deep gasp of terror, and then she came to me and took my face in her hands and kissed me on the forehead and said, "My darling, I love you, whatever happens."

In all of my frenzy to get her to help Orion, it hadn't occurred to me that I'd have to let Mum go in there with him, alone. I'd only thought about how I could persuade her; I hadn't thought about what I was asking her to do. But she didn't give me a chance to say *wait, no,* which I suppose was better than having to decide whether to say it or not. She let go and went straight inside the hut, and the yew branches lowered back down behind her.

I didn't sleep at all, by which I mean I sat down on the ground outside the hut to wait, lay down on my side two minutes later, and was asleep almost instantly. I got up again when Precious bit my ear to wake me, leaping to my feet half asleep with my hands moving to cast a shield spell on instinct, pointlessly. The yew was groaning deeply overhead and light was pouring out of the hut, out of the roof between the leaves and branches, out of every crevice between the stones, turning all the moss into glowing green embers: a light that made my eyes water and my mouth feel cool and refreshed, a light I only remembered seeing once before in my entire life. The moment when Mum had chosen to save me from the teeth of prophecy and had carried me to safety in her arms, in her heart, giving her own life over to making herself a shelter to protect me from my own terrible destiny.

There wasn't anything attacking me; there wasn't anything for me to do. "Mum!" I called desperately. No one answered. I couldn't see her or Orion at all. Inside the hut there was only light, and all of a sudden it was fading back down to nothing, so quick my eyes couldn't keep up and I was left in pitch darkness with the muddled glowing afterimages of the light still imprinted on my vision.

When my eyes finally cleared, there were still a few streaks of light left: the dawn was breaking. All the leaves were coming off the yew, curling up and falling with a faint pattering. The bare branches were wizened and thin, dried up from inside, and then abruptly the lintel of the doorway cracked in two with a sound like a gunshot and came crashing down, smashing the branches across the door into kindling and cracking the threshold straight across. I lunged forward, scrambling over it inside the hut, and Mum was lying in the middle of the floor in a small curled heap.

"Mum! Mum!" I squalled, grabbing for her and heaving her over into my arms, my arms that could completely encircle her huddled body, hideously fragile and light. She was breathing, and when I'd got her over, she opened her eyes and looked at me, glazed over with exhaustion. She didn't reach up and touch my cheek, but her arm twitched a little as though she wanted to and just couldn't quite manage it, and then she tipped her head against me and sank into something between sleep and unconsciousness. I clutched her to me and tried to manage my breathing, and then I looked over at the one small place still shadowed by the lattice of dying branches, and Orion was standing there with his back against the wall.

Orion was standing there: it was *him*. Mum had done it. I could have screamed, I could have burst into tears; instead I reached out my hand to him, in joy, in longing, in the first moment of believing that the miracle might actually have happened, that I might actually have got him out, and he said, his voice hoarse and ragged, "You should have left me there."

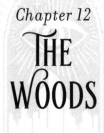

Chapter 12
THE WOODS

I COULD HAVE TORN HIM limb from limb, honestly, but instead I heaved Mum up and snarled at him, "Then stay in here and *rot* if you like," and marched out of the hut.

I wanted to go straight home, but I haven't been raised by wolves, so even though I was blazing up with all the anger I hadn't been able to feel until relief had let it out, I didn't keep going; I stopped outside in the clearing and turned to face the broken doorway and the yew and said, "He might be an ungrateful git, but I'm not. Thank you."

I wasn't sure of anything else to do. I felt deeply that I ought to do *something:* the poor yew was still shedding withered leaves in a small grey rain, and I was sure Mum would have told me what to do if she'd been conscious. But I didn't have any ideas, and if I'd had one, I would have been suspicious of it doing more harm than good. I looked down at my pocket. "Any ideas?"

Precious climbed down me and scampered around and over the tree, sniffing along the bark with her pink nose, until she found a place she apparently liked, low on the trunk, just by the largest forking. She put her paw on the place and looked up at me. I was more than a little dubious, but she squeaked at me firmly. "If you're sure," I said. I put Mum down carefully in a mossy spot, pillowing her head on some dried leaves, and then I laboriously transmuted a fallen branch and a stone into a small hatchet.

I whacked away at the trunk for the better part of an hour, the sun gradually creeping up into the sky, until finally, with a creaking groan, the whole massive forked section cracked and fell, shattering like wood that had been dried and seasoned for a decade. Where I'd chopped it off, though, a tiny trickle of living sap oozed from the trunk.

Orion still hadn't come out of the hut, but once I'd cut down the big section, most of the branches shading him had come down, and he was just left there standing behind the half-height stone walls, almost completely exposed in all his dubious glory—and more of it likely to be on display soon, given the precarious state of his rags.

"Are you going to help me, or do you fancy just standing there being useless?" I said to him coldly. I pushed away the loose broken chunks of the lintel, clearing off the threshold, and then I started going round the hut, clearing the brush back a bit and picking up any fallen stones and putting them back up. I wasn't going to find a new lintel just lying on the ground, but at least I could firm up the walls. After a little while, Orion did start helping, but from the inside, as if he still didn't want to risk coming that near to me.

When I'd done as much as I could see to do, I went back to Mum, who'd got a bit of color back in her face, thankfully. Orion got over himself enough to come out, but he stood off to one side watching me work out some way to carry her, twitching forward a few times as though he wanted to help but couldn't, presumably because he was so horribly contaminated that I *should have left him there,* and with every twitch he made, I grew furiouser and furiouser, because Aadhya was bloody *right,* it wasn't my fault, none of it had been my fault, it had been *his* fault, *he'd* shoved me out, he'd done all this to me, and he was *still* doing it to me, and I stood up and snarled at him, *"You* take her, and mind you don't drop her." After a moment he came jerkily towards us, and I stood with folded arms, glaring until he got Mum up in his arms.

It took much longer for me to get us back to the yurt than it had taken Mum to take us out. Precious sat on my shoulder and gave me nips to the ear to make sure I didn't go the wrong way blundering through the woods, but her vigilance wasn't sufficient. Orion didn't drop Mum. He didn't even ask for a pause until we finally straggled out two hours later, at midmorning.

Aadhya and Liesel were sitting out in front of the yurt arguing about what to do. Liesel's expression when she saw Orion walking carefully behind me with Mum was so utterly disbelieving that it would almost have been funny if it hadn't been very clear that what she couldn't believe was that we were all such colossal idiots and yet had somehow survived, and that she wasn't sure it was a good thing, either.

Orion brought Mum inside the yurt and put her down on her bed when I showed it to him, and then went out again in a hurry. I got her to drink a little water from her jug and settled her under the covers, and meanwhile he put himself at the far side of the small campfire and sat down on a log. He didn't say a word to Liesel or Aadhya at first, until I overheard Aadhya saying to him, "Orion, don't get me wrong, I'm super glad you're not in mindless hunting mode anymore, but you're still looking kind of freaked out. Are you okay?" I looked out through the doorway to listen in—I was fairly curious about the answer myself—but he only stared at her as if he hadn't noticed she was there until then. "Yes? No? A complete sentence, maybe?" she prompted. "If you need an idea, *Thanks for saving me from certain doom* would work."

"I should have stayed there," he said flatly instead.

I surged out ready to do battle, now that Mum was taken care of, but before I could sail into him properly, Liesel said, peevishly, "You weren't going to, no matter what we did. Your mother was organizing a search party for you."

"What?" I said, stopping.

Liesel gestured to Orion impatiently. "You said it yourself! Ophelia did this, she gave him this power. She knew none of the maleficaria could kill him. She knew he was alive. That is why she was so insistent about keeping mana going to the school. She meant to get him out. Did you know she was a maleficer?" she demanded of him.

I'd have asked the same question, if I could have thought of a way to word it. Orion hadn't talked very much about his mum and dad at school, but he hadn't *never* talked about them. If he'd had any idea that his mum was a maleficer, he'd kept it very close. I'd certainly not had the least idea what I was going to find when I'd gone to New York.

"No," Orion said: an odd answer. Either he ought to have said *yes* or he ought to have indignantly said *my mom isn't a maleficer.*

"But you know it now?" Liesel said, alert to the same oddness. "What did she do to you?"

Orion didn't answer her. He just got up and walked away. He didn't go as far as the next pitch; he just went a few yards away to the nearest big tree and sat down on the other side of it.

"Wow, the tact, it burns," Aadhya said.

"We don't have time for tact!" Liesel said.

"Said like someone who never does."

Liesel scowled at her. "His mother *knows*! Do you understand what that means? We were surprised. *She* wasn't. She knew we would find Orion and bring him out. Most likely she has people on the way here already. She must have a tracker on that power-sharer." She gestured at my wrist.

"She can send half of New York if she likes. I'm not letting them take him," I said.

Liesel threw her hands up exasperated. "And what will you do when she stops the mana?"

"Okay guys, before you start yelling, allow me to point out that no one is taking Orion anywhere *he* doesn't want to go," Aadhya said. "Can we maybe worry less about evil schemes and more about him for a sec? I don't know whether it's his mom or killing all those mals or sitting halfway in the void, but he is *not* okay, no matter what your mom did to fix him."

Liesel scowled at her; I could have scowled a bit myself. That was much too sensible and kind, when what I wanted was to shriek at Orion in fury and claw his entire face off for having put me through all of this and having the gall to—not be okay. As he clearly wasn't.

I sullenly went inside and rummaged through the cupboards and got a bowl of Mum's vegetable soup and half a loaf of bread and a plate heaped with pickled vegetables and put it all together on a tray and took it down to him where he was still sitting down on the slope. "Eat something."

"I'm not hungry," he said, except he made it sound like some elaborate doom. And in fact, he didn't actually look as though he'd lost any weight after starving in the Scholomance for nearly two weeks. As if he'd been filled up adequately some other way.

I swallowed down nausea at the thought. "Eat something anyway and see if it changes your mind," I said, and pushed it nearer him, then planted myself on a handy stump to wait.

After a bit he picked up the soup and drank a swallow out of the bowl, and then he finished the whole thing and ravened through the bread and the vegetables at top speed, leaving nothing but crumbs by the time I came back with another round of larder-raiding.

The cupboards were growing bare, and when he finally stopped inhaling partway through the last packet of half-stale crackers, I was relieved: we were an hour shy of lunch, and I didn't really fancy going down to the commune kitchens and trying to get an early meal out of the people on rota. They'd have given Mum whatever she wanted, but I'd never succeeded before, and I was wary of what I'd do if they said no.

Then Orion rested his forehead against his hand and said, rawly, "El. I'm sorry. I'm so sorry."

He didn't specify, but I could have enumerated a long list of things I felt strongly he could have been sorry for. I swallowed them all. "Come have a lie-down," I said instead, because this was what you did for someone who'd just got out of the Scholomance: you fed them a gigantic pile of food and then you put them to bed on clean sheets and then you got them a shower and clean new clothes. The same thing Mum had done for me, the same thing every family in the world did for every one of their returning graduates. And for lack of a better plan, that's what I was going to do for him.

He didn't tell me again that I should have left him back in the school, and he didn't argue. He got up and followed me back to the yurt and lay down on my cot and went to sleep, on the opposite side of the yurt from Mum. I took Precious out of my pocket and left her to stand watch over them both.

I spent the next three days with my head down, following the playbook, providing regular doses of food and sleep and showers and food all while miraculously—for me—continuing to not gnaw Orion's face off. Aadhya long-sufferingly took the van into town—after mending the peeled-open side—and got him new things from Primark: a plain white T-shirt and a pair of jeans, new socks and trainers.

Liesel spent the three days preparing mystical fortifications and defensive strategies, and having hissed consultations over the phone with Alfie, apparently wanting to establish a back channel for negotiations when New York came at us and was repulsed with one of her dozen plans. She tried repeatedly to share them with me until I finally snapped at her over the fire and said crossly—I'm not very good at taking care of people, and between Mum and Orion I was having to do a lot more of it than I ever had before—"Liesel, it's not three days to New York! If they were coming, they'd be here." We all realized as soon as the words came out that I was perfectly correct, and her face went baffled with indignation: how dare Ophelia *not* come after us.

So of course, later that day, she did.

That morning Mum had been able to sit up and walk for a short distance without getting out of breath, but she certainly wasn't up to cooking. My and Aadhya's joint attempt, the first night, had ended up with the fire gone out in a gush of water and all of us trying to choke down half-cooked beans. "My grandmothers always make it look so easy," Aadhya said glumly, putting down her bowl in defeat.

So I'd had to go down to the group kitchens after all. The theory had always been that all comers were welcome to a share, none turned away hungry, and you contributed as you could; very lovely and utopian. In practice, coming down without Mum had always been my idea of purgatory: being asked sharply what I thought I was doing, taken to task over how much food I wanted, why I thought I had a right to it.

But now I had too much else to worry about, and maybe it showed on my face. After the bean cataclysm, I marched down the hill and pitched in with the washing-up that was continuously going on in the back, and afterwards loaded up our two biggest pots with rice and beans and vegetable curry, and nobody made any commentary at all. When I came down the next morning, someone even asked me about Mum, and after that I was getting regular inquiries after her, if she was better.

And that third afternoon, Ruth Marsters came in while I was there and said to me—almost as though I were just another person, with only a very faint air of resentment—"There's a letter for you," and handed me the envelope, smooth and creamy thick paper, the New York seal pressing it closed, addressed to *Galadriel Higgins*.

I took it back up to the yurt holding it between two fingers and opened it out in the woods far away from anyone else, with Precious anxiously watching at a distance in case some sort of smoke or poison came out of it. But nothing did; there was only a small note inside, wrapped around another envelope:

> *Dear El,*
> *I'm very grateful to you for bringing Orion out. I hope he's doing well. Please give him the enclosed letter when you think he might be ready to read it.*
>
> > *All my best,*
> > *Ophelia Rhys-Lake*

Her handwriting was slanted and elegant and easy to read, the signature flourishing just a bit, tasteful and elegant. I glared at it speechlessly. She really was an evil monster. If she'd told me to give Orion the letter, full stop, I'd cheerfully have set it on fire; if she'd threatened me, asked me for anything, I'd have told her out loud where she could get off, and then set it on fire. Instead she'd invited me to keep it from him, as though we were chums on the same side, taking care of poor dear Orion who didn't get to decide for himself, the way *she* hadn't let him decide. It was a tidy bit of manipulation, and even seeing it plainly didn't let me out of it.

Liesel nodded over it in admiration. "And if you withhold it, she will eventually get it to him another way, and ensure he knows you chose to keep the first from him." She thought I ought to open Ophelia's letter at once and read it for myself, without Orion, but I couldn't stomach doing that; then she thought I ought to give it to him at once, and get him to show it to me, so I'd know what Ophelia was after. I couldn't quite bring myself to do that either.

Orion wasn't wiped out physically the way Mum was, but he still wasn't anything like *okay*. If allowed, he would have spent his days huddled next to the woodpile on the far side of the yurt like a goblin, trying to pretend he *had* been left behind in the Scholomance. I wasn't having it, so I'd aggressively reorganized the woodpile round him, scattering crawling bugs and bark all over him, and handing him stacks of logs to hold for me and making pointed comments about how we'd need more laid in for the winter, until he actually said words, namely, "Do you want me to get you more wood?"

"That would be lovely," I said sweetly, and handed him a hatchet.

He then brought back an armful of green saplings that he'd mangled apart, combined with some completely rotten chunks of a fallen tree, already half eaten and probably dripping termites, and I just barely managed to head him off before he popped it onto the rest of the pile. But after that, he went off into the woods on his own each morning, which seemed to me like an improvement, although I hadn't got any more words out of him since; he only came back to eat monosyllabically on the far side of the fire and sleep again. Aadhya had got herself a long twiggy stick that she used to jab Liesel whenever the urge to start another interrogation began to come over her. It didn't get used above five times a night.

Yes, all right, I got jabbed regularly too. If Mum had been able to stay awake for longer than it took to go to the loo, she would have approved of everything I was doing: living in the moment, one to the next, getting a meal, going to sleep, not thinking about the future. I hated it. The first night we'd laid out yoga mats for sleeping, and after that first night, Aadhya and Liesel had gone down to the commune offices and paid to stay in the nice tourist cottages instead. We *were* on holiday, having a rest cure after the success of our impossible quest. But it wasn't going to last. Sooner or later—sooner— Aad was going home to her good sensible loving family and her good sensible healthy future; Liesel was going back to London and Alfie and her thirty-year plan, from which this was only a brief detour. And I was going to—? There was an enormous blank space at the end of the sentence. I didn't have any baseline to go back to.

I could have made one up. I could have gone over to the box on Mum's worktable and taken out the sutras. I could have told them we'd be getting started soon, getting on with the grand project. Or I could have started building a stockpile of weaponry and bleeding mana off the power-sharer, if I was going to go back to New York and pick a fight with Ophelia. In theory, at least; I doubt that particular plan would have got past Mum if I'd actually started in on it, but I could have tried.

Or I could have told Liesel I'd go back to London with her after all. At least *she'd* have been well chuffed. After the letter turned up, she cornered me privately for a conversation about the future, and I let her, mostly because I was sure Mum would look at me disappointedly if we didn't talk about our feelings at all under the circumstances, although personally I felt I'd had far too many feelings lately and would have liked to repress a lot of them. I had barely started on grieving for Orion, and now he wasn't dead, and while I still intellectually believed in all my extremely sensible ideas about seeing other people, all I actually wanted to do right now was keep seeing *him*. Although at the moment that was less a romantic impulse than the literal sense of wanting to have my eyes on him regularly until the still-gibbering inward part of me calmed down and finally accepted that actually he *was* alive. It still felt unbelievable every time I looked at him. Also I hadn't lost an ounce of the passionate desire to beat him over the head with a large stick, and surely that was a sign of true love.

So where that left me and Liesel, I hadn't any idea. Thankfully, this was Liesel I was dealing with, who only said with a tone that was the equivalent of eye-rolling, "What do *feelings* matter right now? There is about to be an enclave war. What are you going to *do*?" She made absolutely no secret of what she thought I *should* do, either. "We should all go back to London and help Alfie's father secure control over the council and repair the damage. Then we will have one of the most powerful enclaves in the world supporting us."

"You know I won't, so stop suggesting it just because it annoys you that I won't be sensible!" I said, which was accurate enough to make her glare at me. "Look, Liesel, you can make yourself Domina of London if you like, and get back at your horrible dad and his horrible wife, and odds are, you won't be any worse than Christopher Martel or Sir Richard or *them,*" which made angry red color come into her cheeks, her lips pressing tight, "but I *can't,* and you know it!"

"So what *can* you do?" she bit out, and of course I couldn't answer that question, because I hadn't any idea what Orion was going to do with himself, and it seemed that I couldn't work out what I was going to do with myself in the absence of that information. I couldn't even decide what I *wanted* to do. Which was infuriating on multiple levels. I halfway wanted to give Orion the letter, to make something happen, and I didn't trust the impulse.

Mum was finally well enough the next morning to ask me to help her out to the nearest clearing in the woods, where she sat for several hours with her eyes closed, breathing deeply, and after that she came back to the yurt slowly on her own and sat down by the fire with a long sigh instead of going back to bed. But she couldn't give me any advice. "I don't know," she said, a whisper, rubbing her hands up and down her arms, a chill in deep July, when I asked her what had been wrong with Orion, what Ophelia had done to her own child to get an unstoppable mal-killing machine for New York. "I don't know. Whatever it is, I couldn't do anything about it."

I stared at her. "You did do something! Orion's all right now!"

Mum looked at me, her face still a little pouchy with exhaustion, her blue eyes small and tired, but she reached out and put her hand on my cheek and shook her head a little in apology. "I couldn't set him right. I could only give him hope. And I don't know if I should have." She closed her eyes, drew a deep breath, and then she got up and went into the yurt and went to sleep again.

The next day when I came up from the kitchens with

lunch, she'd taken Orion out into the woods with her. I went hunting them, and it's possible that I crept more quietly than usual for the chance of listening, but I might as well have gone trampling round like elephants. He was kneeling in front of her in the woods, and she had her hands on his head, tears running down her face, and when she took them off, she said, "No, love. I'm sorry. It's not something that I can bring out of you."

Orion bowed his head like someone had told him he was going to be executed. "It's just me."

Mum looked down at him, sorry, so sorry, the same kind of sorry she is when she's telling someone their child is going to die, and she can't stop it. "It's not all of you. It's not the part of you that's asking. The part of you that loves El."

Orion stood up. "But it's the part that matters." He turned and saw me.

"*What* part?" I said, but he only stared at me and then shook his head and walked past me. "Lake, you plonker, bloody *tell* me!" I yelled after him, but I didn't get a response.

"El," Mum said, gentle, meaning *please stop hitting my patient with a stick,* but why should I, since that was the only thing that seemed to be doing any good?

I stormed after him, and as if he understood he wasn't getting out of it, he kept going until he reached one of the inconvenient pitches further up the hill that had been abandoned, well out of sight, with the firepit overgrown and a couple of saplings going up inside through the falling-in roof of the old yurt. He wasn't trying to get away from me, I don't think, but I also didn't care if he was. At least he sat down on one of the logs and didn't get up and flee when I sat down next to him.

I probably oughtn't have given him the letter then, either, but I couldn't think of anything else to do. I didn't actually think he was ready for it, but he wasn't ever going to be *ready* for Ophelia to twist a knife in his gut. And at least I'd know what I was up against, I thought; so after a few moments of stewing, I pulled it out and handed it to him.

He turned it over in his hands, looking at his mother's handwriting for a while before he opened it, and I watched his eyes skip over it, tiny reflection of cream paper in the pupils, and then he folded it back up and creased it over and just sat there without saying anything. I held my hand out for it, and he gave it to me without the least objection, which made sense after I'd read it, because it didn't give me the slightest information.

My star boy,
I don't know if you'll let me call you that anymore, but this once I will.

I know you must be angry and upset with me. You have every right to be, and I can't even apologize, because if I had made other choices, I wouldn't have you. So I can't ever be sorry. I want you not to be sorry either. Whatever you're feeling, whatever you fear, I need you to believe in yourself, and if not, believe in me and Daddy. We love you and trust you, and if you need help trusting yourself, know that you can always come to us and we'll do whatever it takes to help you.

We've met El. She's an extraordinary person. I only wish I'd found her sooner. But you found her yourself instead. I know she's afraid of me. But she's not afraid of you. That's a gift. I don't think you need me to tell you to treasure it and be careful of it. I'm just happy that you have it.

Don't be afraid. When you're ready, come home. We love you.

Mom and Dad

I was near tearing it into shreds after the first outraged pass. I could tell there was all sorts of hook-yanking going on in there, only I couldn't follow it, because Ophelia had planted all of her hooks years ago, out of my sight. It was like watching her trundle a wheelbarrow full of paving stones and landmines into a garden, hearing her digging busily on the other side of the hedge, until out she came to cheerily show off the delightful path she'd laid, and now I had to walk down it without any idea which step was set to blow me to bits.

"What is she talking about?" I demanded, even though I already knew Orion wouldn't say, and he didn't, not a word. "You're *not* going back to New York," I told him savagely. He didn't even raise his head. I grabbed him by the shoulders and made him look at me. "We're taking the sutras to Cardiff," I told him. "You're going to hunt down whatever random mals are scattered round, and I'm going to put up a Golden Stone enclave for the circle there, and then we'll move along to the *next* place. Just like we planned."

His face crumpled a bit and he said, "El . . ."

"Shut up unless you've got any *better* ideas." I shook him. "You're *alive.* You're not in the Scholomance anymore. And that's more than any reasonable person could hope for— that's more than any reasonable person *got,* the last century and more, so whatever else you think is wrong, whatever else is the matter inside your head, you haven't any excuse to moan about it. Stop trying to put yourself in the ground. You're alive, so get on with *living!*" I was snarling in rage by the end of it, and he put his arms around me and pulled me close and buried his face on my shoulder. He smelled of sweat and smoke and the woods, and I put my arms around him, and he shuddered all over. Tentatively, slow and lurching, he raised his head. My breath was catching with hope as his cheek and his lips went bumping soft and warm over my skin, until he reached my mouth and he was kissing me.

Only just barely, the lightest brush, but I didn't leave it there; I caught him round the back of the head and kissed him harder, kissed him without bothering to get my breath in between until I had to stop, gasping, and he'd got the idea by then and he had his arms round me and was kissing me wildly, kissing me all over, along my jaw and down my neck, like he'd been desperate to be kissing me all along and now had just let himself go. He yanked loose the drawstring neck of my dress and I wriggled my arms in from the sleeves and out the top of it, letting it slide down to my waist; he went on kissing me, down between my breasts, as I clawed his T-shirt out of his jeans and paused only so we could get it off over his head.

I stood up and let the dress fall the rest of the way off me. He stood up to meet me, and we got straight back to kissing while I unbuttoned his jeans and shoved them down off him, and then we stopped again to grab my dress and spread it out on a thick patch of grass in the sunlight, and we lay down together, and with his body against mine, so unbelievably warm and good, I said, gulping for air, "You absolute bastard, I could kill you," because we could have been doing *this,* we could have been here together, in the sunlight and the grass and the world, instead of the horrors he'd put himself and me through. He made a choked gasp, something between a sob and a laugh, and said, "El, I love you," and impossibly he *was* alive, he was *here,* and we'd made it out; we had got out of the Scholomance after all.

Mum looked at me with worry and sorrow when we came back to the yurt. There wasn't any great mystery about what we'd been doing; the dress was going to need a good laundering, and so were the two of us, really, glowing and sweaty. But I could forgive her, because she was worried for us *both*, and she even smiled at me a little when I asked her how she was. "I'm better, love," she said, and when I told her my plans, our plans, she still looked sad, but she nodded and didn't tell me it was a terrible idea.

I brought the box with the sutras to the fireside and opened it up, and they were still in there, the gilt and leather shining richly, and I put my hand on it with a lump in my throat. I brought out the leather oil Mum had on her shelf and some rags and gently cleaned and buffed the cover, every inch, just as I'd promised them ages ago, and I told them softly, "Sorry for leaving you alone so long. I won't do it again. We're for Cardiff soon—maybe even the day after tomorrow," and then Aadhya said, "El, get over here," from the other side of the fire, where she'd been on her phone. Her face was stricken.

"Something's happened to your family," I said, horror gripping me—Ophelia had gone after them? Why hadn't I thought of that, why—

"No, it's Liu, and something's seriously wrong," Aadhya said, and I scrambled over to the other side of the fire with the sutras still in my arms, and Aadhya put Liu on speaker.

It didn't really help. She was crying softly, small gulps over the line, wordless. "What's happened?" I said, panicky, still thinking of Ophelia. "Has New York come after you? The war's started—?"

"I don't think that's it," Aadhya said. "I talked to her on the drive from Portugal. She was in Beijing. Her family made the deal, Beijing enclave was going to give them all the enclave-building spells they still needed, and they were going to put up their new enclave attached to what's left of Beijing enclave and shore it up."

"Then what's gone *wrong*?" I said. It was certainly a good plan for Liu's family on the face of it: they were based around Xi'an, so they'd have to collectively move away from home, but that's nothing compared with saving the thirty years of work and the healthy ration of luck they'd have needed otherwise to finally get up their own enclave.

"I don't know!" Aadhya said. "She literally hasn't said anything! I've called her twice in the last two days, she didn't pick up, and this time she answered but she's just crying!"

Liu still didn't say anything. She wasn't sobbing uncontrollably; it was barely more than breathing, tiny soft gasps that sounded oddly far away, and then Precious jumped out of my pocket and squeaked shrilly at Pinky, who came out too and ran up Aadhya's arm to the phone and put his paw out to press the button to start a video call. A moment later the video came up, with Xiao Xing's pink nose almost filling the screen; he pulled back a moment later, and behind him we could see Liu, her face tear-streaked and reddened, looking back at us. I thought the phone must have been propped up on a desk or a table somewhere; she was sitting across from it on a wooden bed with her knees pulled up and her arms wrapped round them. The room had a certain bare uninhabited quality, but it didn't look like a prison, and she wasn't bleeding or beaten or chained up. But she still didn't say a word; she didn't even make a gesture. And it wasn't that she didn't know we were there, calling. She was looking straight back at us, tears spilling over.

"Okay, what the actual fuck is going *on*!" Aadhya said, staring at her.

"She is under a compulsion, obviously," Liesel said, having come to peer over our shoulders. "She cannot tell you anything or ask for help."

"There's no one in there with her!" Aadhya said. "Is there,

Xiao Xing?" Xiao Xing could talk, or at least squeak in what sounded like confirmation to us all; Precious and Pinky both set up their own chorusing squeaks of agreement. "I've never heard of a compulsion spell that can stop anyone from even whispering *help* while you've just let it keep going from another room."

As it happens, I knew seven, but it wasn't any of those, because all of them essentially turned the person into a mindless zombie minion. That said, Aadhya wasn't wrong about the basic principle. It's really difficult to both completely compel someone and yet let them keep their own feelings on display. If you've left them that much control over their own face, they usually *can* manage at least a whisper, or for that matter pushing a button to pick up the phone, or some other clever little workaround. This wasn't like that. Liu's own brain was working for the enemy, and there's only one way to get that kind of a hold on someone.

"She consented," I said. "She agreed up front not to tell anyone anything about whatever is happening." And as soon as I said that, I knew the rest. *Enclaves are built with malia,* Mum had said to me. "It's the enclave spells. Beijing gave them the enclave spells, under a compulsion of secrecy, and there's something awful in them, but Liu can't tell us about it."

I was almost sure that Liu wanted to cry harder, but the compulsion was tidy and proper: she couldn't even do that. She just kept looking at us and the tears and snot kept coming exactly as before. It didn't matter, though; I knew I was right. The problem was that I didn't see what to do about it. I could get on a plane to Beijing and sail into the midst of the ceremonies and disrupt things, me with my handy New York power-sharer, but then what? Beijing would collapse, we'd have an enclave war for sure, and someone else would start some other enclave somewhere else. I couldn't stop anyone from ever building another enclave.

Then I looked down at the sutras in my arms, and I said slowly, "Liu, you can't talk to us—but can you talk to your family? I've got another way to build an enclave. Maybe I can use it to save Beijing. If they're willing, I'll come and give it a go. And if it works, I'll make you an enclave, too. It won't be a skyscraper or anything, but it won't take malia, either. Will you tell them?"

"She can't tell you if she agrees or not!" Liesel said. "She would be confirming your guess. It would be too easy to get information out of someone if the compulsion was so incomplete." She looked at me, frowning, and then added with decision, "We will go to Beijing and go to a hotel in the city, and text her from there. If they have agreed, she'll be able to talk to us then."

I didn't like ending the call with Liu still sitting there looking at us, still in tears, but we weren't doing her any good by staring at her and running out the battery on her mobile. So I told her, "Just hang on, we're coming," and Aadhya hung up.

My bag was already packed behind me, and when I turned round to get it, Orion was standing there, holding it: he'd been listening. "We're going to help Liu," I said, even though he'd just heard me.

But it was a question, and he swallowed and answered it. "I'll come with you," he said—but for just a moment, he looked afraid again: the same fear he'd had on the threshold of the hut, before he'd gone inside.

Chapter 13
BEIJING

I WAS A LOT MORE FUNCTIONAL on this journey, more amazing jet lag notwithstanding, so I balked at yet another luxury hotel, much to Liesel's annoyance and even Aadhya's muted protests. "Someone's paying for it, if it isn't us," I said. I wasn't really inclined to take anything from any enclave right now. It was one thing to know in a more or less academic way that enclaves were built with malia, feeling it churning under my feet as I walked through their halls, and another to know that all of them were built on something horrible enough to put that misery in Liu's face.

Obviously I was still wearing that power-sharer from New York, but consistency is the hobgoblin of small minds, so I dragged them all to a hostel, which was the only kind of hotel Mum ever booked us into, although we almost never stayed in one for more than a day before we were being invited to stay at someone's house. I suppose, technically speaking, that was more or less what happened to me as well, only with appropriate differences.

We got ourselves a room and texted Liu's phone and then

sat exhausted in the courtyard drinking lemonade and didn't discuss the excellent question of what we'd do if no one came to get us. None of us knew where the entrance to Beijing enclave was, and my one year of Chinese was distinctly inadequate for getting round. I was absolutely fluent in at least thirty different ways to tell someone to dodge something that was about to kill them, so I'd be ace if I happened to spot someone walking out in front of a lorry, but the only reason I'd managed to successfully get directions to the aforementioned hostel was because we were in a tourist zone, and everyone I'd spoken to had answered me in English.

Fortunately, I suppose, the question didn't arise. A woman set up a stringed board instrument in a corner under the gate and began playing soft harmonious music, and it was hot and muggy, and we had just been on an aeroplane for eleven hours—not in business class either, this time—and we all started drifting off until Precious squirmed out and bit my ear, and I lurched back up to my feet wide awake with eighteen wizards making a circle round us, armed with long tubes the shape of plumbing pipes.

The instant they saw me move, they all activated them, and each one linked up with the ones on either side, split open, and started launching a massive net of interlaced beams of light. I was trying to fight off the groggy heaviness of the music well enough to work out the best way not to kill them all when Orion glanced up—not jerking free of the spell, just lifting his head from the random tourist brochure he'd picked up, as if he hadn't been caught by it at all. He reached up and grabbed the net with a hand, and the whole thing pulled loose from the tubes and went *into* him as if he'd sucked it up with a straw.

I gawked at him at least as much as our unwelcome visitors did. But then one of them dropped his tube and went for another weapon. Orion got up and started to—*move* at him, and everything went hideously wrong. It looked as though Orion was taking a step, but there was something off about it, the air distorting around him as if he wasn't *really* taking a step, he was just swimming through reality somehow and the step was only my own brain trying desperately to fill in with something that made sense.

It wasn't only my reaction; the man went sickly greenish, and all the other wizards on that side lurched back away in unison, breaking the perfect curve of the circle. The other half of them were yelling panicky instructions that I understood no bother: *hold the line, don't let them break out, get up a shield,* et cetera, only the people backing away were the smart ones, because nothing else was going to make this work out even decently for them. *Or* for Orion. I knew if he touched them something unbearable was going to happen.

I planted one foot and called an old vicious spell that someone had meant to drown an entire fishing village, drag it down into an ocean maelstrom, only I threw it into the air instead and whirled round in a circle with my hand cupping the power, a scream of protesting wind following me round. It started grabbing at all of them, whipping their clothes like snapping flags, sending the tubes flying out of their hands. I turned round once more, and it was dragging them off their feet, the air starting to churn into visible streams as it picked up dust and leaves from the ground, then a couple of stray chairs in the way, and the third time round it took them all off their feet in a howling vortex, and I shoved the whole thing up and away onto the roof.

Our visitors must have herded the hostel staff and all the other guests well away from the courtyard before making their approach, but launching a tornado and dumping eighteen people onto the roof was still a bridge too far. Mundanes started to stick their heads out of the windows and doors to see what on earth was going on, which meant that none of the wizards I'd just flung onto the charming slanted roof could cast anything to stop themselves rolling straight off and plunging the two stories straight down to earth. But that was a good bit better than whatever else had been about to happen to them, even if they landed on concrete, so I wasn't fussed.

"Come on!" Aadhya yelled. She was hauling up Liesel, who hadn't had a mouse to wake her up and was still fighting off the grogginess of the musical enchantment. Orion was just standing there, and I ran over and shoved him until he started moving in the right direction with his legs like a human being again. We went past the one wizard left standing—the woman with the instrument, who hadn't processed the sudden change of situation well enough to panic yet—and we ran through the hostel and into the street, my bag with the sutras in their case thumping against my chest.

I don't know where we were going, we barely knew where the nearest metro station was, but we didn't have to work it out. By the time Orion and I got out into the street, Aadhya and Liesel were beckoning us wildly into a waiting minivan taxi, and when we jumped in, Liu's cousin Zheng was in there, huddling back into a corner so he couldn't be seen from outside and visibly scared to bits.

The driver had already been told where to go, apparently with some urgency; the instant we had the door slammed behind us, we took off careening into the streets at the top speed the traffic allowed and somewhat beyond it. "Where's Liu?" I demanded. "What's going on?"

"I don't know," Zheng said. He started crying as though he'd been crying very recently and had only briefly had it on pause; he wiped his face. "We haven't seen her for five days."

"Are you under the compulsion?" Liesel said sharply. "The enclave spells—"

He shook his head. "Me and Min aren't old enough, and Nienie is too old. We didn't go to the exchange ceremony. And nobody from our house came back. One of our other cousins came to our hotel room and told us we only had to be patient and everything would be okay, but we knew it wasn't true. He looked really upset." His voice was breaking. "And Liu's myna keeps coming to the balcony and telling us to help her."

"Wait, what do you mean, nobody from your house?" Aadhya said. "It's not just Liu missing?"

"Liu and her parents, and Ma and Baba, none of them came back," he said. "Everyone else from Xi'an, the rest of our family, they all came back to the hotel. But not them. And nobody will tell us what's going on."

His brother Min and Liu's grandmother were waiting for us in a little park a few blocks away from their hotel, and the myna was perched on the branch of the tree above them. It hopped to a higher branch as we came close and tipped its head, a bright black eye fixed on Orion, even though he was behind the rest of us.

Liu's grandmother was tiny as a doll, frail and grey-haired: she'd sent six children to the Scholomance and got two back—beating the odds, but they'd been her two youngest. She'd started late, after a long run of working flat-out for her family, and then she'd run into the one-child policy, which meant she'd had to wait until each child had gone off to the Scholomance and effectively vanished off the face of the earth to have the next one without attracting too much attention. So she'd been in her fifties when she'd had Zheng and Min's father, and in her sixties when she'd had Liu's; if you're thinking there was magic involved there, you're right, and undoubtedly it was why she looked so fragile now, part of the price she'd paid. But there wasn't any shortage of fire in her eyes, and she reached out her gnarled hands to me and Aadhya and gripped ours. "Tongzhimen," she said. She didn't speak English, but she didn't need to; all of us knew the word for allies in almost every language spoken in the Scholomance.

"We're going to get Liu out," Aadhya told her. She nodded when Zheng translated.

"Can you ask her if she's got any idea where they're keeping Liu?" I asked, urgently, but she slowly shook her head and told us, low, that the rest of the family had all been summoned back to Beijing enclave a few hours ago, which wasn't a good sign. By now, whoever had Liu penned up knew that their ambush hadn't worked. If we were unlucky, they were going to rush into whatever sickening plan they had. And it had to be something really monstrous, because it wasn't *just* Liu objecting. Liu's mum and dad had deliberately sent her off to the Scholomance with a cageful of mice to become a tidy small-scale maleficer; *they* weren't going to be turning up their noses at some modest use of malia.

Liesel made a grimace when I said as much, and when Aadhya and I both immediately gave her narrow looks, she said sourly, as if she didn't like admitting it, "The process of building an enclave must need a *sacrifice*. They are going to do something *to* Liu, or perhaps one of the others, and the rest of the immediate family objected. That is why they all had to be restrained."

My gorge rose, but I was instantly bog-certain that she was right. That was what I'd felt, the horrible nauseating squish of malia underneath my feet, in the beautiful gardens of London, in the shining vast halls of New York: a *sacrifice*. And of course they'd do it, they'd all do it. What was one life, after all, compared with all the lives that an enclave would save? Ophelia wouldn't have batted an eye. *Enclaves have their own unique costs.*

"But why one of *them?*" Aadhya said. "It doesn't make sense. Liu's parents are high-octane in the family, and her uncle's in the running for council. Even Liu—maybe she didn't tell them she's seeing Yuyan, but they must know she's made friends in Shanghai! Not to mention *you.* If there *was* some kind of human sacrifice involved, why would the family pick any of them?"

Liesel shot me a glance that made me fairly certain that she had an idea why, but she only shrugged and wouldn't speculate. "It doesn't matter," she said. "Are you questioning that *something* bad is going to happen?"

I didn't question that at all. "Could you lead us to her?" I asked the myna, in Chinese, but it only cocked its head at me and said, "Liu! Liu! Liu!" in three different human voices that all sounded like cries of horror.

"We do not need to be led," Liesel said. "We know what they are doing, and there is only one place they can do it." She looked at Zheng. "Does your grandmother know where there is an entrance to Beijing enclave?"

It was a long ride to Tanzhe Temple, and every minute felt twice as long as it was, stretched out and cold and blank. I didn't know what I was going to do. Liesel's plan was tidy: just get through the gates of Beijing, and then tell them that if they didn't hand Liu and her family over straightaway, I'd give the whole enclave a good whack and send it sliding the rest of the way into the void.

I hadn't been able to say *no, I won't do it.* I couldn't say that, not when Liu was locked up in a room somewhere with a knife at her throat and I had no other way to save her. But I felt the prophecy closing in round me like a physical thing, a thin clammy layer over my skin. *She will bring death and destruction to all the enclaves in the world,* and what if it started here, with all the best reasons in the world, all the justification I could possibly have needed, and never stopped again?

The taxi dropped us out in front of the elaborate gate, and we went in past the scattering of tourists; we were far enough from the city center that they were relatively thin on the ground. The place was in beautiful repair—fresh paint in vivid colors, golden Buddhas, gilt everywhere—and it was the opposite of that pagan playground in Sintra: people still worshipped here, true believers and not just playing at it, all of them reaching out for something past the limits of reality. The structures were all nestled among old, old trees, and when we got out past the biggest buildings, the more recent ones, we found a whole garden full of stone pagodas, silent among trees and flowering shrubs.

It wasn't like trying to find the Scholomance doors. There we'd been given the coordinates and sent by a person with authority, and in some sense, it had been *our* place to begin with, Scholomance graduates one and all. Here, the enclave didn't want us to find it. We were exactly what the wards were there to guard against, the enemies at the gates. Zheng tried his best, but he wasn't going to be able to get past the wards easily himself. He wasn't *in* Beijing enclave, not yet, and enclave wards are just as keen on keeping out local wizards as distant enemies, if not more so.

His grandmother had told us this gate wasn't used much anymore. But it was still standing after the attack, because this was the way into the most ancient part of the enclave, the one that had been here for a thousand years. The enclave's center of gravity had shifted along with the city itself, leaving this part to become the equivalent of London's upper reaches. Probably only wizards far down in the rankings had still lived in the poky older section, and even they had probably used the main entrance most of the time instead of coming out back here.

We could tell that the entrance was *somewhere* round here, but we could also have walked round in circles for weeks without actually finding it. The wards were running through the ground beneath our feet, pulsing a bit; I could have started ripping them up wholesale, but if I did that, there seemed reasonable odds I'd send the remaining chunk of Beijing enclave sailing off into the void by accident, with Liu and her family still in it.

But I was running out of other options, as far as I could tell, and then finally Liesel turned round to Orion, who'd been slouching along behind us the whole time, head bowed and silent; he hadn't said a word since we'd run away from the hostel. If I hadn't been frantic with worry about Liu and about me, I'd have looked up a stick to hit him with; he was looking as though he could have used it. "Any mals near here will be trying to break through the wards and get in, while the enclave is weakened. Can you try to hunt them?" Liesel asked him.

He lifted his head and blinked at her as if he were vaguely surprised to see her, and then he said, "What?"

"The enclave entrance we are trying to find," Liesel said pointedly. "Could you follow some mal to find it?"

He stared at her, his brow furrowing a bit, and then he said, "Uh, the entrance over there?" We all stared at him, and then he went past us and out of sight behind one of the pagodas, round a curve of the path that we'd tried at least twice, and when we followed him, he was standing in front of a narrow mostly overgrown footpath leading to a worn old stone pagoda that very much hadn't been there before. He looked at us with a quality of doubting both our sanity and our general competence.

"Yes," I said through my teeth. "This entrance over here, which we've been trying to find for half an hour. Lake, is it too much to ask you to pay the least bit of attention while we're doing our best to barge into an enclave uninvited?"

He glared at me. "It's right there!"

"It *wasn't!*" I snapped back, with grace and maturity.

"Is it too much to ask that we now try to get *in?*" Liesel said pointedly.

The first hitch: our newly discovered pagoda was built of solid stone, and there wasn't a door to go through at all. There was only a small carved stone opening like a window, and it was a dozen feet off the ground. "Can we pry it open?" I asked Aadhya.

"No, that's not even a real opening, it's just carved to look like one," she said. "I remember reading about this in school. Old Chinese enclave architecture used spiritual entrances, not physical ones. You don't go through a door with your body, you go through it with your mind. I think we have to meditate our way through."

I wasn't in much of a frame of mind to meditate, but on the bright side, I almost never am, so it wasn't as hard to force myself as it might have been. But we looked like right wankers, all of us sitting cross-legged round this one obscure pagoda, so every time a mundane tourist wandered along the path behind us, they stared at us—they weren't having any trouble seeing the pagoda now that we were camped round it—meaning we couldn't possibly get through until they'd gone. I wasn't a fan of modern enclaves in almost any dimension, but I'll say right now that physical doors were absolutely an upgrade.

And we didn't really think it through; we just all sat down and started trying at the same time, because it was in front of us and we were all frustrated and jet-lagged and frantic to get inside, and so obviously what happened was that the first of us to make it through was *Zheng;* with my eyes closed, I felt him sigh out deeply next to me, and then he just got up and went and wasn't next to me anymore, and for a moment I was massively relieved: he'd got through! And then I realized I'd just sent a twelve-year-old child alone into an enclave that was very likely going to try to kill him.

"Zheng!" I yelled, opening my eyes. "Wait! Zheng, come back!"

Which worked not at all, except to make a few mundanes just out of sight start coming towards us to find out what all the yelling was about, and then Orion said, "I'll go after him," and by the time I turned round to tell him off for not doing it sooner if he thought it was that easy, he was gone, too. I was left with Aadhya and Liesel, and four temple visitors frowning at me for disrupting the atmosphere. They didn't leave again for several disapproving minutes of muttering amongst themselves, obviously trying to embarrass us into decamping, but when we stayed aggressively put, they finally gave up and left again, and I shut my eyes again and got back to trying to find my extremely elusive zen.

We were all just sitting there taking deep breaths, slightly furious ones in my case, and then Aadhya reached out and took my hand and said quietly, "Let's go get Liu," and gave me a comforting squeeze. I took another breath and let the anger all out: right, that's what needed doing, no more faffing about, and I got Liesel's hand on my other side without opening my eyes, and together we all stood up and stepped into the enclave.

The entryway was a short wide corridor, the old worn

walls plastered, leading to a doorway that faced onto a stone wall carved with an odd-looking dragon shape. Instead of being sculpted out, someone had carved it in reverse, the scaly indentation of its body set into the stone as if it had laid itself down in some wet concrete and then climbed out and gone away afterwards.

Then I looked over at Zheng, who was plastered with his back against the wall right near the doorway, panting, his face pale and stricken, and I realized something *had* climbed out of the carving: there were four parallel claw marks scored shallowly down the front of his shirt, a few drops of blood staining the edge of one of them. But that wasn't the source of his fear. He was staring at Orion, who was all the way at the other end of the corridor with his back to us, facing the stone wall, his shoulders rigid.

I ground my jaw and went up to him. There were some claw marks dug into the floor, too, as though something long and snaky had been trying futilely to stop itself being dragged towards him. "Are you all right?" I said, reluctantly. I hated asking. What I wanted to do was punch him in the arm and tell him to stop being a lump, only I couldn't, because he *wasn't okay,* and I hadn't any idea what to say or do to help it.

"Let's just get going," he said shortly.

We went cautiously round the stone wall and came out into the courtyard of the house. A rocky pool stood in one corner near us, with a streamed running through to the other side, a little bridge going across—very pretty, only they had all run dry—and a couple of old dead trees that had been reduced to nothing but bone-dry skeletal branches. There was nothing overhead but the empty void. We were all used to that, by which I mean, as used to it as you could get after spending your entire Scholomance career with a section of your dormitory cell gaping wide. That was the odd thing here: the rest of this house had a grey roof made of clay tiles, and the inner walls of the pavilions around us were made of removable panels, the kind you'd pop out to let in the nonexistent light and air, as though someone had built this tidy little house outside.

Which was probably what had happened, I realized, as we took a few more cautious steps forward, because there *wasn't* any churning horror underfoot. This place didn't have a whiff of malia to it. This place had never been pushed out into the void. Instead, wizards had built this house, somewhere on the temple grounds, and they'd lived in it, done magic in it, while the rest of the world went by outside, until finally the whole place had quietly slipped all the way out of the world: one of the vanishingly rare natural enclaves in the world.

But Beijing enclave hadn't been satisfied to stop here. In fact, I doubted any Beijing enclavers still lived here, even the lowliest new recruits. The floor showed recent footprints disturbing thick layers of old dust, and the boxes and chests crammed into the side buildings and spilling out into the courtyard looked like recent additions: attempts to save something from the oncoming wreck. We followed the trail of footprints through the courtyard and into the main building, and they continued on—straight until they met the perfectly unbroken back wall. There was even a half footprint that intersected with it.

I was ready to have a go at bashing an opening, and then Precious gave a squeak, and I looked over to the side: the main hall was partitioned into three sections, and on the left there was an old, thoroughly whiskered man sitting quietly at a low table, in elaborate robes like a costume out of a historical film, doing calligraphy with an ink brush under a glowing orb of light.

He didn't seem about to leap up and come at us or anything, but on the other hand, he could have been writing out the most massive curse ever known to man. "Wǒ cào," Zheng said faintly behind my back.

"Do you know who he is?" I hissed at him.

"I, uh, I think that's the Seventh Sage of Beijing," Zheng said in barely more than a whisper, still staring. The old man was going serenely on with his brushstrokes as if our presence and time itself didn't matter. "The one who founded the enclave."

"This enclave is a thousand years old!" Aadhya said in protest.

"He was the seventh teacher, the one who was here when the house left the world," Zheng said. "They say he never died. He kept teaching anyone who came here, until one day he just disappeared. There are stories that he comes back sometimes when the enclave is in a lot of trouble, but no one's really seen him in hundreds of years."

"Right," I said, grimly. I hadn't any idea how powerful you had to be to arrange all that, but it sounded impressive. "Is there anything in these stories about what he *does* when he turns up?"

Zheng just shrugged a bit helplessly, but the old man had finished the last brushstroke on his paper, and after he carefully set his brush aside, he turned and beckoned to us. None of us moved, not being idiots, but he just sat there waiting with the faintly familiar air of deliberate patience that Mum would occasionally get when I was small and screaming wildly at her about something. I liked it now about as much as I did then, but it was also a bit comforting to me, or at least as comforting as you could get when you'd just broken into the house of a thousand-year-old wizard who pops in and out of reality at will. Anyway, I could see we weren't getting out of it. We needed to go through the door that should have been standing in this back wall, and I was willing to bet I wasn't doing that without talking to him first.

So I went over, and he kept emitting patience until I grudgingly sat down on the floor in front of another side of the table, and also until I bowed, not very gracefully. But the attempt satisfied him enough that he said something to me, which I understood about as well as a student in their first year of English would have done with Chaucer. I looked over at Zheng; he looked hard-pressed but said, "I think he said—'Don't be afraid, daughter of the golden stones'; does that make sense?"

My arms went to clutch round the sutras, which were still slung across my chest. The sutras, which my dad had wanted, because his family had lived in and lost a Golden Stone enclave. An enclave like this one, an enclave made without malia. "Yes," I said. It made sense, but it didn't work; if anything I was more afraid. The old man was looking at me with a little too much gentleness, like he was sorry for me.

He told me something else, and I picked Liu's name out of it before he held out the huge scroll he'd been painting on. Zheng caught his breath and then said, "He said, 'This will bring you to Guo Yi Liu!'"

I took the scroll: the characters were stylized and I wasn't sure of them—the handful of Chinese spells I knew, Liu had taught me by ear—but I believed him anyway; looking at it felt like looking at a map, something meant to help you get somewhere. The old man nodded to me and said a phrase I did recognize: "Finish what you started."

Then he added something a bit more dry, and reached up and touched the glowing golden ball of light with a finger. It went out instantly; by the time my eyes had adjusted, he wasn't there anymore; only the table, thick with untroubled dust, and the scroll hanging between my hands.

"Uh, I think he said—'I'm tired of demons in my house'?" Zheng said, doubtfully.

"Who wouldn't be," I muttered, as I scrambled up. I ran back to the blank wall and put the scroll up against it. As soon as I did, the letters glowed with the golden light, and then the whole paper illuminated round the border and burnt up in a single rush, leaving a tidy narrow rectangle opening out to a tidy narrow alleyway—and it was an alleyway, not a corridor; the top of it was open to the void—with the walls on either side broken up with doorways that were standing in shadow. All the lanterns hanging next to them were dark, except a single gleaming of red outside one door at the very end.

I stepped through the opening while the edges were still glowing with embers, and as I did the whole alleyway blurred towards me, or I blurred through it, and I staggered a bit as my foot came down right in front of the door with the lit lantern. I waved my arms wildly to get my balance and keep from tumbling down: just past the door, the alleyway plunged down an ink-dark stairway that looked a great deal like the Beijing metro.

A low uneasy rumbling was coming up out of it, and underneath me the floor felt as though it was all bending away, a deep creaking. Like in the Scholomance: a giant just barely holding on by its fingers, on to the deep-rooted strength of the one small house back there. But the weight was too unbalanced. I didn't know how much of Beijing enclave was down there, but it was clearly the vast majority of the place. A thousand years ago, the sage's house had slipped out of the world all on its own, and become the first foothold in the void. Other wizards had slowly expanded it little by little, adding on this long alleyway full of houses, building a community. Then—a few decades ago, they'd built themselves a major expansion based in the bustle of modern-day Beijing's city center, just barely linked back here by a metro line of their very own. There on the other end would be the laboratories, the libraries, the massive blocks of flats. All of them now on the verge of toppling away into the void.

And on the other side of the door in front of me, I could hear heavy rhythmic thumps coming at regular intervals, each one sending trembling waves through the ground: some kind of major arcana going. Whatever spell they were working on to try to save the enclave. The spell that was going to hurt Liu.

I looked towards the sage's house: everyone else was still in there, Orion framed inside the singed rectangle looking out at me. His knee was suspended in midair, caught in the motion of taking a step, frozen. Whatever magic the sage had put on the scroll, apparently it had only been good for one, and there must have been some sort of delaying spell on the alleyway.

I had the strong suspicion that the sage had only shown up to offer his help because he'd known we wouldn't be in time without it. Anyway, I wasn't going to wait around and make certain. The door was locked, but I put my hands on the framing posts on either side of the doorway and spoke an incantation that a Roman maleficer had used to rip open a mystically fortified Druidic site during Caesar's wars, so he could get at the mana store they'd kept inside. Not at all the spell you wanted when the lock on your dormitory room had jammed and you were trying to get to the cafeteria for breakfast, which was when the Scholomance had handed me that one, but I was grateful for it now, because the wooden door instantly exploded before me, spraying splinters over the chamber at high velocity.

The room beyond wasn't very impressive: round and small, and the one tiny spell-globe was so dim that the lantern outside the door was letting in more light, striping a bright-red-tinged rectangle into the space. It fell over Liu's mum and dad, and her aunt and uncle with them. She'd shown me a tiny photo of them in the Scholomance, but even without that, they would have been easy to pick out, because they were all tied with their backs and elbows and wrists together, securely gagged and blindfolded, on top of a rough metal grating very precariously placed over what looked like a massive sewer opening plunging out of sight.

There were eight other wizards in the room—the council-to-be of the new enclave, I strongly presumed—all busily at work on a piece of artifice a short distance away from the sewer: a round metal cylinder the size of a small table. The outer shell of it was thin—it looked like a bigger version of the sort of ring mold you'd use to construct an elaborate dessert, made of glossy black metal with narrow slots punched through all the way round the bottom to let air out. Inside the ring, there was a disk made of blue-tinged metal that was being pressed down inside the ring underneath the weight of small bricks. One of the council wizards was taking bricks from a small stack and laying them on top one at a time, neatly, filling in the circle. The others were ferrying more of the bricks over from a hatch in the wall that flipped back and forth like a postbox. Even as I came bursting into the room, I saw it go over empty, and come back full, as if someone had popped a brick in on the other side, from a room where no one could see what was happening in this one.

The future council members weren't slouches. I had barely set foot in the place when they started throwing killing spells straight at me. They'd have done better lobbing nerf balls; I caught the spells more easily. I could have just slung them right back, but I deflected them over my shoulder into the alleyway instead and threw my own spell: a sprightly little charm I've got that turns people into stone. The only down-side of it is that people really don't enjoy being stone even if you turn them back after, as I'd discovered from using it to save people's lives on the obstacle course last year. Under the circumstances, that was a price I was willing to have the council members pay.

Unfortunately, these wizards weren't voluntarily running an obstacle course with me of their own free will, and they also weren't terrified kids still in the Scholomance. Almost as soon as I'd cast it, all the statues were flexing and moving as if something inside was moving, working to get out. I'd never chipped away at the stone surface to find out how far down the transformation went, but it clearly wasn't going to last long. I ran across the room to Liu's mum and yanked her blindfold and her gag off. She shook her head, having to blink hard up at me to make her eyes come clear, and she flinched back, but I didn't have the patience to even get upset; I didn't care if it was because my eyes were glowing ominously or I was giving off my usual aura of dark-sorceress-in-training. "Liu!" I said, even while I flicked the ropes off her wrists. "Where is she? Liú zài nǎlǐ?"

"There," her mum said, with a gulping ragged sob. "She's in there."

I turned to look round the room again, baffled, and then—there was a moment of blank horror, and then I was running to the metal ring, shoving my way through all the flexing and shuddering statues round it, to get the weight off that sinking disk.

The bricks didn't want to come off. I grabbed the highest one on top, and it was like trying to lift a hundred-pound magnet off a floor made of iron. I had to drag it at a gro-tesquely slow pace all the way to the inner rim and then drag it up the side without dropping it until I could tip it up and over the edge to go crashing to the floor. By the time I was done with the first brick, the council wizards were already starting to break loose, stone chipping away from fingertips and noses and lips that were gasping for air.

I started in on a second one, my teeth gritted. Liu's mum ran over and started trying to help me, but she couldn't shift the bricks as much as a millimeter, no matter how she threw her back into it. She'd got her husband loose first; in a moment he was with us, and her uncle and aunt as well, but even pushing all together they couldn't move a single one.

"Just keep those other wizards off as long as you can!" I said. Sweat was trickling down my face, dripping off my eyebrows, running down my arms and my back as I dragged the second brick up the rim, my fingers getting slippery. It wasn't a physical weight. I could tell what the bricks were, as soon as my hands were on them: *mana* and *will*.

On the other side of that wall, some wizard had just crammed thirty years or more of mana and work and longing into this brick. They'd built it out of their longing for an enclave, and it didn't really matter that they didn't know exactly what was happening in this room. Because they did know, they had to know, that *something* evil and horrible was going to happen in this room. They were only over there in the other room because they didn't want to *watch*. They would surely have rather been somewhere even further away, but they couldn't be; this spell needed both their power and their *intent,* so they had to be here, they had to be part of it.

But they had found this way to keep their eyes shut and their noses pinched. They just had to be willing to hand over their work to these eight people, the people who were so hungry for council seats and power that they were willing to get their hands really dirty. And everyone over in that room was willing to do that, just so long as *they* got to walk out of that other room as enclavers, with their futures of safety and luxury assured. So they wanted their brick to stay right where it was, and that was why I could barely move it.

Liu's family had put themselves in front of me with their backs to the council members, except for her uncle, who had turned to face the other three. He began leading them in an intricate flowing pattern something like a group of people doing tai chi, but perfectly synchronized. It was a mana-building exercise that they'd clearly practiced together for years and years, slow and very deliberate, and as the council members struggled out of the stone one by one, it *snagged* them, and they had to join in.

I had to look away because I could feel it trying to nab *me*, too. I put my head down concentrating and kept dragging the brick up the side, millimeter by millimeter. It was going to take an agonizingly long time to get Liu out, if I could do it at all. They'd already filled the top of the disk almost halfway. The room was so dim I couldn't be sure, but there might have been something wet trickling out of those slots at the bottom, those slots that hadn't only been made to let out air. I wanted to burst into tears. "I'm coming, Liu, hold on," I panted out, in case she could hear me. "I'm coming. Precious! Precious, can you see her?"

Precious put her head out of my pocket and jumped down to the disk, and then without even going down the side, she squeaked up at me urgently and put her paw down on the surface, and her white fur started glowing, literally. In the light, I could see the disk was engraved all over in Chinese characters.

I could make out enough of them to know that it wasn't a single spell. It was like the gates of the Scholomance: a compilation of spells all doing the same thing, reinforcing one another, and even before Precious's light faded out, I'd picked out the same phrases being repeated over and over in different ones: *eternal life, longevity, deathlessness,* and I understood in a mingling of relief and rage: Liu *was* alive in there. Because she wasn't meant to get out of this too early. She was meant to die *slowly.* Even if her body was being shattered and her hips and shoulders had been crushed under the weight of all these bricks, these *fucking* bricks that wouldn't *move,* and I gave a howl of rage and heaved the second brick up and over the edge. The disk even shifted slightly up, a millimeter maybe.

But that was only the second brick. My arms and back and legs were all shaking with effort, and my time was running out. Three of the council members had started chanting an incantation: they were still being forced to go along with the mana-building exercise, but it wasn't going to stop them casting whatever they were doing, and from the words I could overhear, it wasn't going to be very nice. These strangers who were trying to murder my friend, these strangers who agreed with Ophelia in New York, with Christopher Martel in London, with Sir Alfred Fucking Cooper Browning and the rulers and founders of every other enclave in the world, that it was worth doing this one horrible thing to someone *else,* to avoid all the other horrible things that might happen to *them.*

I didn't know what to do and I knew exactly what to do. I could have pointed at any one of them and just whacked them off the face of the earth with a careless flick of my hand, the insignificant insects that they were, troubling me. I could have sludged the marrow of their bones and let it run out of their bodies while they collapsed, writhing and screaming, the way they'd been about to do to Liu. I could have clawed their brains out of their skulls and made them into the obedient minions they had made out of everyone in that

THE GOLDEN ENCLAVES ✦ 271

other room who'd agreed to hand her over to be mangled in this ritual.

Instead I turned to the wall with the postbox hatch in it. It was made of stone, so my Roman spell wouldn't do, but that was all right. We were inside an enclave, and that wall was barely even there; it was a polite fiction, a curtain for all of them to hide behind, in both directions, from each other and from what they were doing. "*À la mort,*" I said, and waved the whole thing out of existence.

Liu's mum gave a squawk of protest. On the other side of the wall was a massive auditorium, nearly the size of the Maleficaria Studies room back at school, and it was full of wizards sitting in small orderly groups. The last few were waiting to come down to a stamping machine artifice that was making the bricks—which apparently weren't the product of one wizard, but *ten* of them.

The council members had stopped chanting their spell, possibly out of bewilderment that I'd done anything this apparently stupid; the wizards on the other side were all still frozen in surprise and confusion. They were all laid out in the amphitheater as tidy as you like. For one instant I had a beautifully clear opening for anything I wanted to do, to any and all of them.

I clenched my hands into fists at my sides and used the stupid little compulsion spell I'd made up as a furious child, the one I'd eventually stopped using because every time I tried it, Mum gently untangled it before I could get anywhere with it, and then sat me down for a really long conversation about why we couldn't force people to do what we wanted, which obviously every last one of these wankers had missed. "*Do as I say, and not as I do, and what I want, I'll make you,*" I chanted, clearly a masterpiece of high arcana, only I pushed it out at all of them with a massive wall of New York's mana behind it, and then I said in Chinese, "And what I want is for you to stop and listen to me, so I don't have to *kill you all!*"

I meant it with total sincerity, and since they didn't want me to kill them all either, that had the extremely helpful quality of aligning their self-interest with my compulsion. A total silence descended as everyone stopped; even the ordinary background rustling of clothing and faint coughs went still.

I dragged in a deep breath and gestured to the cylinder pit. "This is what you're doing. You've put a living girl inside that thing, someone who trusted you, someone who wanted to help you, and you're crushing her slowly. You're *all doing it.* All of you. That's what you're doing to make your enclave. That's what you're putting at the very heart of it. Torture, and pain, and betrayal, and—"

I stopped. I'd been going to say *murder,* only I understood, suddenly, with a terrible nauseating clarity, that murder was the one thing that wasn't on the agenda at all. Of course it wasn't. *Deathlessness, eternal life, longevity.*

"A maw-mouth," I said. The words came out of my mouth small and quiet, and they dropped into the silence of the room like stones going into a deep well. "You're making a maw-mouth."

It was obvious once I knew. The tiny slots cut in the bottom of the cylinder, for something to come oozing out. The sewer grating where they'd tied up four people, bound and gagged so they couldn't shield themselves against the hungry newborn monster looking for its first meal. And then it would drop through the grate while it digested. Tidy. You wouldn't have wanted it to turn round and have a go at the council members, after all. Surely the sewer dumped out somewhere into the real world, maybe into the streets of Beijing, where it would go creeping away to hunt amongst the independent wizards of the city, all those poor bastards hovering round the enclave hoping for work.

And as soon as I knew what they were doing, I also knew why. A maw-mouth took *everything*. It extracted all the mana you could make, everything that came from your desperate failing struggle to keep it *out of you,* and it kept squeezing you forever. It didn't just get you and your agony, it got all the mana your agony could ever build, borrowed in advance. And they needed that to build an enclave . . . because the final working had to be done all in one go, by a single wizard.

I'd noticed that bit ages ago in the Golden Stone sutras: *one voice calling to the void, in a single breath.* A circle of wizards wouldn't do. One caster only, convincing the void that no, really, this one part of it was fixed and permanent, even though the void was the exact opposite, and wanted to be nothing and everything all at once. Channeling a vast torrent of mana into that persuasion.

I simply hadn't paid that particular constraint much attention, because it wasn't going to be my problem. My problem was going to be making certain I didn't get anything wrong out of the twenty-six different incantations that had to be combined into the casting. That was what I'd been working on, trying to learn. As soon as I'd got that nailed down, just hand me a truckload of mana and let me go, and I'd knock you up an enclave quick as you like.

But of course it *would* have been a problem for any other wizard in the entire world. It made sense, after all, of why the sutras had been lost. That ancient long-ago wizard who'd written the sutras, who'd gone round India knocking up the first-ever constructed enclaves for other wizards—he'd been like me, a *tertiary-order entity,* or at any rate someone who could cast that great final working. So even though he'd written it down for others, it had been useless, because no one else could make it work.

Those other wizards still desperately wanted to build enclaves of their own, though. Purochana had shown them it *could* be done, you could *make* an enclave, so once they'd understood the general idea, they'd tried and tried and eventually some sufficiently clever and vicious bastard had found a solution. A way to get that much mana through a single wizard, to narrow the power down to that one singular point. Alas, the process produced a very unfortunate side effect, but oh well. You could shoo that nasty maw-mouth right out to fend for itself. And if it fended for itself by eating other wizards' children, well, from inside your tidy new enclave you'd never have to hear them screaming.

There were tears running down my face. I wasn't the only one. No one else was saying a word, but there was an amphitheater of faces staring down at me full of horror, refusal, recoiling. I could hear my own ragged choked breathing rasping back at me off the walls, mingled with theirs. The way you heard a maw-mouth coming from a distance, full of strangled human voices.

A maw-mouth is the worst thing that can happen to a wizard. They're the monsters that keep us awake at night. Probably every last wizard in that enormous amphitheater had made it out of the Scholomance, running past Patience and Fortitude, inches away from endless hell. All of these wizards, they'd known that something bad was going to happen in here, that Liu wasn't going to come out again, but they hadn't known *how* bad. Surely they'd told themselves a story—it was just one death, one sacrifice, for everyone's sake. Maybe there had been a lottery, something they'd told themselves was fair.

And the eight people in this room—who wouldn't meet

my eyes when I looked at them, who'd known what they were really doing—they'd told themselves a different story: Ophelia's story. The story that every council member in every enclave had been telling themselves for thousands of years, since the very first time someone had *built* an enclave out of death instead of gold. It was their *responsibility* to do the terrible thing for everyone else. To bear the scars of it like a burden, as if there was something noble in doing something so horrible that most people couldn't stand doing it, for the sake of those squeamish people.

I wanted to sweep all of them off the face of the earth. But they were just ordinary people, after all. The people in this room weren't any worse than the enclavers I'd known at school, and *they* hadn't been any worse than the losers I'd known at school, except that they'd been enclavers, and that hadn't been their choice, not really, or at least not a human choice that ordinary people made. The enclavers had been born enclavers, and the losers had been born outside, and I was more or less the only loser in the world who had *chosen* not to be an enclaver.

And that was a choice I hadn't wanted *myself.* I'd tried not to make it. It was Mum's choice, and I knew that at the heart, that was the choice to care about, to forgive, even the Philippa Waxes and Claire Browns of the world; even the *Ophelias;* the most horrid and miserable people, who didn't deserve to be forgiven, because otherwise no one deserved to be forgiven.

And if Mum *hadn't* made that choice—if she had ever chosen *not* to forgive someone, if she'd chosen to refuse healing and care to someone because they had been just too awful— then the worst thing that would have happened was, that one person would have gone off into the world, sick and desperate. But for *me*—my choice was to find some way to forgive these people, these horrible people, or sail out and start blasting the whole world bare. Because enclaves all over the world, every enclave built for thousands of years, had been made this same way. *Enclaves are built with malia,* Mum had said, and how right she'd been. If I was going to eradicate this one, why *wouldn't* I keep going? The people in this room weren't any worse than the people in the cold polished vaults of London, the ones who'd been so grateful for my help to fight off a maw-mouth at *their* gates, after they'd made one of their own and sent it roaming the world.

So why wouldn't I go back to London and rip it down, with every man, woman, and child inside its walls? Why wouldn't I head to New York straight after, and go down the line from there, bringing death and destruction to all the enclaves of the world, right on schedule? Just because I hadn't watched their ceremony firsthand, just because they hadn't picked on my own friend? That would make me exactly like these people in the amphitheater, hiding behind their comforting wall.

But I *was* like those people, surely. The only difference was the wall. I didn't have one. I had to hold the power and I had to commit the act, both, inside my own body and mind. I couldn't hand a tidy bit of mana over to someone else to do the dirty work, and I also couldn't tell myself that I was just doing what everyone else wanted me to do, and if I didn't, someone else would. I had to look my own selfishness in the face, each and every time. And I didn't like doing it, did I? The wall wasn't for nothing, after all.

And that didn't mean they wouldn't still do the wrong thing if they had the chance. They could tell themselves, after all, that everyone else in the world had done the same wrong thing. But I made myself look up at their faces, and look at the tears and the horror, and believe in it enough to give them a choice, the only choice I could think of.

"I'm not letting you do it," I said. "Not if I have to bring the rest of this enclave down with all of us in it. I did it to the Scholomance and I'll do it here. And you can't stop me." My voice echoed off the walls and around the massive space, ringing through the enforced silence. Nothing else broke it. I gestured to the circle of bricks, that horrible weight. "Or you can take these off her, and I'll try to save this enclave for you. I don't know if it'll work. But if you'll give the mana to me instead of using it for this, I'll try."

The compulsion faded, and a low murmur started, rising louder all around the chamber as people turned to their neighbors: *Did you know, I didn't, I didn't know,* all of them telling each other that half lie. I was disgusted with it and hoping for it all at once. I needed them to want that lie enough to agree, to try another way.

But one of the council members abruptly said to me, "We'll let Guo Yi Liu out, and you can go—"

"*No,*" I said, in a howling that echoed off the walls of the little room, like a pack of wolves ringed round him. He shut up. "Those are your choices. Don't bother looking for a third. I'm not letting you do it to Liu, and I'm not leaving you with this tidy pile of bricks to do it to someone else. If you don't want me to try saving the place, you can dump them down that sewer and evacuate for all I care."

"Most of the stored mana is *ours,*" a different council member said—a middle-aged woman, young relative to the others. "We chose to use it to help Beijing and not just to make our own enclave, but we are not going to give them the work of our entire family for generations—"

"You took the work of your entire family for generations and chose to use it to *make a maw-mouth,* so shut it!" I said, but that was only a seething of outrage bubbling up and over from the simmering pot; I knew there had to be a real answer. "And fine, if it's not Beijing's to give, then I suppose if they want me to have a go, they'd better make you a decent offer."

It was still mostly an explosion, but a useful one; I imagine they'd spent most of the last week, with Liu sitting locked alone in that room waiting for this to happen to her, negotiating urgent points like how many council seats went to the original Beijing team versus the newcomers, who got to live in the fanciest bits of the joint enclave, how many places they'd make for new wizards and who would get to hand them out. So now I'd put them on comfortably familiar territory, even if I'd also taken away half the spoils they had to haggle over.

They started to discuss hurriedly amongst themselves, huddled in low voices, but then someone stood up abruptly in the amphitheater: a boy I recognized from the Chinese obstacle-course runs, Jiangyu, one of the Beijing enclave seniors. He'd been one of the very last kids to join up, less because he'd thought I was secretly trying to kill everyone than because things were *not* going according to the rules, about which he had extremely passionate feelings. Even after he'd finally come round and done a first run in our chummy little group of five hundred, he'd come up to me and Liu afterwards to complain that our tactics went against the advice in the graduation handbook—which had been completely useless for several months by then. We'd eyed him sidelong and another of the Beijing enclavers had shown up and towed him away with an air of weariness, but now he got up and said stolidly, "I wish to say that if there is not enough room for all of us, then if Xi'an will agree to save Beijing, I am willing to give up my own place."

His mum, sitting next to him, was grabbing for him with an alarmed expression, but nine other kids stood up with him, all the rest of the senior Beijing enclavers, and started declaring the same offer, and as if they were a cork popping out of a bottle, all of a sudden the room dissolved into a quiet but general pandemonium. Beijing enclavers were standing up, looking round for anyone from Liu's clan and talking to them directly—they outnumbered them, nearly three to one, and there *could* be enough room for all of them, surely.

Assuming the enclave didn't just come down in a heap when I tried. But I couldn't be fussed about the possibility if they gave me the chance to try it. It was the only way out of here for me at all. Because I meant it; I couldn't walk out of here knowing they'd do this to someone else, but I also couldn't walk out of here and become a destroyer of worlds. I *wasn't* going to. If I had to bring this enclave down, if I had to fulfill that much of the prophecy to stop this from happening on my watch—my watch was going to have to end here, too. And maybe that wasn't any real solution; Liesel would tell me I was being an idiot, and if I was going to let all the other enclaves in the world off, I could simply choose to do that instead of throwing myself into a pit. But fine, I'd have to be an idiot, because I couldn't do anything else. I've spent my whole life fighting as hard as I could not to fulfill the prophecy, not to turn into a monster, and I wasn't going to give up now.

The council members had all stopped negotiating amongst themselves and were staring out at the rest of the wizards in dismay, the reins slipped out of their hands. Which meant there wasn't anyone who could turn to me and say *all right, we agree, go ahead,* but there was a faint grinding noise from the pit: the disk had risen a bit. I tried one of the bricks again, and I managed to pick it up: not easily, not like a simple ordinary brick, but at least like a brick made out of lead instead of a brick made out of black hole, and I gave a heave and let it

go flying off, then went for another. The crash made everyone jump and look, and as I kept going, hurling bricks out,
the remaining ones got lighter and lighter, everyone coming
round, until Liu's mom could take one off too, and then Jiangyu and some of the other Beijing seniors came in to help,
with the rest of Liu's family, and we got the last one off and I
put my hands on the disk, risen back to the top—

I didn't really pause, but there was a moment inside my
head when I wanted to. I couldn't read the inscriptions without a better light, but I felt them under my fingers, and if
they'd gone too far—if they'd already hurt Liu badly
enough—then when I took this thing off her, she'd die. And
I'd promised them, so even if I took it off and she was in there
crushed and bleeding and I had to watch her die, I was going
to have to help the people who had done this to her. I was
going to have to save their enclave anyway.

Then I finished taking it off and threw it violently aside
like a discus to smash into the wall, and Liu's mum and dad
screamed and were reaching down for her: she was in the
bottom, naked and strapped tightly into a curled fetal position with leather bands marked up with runes. I remembered
with lurching nausea the shape I'd seen inside the maw-
mouths I'd killed, the crushed body at the very center. I'd
vaguely thought it was the remains of some maleficer—
someone like Jack, only more successful, who'd just kept
sucking people dry until they finally collapsed in on themselves to keep on devouring endlessly. I'd been afraid of becoming one of those people.

Instead it would have been Liu, kind quiet Liu, who'd only
ever touched malia to save her little cousins and had sworn
off it as soon as she'd had the chance, bound inside there forever. Her arms had been wrapped around her, and the poor
hand on top, the one she'd used for fingering on the lute, had

been crushed bloody against her shoulder where it had been strapped down, and along her side there were horrible purpled stripes where her skin had been ground against her ribs, raw in places and starting to rub off. When her parents got the hood off her head, there was blood on her mouth; her shoulders and hips looked all wrong. Her eyes didn't open.

But she was breathing, and she kept on breathing. She moaned faintly when they cut the straps loose to move her, but a couple of healers were dashing in from the amphitheater room; they cast half a dozen quick healing spells on her, the equivalent of giving her some morphine and an oxygen mask, and under their direction, together all of us reached down and lifted her out with many hands. Some other people had transmuted one of the amphitheater chairs into a waiting stretcher. As they got her on it, Xiao Xing squirmed out of the hollow of her throat and reached up to me with his little paws. I picked him up and cuddled him against my cheek, tears dripping. "She would've wanted you to get away," I told him, but he just squeaked at me and wriggled out of my hands again, and jumped back to curl up under her ear as they lifted the stretcher.

Her mum was by her side, but her dad turned back to me for a moment. His eyes were wet and his mouth was hesitant, as if he didn't know what to say, and then he gave it up for a bad lot and just put his hands together and bowed to me, a thank-you, and I did it back, which probably wasn't the proper thing, but it didn't matter. Liu mattered, and she was alive and out, but even as her dad straightened back up, the room swayed a little around us, with the heaving of a large ship in choppy waters.

"Get her out of here!" I said to him, and then I turned back to the pile of bricks scattered all over the floor, and stared down at them a moment. I wasn't wholly at sea. The first half of the Golden Stone sutras, taken all together, were an instruction manual for creating the equivalent of those bricks, only the ones you made with the sutras were pebbles, and each one was only a year's work by a single wizard, instead. But it was the same idea: they were *building materials*. Of course, I didn't need that part of the sutras here. Just as well, really, since apart from the year-of-work required, even the process of compressing the pebbles was the undertaking of a week we didn't have.

The second half of the sutras—which I knew much less well than the first—explained in detail how you very carefully opened yourself a White-Rabbit hole out of the world and into the void over the course of three days. Again, that part was already done, since we were standing inside it. And then the last three pages—which I'd given a few brief skimmings— were about that great final casting, where you took all your pebbles and used them in a grand working uniting all the rest of the spells to build the foundation of the enclave.

The original Sanskrit text had mostly treated this final casting as something quite obvious, which I suspect it might have been after you'd gone slowly and laboriously through parts one and two. The medieval Arabic commentary had treated it as an outdated and quaint little process, included only for historical interest, more or less the way some manual of modern architecture might describe putting up a one-room mud hut: not anything anyone would actually want to do themselves, of course. Obviously they'd already advanced to the much more convenient technique of infinite torture by then.

So I wasn't at sea, but I *was* on a random uncharted island with a broken compass and a fragmentary map, and good luck getting to my destination. I didn't think I'd share that with everyone looking anxiously at me, though; I didn't need *their* doubts making the job harder along with my own. "All of you had better clear out before I try this," I did say to Jiangyu. "If this doesn't work, you won't want to be in here. Get Liu out, and—"

Jiangyu was already shaking his head. "No one can leave. The enclave is being braced from the outside by a circle of wizards. That is why we could come back inside to fix it, after we had evacuated. But we were warned that if any of us tried to go out again, before we finished the new enclave, we would push in the opposite direction, and the bracing would collapse. Then the whole enclave would fall." Wonderful.

"I have confidence that you will succeed," he added, with apparent sincerity. How very nice for him. I would have preferred if he'd told me sneeringly that I was a fool and I wasn't going to get on at all; I always do my best work angry.

"Thanks," I said sourly, and shut my eyes and took a few deep breaths, trying to clear the decks for the casting, to imagine my way into it. But I still had a strong impulse to get out of this room, and after a moment, I realized it wasn't just revulsion: this was the wrong place for me to be. The council had been about to build a *new* enclave, and then attach the old one on to hold it up. That wasn't what I was going to do. The Golden Stone sutras couldn't build a gigantic modern enclave. My only chance was to try to fix the old one. I opened my eyes and looked at Jiangyu. "Where's the foundation of the old enclave? The one that's broken."

Even Jiangyu had a hard time prying the information out of the council members: they certainly weren't nearly as sold on my prospects of success as he was. But they didn't have much of a choice either, which was emphasized by another barrel-roll of unease that went swelling through the floor and walls around us. When it subsided, the council finally stopped arguing amongst themselves and led me back out into the alleyway.

I could still see Orion and the others down at the far end, still caught out of time: it looked like he hadn't even moved, his knee still hanging midair. "Let them out of whatever that is," I said to the councilwoman, but she was staring out at it with real alarm of her own.

"That isn't a spell," she said. "The connection to the original enclave is breaking. They are on the other side."

It hadn't been a spell of speed after all; the sage's scroll must have heaved me over into Beijing enclave, straight through what was clearly a disjunction in the void. And if it opened up the rest of the way—down we'd all go.

There wasn't any more hesitation on their parts. Across the alleyway, next to the metro entrance, stood two imposing townhouses, and between them was a small gap, just barely noticeable if you looked up above the shared front wall that ran across their ground levels. Two of the council members went to it and put their hands on either side of the gap and pulled, and the wall split open and revealed a short narrow passageway running between them that opened into a small chamber on the other side.

I went in with my stomach turning. They'd got away with it, in here. Fifty years ago, a hundred years ago, a group of wizards had got together in this room and had put someone like Liu in a tin and crushed them into an endless hell, because they needed the grotesque power of that act to make not even an enclave but just a *bigger* enclave. I had to force myself to go inside, braced to feel it in the walls, in the ground under my feet, the monstrosity that had been made in that room. But when I stepped over the threshold with my fists clenched tight—it was only an empty room after all, bare and dull.

There was a single round disk on the floor, like a manhole cover with a square hole cut out of the middle and a four-character phrase carved out that I recognized from the lists of proverbs I'd had to memorize at school: *escape from certain death*. Much less complex than the one they'd been using today; it's always nice to see modern advancements in artifice and incantation at work. But the disk had cracked apart into four chunks, separating the characters, as if some giant had slammed a fist right down into the middle and smashed it. The only thing left here now was a hollow space where the foundation had been, where the unleashed void was doing its best to go back to formless chaos. The enclave was only hanging on because of all these wizards still believing in it, and that wasn't enough to keep up an entire magical city.

That's how the maleficer was bringing down the enclaves, I realized abruptly. They'd learned the secret of enclave-building and found out that this central point of weakness existed in every single one. Presumably they wriggled into the enclave and hit it, and while the enclave went reeling with all the wards coming apart, they sucked all the mana out of the place that they could, and left the rest of it to go tumbling down Humpty-Dumpty.

And in the end, I didn't want that to happen. I didn't want to rip Beijing off its foundation and push it off into the void. Jiangyu was out there organizing a bucket brigade of people to ferry the bricks in to me; he didn't deserve that. None of our schoolmates, who'd risked their almost certain escape back in the Scholomance just to help make the world safer for everyone, deserved it. Even the rest of the people in that amphitheater, who in the end had collectively let me take those bricks off Liu, didn't quite deserve it. Or even if they did, still it wouldn't have done any living person any good to smash all the towers and burn the metro line, bring down those libraries and laboratories. I did have to stop it happening *ever again;* and after I got done here, I'd have to think about what it would take to stop it, to make everyone in the world stop putting up new enclaves. But I didn't want to let the place collapse, any more than I'd wanted to send London's fairy gardens sinking into the void.

So I unslung the sutras from my back and took them out, and opened them to the first page marked with the illuminated border filled with gold leaf, the beautiful calligraphic heading that marked it as one of the *Golden Stone* castings, the ones that you had to use in the final working, and I took a deep breath and dived into the spell.

I'd cast bits and pieces of the sutras before, but never any of the major workings. But I'd spent so much time looking at them, dreaming of them, about all the things I'd do with them. The ancient Sanskrit came flowing through my mouth like a drink of cool water, a breath of sun-warmed air, the taste of honey and roses, and my eyes were prickling with tears, because it didn't feel like any of my spells at all. It felt like one of Mum's spells, something beautiful and full of clean light.

In that moment, I knew with clear glad certainty that it didn't matter to me how the sutras had come to me or what I'd paid for them. I couldn't get that price back, any more than I could undo what had been done to make the enclave around me. This was still the life's work I wanted to belong to. And I felt also, for the first time, that it wanted to belong to me; that the sutras really were *mine,* in a way I hadn't quite believed in before, despite all the time carefully polishing them and cuddling them and tucking them safely in at night.

As if to agree with me, the pages began to glow with soft golden light, illuminating themselves in the dim close room. A moment later, the book tugged gently, and when I uncurled my fingers, it rose up into the air and hovered just before my eyes, freeing my hands just as the page turned and I needed them for the next part of the work. The incantations kept flowing out of me, almost a song, and I turned and took the first brick from Jiangyu, at the end of the bucket-brigade line. I knelt down still chanting, and with both hands I pushed the brick down into the very center of the broken disk. The sharp points of the triangular pieces crumbled away. I felt the brick stick for a moment, and then almost as if I'd pushed it straight into a bog, it was sucked out of my fingers and sank away into the dark underneath the disk.

Only that wasn't just darkness. It was the void, ready to start swallowing the whole place up. A bit more of the disk crumbled away into it, and thin fracture lines of void began to spread out, following the cracked lines of the disk. I just turned back and grabbed the next brick and put it down as fast as I could, and the one after that, trying to catch the sinking brick just a bit before it went down, as if I could give the next one someplace to stand.

It was easy at the start, but that was only, as it happens, because I was dropping the bricks straight into the void. The first time I actually managed to put two bricks together, I felt it at once. I put down a brick, the ninth or tenth one, and a jarring shock came ringing back up my arms and through my body, and out from there into the whole enclave, a shivering ripple of—it wasn't power; the only word for it was *solidity*.

You might think that would have been encouraging. The trouble was, as it came through, you really couldn't help noticing the contrast between that and *everything else round you*, because the totality of the enclave was in fact being held up by pixie dust and good thoughts, or rather selfishly greedy ones, and as powerful as those are, they don't actually have anything to do with material reality. And that's what was coming for us: reality, with the pointed message that this whole enclave was a sack of made-up nonsense and what had ever given us the idea we could exist inside it?

So at the same moment, all the thin fracture lines of void ran away with it, spreading out of the small chamber like growing trees, and not like cracks in an earthquake, either. They went as though the enclave were a really magnificent painting by an old master, full of the illusion of richness and depth, but cracking all over its *flat surface*. Lines went crawling in nonsensical directions, one going along the ground of the narrow passage and then straight up the wall of the alleyway that was visible behind it; others, even more alarmingly, were putting partial outlines round some of the people in the brick-ferrying line as though they were characters in a comic book instead of people in the world.

I stopped looking at them and just focused on the bricks, but those were getting heavier again, heavier with each one, and my shoulders and back were already strained and tired. I had to start swinging, taking each brick from Jiangyu at the top of an arc and carrying it in the same movement over and letting it drop onto the pile I was making in the center, which wasn't nearly as tidy as the beautifully manicured circle the council had been building on top of Liu. I was trying to land the bricks in some connected way, getting at least one end onto some of the others. It was working in one sense, and in another I was thoroughly smashing up the disk that had been carrying the entire weight of the expanded enclave, all these years, and my replacement wasn't to the proper building standards.

Jiangyu was having trouble with the bricks himself, but despite that he crept a bit closer to help shorten the distance for me, although he was clenching his jaw and trembling all over with it. Then one of our classmates behind him, I thought her name was Xiaojiao, said in Chinese, "Double up! We need to double up!" and when he passed me the next brick, she didn't give him the next one, she just stepped forward, in a staggering waddle the way you'd carry a loaded bucket, and got him to take the other end without letting it go.

The two of them together got it closer to me still, and that gave me much better control: I was able to place the brick into an empty gap between two others, and firm up a space between them. The line of the brigade rippled forward slowly, compressing as everyone moved up the next brick and more people joined the line at the end, and even before the whole line had shrunk, Xiaojiao was beckoning urgently to the person behind her, and all three of them passed the next brick to me.

Everyone was in the line by the end of it. The later bricks didn't get passed along so much as they surfed over the crowd, hands beneath hands beneath hands holding them up. They were getting bottled up in the narrow entryway: there were thirty people crammed into the tiny chamber with me by then, and even the council members had joined in the work, but not enough people could get a hand on the bricks to support them properly. A man in the entryway gasped as the next one came in, and he and two other people went to their knees and the brick slid out of their hands and smashed down through one of the fracture lines and was just gone, sending spiderwebbing cracks everywhere. One of them went straight over the man's leg, horribly, and when he screamed and tried to grab at it, the rest of him moved and the part that had been cut off didn't; it was just standing there, disconnected, and then just stopped being there as he fell over.

I had to keep chanting the incantation, so I couldn't say anything, but I grabbed at Xiaojiao and pointed at the walls of the chamber, urgently, and she got the idea and called out, "Open up the wall! Break it open!"

Some people either misunderstood or overachieved, and in moments *all* the walls around us came down: people had dashed into the two townhouses on either side of the secret little chamber and torn apart the side walls. The whole crowd pressed in around me with the remaining bricks, so close that I scarcely needed to take them at all. Which was just as well, because within another three, they had become nearly impossible even for me. I didn't really *place* the next one; I just barely got it over an empty spot and it went slipping out of my hands the last inch to thump into place, marked damp with my sweaty handprints, and then Xiaojiao put out a hand and stopped me reaching the next one. She turned and waved her arms wildly to get everyone to come in closer, gathering round the solid circle I'd laid down with the last bricks. "All together, all the rest!" she said, and of course she was right: if I took those bricks one after another, the ones left would just get heavier and heavier, and I wouldn't be able to do the rest. This was why the golden enclaves hadn't been very big: not even *a tertiary-order entity* could build a foundation this big on their own, something that could take the weight of modern towers and underground lines.

So instead I took a step onto the center of the bricks, getting out of the way. The sutras came hovering along with me, and I kept the incantation going while all round me everyone chanted together: *sān, èr, yī,* and put the bricks down at the same time, finishing off a single bordering ring around the rest, smashing the last chunks of the old disk beneath them as I sang out the last words.

The whole enclave shook, and the fissures began to widen, a deep groaning all round. I didn't know what else to do; I was on the final part of the incantation, the last page with a golden border, the last one with any commentary. The remaining pages of the book were only an afterword where the scribe thanked his patrons effusively for the honor of deeming him worthy of a place in Baghdad enclave after his entire family had been killed by maleficaria, and it had made me angry enough that I'd only looked at it once.

But as soon as I finished the incantation, the last few pages of the book were turning: they whiffled to the back of the very last page, and there was one final line of Sanskrit written there in plain black ink, as if the scribe had copied it down and then hadn't bothered to illuminate it, because he hadn't thought it was part of the working. I'd never read or translated it, but it was so simple I could do it out of my head, and even at a glance it wasn't remotely like the inscriptions on the disk. Nothing about deathlessness or permanence, nothing forced; it was only a request, a cry of longing: *stay here, please stay, be our shelter, be our home, be loved,* and after I'd sung it out in the Sanskrit, I translated it off the cuff into Chinese, as best I could, and called it out urgently.

Everyone was sagging, panting for breath, many of them clinging to each other with eyes closed or staring fixedly at the ground, all of them trying not to look at the terrible fissures opening up round us. But back in the other room across the passageway, the room where they'd tried to crush her, Liu had heard me. Very faintly I heard her voice, thready and fragile, calling it back to me.

Other people joined in, voices picking it up all round—the words changing a little as it was passed along, like a children's game, but that didn't matter: the meaning was the same, and everyone was saying it together. As it swept through the crowd, all the people round me taking up the chant, I called it out again with them, and golden light came welling up through the loose bricks like mortar, joining them into a single round mosaic. It reached the final border and suddenly shot out at high speed, filling into all the cracks of void and patching them up, the red lanterns coming alight all along the alleyway, revealing second and third stories on all the buildings, and a neon sign above the metro suddenly blinked into improbable existence as lights came on in the stairway going down.

The sutras slammed shut, and I just barely caught them out of the air and then went the rest of the way down with them, not because they had gone heavy but because my legs had simply stopped working without notice. All round us, everyone was crying and laughing and embracing in the drunken relief of knowing they weren't all going to die and their home hadn't fallen in on itself. They went pouring back out into the alleyway to find their friends and family, dancing and rejoicing like a massive party-going; some of them even began flinging up fireworks into the void.

Sitting in a cross-legged heap on the solid bricks, I wrapped my arms round the sutras and bent my head over them, hugging them against me, and whispered, "Thank you," to the book, to the scribe, to Purochana, to the universe; for the gift of being allowed to do this, *this*, instead of the destruction and the slaughter I'd been destined for.

And then Precious squeaked shrilly, and I jerked my head up. The council members *hadn't* gone anywhere. Five of them had now stepped between me and the rest of the crowd, blocking their view, and the other three, their hands joined, were about to hit me with a killing spell.

Unfortunately, the warning wasn't any help. I hadn't anything left. I couldn't even kill them. I could only just watch it coming, my arms tightening round my book, and then they were all screaming, screaming horribly, so horribly I almost could have killed them after all, just to save them from whatever it was that was happening to them, but before I could even move, there was a sort of *yanking* motion, and all of them were just—gone. Gone as if they'd never been there at all.

Orion was in their place, just behind them. For one moment, his face was blank and utterly unmoving, and then he looked at me, and I should have said, *Fine, fourteen for you; I suppose we're tied again,* but I couldn't say that; I couldn't say anything like it, and he turned without a word and left, and everyone shocked and staring outside jerked back from him, pushing and shoving at everyone who'd wanted to see what was going on, a wave of empty space rolling with him through the crowd.

Chapter 14

DUBAI

CAUGHT HIM at the airport, thanks to Liesel, who'd grudgingly said, "He is going to New York, obviously!" after watching me all but crawl out of the enclave and start lurching round the temple grounds looking for him. She did first try to talk me into having a lie-down and not worrying about him, but gave in after it didn't work.

"You're *not* going to New York!" I snarled at him, standing between him and the security line. "I'll start yelling you're a terrorist and get us taken up, I swear I will. She's not getting her hands on you again! Are you out of your bloody mind?"

He didn't shout back. He just went on standing there in the middle of the concourse, looking far better than he had a right to in the still-pristine white T-shirt and jeans we'd got him at the commune, his silver hair artistically floppy; opposite him I looked like a ragged urchin, my clothes filthy with sweat and dust, stained all over with faint red marks from the bricks, torn in a few places. I wasn't getting him taken up; if I started howling, any policeman would look at the two of us, and I'd only get myself taken up instead, and be locked up somewhere for weeks until Liesel and Aadhya got me out somehow, assuming Liesel didn't sabotage the process to *keep* me locked up for her opinion of my own good. People were already giving me sidelong looks.

But Orion was staring at me like I was a drink of water, so I drew a few deep breaths and forced myself calm. "Lake, I know she's your mum, but she's a *maleficer,*" I said, level and measured. "Whatever's wrong, it's *her fault.* She's *done* it to you. And she won't fix it for you, either."

"She's the only one who might be able to," he said. "If anyone else could have—" He stopped, and I remembered Mum with her hands on his head, sorrowing, after everything she could do. *I couldn't set him right,* she'd said. All she'd been able to do was give him hope. Enough hope that he'd taken himself back out of the despair he'd fallen into, let himself believe that he deserved to live after all, no matter what was wrong—wrong *with him,* the words I hadn't said, but they were in him already.

"You don't *need* fixing," I said, and tried to mean it. "You've spent every minute of your life *saving people.*"

"No," he said. "I've spent every minute of my life *hunting mals.* I wanted to—" He looked away, a shine of misery in his eyes. "I wanted to think I was saving people. I wanted to be a hero."

"Oh, shut it, you absolute block, you *are* a hero!" I said savagely. "You *did* save people. You saved bloody all of us!"

"*You* did that," he said.

"I'd've been eaten ten minutes in, along with everyone else in the hall, when the horde came back down!" I said. "I couldn't have tried it, anyway. I couldn't have done a thing if you hadn't been there; we'd never even have fixed the machinery in the first place if you'd just faffed round and took out mals when you were bored." I was grasping wildly round.

"You cleared *the whole Scholomance*! You killed half the mals in the entire world—"

"I *ate* them!" he burst out.

I pulled up short. "What?"

"I ate them," he said again, his voice raw-edged. "All those mals in the school. I didn't kill them. I just—sucked them up. They tried to fight me, and it didn't do any good." He looked away, his face twisting with something horribly tense. "I'm pretty sure that's what I've been doing all along. Not killing them."

"I've seen you kill mals!" I said.

"I was doing it the hard way," he said. "Maybe I needed to—to get through their skins, before, somehow. But I don't have to anymore. I just have to get hold of them, and then—" He made a horrible gesture like someone slurping up noodles. "I can take *everything*."

"What, like a *maw-mouth*?" I said, a howl of protest, and stopped, my whole stomach gone into free-fall.

"Yeah," Orion said, smiling at me, an awful and utterly mirthless smile. "Just like that."

I wanted to scream questions at him, but I couldn't, not with that look on his face, gutted of hope. I'd have been pretending I didn't understand. I didn't *want* to understand, but I did, with horrible clarity: this was what Ophelia had done to him. The monster that couldn't be killed, the monster that all the other monsters feared. The monster that extracted every last ounce of power from its victims. She'd found a way to put that horrible devouring power into a *person*—and then she'd taught the person to feed the malia he gathered back into her enclave—where it superficially became mana again, purified by the act of being freely given. Beautifully efficient.

It was like I was back, *we* were back in the Scholomance, in those final moments just before the gates, with the worst horror in the world bearing down on us. I'd been yelling at Orion to run, I'd told him we had to run, and he—he'd been staring up at Patience, the whole time. He'd never fought a maw-mouth before; he'd never even seen one before I don't think, not that close, not *in range*. He'd gone hunting for the one in our junior year, but he'd never found it. I'd killed it before he ever got there. But in the graduation hall, he'd come face-to-face with Patience, and he'd seen—something he recognized. A mirror held up before him.

And when I'd screamed at Orion that we *had* to run—that there was nothing to do with a monster like that, with that unkillable horror, but leave it to fall away into the void—he'd *agreed with me*. So he'd shoved me out the doors, and stayed behind. As if I'd *told* him to.

He was looking at me now the same way he'd looked at me then: as if for the last time, storing the memory of me up inside, getting ready to shove me out the doors again. And I was already falling, falling into horror, but Aadhya had been right. I hadn't left Orion behind. That wasn't a thing that I would do. No matter what. I couldn't speak, but I took a step towards him, reaching for him.

But Orion didn't let me touch him. He backed away a step, tensed up for flight. "Don't," he said. "Don't. I've got to go. I have to."

"Listen to me," I said, raggedly; my throat was swelled up choking-tight, but I forced the words out. "Orion, listen to me. As long as I can remember—I've had the power to do the most monstrous things I could imagine. And all I've ever wanted, all my life, is for someone to tell me—that I was in the clear. That I'd never do something so horrible I couldn't walk away from it. But there's no one. There's no one who can hand you a badge and make you all right. The only way to be all right is to keep on being all right, as best you can."

"I *can't* be all right," Orion said flatly, and silenced me. "El, you can't look me in the face and tell me there's anything I can do that can make me all right. Not like this. You know what maw-mouths are. What they do to people. And that's what I did—that's what I'm *doing*—to those people in Beijing," and for a moment I was back on my knees in that narrow chamber hearing the screaming again, the unbearable screaming of people being taken by a maw-mouth—only a maw-mouth that didn't need to bother hanging on to their eyes and mouths, because it had eyes and a mouth and hands of its own—hands that could even cast spells.

"I thought—after your mom helped me, I thought— maybe I could control it," Orion said. "I thought I could just keep hunting mals, and that would be okay. But I can't. I *can't* be all right. I don't even know if—" He swallowed. "I ate— *Patience*. And I don't think . . . I don't think that *destroyed* Patience. I think all those people are still—"

He stopped, but he didn't need to keep going, because I did know, in horrible detail, what maw-mouths were. All those people, all those devoured lives, were still in him, still screaming, being shredded to exhaustion and still not allowed to die, because that was what maw-mouths did to people, and he was right; I couldn't say anything. For all I knew, one of those screaming people inside him was my *dad*.

Maybe the horror of it was in my face. I hope it wasn't. But Orion said rawly, "El, if my mom can't undo this—"

I didn't want him to keep going. "If she *won't*," I snarled.

"Either way," he said. "If she *doesn't*—"

"It's not your *fault*," I said, just a howl into the universe, which cared as much as it ever did. He hadn't been asked for permission any more than I had, but here we were, still stuck with the consequences: a maw-mouth and a maw-mouth killer, and I knew what Orion was trying to ask me, and I couldn't bear to let him.

He didn't try again. He shut his eyes, and then he took one small lurching step towards me, moving so fast I didn't even have a chance to clutch at him, and he caught my face in his hands and kissed me, tears sticky between our mouths, and then my fingertips were just catching at his arm and sliding off as he went away from me, through the security gates, and was gone.

I was sitting on a bench in the concourse, staring into space when Aadhya eventually turned up and towed me back to the enclave. Not the new section; Liu's family had set up shop in the sage's house. There seemed to be a tacit agreement to leave it to them, even though the rest of the enclave was fairly crowded now: all the former enclavers were having to give up hard-won rooms in their flats and divide up the working space to make room for the newcomers who'd provided all the mana.

And Liu did need to be inside the enclave. Three of the top healers were working on her, taking it in turn round the clock to keep her hovering in some kind of complicated healing spell in the middle of the courtyard. It took me aback when Aadhya led me back in. I wasn't paying much attention until then, but when we came inside, the whole house was different: the fountains had been refilled and the water was running again, a soft gurgling over rocks, and the trees and shrubs had all grown new leaves; a narrow vine was putting out flowers. And Liu was floating three feet off the ground in a glowing cocoon that one of the healers was spinning round her.

"It's okay!" Aadhya said, when I pulled up in alarm. "It's a regeneration spell."

The cocoon was made of filaments of water coming up out of the stream, which were being interwoven with thin lines of fine powders coming out of two dozen porcelain jars arranged in the courtyard. Some were enormous waist-high things that I could almost have climbed inside, and others were the size of a sugar bowl, and one tiny casket made of solid gold emitted a single glowing-red grain every ten minutes out of a minuscule opening in the top. It was certainly impressive, and when I went up as close as I could and peered through the translucent shell, Liu already looked better: her shoulders and hips had straightened out, and her skin was glowing faintly and evenly all over, the livid marks gone.

I made the mistake of trying to ask one of the healers' apprentices how much longer the treatment would take, and got an exhaustive explanation that I couldn't understand at all. It was given to me in English, not in Chinese, but that didn't help. The Beijing healers weren't like Mum; they were the kind of healers who'd come out of the Scholomance, went straight for advanced mundane medical degrees, then apprenticed for another ten years to a senior healer. Anyone who emerges from the process talks in jargon so rarefied that I doubt any other human being could understand them except other wizard healers. Occasionally those sorts come to see Mum to try to understand her work, and usually go away again seething in frustration after a few days.

Except in one way it turned out they were exactly like Mum. I finally gave up on understanding what they were doing and just demanded to know specifically what hour, day, week, or year Liu would come out of the chrysalis, and they said, *When she is ready.*

Liesel and Aadhya both asked me—with differing degrees

of tact—what had happened with Orion, what was wrong with him. I couldn't tell them, not even Aad. I couldn't put the words into the world. If I didn't say them, if I didn't think about it, I could put myself back into the story I'd already written for myself, well before graduation: a jilted girl, the school romance come to an end, ordinary and expected. Orion would be alive in New York, choosing to be there of his own free will. And I could go on with my life after all.

I suppose on some level I already knew that as soon as I tried, I'd find fairly quickly that I couldn't. But I didn't know what there was to be done, and I had still less idea of what *I* could do. Ophelia deserved to have her entire brain taken out and shredded like cabbage, but Orion was right: if she couldn't undo whatever she'd done, no one could. Mum had already tried, and I didn't believe there was any healer in the world who could do more for him. And I couldn't see any way for me to be of any use at all. The only thing I could have done was the only thing I could do to any maw-mouth, and I wasn't going to do it to Orion. He was alive, he *was,* and he deserved to live if anyone ever had, and I wasn't going to look him in the face and tell him he was already dead.

But I didn't know what else I could do. I ended up just sitting in the courtyard with Zheng and Min and Liu's grandmother, watching the cocoon turning gently round and getting more and more angry, like a supervolcano building up pressure deep underground, ready to erupt in one direction or another. Aadhya and Liesel had both been taken off by Liu's uncle and father to go help negotiate various terms with the rest of the new and old enclavers—as proxies for me, I gathered, which was probably just as well for everyone concerned, since seething rage doesn't really make negotiations go smoothly.

Out of the back of the sage's house, there were faint warm

gleams of light coming out of the shutters of every house along the alleyway, and the red lanterns had dimmed, but deliberately. Everyone had been tucked into some corner or another for the night, and the enclave was starting to settle, a general quiet descending. There were even a few crickets making soft singing noises together in the courtyard, as if they'd snuck in or been brought in. You couldn't tell what had almost happened here. Except for Liu, still floating, eyes closed, still not ready to come back out of what everyone in this place had tried to do to her.

"There was a lottery," Jiangyu had told us, with perfect serious earnestness, and looked perplexed when I'd brayed a laugh in his face. There hadn't been a lottery, or at least not a real one. Oh, surely there had been some nicely arranged set dressing, but it hadn't been random at all. I knew that, because now that I'd cast the final incantation, I knew why it had been Liu. Because the person touching the void for everyone, the single voice asking the void to *be shelter,* had to be strict mana. They couldn't be even a little bit of a cheat, they couldn't have any anima scarring at all. The mana had to flow perfectly smooth.

And even though Liu *had* been a reluctant maleficer for three years, she'd done it out of love for her cousins, and then she'd been the involuntary recipient of a really bang-up spirit cleanse, thanks to me. She'd stayed strict mana ever since. For a whole year in the Scholomance, even under all the weight of fear and graduation: it had probably been the equivalent of physiotherapy for her anima.

It must have looked like a golden windfall to the council members. It's not that easy to find a wizard who's strict mana. Almost everyone cheats a bit, now and again. I would guess most of the time they have to use someone who's strict mana by accident rather than design: a loser kid fresh out of the

Scholomance, one of the kind that don't have enough power of their own to steal anyone else's mana when the only available targets are other wizard kids, who just barely squeak out on the minion track by building mana of their own frantically, getting lucky enough that they don't have to use it themselves, and then letting other people have it for graduation.

But the council here hadn't had to do that. They'd had a witch with real power, who consciously refused to sneak even a drop of unearned mana—which always means stolen from some other living thing—and they'd deliberately taken her and made her their conduit for the void. That probably would only have made the spell work better, too. That Liu was someone like that, and that they'd chosen to do it to her. And no one had stopped them.

Except me. I'd stopped them. I'd stopped them, but I hadn't done it by killing them; I hadn't done it by destroying their enclave. I'd done it by giving the ordinary, mostly decent people, the ones who hadn't been able to watch, *another way*. I hadn't destroyed Beijing. I'd *saved* Beijing, just like I'd saved London. I *had* made Mum's choice, every time it mattered. I'd made it here, and I'd made it in the Scholomance with Jack's knife deep in my belly; in the library corridor, watching a maw-mouth go after a hundred helpless freshmen. I'd made it over and over, all through senior year, with graduation looming closer every day, and I was never going to turn into the monstrous vile destroyer of worlds that my however-great-grandmother had said I would, because if I was ever going to, I'd have *done it already*.

And that meant that much to my rage and sorrow, I couldn't go to New York and destroy Ophelia, who deserved to be destroyed if anyone in the world did, and since I couldn't do that, gradually I realized that what I could do, what I was going to do, was go and beat down the doors of Deepthi Sharma's bloody compound and make her look me in the face and admit that *she'd been wrong.*

I started trying to use my phone to work out how to get from Beijing to Mumbai. That went as well as you'd expect given that I'd literally never used one until a week before, until Zheng, who was sitting next to me, couldn't bear watching my incompetence anymore and took it from me and started showing me the flights. I couldn't actually book any of them, since I still didn't have any money or a credit card, but I'd just decided that I'd go back to the airport and muddle through it somehow, when Liesel and Aadhya came back in from the alleyway, and Aadhya immediately said, "Don't freak out."

Obviously the first thing I wanted to do was *freak out,* but before I got a word out, Liesel said, "No, the enclavers have not done anything!"

"Yeah, no, it's not anything here," Aadhya said. She held up her phone. "Ibrahim's texting me from Dubai. Jamaal asked him to help get hold of you. He's begging you to come out there. He says they're going to be the next enclave attacked."

"What do you mean, *going* to be?" I said. "And since when do people think I'm on call to every enclave in the world?"

"Excuse you, you're *not* on call to every enclave in the world, *I am,*" Aadhya said, pointedly.

"And since seven hours ago, when you have now saved *two* enclaves from collapse, that is when," Liesel said, equally unmerciful.

"Well, I'm not going to be," I said. "If they *know* it's coming, they can all clear out and go live like ordinary people."

"But they won't do that," Liesel said. "They will empty the mana store, and take all their most valuable artifice and their books, and their money, and when the enclave is destroyed, they will take all the space which they already own, in the mundane world, and the enclave-building spells which they already have, and they will *make a new enclave,*" which was so patently true that I couldn't argue with it in the least. Even if I broadcast the truth all round the world, told every single wizard what the enclavers were doing to make their snug little pockets in the void, it wouldn't stop anyone, not for long. People would hesitate, they'd recoil, and then little by little they'd reconcile themselves to the idea. Because they'd look at everyone else living in their own tidy enclaves, each one of them made the same grotesque way, and they'd say *why not me,* and that was a fair question, after all. Why *not* them.

I got up and stormed out of the enclave and into the temple grounds. All the tourists had gone; it was well after dark. It was still sweltering-hot outside compared with the cool dimness of the enclave, but a breeze was whispering through the green growth everywhere, and I found a bench and sat sullen and seething. After about fifteen minutes, Aadhya came out and sat down next to me.

"You're going to Dubai," she said. She sounded a little bleak.

"I'm *not,*" I said ferociously. "I'm going to—" She was holding out her phone. I took it out of her hand and looked at the last messages on the screen.

Please, tell El, she's got to come, Ibrahim had texted. *We don't know anything else, but we know it's going to happen. The warning came from the Speaker of Mumbai.*

I stared at it, mounting rage swelling up in me. It made sense of their panic: as far as I know, of all the many, many prophecies made by the Speaker of Mumbai since she was four years old, the one she made about *me* remains the single solitary exception that hasn't come true yet. *Yet:* the shadow

that I've lived my entire life inside, ever since she'd prophesied that I was doomed to bring death and destruction all
over the world. It was like she'd *heard* me thinking about
coming to yell at her, and she'd found a way to get someone
else to grab me by the ankles and slow me down.

I shoved the phone back at Aadhya. "I'm not going," I said.
"I don't want to go!"

She didn't argue with me. She just put her arm round my
shoulders, and I turned in and hugged her, and she hugged
me back, hard, letting me hold on.

"I'll stay with her," Aadhya said, holding my hand tight as we
stood and looked at Liu, still floating in the cocoon, still not
ready to come out. "I'll let you know as soon as she's okay."

"Text me every day," I said.

Even sitting in the taxi on the way to the airport, I was still
giving serious thought to getting a plane to Mumbai instead.
But Ibrahim had managed to wheedle my number out of
Aadhya, and halfway there he phoned me directly. It was the
first phone call I'd ever received, actually, which was why I
answered. The ringtone came yammering out of my pocket
at full volume, loud inside the car, and I pulled it out and
pushed and swiped until the noise stopped and then Ibrahim's voice was coming out of it tinnily, "El?" and he sounded
almost on the verge of tears.

I put it to my ear and said, "Yeah," grudgingly.

He hadn't an excuse to be sniffling. He wasn't even *in*
Dubai enclave. But obviously this was his chance, a precious
once-in-a-lifetime crack at an enclave place, and—even
though any sixteen hundred people you asked would have
universally agreed that he was infinitely more likable than me

and far better company—he was only getting that chance because he could get me on the phone.

"Thank you, El, so much," he said, as if I'd already agreed to go. "I know you don't like enclaves. I even warned Jamaal, I didn't think you'd do it. But he begged me to ask. His sister's about to have a baby. They've already moved their whole apartment out of the enclave, but the healers can't work nearly as well outside. She'll have to go to hospital. And everyone here is really scared."

I'm sure they were. I half wanted to tell him how they'd built the enclave he wanted me to rescue, and ask him point-blank if *he'd* have chosen to do it at the price. But why should I have made Ibrahim feel bad? I knew without asking that the answer was no in any practical sense, not because he was pure and selfless, but because he'd never in a thousand years end up in the position of having to make the choice. None of us talked about our plans for the future in the Scholomance, nothing specific, but we did share our dreams and fantasies in sidelong ways: *wouldn't it be nice,* or *if you had to choose* or *the best day would be,* and all of his fantasies had more or less been sitting peacefully in a beautiful place with three or four friends and chocolate ice cream. He'd never get near a council seat; he didn't want power. He just wanted to *live.*

"If they want my help, they can have it," I said instead, and cut him off when he started bursting into thanks, "but that's *if.*" And then I told him that they'd have to chuck out everyone on the council, and then recruit enough wizards to get the mana I needed to replace their foundation stone. They were going to be even more crowded than Beijing after, since they didn't have a convenient clan nearby who had spent several generations saving up.

"But you can tell them at least they won't need to find anyone strict mana," I added, savagely. He didn't understand my anger, but he did understand that I meant it; he didn't even try to argue, just said he'd pass the requirements along, and get back to me.

I half expected not to hear from him again. I imagine if he'd been deputized directly by the Dubai council, I wouldn't have. But Jamaal's grandfather and his three wives, a team of gateway builders, had joined the enclave as founding members some forty years ago after a bidding war. They weren't on the council itself, but they had a great deal of influence in the enclave and couldn't simply be shut up. I suppose they and everyone else considered ditching the council members a reasonable price to pay.

In any case, Ibrahim had sent me plane tickets before we'd even got to the kiosks, and when they came through, I stared at them and Liesel said, "Well?" with an air of impatience, and I clenched my jaw and made Mum's choice *again* and said, "Fine, we're going."

The tickets were first-class, naturally. Liesel was still monumentally irritated with me, and vice versa, but after we got on board and the flight attendants showed us the elaborate private shower cabin on the way to our seats, we both sat silently through takeoff, without exchanging so much as a sidelong glance, and then she got up and went. After a moment of debate with myself, I slipped Precious out of my pocket—she gave me an up-and-down look and then burrowed into the blanket without further commentary—and snuck off after her.

It was the sort of stupid prank I'd have rolled my eyes at, if someone had tittered about it to me. Why would you want to cram yourself into an aeroplane loo when you could just wait to be on the ground? But actually being on the plane, in this strange and transient bit of the world, made it easier.

And Liesel was right: it helped to feel good in my body, her hands and the water running over my skin reminding me that I was whole, even if I didn't feel that way, telling me I was still all in one piece at least on the outside.

Liesel predictably tried to pry some information out of me afterwards; we were toweling off when she asked abruptly, "*Now* will you tell me what happened? Why did Orion go?"

And it turned out that was the real reason I'd done it. It was easier to tell her here, and I did have to tell her. Because I didn't know what I could do for Orion, and that meant I was going to have to ask for help to do it: the lesson I'd had thumped into me properly last year in the Scholomance.

So I sat down on the lid of the loo and told her right there, with the roaring of the plane going all around us, trying not to listen to the words I was dragging out of myself. I wanted desperately for her to sniff and tell me I was an idiot, over-looking the manifestly obvious thing to do. Instead when I was done, she went and sat down herself, on the narrow bench inside the shower stall, and just stared at the wall for a while with her brain ticking away, and then she shook her head and said briefly, "Ophelia is very clever," in something too much like admiration. Then she got up and patted me on my shoulder, a bracing *nothing to do but carry on* kind of pat, and said, "We should go and sleep."

Ibrahim and Jamaal met us at the airport, both of them fretting themselves ragged with anxiety. My appearing didn't lift their spirits—it rarely does—and only added the extra layers of faint hope and unease. We didn't speak much on the way, except I asked Ibrahim about Yaakov, and Ibrahim looked down and said, stifled, "I've heard he's all right," so I might as well have jabbed him with a hot poker instead. That might even have been why he was so desperate to find a way in. I'd found it too large an ask to make myself, inviting someone to come away from his home and family to yours. I'd tried to run away from Orion even making the offer in the other direction. It was too much, a debt you could spend the rest of your life trying to pay off, and that was even before you got to Ibrahim and Yaakov's additional problem that un- less they went it totally alone, then whichever family side they lived with, the other one of them would face suspicion and possibly even hatred, from the surrounding mundanes if not literally the other's relations.

But everything would change if Ibrahim could offer in- stead a place in Dubai enclave, which is big and modern and firmly aboard the tolerance train, meaning they'll welcome anyone, regardless of their religion or their nationality or who they like to go to bed with, and let them live exactly as they like, so long as they're either spectacularly powerful in some way or have twenty years' worth of mana to buy their way in with.

The entrance to the enclave was in a mid-height office building on the other side round of the fantastic view of the Burj Khalifa; half the doors we passed along the corridor were unlabeled, and you had the sense that if the building had been a boat, it would have tipped over from the weight of everyone hanging on the opposite rail.

Except right now all the unlabeled offices were crammed with enclavers, sweating and scared in the dark. They'd re- turned all the space they could back to the real world, and come out to hide in it, but of course they didn't bother hav- ing electricity or water in the offices they borrowed, and they also had to keep quiet or else risk the mundanes in the rest of the building nosing in to find out what was going on.

Jamaal took me to the big conference room at the very end of the corridor, where the senior wizards of the enclave had gathered—minus the former council members. The room was stifling-hot, despite two banks of palm-frond fans in carved wooden handles that heaved back and forth on their own.

They welcomed me with what I got the sense they considered to be an unforgivably abbreviated hospitality, the splendid table creaking faintly but literally with the weight of food spread upon it, a banquet that the massed company couldn't have polished off in a week. Not a single one of them were actually eating any of it, though: *your enclave is about to come crashing down* had stifled their appetites. But they pressed me and Liesel urgently to have some, and poured me a cup of tea out of a beautiful antique pot that smelled faintly of a *be well disposed to me* charm. I pushed it aside and said rudely, "I'm not here to waste my time."

Predictably they moved on to asking if I'd really meant everything I'd told Ibrahim, and surely there were some alternatives to this or that piece of the plan. I remained my usual disappointing self. "And you can't just *hire* the recruits, either," I said. "It's got to be *their* home that they're building."

"Dear child," Jamaal's grandfather's eldest wife—his grandmother was the third—said, "surely your method could be used to simply reinforce the existing foundations of the enclave, at much less cost in mana."

"You'll do it without me, then," I said, and Liesel sighed noisily and interrupted to tell them how their *existing foundations* had been made. I got up and went to the loo while they talked, so I didn't have to listen to either the explanation or everything I assume they said: the appropriate displays of shock and horror, the delicate inquiries about whether I was really intractable on the subject.

I assume Liesel and Ibrahim and Jamaal managed to satisfy them on that point; in any case, no one else made me any other clever suggestions when I came back. And lucky for them, they'd been making the preparations in advance anyway: motivated by the alarming consciousness that the warning hadn't specified *when* the attack was going to come, and the even more alarming consciousness that when it came to age and stability, their forty-year-old enclave was far closer to Bangkok and Salta than to London or Beijing, and it was good odds that the whole place would go.

It hadn't been hard for them to recruit help, even without any assurances: *there's a very small chance we'll be offering enclave seats at the cost of two years' mana* is the kind of announcement that will have a thousand eager wizards queuing up at your gates quick as winking, just the way they had come running to London's gates on a rumor. They only had to decide to go ahead and do it, which took them much more time than I would have liked, and much less than they would have liked, since after fifteen minutes of urgent discussion, I got fed up and said, "I'm not sitting round here for hours waiting for you to decide whether you'd rather share your enclave with the plebs than have it knocked off into the void. If you don't want me, I'll be going."

At that point, Jamaal's grandmother—the youngest wife—burst out, "We must stop arguing! The attack could come at any moment, and we will all have to *go inside* to perform the casting." It was a potent argument, as was their very obvious lack of any better alternatives than me, for which they'd surely have given a great deal.

So finally they led me inside, through a blazing-hot server room full of flat narrow computers stacked up in metal racks and the uncomfortable blasting of fans, and into a small back door marked ELECTRICAL in English and Arabic. It opened to reveal a long panel covered with rainbows of thin wires, and *that* pulled open to reveal a small opening in the wall, just barely the height of my shoulder. I had to duck my head down to get through, and I straightened up a hundred years in the past, or at least it felt that way.

Jamaal's grandfather took us through a narrow lane between the smooth unbroken golden-brown walls of houses rising up on either side. Sail-like shades hung overhead between the buildings, high enough and overlapped so you couldn't see between to whatever artifice they were using to bring in the sunlight. You couldn't see into any of the houses: the dark wooden doors were all shut up tight, the windows shuttered; the few courtyards we passed were curtained off with heavy opaque hangings.

This place wasn't tipping off into the void, like Beijing had been, but I almost would have preferred it otherwise. Instead I felt it under the soles of my thin sandals, the grotesquely soft support beneath, yielding and fleshy. *Enclaves are built with malia. You can feel it when you're there, if you let yourself.* And now I knew what I was feeling, what I'd felt in New York, in London. I had to feel nauseatingly sorry now about having howled at Mum, when I'd been a kid, begging her to take me to the safety that any enclave would have given her for the asking, to have her healing inside their walls. Once she'd even gone to visit an old enclave, famous for their own healers, and she'd come back before the end of the day and told me she couldn't do it; she couldn't give me what I'd asked her for. And I'd raged and screamed at her for weeks, because she hadn't been willing to live on top of a putrefying heap of murdered corpses.

All the while, a cool pleasant breeze came steadily in my face with a faint hint of dampness. It wasn't like London's magical sunlamps, either; the sun and the wind were real sun and real wind, the same color and flavor as the outside. We reached the end of the alleyway and I saw the sun and air were coming into the enclave through wind towers—square hollow towers built outside a century ago or more, meant to catch and funnel breezes into the walled streets. When they'd brought the old buildings in, they'd left the tops of them outside, sitting on some skyscraper roof I suppose, and added small enchanted mirrors to coax the sunshine in along with the wind.

I knew it even as Jamaal's grandfather led us towards the middle one and unlocked a massive iron-banded door: the foundation stone was inside. Some sort of twisted irony, having the lovely comfortable breeze blowing at you, the sunlight glowing above, all of it flowing to you over that piece of hideous work. Of course it wasn't just irony at work. These towers weren't magical buildings on their own, like the sage's house in Beijing; they hadn't been imbued with power by seven generations of wizards. But someone, some mundanes, *had* built them with the right passionate intent, with care and love: trying to make shelter, a place of coolness and relief in the desert. The founding enclavers had probably done a mystical survey and settled on them as the perfect spot, just the right place to punch a hole through into the void. Just like finding someone strict mana to put under their stone.

I didn't go inside. "You'll have to tear the walls down round it," I said.

The work went a little slowly at first; not because they weren't desperate to save their enclave, but because they couldn't quite believe in the oncoming attack. The enclave was still there, still solid all around them. It was a warning of hurricanes with a clear blue sky above stretching for miles in every direction. Even the senior wizards, who'd already agreed with their own mouths, had a hard time putting their metaphysical pickaxes to the tower and opening it up.

Or maybe they just didn't want to open the tower up, so

they wouldn't have to see what they'd done. Because once they had fairly started, the first large chunk taken out of the doorway and their borrowed sunlight hitting the smooth round disk of iron set there in the floor, so all of them could see it, the pace began to quicken. And by the time they'd got the last bits down, they were all going full-tilt, pulling it down in massive chunks, leaving them in a great massed heap, dust rising in a cloud all round us. But none of the dust clung to the iron disk. It stood stark and heavy against the warm golden stones, and no one went near it.

The rest of the enclavers had already begun making their building-blocks. They didn't need me to bring out the sutras for that, though, since they had a piece of artifice to do the job. It wasn't the same as the massive stamping machine in Beijing—that one had been very expensive, I imagine—and looked more like a small oven. But they had a dozen of them lined up: each wizard stepped up to it and put in a double-handful of the dust and broken chunks from the shattered tower, and they put their hands on the oven and sent the mana in, and when the light faded, they reached in and brought out a single flat stone, all of them in different colors, some smaller and some larger, polished and rough.

It took a few increasingly frantic hours, all the new contributors coming inside one after another down the central lane to get their paving stones and then go line up in the other two lanes, waiting huddled together. Ibrahim came away with a polished green disk barely the size of a pound coin—he hadn't had enough time out of school to save up anything, but he'd obviously been let in for services rendered in bringing me in, and I couldn't help but be glad for him. His brother and sister-in-law, who'd both been working for the enclave for years, were there, too, that narrow uneven bargain they'd made suddenly paying off in spades. His parents hadn't any other children who had escaped the grinding teeth of maleficaria, but his aunt and uncle had come with their ten-year-old daughter and their six-year-old son, who'd never have to go to the Scholomance just for the thin hope of survival. His family had collectively scrounged up all the mana they could, hurriedly selling off a few magical heirlooms and mortgaging years of their work, to get together the two years of mana that the most vulnerable members of their family had to pay to get in.

It was an absurdly low price for an enclave place. Almost any wizard could pull together that much. Of course, there was one other significant price: having to come inside a condemned building. Everyone knew about the warning. The pressure built with every other person coming nervously inside to make their paving stones, then going to line up in the alleyways and wait, tensed and watching the walls around them for the first sign of cracking, for the storm to come rolling in, all of us together in a race we were running against a rival we couldn't see.

But any wizard would still take the chance at the price, because it was a price they *could* pay, a reward that *would* be given, if we all made it to the other side. It wasn't a lifetime of drudgery and constant fear with nothing but a thin scrap of hope to help you along the way. And to give them this much credit, the enclave could have made more of a bidding war of it, thrown the call open worldwide and driven up the price. Instead they'd come down on the side of letting in people they'd already vetted: all their workers, all the Scholomance allies the recent graduates could ring up, whoever could make it quick enough.

I spotted Ibrahim and Jamaal's ally Nadia in one of the queues, and before the process had finished, Cora arrived too, fresh from the airport without even a bag, running to hug Nadia and Ibrahim and Jamaal fiercely, wiping tears away, before she got in the queue; and then she saw me and after a moment got out of the queue and came to me. I waited there like a block wondering what she wanted even straight up to the moment when she put her arms round me, too. I managed to behave like a human being and hug her back, my throat tight.

Ibrahim kept watching the last trickle of people streaming in through the central lane while pretending he wasn't, turning his green stone over and over in his hands, and then he put it away in his pocket and turned his back as the stragglers brought up the end, the last of the enclavers coming back in from outside, the oldest wizards and mums with small kids, going one after another to put a handful of dust into the baking ovens, even the babies bringing out pea-sized pebbles with their mums' hands cupped round theirs. The houses were thickening up, gaining a sense of solidity as the last of the borrowed space eased back in with them, from all those conference rooms and empty offices.

I looked at Ibrahim, who'd stayed with me by the ruined tower the whole time. "I'll wait."

Ibrahim didn't look up. "I don't know if he's even got the message." His voice was a little ragged, thready, and then Nadia gave a cry, "Ibi!" and he turned and was running down the alleyway, dodging people left and right: Yaakov was coming in with the very last three people. A frail ancient man, bent almost double, was creeping precariously balanced between Yaakov's arm and a spindly walking stick whose carved inscriptions weren't powerful enough to keep him upright alone. An only ordinarily old woman with exhausted eyes was on his other side, carrying a small child limply asleep on her shoulder. Ibrahim stopped just short of them all, and then Yaakov reached out his free arm and they had buried their faces against each other's necks, standing together.

For just a moment: everyone was impatient with fear, longing to hurry them up. I couldn't help but feel it too: the old man's every creaking step stretched out agonizingly long, even with Ibrahim helping on his other side now, and I had rotten sinkhole ground beneath my feet and the weight of a thousand innocent lives on my shoulders, all the people who'd come here because I'd *told* the enclavers to let them in. I could see Jamaal's grandfather glancing at me, wanting to tell me to go ahead and get on with it, wondering if I'd do it, and before he could ask so I'd have to find out, I went to the almost gone heap of tower bits and grabbed a chunk and started dragging it on the ground round the iron disk, making chalky circles like places to stand, as if I were getting ready for a casting, even though it wasn't necessary, while Yaakov and his family got their paving stones.

Liesel either realized what I was doing or couldn't resist the golden opportunity to organize something into better order; she started corralling some of the enclavers and telling them where everyone ought to stand, and having them establish a tidy traffic pattern so everyone would flow out of one lane to make the next circle, and then away into another. "In Beijing," Liesel said to me abruptly, after everyone had got the idea and was on their feet and queuing up. "You said at the end, replacing the foundation, they put the last bricks in together."

I nodded. "I couldn't have lifted them by then."

"Why not *all* the stones at once, then?" she said.

So I didn't touch a single brick with my own hands; instead, Liesel and her helpers counted off a precisely calculated number of people in from the lane and had them form up in a circle round the iron disk with their own paving stone. Then each of them cast a little bog-simple *hover* spell on the thing, parents casting them for children too small to do it themselves, and left it floating there in midair just a few inches above the ground. Then off they all marched down into the other lane, making room for the next group.

It was a tidy way to keep from making the stones grow unbearably heavy along the way, and then at the end, five of the loudest-voiced men bellowed out a count, just like they had in Beijing. Everyone ended their hover incantation at once, and the paving stones came down like an inverted explosion, the outer ring landing first and each inner one coming down with more and more force, until the inner-most ones smashed down onto the iron disk, burying it some-where far beneath, and together we all called out the final incantation—a better translation this time, since I'd been able to give it to some professionals with a bit of warning—and the shining spell welled up in brilliant glowing from under-neath to a massive ululating chorus of voices calling in unison, *stay, be shelter, be home for us.*

The banquet did get eaten, afterwards. The doors and court-yards were all flung open to celebrate, all the newcomers in-vited in somewhere by one enclaver or another. Dancing and music spilled out into the alleyways, everything from tradi-tional songs to modern pop from seventeen different coun-tries, while people rapidly got drunk on liquor and enchanted vapors and relief.

And for once—I was *wanted.* Ibrahim and his allies reach-ing out to put their arms round me and Liesel, wanting to take us back with them to Jamaal's family compound, a mas-sive courtyard house right there at one end of the right lane.

I would have been so desperately glad to join in the massive catharsis, to find release somehow. Liesel took my hand and looked an invitation at me, and I wanted to stay, but I couldn't.

Because *it was still there.* We'd built the enclave a new foundation now, a wide round plaza full of those beautiful stones—but the old one was still there, a spongy mass beneath that I could still feel even when apparently no one else could, a horrible version of the princess and the pea.

"I've got to go," I said, brutal and crass, and I pulled my hands away and forced my way through the lane, past all the joyful press of bodies that kept wanting me to join them. People whose faces I'd only glimpsed for a moment were looking at me and *smiling,* reaching out, and I couldn't reach back to any of them. I just put my head down and bulled on through to the other end, which was just as crowded, and there managed through sheer desperate insistence to make the way out open up for me, a low hatch falling open in a wall when I banged on it. I ducked through and came stumbling out of the door, a janitorial closet tucked away behind the impersonal marble lobby of the office block. The security guard did a double take when I burst out past him, and got up frowning as if he half thought of coming after me, but he could see I wasn't carrying anything, and I was moving fast, so he gave it up for a bad lot and sank back down in his chair.

I kept going bang out of the doors and into the sweltering heat of the Dubai afternoon. It dragged me to a stop sooner than I wanted; I had to stagger into a massive mall the size of a small city itself and sit down by a fountain just to breathe. I was feeling too many things at once: the ferocious joy of the foundation spell, the power and longing of all those people's hopes still running through me, and my own recoiling from the deep horror beneath, both of them twisted up with my own longing for Orion, who was out there in the world living with that same horror buried under his own skin, impossible to escape. My body was shaking with exhaustion and heat and energy, and my mobile buzzing madly in my pocket until I just turned it off. I sat there for fifteen minutes getting my breath back and letting everything else settle, until one single feeling came up to the surface above all the rest, and if you can't guess which one it was, presumably you've only just started reading at this particular point in the story.

The attack, the prophesied attack, hadn't come. It hadn't come before I'd got here, and it hadn't come during the casting, and now it would *never* come. Why would it? I'd buried the vulnerability beneath that new foundation plaza built of mana, mortared with hopes and dreams and love, and there wouldn't be any chance to steal mana from the place. Why would any maleficer bother wasting their time attacking it? So that was *two* prophecies that hadn't come true, now. Like the one thing my great-grandmother couldn't properly foresee was *me* and my choices; as though her *gift* was assuming the worst of me, the same way everyone else in the world always had.

I got up and went out to the taxi stand. I'd noticed on the way in from the airport that loads of the drivers here seemed to be Indian, come over to work for the mundane version of enclaves. Three of them were standing outside together smoking, and I said to them in English, "I need to go to Mumbai."

"I'd like to go to Mumbai," one of them said, wistfully. "Are you from Mumbai, pretty girl?"

"My father was," I said, in Marathi.

They told me to wait until one of them got a ride to the airport, and then he let me sit up front with him and ride along. After Iqbal dropped off his passengers, he took me over to the terminal with the cheaper regional flights. I lay down on a bench in a quiet corner and catnapped until it got late, the whole place going quieter and quieter. When the security lines were empty, I went into the loo nearest to the gates, where I was now the only person. There was a cleaning cart inside. I took the spray bottle of blue cleanser off and used it to make a dripping outline of an archway on the back wall, and then I balled my hands into fists and rested them on the wall inside, shut my eyes, and recited a useful modern American spell: *"Get ready, get set, and go, go, go,"* thumping on the wall along with the punctuation, and on the last one I dropped my hands to my sides and just walked straight through and out the other side, into the facing loo on the other side of security.

There was one flight to Mumbai on the board. I went to the gate and waited until everyone had boarded, and then I asked the people on the desk if there were any seats left, and if I could have one. The woman attendant started telling me officially how I was to get on a standby list, but I stopped her. "I know I'm not allowed," I said. "I haven't got a ticket and I haven't got any money. If there's a seat empty, and you'll let me go sit in it anyway, I'd be grateful, that's all."

She and the other two people at the desk all stared at me in confusion. "Is this some sort of joke?" she said.

"I just need to get to Mumbai," I said. "How would you do it?"

"I'm going to call security," she said.

"Why?" I said. "You can just say no. I'm not going to punch anyone and shove my way on board."

I think she was about to do it anyway, but one of the people hanging round the desk was an attendant; he laughed and said, "Wait, no," to stop her, and then went inside the plane for a quick conference with the captain. Apparently one person had called in sick, so now they were shorthanded, and they quietly snuck me on board in exchange for helping out in the galley during the flight. I wasn't surprised, somehow. It almost felt like the way things worked out for Mum, when she wanted to go somewhere. It hadn't occurred to me that she paid for that help, all the time, giving away her own work and help to anyone who asked her. The way I'd helped, now; in London, in Beijing, in Dubai. Even to the people I didn't want to help.

And the universe wasn't giving me back a ride on a private jet, but I didn't mind that. I preferred hanging out in the galley and working with the crew to having to be nice to the owner of a private jet, and for that matter to sitting in a first-class seat without anything to do but think, and absolutely nothing tried to kill me on the way, which put it well up on the many times I'd been on maintenance duty in the Scholomance.

On the other end the attendant who'd brought me on board said to me half apologetically, "I'd better take you to security now and sort out where you belong."

That would have been a tall order. I looked at him and said, "Thanks, but you're better off forgetting I was ever on board," and it wasn't a spell exactly, but I put some mana behind it, and the statement was so obviously true that his brain got on my side and helped; he turned away a moment frowning in thought, and I slipped into the stream of people disembarking and out of his memory at the same time.

It was nine hours all told before I made it to the compound. If you're thinking maybe that was enough time for me to cool down, you'd be wrong. I was only angrier and angrier with every step of the last three miles, which I had to walk, a litany of rage running over and over inside my head. I didn't know what I'd say to Deepthi, to any of them, except to call her a liar, a monstrous liar who'd weighed my whole life down with false prophecy, and tell her I wasn't having any more of it.

I knew where the compound was, because Mum still had the letter from Dad's family, the one they'd sent her all those years ago, asking us to come. It was tucked inside the small flat box, waterproofed with beeswax, where she kept our birth certificates and all the notes Dad had written to her on the inside, and the sketch she'd made of him after graduation, the paper worn down in places because she'd had to erase and try again and again, on paper she'd cried over, trying to make a memory that she could give me when I was born. I never looked in the box, except for all the times I went and looked in it; I never read the letter, except for all the times I took it out of the envelope and read the false promise of it, *We will love you and her as we loved Arjun,* and tried desperately not to wish that I was someone else, someone to whom they could have kept that promise.

And now I was someone else, someone who had proved that Mum had been right all along, right to save me, right to love me, the way they'd chosen not to; now I was someone who had proved them wrong, because I was saving people, even saving enclaves, one after another all round the world, and I was going to rub their faces in it and make my great-grandmother admit that she'd been wrong about everything to do with me, over and over again.

I promised it to myself with every step, panting up the drive walled in on either side with the lush chirping of vegetation and life, cicadas and birds and small monkeys squabbling with one another all round, a surrounding jungle of protection from the skeptical eyes of mundanes. My head was pounding at the temples with fury, and I was ready to get to the gates and smash them to pieces, tear them apart and make them listen, only I came over the final crest and then had to stop, because I was second in line.

There was a maw-mouth at the gates.

It hadn't made it through the warding yet. There was a faint golden glimmering over the surface of the doors and the walls to either side, tracing each of the tentacles splayed out across them. Everyone inside the walled compound had to be casting together, holding up the shields as long as they could. But that wasn't going to be for much longer. The golden light was pulsing and fading all along the line, a sense of struggling and growing weakness. The maw-mouth had been at it for some time, patiently working away on the lock. It wasn't in any hurry. It would get through eventually.

You'd have thought that a great prophet would have been able to warn her own family that they needed to move house, or else they'd all go into the belly of a maw-mouth. And the only reason they wouldn't was because I was here to rescue them, the child they'd betrayed for nothing but a false prophecy: *she will bring death and destruction to all the enclaves of the world,* and now here was a maw-mouth at their gates that one of those enclaves had sent out into the world to roam freely, and if I hadn't been here to destroy it—

I stood there a long, blank moment staring at the maw-mouth as it probed at the gates, trying to poke its way inside. It wasn't anywhere as big as Patience, or even the one I'd killed in London, but it was bigger than the one I'd killed in the library. Loads bigger than the little one I'd killed at graduation. But then, Bangkok and Salta had been young enclaves. There probably hadn't been more than two hundred wizards in Salta when the whole place had gone down, taking all of them with it.

I took my phone out of my pocket and turned it back on.

It started piling up notifications in stacks, but I ignored them all and called Ibrahim. "El!" he said, picking up instantly; I heard a background babble of voices pick up round him at once. "El, where are you? We've all been worried, are you all right? Everyone wants to thank—"

"The attack's about to happen," I said. "I don't know how well the new foundation will hold. You've got half an hour to get clear."

"What?" he said. "El, how do you know? El!"

"Sorry," I said. I hung up and turned the mobile off again, and sat down on a rock to wait for half an hour before I destroyed the maw-mouth, the maw-mouth that had been made forty years ago, in the dark, in Dubai enclave.

Chapter 15

MAHARASHTRA

I PUSHED OPEN THE DOORS after the maw-mouth finished draining away down the road. They opened easily. The wards didn't stop me, and there wasn't a physical bar across them. I had a hazy memory of the colonnaded courtyard on the other side: the fountain gurgling, flowers exploding in profusion over the walls and climbing up the archways. When I came in now, the flowering vines had all withered, and the fountain was silent, but even as I came inside, the water made a choked splutter and then started again, a few brief spurts at first and then back into a steady shimmering fall, and new leaves and even a few flowers began to open off the woody vines.

It was empty, except on the far side, a very old woman was sitting alone in the shade under the awning, waiting for me. I crossed the courtyard and went to stand over her, and she looked up at me, her eyes and the wrinkled folds of her face full only of sorrow and not fear, and she reached out with her trembling wizened hands to close them around one of mine, the skin papery-soft and thin, all the bones pokey through it.

I let her have it. I let her have it, and I didn't howl at her, I didn't scream. I couldn't call her a liar, after all. She'd told the absolute truth. I *was* the one bringing death and destruction to the enclaves of the world. Each time I destroyed one of the monstrosities that all of them were built upon.

"Why?" I whispered, instead. I couldn't ask anything more. I could barely make a sound.

"You already know," Deepthi said. She was stroking my hand, gently, letting the tears drip off her face; they made dark splotches on the fabric of her sari. "To speak the future is to shape the future."

"And *this* is the one you wanted to make?" I said, raggedly, groping after the shredded remains of my anger. She'd seen the future. She'd known, she'd understood, that I wasn't going to be a maleficer, and she'd made a deliberately mis-leading prophecy anyway.

"This is the only one where you ever came home," Deepthi said. "This is the only one where she did not find you, before you were old enough to protect yourself."

"Who?" I said, but Deepthi was right; she was right, as she was always right. She'd never been wrong yet, and even while I was asking, I did know. *We've met El. She's an extraordinary person. I only wish I'd found her sooner.* That was what Ophelia had written to Orion. Ophelia, who had made her own child into a maw-mouth, a creature that only I could kill. "I wasn't killing maw-mouths at five!"

"She was searching for you already," Deepthi said. "She knew you must exist, someone or something like you." She brought my hand to her face and pressed the back of it to her cheek, closing her eyes a moment, and then she straightened up and reached out to pat a low cushioned seat that had been set next to her chair, like a footstool. I sank down on it, my knees wobbly. "She made a great working of darkness. So great she took the lives of many children to make it. A year where no one left the Scholomance at all."

I'd heard about that year. But in the history books, it was a dramatic cautionary tale reminding us to keep a sharp look out for maleficers among us. Supposedly a dozen maleficers had banded together and revealed themselves in the graduation hall, and had taken out the entire senior class for malia to make their own escape. They'd quickly been hunted down by all the vengeful enclavers; that made it also a cautionary tale to any would-be maleficers reminding them to avoid enclavers' children in future. And in those history books— Ophelia Rhys-Lake had been the chairwoman of the Board of Governors. She'd overseen the effort to hunt down the vicious maleficers.

And during that following year, in New York enclave— Orion had been conceived. And so had I. Because Mum and Dad had been in the next year after at school.

"You are the balance," Deepthi said softly. "The gift that Arjun and your mother gave the world, to bring light out of the dark."

There were tears coming down my face. Deepthi reached out and stroked my hair back behind my ear, looking into my face like she was searching it for something that she'd lost.

"I saw many paths where Arjun would come out of school," she said. "Many things that I could have said, warnings, that would bring him home. But not for long. Because in all of them, he would still have loved your mother, and he would have seen her taken instead. And so . . . he would have gone back to the school. He would have gone through the doors, and let the maw-mouth take him, too."

"What?" I said in horror. "Why?"

"Because he understood my gift," Deepthi said, low and terrible. "The Arjun who followed my warning, who lived, would have understood that I had made a choice. That I could have saved *one*—and so she, and you with her, had been taken in his place. And he refused that choice. There was no future in which he let me save him. So I didn't warn him. I only gave him my blessing, and let him go."

Let him go despite her own grief, to have a brief time of love uncomplicated by fear, and to make the gift that he'd after all chosen eyes wide open to hand to Mum and to me, in every possible future that Deepthi could see. Her and Dad and Mum, all of them one after the other in a line putting love and courage and the deep mana of willing self-sacrifice into the universe.

They hadn't got the sutras because they'd handed me over in trade, after all. When Mum and Dad had asked the universe to give them the sutras—huddled together in the dark depths of the Scholomance library, in the tiny circle of light they'd made for one another in that horrible place—what they'd really wanted was to find *another way*. To stop the horror of enclaves being built on maw-mouths. And when they'd offered themselves up, wide open, in return for that request, they hadn't just got a spellbook. They'd got what they really wanted. A child who could destroy the maw-mouths, and lay foundations of golden stone instead.

And part of the reason they'd got what they'd wanted was that at the same time, back in New York, Ophelia had been making a terrible gaping wound in the world—tearing malia out of hundreds of lives to build her perfect, perfectly efficient tool. A new and improved maw-mouth that would go round vacuuming up all the scattered maleficaria in the world, accumulating the power they'd devoured from wizard children and pouring it back into her power bank, tidy and sanitized. And hoovering up councils of rival enclaves, for that matter. A maw-mouth that she could raise up properly and train with flash cards to know who really mattered, which people you oughtn't eat.

"Orion," I said, my throat tight. "How do I help Orion?"

But Deepthi only trembled a little, her shoulders hunching in: the same terrible, shuddering look that I'd seen on Mum's face. "I cannot see him," she said. "I never knew what she had done. I saw only the darkness."

"I have to . . ." I put my hands up to my face, wiping tears away to either side. I didn't know how to finish the sentence. I only knew I had to do something. "I have to go to New York—"

"*No,*" Deepthi said, turning on me with a startling jerk of speed. Her hands didn't have much strength to them, but she seized mine and closed them both around them, clutching clawlike as if she were trying to shelter all of me between them. "You must never go there again while she lives. *Never.* That is the place of her power, and now she knows about you. She will be ready."

"I can't just leave him there!"

Deepthi was shaking her head, urgent, leaning towards me; her mouth was downturned and sagging in deep folds on either side. "Galadriel. I have never been able to give you anything but pain. But listen to me. Listen: I loved Arjun. I knew what he had given for you, not only in this lifetime but in a thousand others he might have lived. I wanted with all my heart to give you and your mother all the love he could not, and so did all of us. Instead I cursed you with my own mouth, so terribly that none of our family would stretch out a hand to help you, and sent you both away in the night, alone, to live among strangers."

I flinched, salt on the wound that was still raw, and her face crumpled as she saw it, more tears rolling down. "I know," she said. "I know you lived in fear. Every time a cruel death came near you, I saw every one. Because of the future that I spoke over your head, my own grandson Rajiv, Arjun's father, might have torn you from your mother's arms that very night. He would have taken you up to the top of the mountain and still holding you in his arms, he would have leapt. I *saw* this. In many paths, it happened. And still I spoke. Because *it was better.*"

There was an absolute, iron finality to her words, like metal stakes going into the ground: nailing down the boundaries of possibility. She never let go of my hands. "If ever Ophelia tries to lure you back there," she said, "whatever she does, whatever evil she threatens, you *must not go*. You must hold tight to the memory of the pain I gave you, and all the love and comfort we would have given you and never did, and know that this is true: *it was better.* You must never fall into her power."

She didn't tell me exactly what she'd seen, but I didn't need her to. I'd lived with it, every day since she'd first spoken the words of her prophecy. She'd seen the maleficer I could have become, the dark queen I'd spent my whole life struggling not to be. That was what Ophelia would have made of me. What she'd still make of me, if I ever gave her the chance.

⚮

Deepthi had me push her chair along the next colonnade and into the biggest wing of the house. I smelled the incense first, then heard the chanting, and we came into a hall with everyone gathered round a raised altar in a many-ringed circle of power, singing together, spells of shielding and protection, still holding the wards up against the maw-mouth that was gone. The children were gathered in the center round the altar, a handful of them old enough to be afraid, huddling near their mothers. They noticed us at the back of the room, and one of them called out, "Aaji! Aaji!"

People began turning to look without breaking the circle or the chant, but then a woman turned, and it was my grandmother Sitabai. Even after the prophecy, she'd secretly kept in touch with Mum by email for years, begging her for photos like table scraps. I'd never wanted to see the ones Mum asked for in return, but I'd glimpsed enough of them to recognize her. And as soon as she saw me, she gave a loud cry, and the circle fell apart in confusion.

Just as well I'd taken out the maw-mouth already.

There was rather a lot of shouting on multiple fronts, until they quieted enough to listen to Deepthi and grasp that the maw-mouth was gone, and also that it was time to welcome Arjun's daughter home with open arms. As you might expect if you'd just asked someone to get a cuppa for Pol Pot, there were a handful of initially bewildered looks, but they very quickly started to shift into realization. They all understood Deepthi's power too, like my father had: *when you speak the future, you shape the future.* They must have been used to her prophecies coming true in unexpected sidelong ways.

But my grandfather went rigid and motionless, something awful in his face, and even as people started to murmur, he came up to face her at arm's length and cut through the rising noise, saying in a terrible voice, "We are leaving your house forever." He turned to my grandmother and told her to pack, and then he turned to me and said, "Forgive me, forgive me, forgive me," and then put his face in his hands and wept like someone had torn out his vital organs.

It was almost down to the exact words a match for one of the many dozens of delightful fantasies I'd had over the years: me swanning in triumphantly, an acclaimed noble sorceress of great renown, having saved them all from some horrid fate and dramatically proving the prophecy false, everyone falling over themselves to apologize for having believed it and condemning my great-grandmother, only it was awful instead. I reached out to him and pried his hands away from his face, and when I got them he put his arms around me instead, and my grandmother ran in and wrapped hers round us both.

I woke up at four in the morning with my eyes sticky and dry with salt, and when I turned on my mobile there were thirteen voicemails, twenty-seven missed calls, and nearly forty texts from Ibrahim, starting with alarm and *how do you know* confusion, moving into *we've checked but no one's broken in,* and *we're guarding the foundation to make sure.* I nearly howled at past-him in rage. Then the texts moved on into the terror of *something's happening! the whole enclave is shaking!* and *we're still inside!* and pleas for help and where was I, please come back, how soon could I get there, settling only a few minutes later into *the shaking has stopped,* and *it's over it's over* and *it's all right* and *the enclave's staying up! Only a few of the—* and I deleted that and all the rest of his messages without reading them, the ones that would have told me how many people I'd killed, what I'd destroyed, when I'd ripped the maw-mouth out from under their feet.

There were a couple of messages from Aadhya, too, telling me Liu had woken up and was okay, and then another demanding to know what was going on and why was I in India; I wasn't sure how she even knew where I was until I inspected my mobile settings and discovered that at some point she'd quietly turned on my location sharing.

I didn't turn it off. But I didn't call her back right away, either. I didn't think I could tell her over the phone. Or at least, not by calling her. I could probably have managed a text: *everything ok, made up with my dad's family, btw turns out I'm the maleficer destroying enclaves, just had a go at Dubai, talk soon.* But I didn't really think that was the best idea. So I settled for *long story there soon* instead, and as soon as I'd sent it, I wanted to make it true; I wanted to get on a plane and get to Aadhya and Liu and tell them everything, as if I could pour it out of me and into them and be shot of every last feeling for a little while.

Next were half a dozen texts from Liesel, all telling me to stop behaving like a child and to call her back if I wasn't in a hospital with heatstroke. But the last one was hours after the others, and it just said: *So now you know.* I stared at it, and then I called her back.

"Yes," she answered, as if she'd expected me to call, which I suppose she had.

"How long have *you* known?" I demanded, a bit waspishly. "Didn't occur to you to mention?"

"It was better *not* to mention," she said, very pointedly, and fair enough; I didn't actually want all the enclaves of the world to know that I was the one blowing them up. I didn't think they'd care that I hadn't been doing it on purpose. "I wasn't certain anyway until yesterday. What are you going to do now?"

"Go back to sleep," I said. "After that . . . I've got to do something about Orion."

"You cannot go back to New York," Liesel said immediately.

"So I've been told," I said. "Any better ideas for me?"

She didn't have one off the top of her head, so we hung up. I did try to go back to sleep. It was still hot, but I was on a hanging bed on a porch outside my grandmother's room, draped with vining flowers and thin shimmery netting that had been imbued with a gentle spell encouraging mosquitoes to go elsewhere and dragonflies to come near: they darted around, the swaying lamp shining iridescent off their bodies, and the fountain gurgling was distantly audible, one court-yard over. It wasn't like Wales at all, except it was just like it, just like being in the yurt. There wasn't any evil lurking down beneath my feet.

I was still so exhausted that my skin felt scraped-tender, but my brain was humming as if the dragonflies had got inside my skull. The real answer to Liesel's question was, I hadn't the foggiest clue what I was going to do next. I had only just barely grasped what was going on. When I destroyed the maw-mouths, I wasn't just destroying the monster. I was undoing the grotesque lie of deathlessness that had created them in the first place, the lie that anchored the enclave foundations into the void. And so . . . down went the enclave, and all the enclavers with it, from the most guilt-stained council member to the most innocent child. Sudarat, that poor kid, telling me her story last year in the gym: *I took my grandmother's dog for a walk and when I came back, everyone was gone.* Her grandmother, her mother and father, her little brother, her home. I'd done that to her, left her standing alone in the street with a small dog, utterly bereft in a world full of things that wanted to devour her.

But I couldn't be *sorry* for it, could I, because my other choice had been standing by while the maw-mouth that kept her home standing devoured dozens of equally innocent freshmen and piled them into the endless agony of feasting going on and on inside its belly. Maw-mouths never got full. They never stopped hunting. Nothing killed them. Except me.

But now if someone called to beg my help with killing one, I'd know that I was taking out an enclave along with it, and everyone inside. I'd savagely resented enclavers at school, but they were still just people. And even if an enclave had been started on a heap of malia, I didn't see what the use was in just smashing the whole place apart. It wasn't the fault of the buildings, or even of most of the people inside them. I'd been caught by the dream of London's fairy gardens, even though I was also the one who had wrecked their wards by frantically ripping lives out of Fortitude at graduation: the maw-mouth they must have tucked inside the Scholomance to feed.

I wasn't sorry to have saved their gardens; I wasn't sorry Beijing and Dubai were still standing, now with more people safe inside them. And I *was* sorry about Salta and Bangkok. But I also wasn't sorry I'd destroyed the maw-mouths. The people who'd died in Salta and Bangkok had only *died*. They weren't being endlessly tortured to death so someone else could live in luxury on their graves. Death was what you *hoped* for, if you were inside a maw-mouth. Death was your only chance of escape.

So what did all of that mean? I knew what Mum's answer would be: *first, do no harm.* But that answer didn't work for me. If someone called me in desperation, trapped with a maw-mouth coming for them, I couldn't let it get them. But if I destroyed it—I'd be sending an entire enclave tipping off into the void, and very likely with every last person in it. My own personal trolley problem to solve.

I gave up on any more sleep and went to go and sit by the fountain, letting the sound of the water fill my ears. I opened the sutras, turning the pages and looking at them without trying to read them, just seeing them as art, the sweeping beautiful lines and the gleam of gold and vivid jeweled colors in the ink. A shining promise of safety that people were ready to buy with murder. And they wouldn't stop making that bargain, because they couldn't get it any other way. I couldn't build enclaves for all of them, I couldn't even fix all their enclaves, and they wouldn't want my enclaves anyway. Surely there were already people in London and Beijing and Dubai who were starting to feel resentful and angry about the space they'd lost, the power they'd have to *share*. Wizards who knew the secret of building enormous enclaves, who knew all the spells, and could cast them again. I didn't know how to stop any of it.

The sky was coming on towards dawn, birdsong rising, and Deepthi came slowly out of the inner courtyard and sat creakily down with me. I wasn't sure if I wanted to talk to her. She'd shaped my entire life with a handful of words, and even if she'd done it to save me from horror, I couldn't quite make myself be grateful. I didn't want her doing it again.

She didn't say anything though, just sat with me, being with me the way Mum did, and slowly a sense came growing over me that she'd gone through this before. All her life, she'd had to choose for the people she loved, knowing she might kill the love in them while she did it. My grandfather hadn't walked out of the house last night after all, but he hadn't forgiven her. He'd known that her prophecies sometimes came true slantwise, but he hadn't been able to imagine that she'd say those words, condemn his son's only child, if they hadn't been true in spirit and not just in the letter. *He would have taken you up the mountain and holding you in his arms, leapt.* That was the only answer he'd found inside himself, the only way he could have borne to save the world from me.

I wasn't sure if I was going to forgive her either. Like Sudarat might not forgive me, when she knew the truth. Like the seniors from Salta, who'd escaped the Scholomance only to find their home destroyed and their families gone.

"How do you stand it?" I asked Deepthi abruptly.

"Sometimes I didn't," she said. "Sometimes I've tried to make others choose, even when I knew that would be enough to take the choice away. And when I did that . . . I lived with what I had seen, when it came to be in the world. So, when I cannot bear to do that, I choose. And then I hope I have done well."

That wasn't especially comforting, as a road map. At least all Deepthi was doing was saying words to people; they still went off and made their own choices. I was going to be tearing down enclaves with my own hands, every time I took out a maw-mouth. Could I make up for it by putting up new ones?

I handed Deepthi the sutras and let her hold them on her lap; her mouth shaped the words of the Sanskrit as she turned the pages. "Arjun dreamed of them," she said. "Even as a boy. Ever since he heard the story of our old home. *Aaji, one day we will live in a golden enclave again.* If I put him to bed, he would ask me if I had seen it. If I told him no, he would say, *not yet.*"

"I'll make one for you," I said, my throat tight.

She closed them and stroked the cover as reverently as I could have asked, although her eyes were wet. But then she reached out over them to take my hand in both of hers. "But not with this," she said softly.

I looked down: she was holding my left hand. The one with the New York power-sharer on it. I swallowed. I hadn't really been pulling from it. I'd put Dubai and Beijing up with their own mana, not mana taken from New York. I'd got to Mumbai on my own mana. And I'd killed the maw-mouth with my own, too. It wasn't hard to kill them anymore, with my own new spell. Really I was just pointing out an obvious fact. Of course they were dead; they'd been crushed into jelly. Just like of course you couldn't build a house in the void. It was a transparent lie, the same lie on both sides: the lie of *deathlessness.*

But . . . I hadn't taken the power-sharer off, either. I'd had it there in case I needed it. Even now that I knew what Ophelia had done to help fill the mana store that was feeding this one. I slowly unclasped it and took it off my wrist. I held it in my hands, and then I flicked it out of existence. It wasn't hard. A jerk of my hand and barely a whisper of mana and it was gone.

Deepthi gave a small sigh that was relief, as if she'd watched me get safely over a hurdle she hadn't known for certain I would take. "Our family has mana saved," she said. "We will build more. And when we have enough, if the universe wills, you will come back and raise it for us."

I nodded, and then I said, "Where am I going?" because I couldn't come back unless I left, but before she answered, my mobile rang again: Liesel calling. I looked at Deepthi; she nodded a little. I picked up. "That was quick," I said, slowly.

"The war has started," Liesel said without preamble. "Alfie just called me. The Scholomance has been attacked."

"I didn't do anything!" I said.

"Not by you! Why would I be calling to tell you?" I could all but see her exasperated expression. "Singapore and Melaka sent in a team to demolish the doors completely, so they would be released from their mana commitments. New York sent in a team to stop them, but the attackers fortified a position and called in allies. And Shanghai has declared they are coming."

Liesel didn't need to spell things out any further: I could see everything spiraling from there. All the enclavers were terrified. None of them knew who was destroying the enclaves, they all thought they might be next, and they all suspected other enclavers. The enclaves of the world had been a massive powder keg even before we'd gone into the Scholomance. I'd lit the fuse the moment I'd taken out Bangkok, and now the explosion was here, the real fulfillment of the prophecy: the death and destruction I'd already brought to all the enclaves of the world, even if I never killed another maw-mouth at all.

Chapter 16

DOWN
THE WELL

THERE'RE ALL SORTS of formal rules for enclave wars, codified in an elaborate treaty to which virtually every enclave in the world is a signatory, all of which get ignored the instant that doing so nets someone a significant victory. But some of the rules are just practical.

You don't fight to take territory. If you attack someone else's enclave, you aren't hoping to move in, even if you manage to kill all the inhabitants, because they'll have left precautionary vengeance spells all over the place. So the only sensible goal of an attack on another enclave is to smash it up completely and send it careening off into the void.

Or, if you're less vicious and more practical, you're looking to establish a position where you *could* do that, and then you hold the enemy over a barrel and demand a ransom in mana, one so huge that paying it will seriously constrain their operations. You might have a team of seventeen artificers who arrange themselves in a particular pattern within the halls of the enclave; you might have a single incanter who manages to seize control of the mind of your Dominus and gets them to pull some sort of self-destructive maneuver; you might pour in a vat of unstoppable acid or send a small army of gnawing constructs, and some enclave at some point in time has done all of those things to another.

Those sorts of enclave wars are mostly carried on by small bands of wizards carefully maneuvering around each other, avoiding any mundanes in the area of the enclave under attack. The would-be invaders try to pry open the enclave and set some operation going, and the defenders try to stop them.

But there's also a messier version of enclave war that can be summed up as *now fight*! The total combatants of any enclave usually number in the low hundreds at most, so you can undermine an enemy enclave very handily just by getting your fighters and their fighters together in one place and killing off a lot of the enemy, although of course they're doing their best to kill off a lot of yours at the same time.

This was going to be a very messy war.

New York could have kept the conflict much more sedate by letting the tourist horde serve as a kind of dampening effect. You can't have much of a sorcerous war when there's a crowd of mundanes standing round, comfortably certain that your incendiary arcana is actually just fireworks. Instead, Liesel told me, New York had got Lisbon enclave to shut down the entire museum grounds and evacuate all the surrounding streets completely by putting out a spurious story of a gas leak, which further required a dozen fire trucks parked all round with their flashing lights going wild and occasionally bursting out the sirens: perfect cover for all sorts of mysterious noises.

Which meant that now almost anything could go. It was an invitation to haul out your biggest guns and all the troops and pile on in, and more or less a statement from New York that *they* were bringing their own biggest guns, too. And no one with any aspirations to power would want to be left out of the wrangling.

When my plane landed from Mumbai, I came out into the baggage claims area with wizards from seventeen different enclaves all staring at each other awkwardly while waiting for the cars that would take them to the battlefield where they'd start trying to kill each other. No one uses translocation spells in a war, at least not to transport the majority of their fighting crew. That's not a rule, it's just common sense: if you do, and the other side doesn't, you can't start fighting until the enemy turns up anyway, and then guess who has loads more mana when you finally all go at it?

I didn't know any of these particular wizards, and none of them knew me; and unlike them, I wasn't carrying any oddly shaped baggage to store my stacks of dangerous artifice. So I just went straight past them all to the bus. Liesel was on her way in, but she was meeting Alfie and a team from London somewhere in the middle. Dubai and Beijing had already announced they were sitting this one out, thanks to recent events. London had an equally good excuse, but apparently Martel had been officially clinging on to the Dominus position for a few more days, and he'd taken this as a chance to cling for longer. He'd declared London was coming to New York's assistance without even convening the rest of his council: seizing the opportunity of the war to try to get Sir Richard or at least enough of his supporters killed off.

Aadhya and Liu had caught a flight, too, although they had five more hours in the air than I did. I'd tried to talk them out of coming: Liu had absolutely no business getting out of bed yet, mystical healing or not, and Aadhya wasn't even *in* an enclave.

"We're not coming to fight an enclave war," Aadhya had said in exasperation; the two of them had already been in a taxi on the way to the airport. "We're coming to help you *stop* one."

"And what are you even planning to do?" I'd demanded.

"We'll let you know soon as you tell us what *you're* planning," Aadhya retorted, and hung up on me, so I'd just settled for racing to the airport as fast as I could to get out ahead.

I didn't in fact have much of a plan. If I tried to head off the fighting by telling everyone that I was the one heaving enclaves into the void, almost no one would believe me, unless of course I told them in a very convincing way, such as by summoning massive dark powers and thundering at them while I floated overhead wreathed in apocalyptic storm, but at best that would turn the war into all the assembled enclavers trying to destroy *me,* and I wasn't really keen on the idea.

I did give some thought to doing it and then just running away to lead them all off after me, but that would have been a very temporary solution, if it even worked. This war had been coming even before enclaves had started tipping out of the world. I was only the proximate event. And in any case, that was nearly the opposite of what I wanted, because it would be effectively winning the war for New York.

As I'm not completely dim, I'd asked Deepthi for advice before I'd gone. She'd put her hands on my head and sung a soft blessing over me, and then she'd shook her head and told me, "Ophelia will be there, and I cannot see past her shadow." So the only rough plan that I *had* formed was to find out whatever Ophelia was doing and stop it, on principle, and regardless of anything else happening. It had the virtue of simplicity, if nothing else.

How I was going to carry it out was a much thornier question. Deepthi and my grandmother and great-grandmother had loaded me up with golden bangles: heavy and clinking round my wrists with the work that had gone into each one: hours of meditation and focus. The love and strength of my family—*my family*, and I still hadn't stopped feeling my eyes smart from the idea—were in them. But for both good and bad, they were nothing like the power-sharer on top of its oceanic well of smooth, unlimited power, the ones that everyone on Ophelia's side would be using.

But it was the only plan I had to go on, so I got myself out to Sintra on the train—there were absolutely no other wizards on it with me; I assume everyone else was coming by luxurious private car if not helicopter—and then hiked up to the estate on foot, dodging the bored mundane security guards who had been hired to patrol the outer perimeter. It was easy enough to get into the park this time, since there were no mundanes beyond them to stop you from just walking through walls, and unlike most of the other guests, at least I knew where I was going.

I had only barely squirmed through onto the grounds when four different spells came straight at me. They weren't meant for me personally; all four of the wizards I assume had been told by their respective enclaves to watch the perimeter and do what they could to make sure only allies made it through, and raise the alarm otherwise. They saw me coming in solo and hadn't any idea who I was, so they all made the exact same decision: to take me out first and ask questions after. None of the attacks were killing spells; one was in fact a really clever spell of happiness that made you feel so delighted with your situation that you didn't want to change a thing about it, and therefore stopped right where you were. But that one and the nastier spell of equally intense depression would probably have canceled each other out when they'd hit me: hazards of throwing attacks wildly in the middle of a general firefight.

346 ✦ NAOMI NOVIK

The other two were of the physical variety; one strangled you until you just fell over unconscious, and squeezed down again anytime you started to wake; the other one went straight to cutting off blood flow to the brain at precisely timed intervals. I caught them all, and I was about to just send them back where they'd come from when instead I thought of Deepthi telling me, *Your gift is to bring light out of the dark,* and I tried to just *hold* them instead, as if I could take the mana out of them and use it for something else later, almost like what I'd done with the reviser spell in the Scholomance gym.

It didn't quite work. I accidentally squashed the four workings together, which essentially turned all of them into miscastings, so instead they rebounded in bits and pieces all round, to what sounded like the discomfort of all four wizards. But I *did* get a few driblets of mana out of the process, enough to think that if I was only working with one spell at a time, I might be able to manage it. The attempt at least got me past that set of border guards, and into the dark and winding circuit of the gardens.

Where I discovered almost immediately that I had no idea where I was going after all. Under ordinary circumstances, when magic meets mundane, the mundane wins by miles. It's so hard to cast a spell in the face of casual disbelief that most wizards don't even try. But you *can* do it if you pour enough mana behind it and keep going, or if you've got enough wizards around, with our total confidence that magic really does work. And with a battlefield-full, the world began to change around us.

All those circling garden paths, which had been meant to make you feel as though you were wandering lost in the wilderness, were spreading out along those lines of intent, almost as if they were *in* an enclave, new branches uncurling to make room for still more wizards hurling still more mana profligate in every direction. Trees were putting out clawed arms or growing unnatural fruit that tried to persuade you to stop and eat; the many statues were coming off their plinths and out of their niches to join the fighting. Strange pieces of artifice were growing up out of the ground—the kinds of impossible structures that defied the laws of physics so forcefully that ordinarily they couldn't be put up outside an enclave. If a single ordinary person did slip through that perimeter right now, or if there was some poor bastard living rough behind one of the bushes, they would find themselves in the middle of a world that had stopped making sense.

I crept round trying to find the initiation well, while silent terrible killing spells went flying overhead so fast and thick that some of them had to be going at the wrong targets. I got all the practice in harvesting bad intentions that I could want without finding a single fight of my own. I caught murder and maiming and agonies out of the air, stuffing them into my metaphorical sack until the gems on all my bangles were glowing vivid red, the crystal hanging round my neck was full as well, and I felt like my skin was going to split like an overripe plum.

By then I had realized that all of us were caught in a working, some spell of endless wandering that was encouraging us to *stay* lost. I suspect none of the other wizards had ever been round here; no sane wizard would have come anywhere near the Scholomance entrance. So they didn't know what to look for, other than someone to fight, and there wasn't any shortage of them in the twisted gardens. But even full-up on mana, I couldn't get out of it.

Or rather, I could have got *out,* but I couldn't get *in.* After that time of getting lost inside London enclave, I'd made a point of looking up a proper wayfinding spell and memorizing it carefully—it wasn't intended to kill or mangle anything, so I had to work to get it to stick in my head—but when I tried it now, I only got back to the front entrance of the park, where the gates were standing wide open and the fire engine lights going in the distance and the park behind me shrouded in dark: an invitation to be on my way, if I didn't like to stay and be a part of the festivities. I gnashed my teeth and turned round and plunged back into the rising confusion of the battlefield.

Mostly no one was paying any attention to me; your assumption if you saw a teenage wizard trying her best to sneak quietly round the battlefield would be that she was a recent graduate who'd clumsily got separated from her enclave's team, and not worth your notice. But the enclavers certainly did notice that none of their deadliest spells were landing, and neither were the ones their enemies were flinging. I was overhearing people debating whether New York or Shanghai had put some sort of muffling enchantment over the grounds.

But they only got more aggressive in response. More and more wizards were turning up, and all of them went on doing their best to kill each other with the hoarded mana they'd all piled up inside their enclaves. I couldn't hold it all, so I started turning people to stone instead. Each time someone lobbed another attempt, I caught it and took the mana and returned fire, and fairly soon the paths I was wandering began to fill up with elaborate replacement statuary.

Which I had the chance to admire over and over, because I couldn't find the bloody well! It was even worse than the last time I'd been here going in circles under the blazing sun with hordes of tourists; at least then no one had been *deliberately* keeping me lost. And I didn't understand the working well enough, so I couldn't work out what it was meant to do. As I went round yet another time in rising fury, I began to give real thought to going back to the gates and taking that as a vantage point and just ripping the gardens entirely off the earth to expose the underground layers beneath, which was obviously a terrible idea, only it began to seem better than just going round and round and round, and then someone shouted out, "El! Galadriel!" into the dark—a man's voice, familiar.

I was all but frothing by then, as you can probably gather from the brilliant idea I'd come up with, so I didn't give a lot of thought to it before I veered off towards the call, into a little paved sculptural nook that had swelled open off one of the paths. Most of the enclave teams were ensconced in small hidey-holes of the sort, to one side or another, which they'd fortified with defensive spells and shield-generating artifice.

I hadn't bothered trying to poke into any of them, because I could simply intercept the spells they flung out. But this one opened for me, thanks to the invitation, so I stepped in and found myself staring at Khamis Mwinyi, who was making one of a team of four—currently two other people and one charming piece of statuary, which was slowly but surely cracking over the surface and emitting a steady stream of muffled noises that I suspect were curses in Swahili. I've never studied Swahili, but the emotion was fully recognizable.

"What are you doing, you crazy woman?" Khamis demanded of me, as charming as ever. "Why are you turning everyone to stone?"

"It's better than everyone killing each other," I snapped at him. "Why are *you* here? Zanzibar's not got more than five seats, you can't be on the hook for massive amounts of mana. What do you care if the Scholomance stays up or not? You're not even allied with New York *or* Shanghai!"

He made a gesture of exasperation at my stupidity, made more alarming because he was holding a massive ancient spear incongruous with his gorgeous red suit; it trailed faint shimmering sparkles with every movement, as if there were a second spear made out of light just barely out of alignment with the solid one. The point of it was made of old pitted iron that looked ready to crumble, so it wasn't the literal weapon it looked like at first glance. He was an alchemist, so I had a strong suspicion it worked on metaphor, and let him pierce an enemy's shielding so he could hit them with some compound from afar. "That's *why* we are here! That's why all of us are here!"

"What, you're trying to get on someone's good side?" I said sarcastically, and then realized that was exactly it. They were one of those minor enclaves that Ophelia had talked about who hadn't been bound by mystical long-term contracts. They'd been able to withhold their own mana contributions to the Scholomance, and now they had a temporary advantage over the intermediate enclaves that was out of proportion to their size. Which they were trying to parlay into a longer advantage, by using it in this one critical fight. They were trying to establish an early position on the battlefield, something valuable they'd have to offer when New York and Shanghai started going at it properly. "And *that's* why you've come out to kill people?"

"What *should* we do?" he snapped. "You're the one who wanted to destroy the Scholomance, change the world! Now everything will be different. So should we keep out of it, wait until the fighting is over and whoever wins decides to tell us what we must do? At least we will have something to say about it, if we can."

He wasn't wrong. He was ready to make a sack of termites out of himself as usual, but he wasn't wrong. The Scholomance had been the major point of contention among the enclaves, the source of wrestling and arguments for a century and change. But it had also been the major point of cooperation. Everything *would* be different, now that it wasn't the one resource every enclaver needed and wanted, worth swallowing almost anything to get a piece of it. And for some people, different would be better, and for others, it would be worse. Zanzibar wasn't stupid for recognizing that this was their best chance to buy themselves some room to maneuver.

And it wasn't just them, of course—that was why the violence was looking so indiscriminate from the outside. Every single enclave was in it for themselves, and all the little ones were fighting it out here in the gardens while the bigger powers hung back, waiting to decide which of the surviving pieces they'd pick up. We weren't trapped in the gardens. Anyone could pick up and go home, anytime they liked. But you weren't getting further *in* unless you demonstrated your ability and your willingness to do whatever it took to get an invitation to the special VIP party. Just like the enclavers in the Scholomance, picking and choosing their graduation allies from among the losers left standing.

"Right," I said grimly, understanding. "So you're out here wrangling for scraps at the table. I don't suppose you know what's happening on the inside? You do *know* there's an inside?"

He scowled at me—my tone might have been just the least bit snide—and then grudgingly said, "We know New York has set up a defense at the doors of the school. Shanghai and Jaipur are preparing an offensive."

"Which they won't launch until things have been sorted out here and they decide who's to be let into the clubhouse," I finished. "Well, I'm crashing the party instead, and I don't know what's going to happen, but it won't be tidy. You should pack up your statuary and go home."

An older man, who had a handful of scars he had deliberately left on—public notice that he was a significant fighter—said something to Khamis in what sounded like incredulous tones, jerking his chin towards me and then the statue, and without waiting for an answer slapped a lancing whip of sharp red light at me, which I expect would have done a great deal of damage to someone else. The basic idea of it resembled a lovely spell that I got my freshman year, which was intended for decapitating a hundred enemies at a go. I caught his line in my hand and let it wrap round twice, and turned it into that other spell, sending the cold blue-white fire searing back towards him. Wisely, he cut loose just before it would have reached him, and I snapped the line back into a tight coil around my hand and tossed it away. I followed that up by throwing another layer of stone on top of the wizard who had nearly broken out one of his arms; it silenced the cursing.

"If you want to stay here killing other people in the dark and letting them have at you back, I suppose you can suit yourself," I snapped. "But come at me again, and you too can spend the rest of the night chipping your way out of a slab of granite."

Khamis said something to the other two I didn't understand, with a gesture towards me that made clear he wasn't being complimentary. However, my demonstration had made an impression, especially on the third member of the party, an older woman, who argued with the other guy a bit and evidently carried the point; she brought a small flat black sack out from under her aba and tossed it over the statue—the sack remained the size of a small handbag, but the statue vanished into it completely—and then gave one of the handles to the fighter.

She meant to give the other to Khamis, but he said something in a surly way, and she nodded; then the two of them set off with the bag, and he turned back to me and said ungraciously, "All right, I'm coming with you."

"You're never," I said, incredulous. "Why would you come with me?"

"Because you're a stupid madwoman who can't be trusted," he snapped: just the reason to hang about someone, why couldn't I see that? Then he added, deeply grudging, "Nkoyo asked me to!"

"What?"

"When I told Nkoyo I was coming, she asked me to look out for you," he said. "You're her friend, not that you deserve her. I told her if I saw you, I would." The implication was very clearly that, much to his regret, his girlfriend had an unfortunate lunatic pal who badly needed someone holding her leash, and he, being the very best of all boyfriends, had been saddled with the job.

I could *gladly* have spent the next hour explaining to Khamis in small words how little *he* deserved to have Nkoyo so much as speak to him, and how totally useless he'd be to me in every possible way, and if we hadn't literally been in the middle of a massive firefight, I almost certainly would have had a go at it, at least a little. As it was, I just snapped at him, "Tell Nkoyo thanks ever so. If you want to tag along after me, you'll have to keep up on your own," and stormed away back into the garden.

By then, apparently some of the other enclavers had worked out what was going on and who I was. They'd presumably all *heard* about me before now: their Scholomance students had come pouring back out all at once, to tell them that induction was canceled and so was school, forever, and half the mals in the world were gone. The details would have been of intense and urgent interest, and my name would have come up.

Of course, just because someone's notable in school doesn't always mean they're notable on the outside; my name had gone on a list of *people to keep an eye on,* rather than the very short list of *people who can have an effect on an enclave war.* I'd have been bumped up in priority as word started to go round about London and Beijing and Dubai, but everything had happened too quick; the news couldn't be more than sketchy gossip yet for most enclavers, and they all had what they thought were different and more pressing concerns.

But Khamis wasn't the only one of my classmates in the field. You might not think an eighteen-year-old would be the best choice for serious combat, but an eighteen-year-old wizard fresh from the gauntlet of the Scholomance graduation hall is often in the best fighting trim of their lives. Some of them had seen me, and told the older enclavers on their crews, and aside from that, by now I'd circled past all their fortified positions four times, with increasing disregard for whether anyone noticed me.

It's also possible that I literally shook the earth a little as I came stamping out of Zanzibar's corner, and maybe I was giving off a bit of smoke and glowing with a visible greenish aura.

For whatever reason, as soon as I emerged, eleven attacks came flying, and these were very much meant for me personally—a wave of deliberate malice and destruction that would have set me on fire, crushed my bones into powder, tangled my mind into gibbering knots, opened the earth beneath my feet. And every last one was only the shadow and pale imitation of what I could have done to them in return. I felt them launch; I was ready to catch all of them and shred them apart into raw mana, but only nine of them reached me. I looked round for the rest and saw a girl I didn't know casting a psychic shield at my back, and a little way down the path Antonio from Guadalajara holding up a stone disk carved with a face, its mouth a square open hole sucking in the fire blast: they'd both been in our year.

At nearly the same moment, three other people yelled, "El!" beckoning to me from different parts of the path, other kids I recognized. I took a bit of the mana that I *had* sucked out of the ambush spells and threw up a common lux spell; it's the easiest light spell there is, so much that even people who've never studied Latin use it, but I always used more complicated and expensive ones, because otherwise I got this: a blaze and a roaring like Guy Fawkes between my clapped hands, and then wide ribbons of neon light exploding away from me in zigzagging streaks, leaving behind a haze smelling of ozone, and the light itself a painfully bright churning orb like a miniature sun floating over my head, erupting with sinister flares of violet and green.

I amplified my voice and called out, "I'm not here to fight any of you, but if you haven't the sense to go home, you'll have to wait until I've gone to go back to killing each other." There was an ominous roll of thunder for punctuation.

No more attacks flew, at least not immediately. The girl with the psychic shield darted over—I recognized her belatedly after I got a closer look at her face: she was an enclaver named Miranda from Austin who'd been waiting for her transition spells until after leaving school—with an anxious look over her shoulder, as if she'd gone against her own enclave's orders. A moment later all the other seniors who'd been calling came out to join us, converging on where we were standing with Khamis. "If you need help, El, we'll help," Antonio said in Spanish. "What are you doing?"

I looked at them, all round me, and in some part of me, I wanted to say, *No, I don't need help. I don't need your help.* Because they were enclavers, all of them, and not reluctant ones; they were here fighting to put their enclave on top. Because I didn't want to need help. Because I did need help and if I took theirs, I'd be dragging them behind me into a fight I had no idea how to win. But I couldn't say no. They had been here fighting, but they'd chosen to come out of the dark, offering to help me.

"There's a tower dug down into the ground, somewhere round here," I said, instead. "Help me find it."

We were trying to find the way down for half an hour; during that time we fended off a handful of attacks without much trouble. That was all we accomplished. The problem was, all of my new allies were combat specialists, which is why they were *here* in the first place. We would have made a really top-notch graduation team—even apart from me personally—but none of us were the kind of experienced artificers who could carefully and slowly untangle a massively complex working of access and concealment.

We were also all the impatient type. As the half-hour mark drew near, we all agreed amongst ourselves that after all the brute-force method was the right idea, and moved on to discussing which part of the gardens I should rip up first. We had just started transmuting a couple of litter bins into a giant pry bar, to serve as a sort of metaphorical lever, when Precious jumped out of my pocket and ran off.

She came back perched on Liu's shoulder, leading her and Aadhya in. I let go of the pry bar and ran to hug Liu as tight as I dared, which was roughly half as tight as she hugged me back. "Are you all right?" I whispered, and she gave me an even tighter squeeze and whispered back, "No," and was wiping tears when she let go, even though she smiled at me. She *looked* all right: I would have liked to find something I could point at and say, *No, you've got to sit this one out,* but I couldn't; she didn't have so much as a bruise or a scar. If anything, she looked *too* good. She'd brought the sirenspider lute, slung over her shoulder, and she was wearing loose graceful clothes. Her short hair was brushing perfectly at chin height, and I had the vague sense that one of her shoulders and one of her cheekbones *had* been a little higher than the other, and now they were all perfectly symmetrical: like someone on a magazine cover who'd been polished up on a computer. And it did help to feel good in your body, to be free from pain, but this seemed more like she'd been papered over by someone who'd wanted to hide the pain from *their* eyes, something they didn't like looking at that was still there underneath for her.

"Is this going to help?" I asked bluntly, instead.

"Staying away would hurt," she said, simply, and fair enough; I'd come for the same reason, after all.

"Okay, so can we all recognize that this is a totally pointless idea that I'm guessing you all liked because it was fast?" Aadhya was saying meanwhile, examining our jury-rigged pry bar. "They didn't *literally* cover the well with dirt. You could rip up the entire garden and you still wouldn't find it. We have to go through the artifice to get in."

"What artifice?" I demanded.

"Have you forgotten the brochure?" Aadhya said. "The whole concept of the garden is you'll keep being lost in the wilderness if you don't follow the right path. And the whole thing's been reinforced by years and years of mundanes going through it. All New York needed to do was just layer a little reinforcement on top, and now you literally can't get into the well unless you've gone through the steps in the right order. You're not going to be able to just bust through. We're going to have to follow the actual initiation ritual."

The problem was we didn't have any idea what that was. The placards all round the gardens were distinctly vague. We found one of the brochures lying half singed under a bush, but it wasn't much more use: it told us what order we had to go to the various places, and that we had to perform vigils and so forth, but provided no details about any of the oaths or incantations. So we got ourselves out of the gardens and broke into the gift shop at the front of the museum and all sat round skimming urgently through the various tomes about Freemasonry. It was almost like being back in a study group at school, which wasn't a recommendation for the experience: it's not very pleasant knowing your life depends on ferreting out an obscure reference in the footnotes of a history book so boring your eyes and brain glaze over in the first ten minutes of reading.

We really could have done with Liesel just then, so of course she didn't turn up. I even went so far as to text her, with no response. Of course the London enclave team wouldn't have been left to wrangle in the gardens with the little people; they'd have been invited directly inside to hob-nob with New York and the other American enclaves, Paris, and Munich. Probably Lisbon, too; I expect it would be rude to leave the host enclave out, even if they weren't quite the power they'd once been.

Liu started cobbling together something out of a few different books, and I worked on translating her work into Latin. Most rituals become a bit more resilient if you do them in a dead language: something about not having the meaning really solid in your own head means that there's room for interpretation. But partway through, Liu paused and said slowly, looking her own work over, "El, this ritual requires a commitment, up front. *You will steadily persevere through the ceremony*—we have to promise to keep going, once we start. The well could become a trap. If they blocked the way out—we won't be able to get out."

"If we couldn't get out, why not everyone else?" Khamis demanded.

"It *would* be everyone," Liu said. "Nobody could get out, even the person who blocked the path. But someone in there might *want* to do that—if they had a weapon that would make people run away."

Liu had more than enough reason to be especially wary of any ritual where you were asked to sign on the dotted line before you knew what was on the other side, but it would be dangerous for anyone. "I'll go alone," I said.

"I don't think you can," Liu said.

"And you *aren't*," Aadhya said, giving my arm a shove. "I'm coming."

"Me too," Miranda said, a murmur of agreement going round, and then abruptly, almost fiercely, Antonio said, "You got us all out last time. You and Orion," and my throat got tight as he spoke. "You got us out for good, and now they're starting a war over the bones. There's a better way. We *know* there's a better way. And you're trying to find it. We'll all come."

We set off to the chapel and took up positions. We were all playing a part: the grandmaster, members of the order, and the new initiate, who had to be me, as there was a solid chance that the new initiate was the only one who would get through, if our makeshift ritual only halfway worked. And if it went completely pear-shaped, the grandmaster would take the brunt of it, so I couldn't argue when Khamis volunteered for the part, although I'm sure he only did it for the pleasure of getting to have me kneel in front of him, which apparently outweighed a substantial risk of bodily harm. I didn't quite *want* the ritual to go all wrong, but I did feel passionately that it would serve him right if it did.

Everyone made a circle and Khamis smugly intoned his bit, and I knelt down at the altar and promised to be a very good knight, trying not to feel silly—you can cast spells that leave a bad taste in your mouth easily enough, but it's difficult when you feel like an absolute twonk. It helped that it was dark, and afterwards we marched in single file from the chapel to the grotto nearby, everyone carrying small spell-lights cupped in their hands, and Liu playing the lute up at the head of the line to lead us onwards. And from the grotto we climbed up a narrow stair through one of the fairy-tale turrets scattered round, stone walls and dark close around us until the stairwell opened up again to let us back into the path, and it began to feel like something beyond the real, to *work*, as we filed silently out.

We were deep into the gardens by then, but there were no sounds of fighting anymore. But it wasn't that everyone else had packed up and gone. We were on the way: I felt it with sharp certainty. The gardens might *look* the same, but we'd moved onto a completely different part of the space, as though we'd gone onto a higher floor of a building. We kept going along the widest path, gradually rising and folding back on itself several times, passing turreted overlooks and alcoves with statues that I didn't remember seeing while I'd been going round in circles. On the next pathway up, we heard a waterfall going somewhere out in the dark; I remembered the sound from being underground in the tunnels. We kept climbing, a steady burn starting in the back of my calves as though we were climbing a much steeper incline. After the next curve of the path, all of us were panting for breath in ragged gulps, the air going thick and moist and clammy on

our skin; every step became a struggle, fighting our way up-
ward, *inward*—until we finally came to a rocky wall, turning
away, and we were at the top of the well, with only darkness
down below.

I knelt down again. Khamis tied the blindfold over my eyes
and took my hand. At least Aadhya was the one holding the
ritual sword, which she'd formed out of our original pry bar.
I wouldn't have liked trusting him with the temptation of a
sharp blade held at my chest. I got up groping in the dark,
and the others reached out and put anonymous hands on my
shoulders and back, Liu still playing the lute softly as we went
down the narrow coiling passageway, footsteps echoing
strange and muffled in the dark.

It was easier going down, in a very bad way: when passages were unusually quick, inside the Scholomance, you always knew they were taking you somewhere you didn't want
to go. And that's where we were going now, with every step:
somewhere we didn't want to go. We weren't actually just
playacting at a ritual anymore. We were going down, deep
into the dark, and we didn't have any assurance that there
would be light on the other end.

I could hear some of the footsteps fall away as we went, as
if some of the others had taken a turning off the path, gone
the wrong way. I wouldn't have been surprised to be the only
one to make it to the bottom. But when the ground leveled
out beneath my feet, Khamis took the blindfold off, his face
hard and grim, and Liu and Aadhya were there, too. Miranda
and Antonio and a boy named Eman from Lapu-Lapu enclave had made it down with us as well, and a moment later
Caterina from Barcelona enclave stumbled out of the passageway, shivering, to join us.

The mouth of the labyrinth was solidly black—no fairy
lights down here now—and we didn't need anyone to tell us

that it wasn't going to be a perfunctory symbolic jaunt to the other side. We made a chain, holding hands, and I took the lead before we plunged into the passageway.

Our lights went out at once. As soon as we were all in the dark, I could hear other people, other voices, somewhere up ahead. I had one hand on the craggly wall, and when a tunnel mouth opened up, the voices came more clearly, on cold creeping gusts of wind. I stopped and listened, but I couldn't make out words or even language over the sound of our breathing. I wasn't sure whether to turn or not, and I had to decide. Finally I kept going: it felt too soon. We needed to go further in.

We passed another tunnel branching on the right, and one more on the left, whispers of sharp wind biting along my arms. I wanted to turn off even more badly each time, but I felt even more certain that it was too soon. The tunnel roof began to lower, and the walls narrowed in, more oppressive with every step, as if the whole terrible weight of the Scholomance was coming down on us somewhere overhead.

And finally we came to another branch, a narrow crack on the left barely big enough to go into, and it didn't feel as though it would be a relief to go that way. The breath of cold refreshing air blew down towards us from the tunnel up ahead, instead, and I had a faint sense of opening up. I put my hand out overhead, and the tunnel roof sloped a tiny bit away, rising. I turned away from it, and squeezed myself through the tight opening, into the branching passage.

The voices began to get louder almost at once, and the tunnel twisted one way and then another and dumped us abruptly into another well, the same size around as the other one but made of rough-hewn slabs and columns that looked as though they were falling into each other, propping each other up.

There was a spiraling ramp in front of us, and it ran upwards to a wide open circle above that was full of stars and fresh air, but that wasn't the way we were going. I remembered the place from our infuriating tourist visit, when we'd been slogging around futilely trying to find the way in. At the time, this well hadn't been any deeper than the other one. It had stopped here. But now it kept going down. The voices were coming from below, echoing up through the hollow middle from a dark place down below, further in. We went down the spiral, down and down and down three more sloping circles, and then abruptly the ramp bottomed out in the massive cavern before the Scholomance doors, the one Aadhya and Liesel and I had found before.

Only this time, the whole place was full of wizards.

The doors had been fixed up, set back into their frame, and there were dozens of people in front of them, manning fortifications that were growing more elaborate by the moment. I recognized one of them: Ruth, the woman I'd seen in the train station in New York. She was sitting in a folding chair directly in front of the doors, in the middle of the shattered starburst of the floor. She looked just as beleaguered and weary as before, but every few moments she lifted her hand, with the vague impression it was a massive effort, and then she moved it just a bit, the same smoothing motion you'd use to pet the back of a ruffled cat, and another square meter of the ground pressed itself flat away from her. The engraved words of the spells settled back into place as she did it. One of them had just been made whole, and it went flaring gold with renewed power, which was just nonsense: you couldn't *mend* artifice that complex, only obviously she could. She must have been controlling the entire floor on an atomic level.

But opposite the New York crew, at the far side of the cav-

364 of NAOMI NOVIK

ern where the ground hadn't been quite so badly smashed up, a second array of wizards were putting together the mirror image of their work: siege machines. The magical sort, long narrow lances mounted on a lightweight metal frame, piercing spells like Khamis's spear, meant to get through a shield. They were being lined up on either side of a pair of long red banners blazoned with the characters for SHANGHAI in gold, and a pair of golden ones with JAIPUR written out in red.

No one paid any attention to us at first. There were only eight of us, after all, and eight wizards weren't especially important on the scale of this fight. Another dozen appeared on both sides just while I was watching, wizards who hadn't had to take the long way in; near the golden JAIPUR banners there was a horizontal pulley set up, ropes going into a big curtained box like a magic trick. "That's a ghandara," Aadhya said, low. "Long-distance transport artifice. You can pull things in from more than ten miles away." Four wizards were cranking the gears round as fast as they could go, and every four or five turns, the ropes came out with a wizard on the other end clinging to them, blindfolded, to be quickly helped off and sent into the frantic preparations.

I couldn't see what the New York side was using, but wizards were coming from somewhere over there as well, more of them every few minutes, like clowns piling improbably out of a car. There was a command center to one side of the doors, a raised metal floor with sections unfolded out from its sides, ready to shut itself back up again into an armored box when the enemy fire began to fly, loaded with senior wizards in there directing things; I spotted Christopher Martel among them talking to a Japanese woman, presumably Chisato Sasaki from Tokyo, and a tall dark-haired man that Caterina said was Bastien Voclain, the Dominus of Paris. Maybe Liesel's target was over there: Herta Fuchs of Munich was surely in that crowd, and her daughter and son-in-law might have come along. There were a few other American wizards looking sufficiently impressive that they must also have been Domini or whatever the plural ought to be. And seated amidst the rest of them, an old woman with a tidy cap of silver hair in a black dress with a collar of sapphires and diamonds, who might have modeled herself after a Hepburn photo shoot: Aurelina Vance, the Domina of New York.

On the Shanghai side, the command center was less obvious; there were a dozen cloth pavilions up at the back in ornate drapery, red and blue and green embroidered with silver and gold, concealing anything going on inside. But surely they had their own ranks of the powerful and important gathering.

My plan was already well off the rails, because the one person I *didn't* see was Ophelia, anywhere. I would have liked to believe that something had gone wrong for her, that she'd lost her grip on power, but I didn't. If I couldn't see her, that only meant she was doing something even more horrible than anything I could have imagined, and I had no idea what it was or how to stop it. I didn't know which side to go to. Presumably Shanghai's side would have had a stronger interest in helping me stop her, but I'd be more likely to get information about what she was doing on the American one.

I stood there like a lump dithering over which side to go to. It didn't seem like a choice I'd get to make twice. There was a feeling of a critical mass being reached, as if the space couldn't hold much more of us, of *mana*. If I wasn't imagining it, the ceiling was receding up into an increasing dark that didn't belong in the world. This many wizards using this much magic all together was making the place become *less real*.

I'd just made up my mind to head to New York's side and try to find Liesel among the throng when a spell unexpectedly came flying right at me out of one of Shanghai's pavilions. I reached out to snag it like the other spells I'd been plucking like ripe fruit, and I failed completely: the thing slid through my grip like trying to grab hold of a water balloon covered in oil. I flinched automatically from the hit before I registered that it hadn't done me any harm at all; there wasn't an ounce of malice in the thing. It was only someone taking a polite grip on my arm, conveying the intention to save me from stepping into something really unpleasant like dog poo, and to tug me invitingly another way: *please won't you come.*

Which was quite alarming really: whoever had tossed that spell had already worked out, presumably based on gossip and my performance in the gardens above, that you couldn't use malicious spells on me, but *neutral* spells would hit just fine. They could easily work out some way to use that against me. The politeness wasn't a comfort either, more the opposite; if they'd decided I was someone worth being polite to under these circumstances, then they'd decided I was someone really dangerous.

But on the other hand—at least they were willing to talk to me. And I couldn't actually see Liesel anywhere over on the American side, or even Alfie or Sir Richard for that matter. The only person I *did* know over there was Christopher Martel, who certainly didn't feel any affection for me and might not feel he'd exhausted the options for trying to use me for his own stupid selfish purposes. He'd already dragged his entire enclave into this mess, for no reason other than to keep clinging to his own power.

"All right," I said grimly, "I'll come—" which turned into a loud squawking yelp: as soon as I'd said "all right," the polite spell snatched me up and thwoomped me like a yanker spell straight across the field and into the pavilion it had come from in the first place. I wasn't even left to catch my own balance; the spell stopped me and braced me on all sides at the same time, so it felt almost as though actually I hadn't moved and the rest of the world had just been neatly rolled over a little bit beneath my feet to put me in the proper spot.

There was a chair right behind my knees, a beautiful one carved of wood with the legs made of storks, and another one directly across from me. They'd both clearly been placed deliberately, waiting, but no one was sitting in there. The only people inside with me were two fighting wizards, wearing quilted silk clothes and holding what really looked a lot like machine guns. They didn't flinch at my appearance, but I reckon that was because they both seemed to already be as tense as any human being could manage. An odd brazier-looking thing was sitting in the middle of the tent right between the chairs—a spell holder, I realized after a moment. Only normally a spell holder is a pendant-sized thing, and this was the size of a very large charcoal grill and holding a bed of glowing fist-sized coals, each one of them a *different* spell, primed to go off under different appropriate circumstances.

One of them—that tidy yanking spell—was just fading away, crumbling into pale ash. Someone had *prepared* that spell, in advance. It hadn't been based on my rampage through the gardens at all. Whoever had cast it had *already* somehow worked out that malicious spells weren't any use on me, even before I'd understood it myself.

I had a bad moment staring at the heap of spells, wondering which of them were about to go off in my face, and then the curtains at the back of the pavilion opened and a short Chinese man came in, wearing a Mao suit made out of some kind of fabric that looked almost like denim, with the buttons made of metal. The guards looked at me with expressions that successfully conveyed both a passionate desire to riddle me with bullets and also the anguished terror of knowing it wouldn't do the slightest good. The carved phoenix at the back of the chair uncurled its head to peer at me with similar anxiety.

"Ms. Higgins," the man said, then seeing my *ugh no* added, with a faint smile, "or may I call you El? I am Li Shanfeng."

The Dominus of Shanghai.

"El's fine," I said, flatly.

It was no wonder the guards were ready to have at me instantly. Every Dominus was a powerful wizard, the valedictorians of their enclaves and not just of a single year at school; the Dominus of any major enclave was on another level. But Li Shanfeng was just as far beyond them.

All of us at school knew his life story; aside from being excellently dramatic, it was a fairly critical part of recent wizard history. As a boy, he'd survived a maw-mouth attack on Shanghai enclave that had forced them to abandon the place. He'd come out of the Scholomance as the most brilliant artificer graduate in living memory, with offers from every major enclave in the world. Instead, he'd gone home and done what everyone thought couldn't be done: with a circle of wizards behind him, he'd gone into the maw-mouth and destroyed it, so they could take back the enclave.

And then he'd rebuilt his home from an abandoned half ruin into one of the most powerful enclaves in the world. He'd developed new construction techniques that allowed modern enclaves to build vastly larger and more elaborate structures. That mana-brick stamping machine in Beijing had almost certainly been one of his designs. So had those elaborate new foundation disks. Every powerful Western enclave had paid enormously in mana and treasure to get hold of them, and he'd taken that wealth and used it not just to re-

build Shanghai, but to support the other major Chinese enclaves, too, and sponsor dozens more beyond, and ultimately
to force a reallocation of Scholomance seats, so they could
save more of the independent wizards living near their own
enclaves.

It had been a story not just of improbable success but of
even more improbable generosity. Big enclaves often sup-
ported smaller ones in return for various kinds of tribute and
fealty, but he had given away more power than he'd kept,
helped other enclaves become so large they could rival his
own. It wasn't the sort of thing enclavers did; it wasn't the
sort of thing any wizards did.

Except of course—now I knew how he'd been doing it.
He'd saved his own enclave from a maw-mouth, and then
he'd gone off and *made more of them.* For every enclave he'd
helped put up, he'd unleashed another maw-mouth on the
helpless, unprotected wizards of the world who didn't have
enclaves to shelter in, and he'd known, *he'd known* what he
was doing, in a way that even the worst council member
couldn't know. He'd stood inside a maw-mouth and felt that
devouring limitless hunger trying to get at him.

Something of that must have shown on my face, because
the guards twitched—they didn't quite raise their guns, but
they *wanted* to. Because they wanted to protect him: their
hero. I looked at them and said to him savagely, "I'm guessing
they don't know, do they."

Shanfeng spoke to the two guards; they looked horribly
miserable but after a moment they went out of the pavilion
and left us alone. "No," he said. "It's very difficult to tell anyone who doesn't already know. The compulsion of secrecy is
very powerful. It has been attached to the foundation spells
for a very long time—from the very beginning, I suspect."

I suspected, too: it wasn't the sort of secret you could hope to keep *without* magic, after all. Whoever had come up with this lovely way of building enclave foundations back in the distant mists of time had wanted to sell their spell to all the top bidders—but they'd probably been a bit anxious about what other people would think of their clever solution. So they'd worked up a spell to make sure you couldn't tell anyone until they first accepted the compulsion to keep it quiet themselves. "Can't have anyone seeing the dirty washing," I said.

Shanfeng nodded as if it wasn't anything to do with him. "The compulsion also requires you to charge fair market value for the spell before you can share it. And the restrictions even carry over onto any improvements or modifications you make to the spells yourself. They were designed to be controlled. Unlike those." He indicated the sutras strapped across my chest in their protective case. "Please, sit."

He seated himself; I stayed on my feet. "Did you have any improvements in mind for *them*?" I said caustically. "I'm sure they could do loads more if you just added a little mass slaughter here and there."

"I can see you're very angry," he said, demonstrating he possessed all the observational abilities of a dead stick. "You have every right to be. But we don't have much time. Once Ophelia knows that I am here, she will act. And then . . . you will have to choose."

"I don't see much choice between the two of you. She hasn't built forty enclaves' worth of maw-mouths," I said. Although that wasn't entirely true. As far as my gut was concerned, he *was* better. He wasn't a maleficer at all. I reckon *other* wizards had actually carried out the enclave-building spells; he'd just helped them along. Perversely, it only made me angrier, as if there was some virtue in Ophelia getting her own hands dirty.

"Ophelia and I are fighting the same war, and have been for many years," he said. "It breeds similarity—and compromise. I've done many things I regret. But the ones I regret the most are the choices I made without information. That's what I'm here to offer you, if you'll take it."

"By which you mean, you'd like to tell me what a terrible person Ophelia is, and how much better you are," I said. I'd come over here precisely because I wanted information, and to stop Ophelia, but now I almost wanted more to tell him to go jump in a crevasse. But I swallowed the impulse. Otherwise what would I do? I could storm over to the New York side and talk to Ophelia a bit, get enraged at her again, come over here and chat with Shanfeng, get angry at him, and ping-pong back and forth until I just exploded us all in a final maelstrom of fury. "Go on, then. Tell me something I don't know."

If I had ruffled him, he didn't show it. He paused, and then said in a very level tone, "When I entered the maw-mouth, I was inside armor that I'd built, with a circle of everyone I loved—all my living family, my friends, every wizard I could persuade to help me—fighting to keep it whole around me. It was six days before I glimpsed the core of the maw-mouth. But of course, I was not going anywhere, that whole time. I was only making it smaller. By killing all the people inside it, before they could drag me down into their own torment."

He doled out each word at a measured pace, as if he had to keep a firm control over them. It had been fifty years ago, but the tendons in his neck were standing out sharply, and every internal organ in my belly flopped itself completely over in sympathy, sharing the memory of that same horror. I wanted to just scream in his face, or vomit.

"But I couldn't do it," he said.

I stared at him. "What?"

"It was a big maw-mouth. It had eaten a lot of lives when

it broke into Shanghai. Too many: I couldn't kill them all. And my circle was running out of mana," he said. "That's how you destroy them, isn't it? You just kill everyone inside."

"I used to," I said, blankly. I was still trying to deal with the idea that apparently an entire circle of wizards *hadn't* been enough to replicate my method. "Now—I just tell them they're already dead."

He nodded in understanding. "But that works for you, surely, because you've already done it the hard way, once. You speak to them now from the certainty of their death. I couldn't do the same. But I had already studied enclave-building by then. I knew the fundamental challenges of establishing a foundation in the void. So when I got close enough to the core of the maw-mouth, I understood what I was looking at. The foundation of some other enclave. The longing of a circle of wizards for a place where they and their children can be safe and powerful. The bottomless hunger that makes us willing to devour others down to their bones."

He was right, I suppose, but I didn't see what good that understanding would do you when you were six days deep inside a maw-mouth and running out of mana. "What *did* you do?"

"I found only one way to defeat that longing," he said, tiredly, a sound of years of looking in his voice. "By overwhelming it with our own. I had been working on a tool to clarify the will of a wizard, to amplify it—"

"A reviser," I blurted, remembering Zixuan using his version against me in the gym.

"Yes. I had one with me. It didn't help with the killing. Killing is already very simple. But once I was in range of the core—I was able to use it to amplify *our* longing, the longing of my entire circle, to have our home back. To have our own place of shelter and power. And there were just enough of us in my circle that, with the help of my reviser, our longing *replaced* the longing at the core. We created a new foundation for Shanghai upon it. But—"

"The maw-mouth *wasn't* destroyed," I said, sickened, in understanding.

"No. But it was much smaller. The process required as much mana as founding an enclave—and it extracted that mana from the maw-mouth itself. I was left outside. We were able to translocate what was left of it away, before it could take any of us, and put wards up to keep it out. We had our enclave back, even stronger than before, with a doubled foundation. But later that same day, as I lay weeping alone, one of my friends came and whispered to me that another enclave had been destroyed. The enclave in San Diego—on the other side of the world."

It hadn't occurred to me before how odd it was to have a maw-mouth from Bangkok squeezing through the Scholomance gates in Portugal, a maw-mouth from Beijing gnawing at London's gate. But as soon as he said it, with emphasis, I understood at once.

Shanfeng nodded, seeing it in my face. "After the Scholomance was built, more wizard children began to survive. And so more enclaves began to be built. After the Second World War, there was a new one going up in America every five years, sometimes every three years. Their neighbors helped them—for a price. But of course they didn't want those new maw-mouths lurking nearby. So they opened great portals and sent them far away. To countries with few enclaves, or where the old enclaves had been ruined and destroyed, or made weak, and there was no one who had the power to object. Like China."

I didn't demand any proof. It was perfectly obvious. "So you built enclaves enough to even the score, and sent your maw-mouths back the other way."

"I've tried to negotiate agreements with other major enclaves to slow down the pace of enclave creation," Shanfeng said. "But it doesn't work. Why would a circle of wizards in Dublin, with enough mana saved, agree to wait and die so that a circle in Guangzhou could have an enclave and live? And though London enclave could have agreed to open their doors to the wizards of the Dublin circle, to give them a home, instead they sold them the enclave spells to build a new one of their own, in exchange for years of mana. Which London needed to pay off their war debts, because they had built five new entrances to protect themselves, and sent the maw-mouths all to India."

"Wait," I said, appalled. "*Each* entrance—"

"Yes. For each opening to the void, there must be a foundation. And a maw-mouth beneath it."

That was why Yancy and her crew could wriggle through the old, closed-off doors, I realized. Not just because of mana and memory. Because the maw-mouths beneath London's gates were *still out there,* devouring wizards, all to save London's fairy gardens from going down under Nazi bombs.

"We have all made as many enclaves as we could, as quickly as we could, even though we knew that in the end, we were building our own destruction together," Shanfeng said. "And now the pace of that destruction will come more quickly. Because you have killed so many maleficaria, and the maw-mouths have less to eat. So they will have to hunt wizards instead."

Like the maw-mouth attacking London's damaged wards, and the one crawling over my family's compound outside Mumbai. There'd been an arms race going among the enclaves of the world, a race heading to the bottom, and I'd come blundering in and pushed it along faster. I put my hands up, pushing my hair back from my face as if that would give me more air, let me breathe out against the squeezing pressure that was really coming from inside my skull, even if it felt like an external force.

"That isn't your fault," Shanfeng said. "It's ours. None of us could find a way to stop. We debated and quarreled and cheated and made excuses—and the enclaves went up. And so Ophelia decided that she had to break the stalemate—to *force* us to stop." He smiled wryly. "At least, to force *enough* of us to stop. That was what she sought to do."

"With Orion," I said, understanding instantly: *this* was the *information* he really wanted me to have. And I knew that I wasn't going to want it at all, but I couldn't walk away from it, either. "What did she do to him?"

"I must first explain the principle," Shanfeng said. "Fundamentally, a maw-mouth is a method of establishing a point of harmony in the void—a place in the void that can support material reality. The foundation stone is the first core piece of reality that we ask the void to support. Then you can build out from there. But the foundation doesn't need to be *large*. It could be as small as a single atom. You simply couldn't build a very big enclave on it. But Ophelia didn't wish to build an enclave."

"She wanted a weapon," I said.

"She wanted a child," Shanfeng said, correcting me mildly but insistently, refusing to take the opening I'd handed him, the chance to make Ophelia out to be a monster, as if he didn't want it made that easy for himself or me. "An heir, if you will. A conscious reasoning mind that would carry out her goal, with the almost limitless power required to achieve it."

He paused—working out how he was going to hit me with it, I reckon, while I worked at not screaming at him. "She took a single embryo, and sacrificed it to create a very small maw-mouth," he said. "But where enclave-builders use that power to establish a foundation, she fed it back into the child she had crushed. That was how she fused the two together to create the being of her vision: a wizard directly in contact with the void. A wizard who was also a maw-mouth."

I swallowed bile and horror. "How do you know?" I managed, a pathetic desperate stab at fending it off. "Did she give you a rundown?"

"No," he said. "But we have eyes in New York, as they surely have eyes on us. The year that all the children died at graduation, we realized that someone—either from New York enclave, or with their connivance—had done *something*. We didn't know what at first. Then we heard of the child, Ophelia's child, who could kill maleficaria at the age of three. After that, we spent a great deal of effort investigating."

I didn't want to believe him. "I'm surprised you didn't hurry up and make a human maw-mouth of your own," I said through my teeth. "Couldn't find someone to stomach it?"

"I don't have the moral high ground, and I won't pretend to," Shanfeng said, with horrible determined gentleness. "What I do have is an experience, a piece of information, that Ophelia did not have. Because I, like you, have stood inside a maw-mouth. And so as soon as I knew what Ophelia had done, I understood that she hadn't found a solution at all. She had only hastened the end for us all. Because a maw-mouth can't ever be satisfied. It can't ever be controlled. As you yourself must know."

He stood up and walked out of the pavilion opening, past

me. I wanted to just curl up in a ball or even better run away somewhere to the other end of the earth. He was right. I did know. I followed him out, each step dragging.

We'd only been in the pavilion a few minutes, a few sentences, but outside, everything had changed. Aadhya and Liu and the rest of our small group were still in what I thought was the same place—peering anxiously in my direction—but the entrance to the well behind them had vanished. The cavern wall was smooth and unbroken. There wasn't any way out.

And the two sides had almost completely swapped their positions. New York and their allies were swinging their fortifications aside, hauling up offensive weapons instead; on this side, all round me the siege engines were being pushed unceremoniously away and defensive walls were coming up. It was as though the whole thing had been a double bluff, on both sides, and now all the bets had been called and the real cards were coming out onto the table.

"This *was* a trap," I said. "The whole thing's a trap."

"Yes. For all of us." Shanfeng waved his hand in a sweep across the chamber, taking in *all* the assembled wizards, everyone in the place. "There are no real sides, for Ophelia. We all hunger, so we are all the enemy, in the end. She wants to intimidate and control her own allies as much as those of us who oppose her. But I knew she would spring the trap as soon as I came myself."

"So why did you come?"

"Because *you* came," he said, simple and dreadful. "El, when we realized what Ophelia had done—we had to make a choice. When we chose *not* to act, *not* to follow her path, we knew that we were giving up the power to stop her. But we also knew that she had created a vast and terrible imbalance in the world. So all these years since, we have been watching—and hoping—for the counterbalance. We were growing very worried," he added, dryly.

"And now here I am?" I said through my teeth. "What do you think I'm going to *do* for you, exactly?" I didn't need to ask. I already knew what he wanted me to do. He wanted me to do what I was made for, the thing I alone could do. He wanted me to *kill Orion,* and I was going to make him *say* it, I was going to make Shanfeng look me in the face and ask me to do it, to kill my friend, so I could tell him to go to hell.

"But it's not just you," Shanfeng said, gently.

I stared at him, taken aback, and for one incredibly stupid moment, I thought he was giving me some kind of hope, some chance of a reprieve. "There's something else—"

But he wasn't. "It's *both* of you," Shanfeng said. "You, and the child Ophelia made. The boy we heard about from our own children as they came out of the Scholomance each year of the last four. The boy who saved the lives of others, who took no payment, and paid no attention to which enclave they were from. Ophelia got—not the hero she wanted, but the hero she deserved."

There was a sudden flaring of light on the other side that jerked my head round: a hideously expensive portal opening. Ophelia came out through it onto the big central platform among all the other leaders of the Western enclaves, perfect serenity in her body language. They all moved towards her with eager smiling welcome, ready to court the queen; Martel was in the lead, putting on that same avuncular face. And Ophelia was turning back, holding out an ushering hand, as Orion came through the portal right behind her.

He was wearing an outfit that might have come straight from the closet in the fake boy's room Ophelia and Balthasar had made him, aged up appropriately: expensive ironed trousers and leather shoes and a crisp shirt. The only wrong fashion note was the watchbands on both his wrists, as if she'd decided they needed a bigger pipeline going to the mana store. But *Orion* was all wrong, inside it: his shoulders were rigidly stiff with tension, his jaw clenched and his hands shoved deep inside his pockets, a figure held together by wire.

Every last Dominus of all those enclaves was eyeing him with the same exact calculation as every kid in the Scholomance ever had, in the library and the cafeteria and the classrooms, trying to think about how they could get him to sit down at their tables. And he was paying them exactly as much mind as he had then, which was to say none. Less, really; they were all saying things to him, I could see their mouths moving, and Ophelia was trying to introduce him round, but he wasn't even being dutifully polite. He turned his back on all of them and went to the edge of the platform.

I could see him more clearly with every passing moment: they were getting closer. Ophelia's arrival had been a signal to their side. Ruth had stood up from her folding chair with her palms towards the ground, concentrating in real effort. She was *shrinking* the cave, reeling all of us in closer for the fight that was clearly about to start. The fight New York was sure they were going to win, with their new unstoppable weapon.

"We knew that you had to exist," Shanfeng said, next to me. "Some power in the world that could balance what she did. That would have the power—"

"To *kill Orion*?" I spat, wheeling on him in rage: I wasn't patient enough to wait until he got round to saying it himself, after all. "To murder the person who saved all your kids, everyone who came out of the Scholomance—"

"He is already dead," Shanfeng said, steady, gentle; not an ounce of malice, and as brutal as if he'd slapped me hard across the face.

I stopped. My ribs were a cage around my chest as I tried to keep breathing. There wasn't enough air in this cavern, in the whole world.

"I was six years old when the maw-mouth came to my home," Shanfeng continued, and there were tears trickling down his face, along with that horrible, unbearable sympathy: the weapon he'd found that could be used against me. "My father carried me in his arms. My mother ran on ahead, holding my sisters' hands. And then the maw-mouth reached out of a corridor between us. My father turned and ran the other way. Over his shoulder, I saw it take them. El, I would have given everything I had, I would have left all Shanghai enclave to fall into the void, if I could have brought my mother and my sisters back out. But I couldn't. There is only one gift that you can give to the devoured. The gift only you can give him."

I could have beat Shanfeng's face in with my fists. Because he was right. Orion *was* the hero Ophelia hadn't wanted, the hero who had understood finally what she'd done to make him—and wouldn't go along with it. Who wouldn't agree to feed a maw-mouth just to keep the rest of him alive. *I can't be all right,* he'd said to me. Not unless Ophelia could undo what she'd done.

But she couldn't. The parts of him that loved me, and wanted to be a hero, and had asked for help, couldn't be separated out from the rest. Because those were the parts of him that had been fed to a maw-mouth in the very beginning, the parts that the maw-mouth was holding up in the void, like a horrible which-came-first puzzle where the answer was it didn't matter, because in the end, it all went into the pit.

Ophelia had gone over to talk to Orion, a small frown on her forehead, a hint of mild concern. I could imagine the conversation they'd had when he'd come home to her. She'd been completely straightforward and honest in that letter after all. She trusted him. She had confidence in him. She believed he'd use the power *well,* the power she'd gone to all these lengths to give him. She'd even been honest with *me,* too. She wanted exactly what she'd told me: she wanted to stop wizards cheating, and she wanted to stop new enclaves—with their *unique costs*—from being built, and she wanted the ones already out there to *share.*

All the very best ends in the entire world, only she'd used them to justify the very worst means. And when Orion had come home and begged her to undo them, I was sure that she'd explained to him very kindly but firmly that she couldn't, and then she had probably told him that he oughtn't fuss, and to think about the greater good. As if the bloody wanker had ever once in his entire life stopped to think about anything but the pathetically small good directly in front of him: the child that needed saving right now, the mal that needed stopping.

I expect he hadn't bothered arguing with her for long. What was the point? She didn't have the necessary information. She'd never stood inside a maw-mouth and felt it trying to get at her, trying to *take everything.* You couldn't *use* a maw-mouth. You couldn't keep it fed to its satisfaction. It never got full. All you did, each time you fed it, was grow its hunger for more. Ophelia didn't know that. But I knew, and Shanfeng knew, and *Orion* knew. So when she'd asked him to come here, to help her with her grand design of crushing half the enclaves of the world and terrifying all the rest into meek submission, he'd come along, but he wasn't here to help her. Even as Ophelia was talking to him, he was scanning the rest of the room, looking at faces.

Looking for *me.*

And when he found me in the crowd, all the way across

the rapidly shrinking cavern, the worst part of it was—his shoulders came straight down. Our eyes met, and for a single clear bright moment—it wasn't longing in his face, it wasn't even love; he'd've needed hope for anything like that. He looked at me and only me, and all I saw was—relief. Relief, and *trust,* the utter bastard, *trusting* me to— And then he relaxed just as if he'd taken a good long deep breath and let go of some terrible burden he'd been carrying. Only what he let go of was—*himself.* Of the thin fragmentary shreds of hope that Mum had given him, in that tiny hut deep in the woods: the only thing she'd been able to do for him. The relief slid down over his face like a lowering blind that took all emotion with it, and what it left behind was the thing—the *maw-mouth*— that I'd found sitting quietly alone in the Scholomance, because it didn't have anything left to hunt.

But there was a full buffet laid on here.

Ophelia frowned and reached out a hand to Orion, as if she'd noticed something had gone wrong, and then paused, just before she touched him. The thing with Orion's face glanced at her bright-eyed and empty, and she took a step back. It didn't immediately go at her. After all, she was only a single wizard, and a strict-malia maleficer at that, who didn't have any mana of her own and rationed the amount of malia she pulled. She wasn't more than a single broken crisp by maw-mouth standards.

But then Orion looked over towards *Ruth* and pricked up like a hunting dog on alert, sniffing out prey. She had her eyes shut and her hands spread wide, her jaw clenched and trickles of red-stained sweat running off her as she worked: a delicious bonbon, at least, and as if she'd felt the interest, she jerked and opened her eyes and stared back at him, and abruptly stopped her working, her face going blotchy with alarm. She took a step back. All the wizards on New York's platform were starting to back away as well, terror wiping away smugness as they all suddenly noticed there was a bloody *maw-mouth* standing up there with them, ready for dinner.

Ophelia was the only one not retreating. Maybe she didn't feel it the same way, or was too determined not to realize what she'd done. She said something to Orion, gesturing out across the plaza, towards all of us massed together on the Shanghai side—maybe thinking he had just got turned round and needed a reminder of who he was meant to be fighting? I don't know, but the maw-mouth looked over and was apparently willing to take suggestion.

He came down from the platform towards us, a horribly *fluid* movement. Pleased with herself, I expect, Ophelia turned and gestured to Ruth, who had the good sense to eye her in some doubt, shaking her head slightly. But after all, it was clearly an excellent idea to offer Orion an alternative meal plan, so in a moment she did start her working again.

I was standing at the very back of Shanghai's side, with Li. Orion was walking steadily towards us even as the ground pulled in, like moving walkways in the airport, or a conveyor belt going straight into an incinerator fire. The front ranks of Shanghai's side were already starting to throw attacks at him over their fortifications, hurling all the same useless spells that people had tried to throw at me, up above, and they did just as much good. Every spell wanted to rip him apart and kill him and hurt him, and he wasn't catching them and picking them apart; he didn't need to do that much work. He was just absorbing them without a pause.

People fell back as he came closer, frantically shoving the defenses out ahead of them as they scrambled, a wall of artifice and barrier spells. He paused as he reached it, and then—he *reached out,* in some way I couldn't describe. It wasn't something I saw, it was something I felt in the same way I could feel magic, or love and rage. But even though it wasn't visible, it was *there*, a grasping tentacled hunger uncoiling, and everything it touched just—went into him, with shrieks of unraveling almost like human voices. And then it *was* human voices, the first human voices screaming, as he reached through the openings he'd made, and seized hold of the nearest wizards, the stupider or braver ones who hadn't got far enough out of the way.

I flinched with horror, with every kind of horror there was. All of us did. Even the wizards on New York's side were flinching back. I could see small distortions in the air around the platform, the other Dominuses trying to open up portals. They didn't want to watch *this*, I suppose. But none of the portals opened. Shanfeng had been right. This wasn't just a trap for him. It was a trap for all of us. Ophelia did want to take Shanfeng out, because he was the biggest threat: the only wizard in the world who *could* have built a bigger weapon, if he'd chosen to follow her down the path. But she also wanted every last enclaver in the world, even her own allies, to understand that she had a nightmare weapon she could and would use against all of them, and that meant that when she finally let them out of here and they all went home, they were all going to do exactly what she told them.

I turned back to Shanfeng in desperation, looking for anything, any way to get myself and Orion and everyone else out of this trap she'd built. And he *was* holding something out to me, across both palms. A chain with a polished disk the size of a saucer, swirling black and silver, in a powdery black steel frame: a power-sharer, only ten times the size. I could feel the power flowing through it even without touching it. "I can't force you to save us," Shanfeng said. "I can only give you what you need to do it. All the mana we'd stored to build a second school, freely given."

I could have slung it at his head, I could have screamed at him. But I couldn't have heard myself over the rest of the screaming, the struggles of the wizards trying to save themselves. Their shields were already starting to go in bursts of sparks. They were being dragged over the floor by inches, towards Orion.

"Ophelia took her own child and fed it to a maw-mouth, and to pretend she hadn't done it, she dressed the maw-mouth in her child's skin," Shanfeng said. "That is what is standing there. Not the boy you loved, the one who offered himself up to save other children. Would he choose to do this?"

"Shut up!" I snarled at him, so angry it came out of me in a sound of many voices, enough to make him flinch back from *me*. "You don't *care* what Orion would have chosen. Any more than *she* did."

I grabbed the disk out of his hands and turned. I blasted out the evocation of refusal all the way over the entire force, a shimmering dome several inches thick, with a glaze of oil-slick rainbows all over the surface. The screams died away into gulping sobs as the evocation shoved Orion back, pushed his grasping reaching arms away.

The wizards he'd grabbed hold of tumbled to the ground, set loose. They all started crawling away on their hands and knees shaking. I ran through the ranks right up to the wall of the dome. The whole distance only took me three steps, because I was going in the direction of Ruth's pull, and together her intent and mine hauled me straight up to the iridescent wall almost instantly. The dome was covering exactly half the cavern, the curved wall lined up perfectly with the shining golden inscription in the center, MALICE, KEEP FAR, holding Orion on the other side.

But he was looking in at me with bright hungry eyes, interested. He reached out to the dome and put his hands on it, and the surface began to run away from around the pressure of his fingers, swirling. It would hold him for a little bit, but not for long. He'd learned how to get through it already once before. A maw-mouth wasn't mindless hunger. It was made out of the longing of all the wizards together who had made it, their longing to live, all the art and cunning and desperation they could bring to achieve that goal.

And Ophelia had made this one out of the frantic hunger of a whole year of Scholomance students, trying to get through the gates: she'd taken the losers and the enclavers both. Maybe even the enclavers especially, so close they could taste the rest of their enchanted, gilded lives opening up ahead of them. She'd taken all the yearning life out of them, and she'd poured it into the void through her perfectly untainted child, crushing him and then building him back up again around the maw-mouth she'd made.

And even if Orion never looked out of his own face again, she'd still go on trying to use what she'd made. She'd feed the maw-mouth half the wizards in this cavern and afterwards she'd find a way to pen it up until it was wanted once again, and then she'd make a portal and guide it through. And maybe that would even work for a good long while. This thing would go with her, because it would know she was taking it to dinner. She'd have it trained up a treat in no time. And all of those people would go on screaming inside forever and ever, screaming along with the first sacrifice, the single pure soul she'd found to crush down into the void: Orion. And the only person left to stop it was me.

I didn't do it. I didn't do anything. I just stood on the other side of the dome watching him pushing his way through, with tears running down my face and all the mana in the world dangling at my fingertips, only it wasn't enough. It wasn't enough to make a different world.

His fingertips began to work through, and then he closed his eyes and put his face against the dome between them and pushed it through, little by little, the surface separating away from around his nose, and his lips, and his eyes. And as soon as his face broke the inner surface, Orion opened his eyes and looked at me, *Orion* looked at me, and he said, "El. Please," and he wasn't asking me to get him out at all. He was asking me for the only gift I had to give. And if I didn't give it, that thing was going to come through and it was going to take me, and everyone else behind me, and probably it would go on forever, deathless, undying, until on some distant day it had finished devouring every last scrap of mana in the world and then slowly gnawed itself away after everything else was gone.

"El," Aadhya said softly behind me, her voice shaky and terrified and full of tears, but there; she was there, reaching out to put her hand on my shoulder. Liu was there holding her other hand, clutching the lute with tears running down her face. They'd come to me, to be with me, even though everyone else was only desperately trying to get away.

And then Khamis was there too, heaving himself forward with his whole face clenched up with the same determination he'd worn when he'd faced me down at school, and he snarled at me, "Do it! Do it and get it over with, you stupid girl! What else are you going to do, leave him like that? You might as well feed him to Patience yourself."

I could have punched him in the face; I could have kissed him in gratitude, for the single spark of rage lighting up in me, burning off despair in clean hot fire. "No," I said savagely, to Khamis, to Orion; to Ophelia and to Shanfeng. *"No.* I'm not going to leave him like that," full of a sharp-edged golden clarity like the shining letters at my feet, the prayer from the Scholomance doors: MALICE, KEEP FAR.

But malice had been inside the Scholomance from the beginning. Those doors had been built on another maw-mouth, a maw-mouth that had refused to be sent away, because there was no better hunting ground in the world. Patience. And it was still here. Orion hadn't destroyed Patience. The Scholomance was still standing. He'd *devoured* Patience, the way Patience had devoured Fortitude, the way that between them they had devoured a century of children's lives. And all those children were still in there, still screaming, still suffering. I couldn't leave them like that. I couldn't leave any of them like that.

I had to kill Orion Lake.

I put the chain with Shanfeng's massive power-sharer over my head, and then I slung my bag forward and took out the sutras. I opened them and held them up, let the book rise up from my hands, the golden incantations shining. I reached out on either side to Liu and Aadhya, squeezed their hands tight, felt their love and strength in their answering grip.

"Keep hold of me," I said. "Don't let go. Please." Orion had almost made it through the shield, and I could feel their terror, too; their hearts beating through their hands. It wasn't fair to ask, but I asked it anyway. "Please."

"We're here," Liu whispered, and Aadhya said, shaking, "We won't let go." They put their hands on my shoulders, just like when we'd started coming down the well, and after a moment, Khamis put his hands on their shoulders, the contact running through to me like an electrical spark.

Orion broke through the dome. It shattered and went falling away like shards of thin ice, vaporizing before they even hit the ground. He came towards me, and I didn't step back. I reached out and took hold of him and gripped him in my hands, all of him: the horrible seething hunger and all the works built on top of it, everything that required that endless fuel. The school that Sir Alfred Cooper Browning had built to save the children of enclavers; the expansion that London had made to let in so many more. The many dozens of enclaves whose maw-mouths had crept into the Scholomance looking to feed, and been swallowed up by Patience and Fortitude in their turn. And Orion. The child that Ophelia had sacrificed to try to stop a rising tide of maleficaria, and I said to him softly, gently, with all my heart, "You're already dead."

It barely took any mana at all. I was just telling the obvious truth, telling all of those devoured children the truth: Orion, and everyone who'd gone into the Scholomance and hadn't come out, and the crushed sacrificial victims under every maw-mouth that Patience had swallowed up. They were already dead, and that was horrible and unfair and agonizing, but it was the truth, and it did, actually, set them free, as the maw-mouth that had devoured Orion, the maw-mouth that was holding Orion up, heard me, and recognized that yes, of course, it too was already dead.

There wasn't a sloshing rush of flesh and rot: Ophelia's efficient maw-mouth didn't need to keep the bodies round, having a better one of its own. But I still felt them *going*, like one single enormous sighing out. And the mana went with them. The mana extracted from all those lives, which had even to this moment been holding up enclaves all over the world, and the Scholomance itself, and the life of one boy; it all went draining away, and Orion's body shuddered under my hands like the deck of a rolling ship, or the waves beneath it. The ground underneath our feet shuddered and rolled the same way, the bronze doors of the Scholomance groaning horribly. There were cries and shouts from the platform as all the cracks Ruth had mended began to open up again and widen, the whole room wavering. Rocks were coming down from overhead; this cavern had slid halfway into the void itself, connected to the Scholomance, and it wasn't going to survive the school coming down.

Orion was almost sliding out of my grip, as if I was trying to hold on to something just as impossible, a different magical wonder built into the void. But I didn't let go. I held on, to Orion, to the Scholomance, to the teetering distant enclaves that I couldn't see, all of that magic built on top of a tiny single-celled place in the void where the maw-mouth had been. "You're already dead," I said. "But *stay anyway.* Stay with us, and *shelter all the wise-gifted children of the world,*" and made all three of the spells into one: the terrible murderous truth I had to tell the maw-mouth, and the sutras' longing plea for golden shelter, and the beautiful lie that the Scholomance had been built upon, and into that working I poured all the mana that Shanfeng had given me, the mana that had been saved up to build a school to save the lives of children. The work that Orion had tried to make his own.

I repeated the incantation in Sanskrit from the sutras, the incantation that really just meant "stay," and then Liu joined in, saying it in Chinese, the version she'd used in Beijing, and Aadhya said it with me the next time in English, "Stay and be shelter," and even as we were speaking I felt more jolting sparks going through me: Miranda and Antonio and Eman and Caterina had joined our human chain too, behind Khamis, and then there was a thump through us all like a lightning strike: Li Shanfeng had joined the chain behind them.

I gasped with the surge and said it again, *stay,* even though I couldn't hear myself speaking anymore; more hands and voices were coming, everyone on Shanghai's side streaming to join in, power crackling through the line into me, and then Liesel's voice was calling out over the noise, "Not in a single line! Get closer and spread out!" and she pushed in next to me, putting a hand directly on my back, another supporting branch. Alfie was right next to her, reaching to touch me as well with Sarah gripping his free hand. In another moment, his father was there too in a line behind him. Wizards from both sides were crowding in now, all of us saying it together: "*Stay,*" getting louder and louder even as the Scholomance and Orion both shook from their foundations.

He was getting heavier and heavier in my grasp, as if I was trying to hold him up, along with the entire school and all those other enclaves loaded up on his shoulders, against the dragging undertow of all the sloshing power of stolen mana draining away from under them. But everyone behind me was trying to help, trying to hold them—and then Ophelia and Balthasar were there, too. But they didn't join the chain: instead they came all the way up and put their own hands directly on Orion, next to mine.

And then Aadhya, my darling Aad who'd taken that first mad flyer on me, gritted her teeth and put her hand on Orion too, and other people started to grab on to them, spreading out the weight, pouring in more mana. We were all holding on to him and just saying it over and over, *stay,* in all the languages of the world, and beneath our feet a golden light was rising up out of the widening cracks in the carved inscriptions, filling them in, starting to make them whole, and there was light all around us, warm, full of hope, as Orion lurched forward under my hands, like someone who'd just been pulled back onto solid footing. He gasped and reached out to me, reached his hands out to cup my face, and he said in a ragged, broken voice, choosing, "I'll stay. El, I'll stay," and kissed me, through our tears.

Chapter 17

THE
SCHOLOMANCE

T HE TAXI DROPPED ME AND MUM at the gates at the end of the drive, a cloudpuff of small green birds going up out of the trees as we stopped. We waited until the car had driven away before we opened the gates and walked down to the compound together, between the high walls and the jungle singing on either side. It was drizzling a little, but we didn't open our umbrellas, the mist and breeze cool and pleasant on our skin in the heat. We didn't rush. Mum had got more and more quiet as we came, and she'd closed her eyes to meditate a few times in the car on the way. She didn't stop now, but she took my hand, gripping it a little too tight.

We didn't make it quite halfway before my grandmother was running down the drive to meet us, as if she'd been lying in wait with eyes on the road: maybe those birds. She stopped a few lengths away, hesitant, looking at Mum and me with her eyes wet and uncertain too, her arms half held out, and then I felt Mum take a deep breath and let it out, a deliberate release of fear and pain, and she let go of me and stepped forward with her own hands held out. Sitabai almost jumped to meet her, reaching out to grasp them.

The first night, Sitabai and my grandfather had us to a quiet dinner in their own living room; the second night we asked in a handful of other people, second and third cousins who were just a few years older than me. The gathering size gradually ramped up over the course of the visit, until we were eating with the whole family in the courtyard on the last night.

Mum had sat and talked with Deepthi that whole morning, and then she'd gone out into the jungle, to a little waterfall cliff that my grandfather had shown us that he'd said Dad had loved. She'd spent the rest of the day there and come back with her peace—not quite intact, maybe, but expanded, I thought. She'd hugged me and whispered, "I'm glad I came."

I wasn't certain that I was myself, yet, but I thought I might have to keep coming back to make sure.

But I'd had to come back at least the once. I'd put it off as long as I could. I'd been sleeping with the sutras under my pillow again, just like at school. But on that last night, as the platters and the younger children all got carried off to be washed and put away for the night, I finally made myself take the sutras out of their box, and I took them over to where Deepthi was sitting in her sheltered corner of the courtyard, the breezes whispering in through slatted walls.

I sat next to her while she held the book in her lap and opened it to the back with the tidy insertion Liesel had written up, ten solid pages full of casting diagrams and new incantations. I'd spent almost a month working on it with her and Liu and Aadhya: most of it inside London enclave, grimly seasick every single minute with the hideous feeling of all their maw-mouths still lingering *out there,* somewhere in the world, gnawing endlessly on their victims.

"I can't help you with Munich, but," I'd said, on my way to

asking what she'd want for helping me, and Liesel had just waved an irritated hand as if she wasn't letting go of a years-long dream of revenge and said, "Enough. Of course we have more important things to do," and the *we* in that sentence was one that I *could* be a part of, after all.

Alfie had talked his dad into letting us come in and look at all of London's foundation stones, putting together a plan for replacing them. The first one in the council chamber, at the heart of that old Roman villa at the bottom, carved of limestone that had been worn horribly soft over the centuries with the Latin spells going muddled around the edges; the ragstone blocks from the Conquest and the Tudor age that now stood underneath their massive library and the green plaza of the dead children—the dead children that *were*, after all, only the ones they'd chosen to put on display, and not all the ones who'd died to keep the enclave up.

The biggest one was the one forged of steel, the one that was buckled down the center, deeply deformed: the one they'd built on Fortitude's back, in 1908, to put up their fairy-tale gardens in the void. That one didn't make me queasy anymore. All its engraved spells were gone, blurred together as if someone had melted them in a forge, but if you looked at it from a slant, you could almost make out a single word instead: STAY. As if the golden spell we'd all cast together, before the gates of the Scholomance, had gone rolling all the way down through the terrible chain of death, through Orion and Patience and whatever had been left of Fortitude, and fixed the foundation back into the void.

But there were five more besides that, the foundation stones laid hurriedly down in the midst of the war. They'd been built with less mana, so they couldn't support more than a corridor or two on their own, but the maw-mouths had gone out into the world all the same. And they were *still* out in the world, somewhere. Still devouring all the victims they'd ever taken, and looking always for more.

So Aadhya and Liesel had helped me tease apart the sutras to find the lines of power in the spells, those beautiful golden lines I held in my hands as I built a new foundation, as I spoke to the void and asked it to *stay*. And Liu had worked out a way you could perform the spells with a *chorus* of casters at the center, instead of a single voice. As long as they were *all* strict mana.

"Sanjay and Pallavi have already got the incantations down," I said: two of my many, many cousins, who both happened to be specialists in Vedic Sanskrit incantations. "They'll be able to teach the others."

Deepthi nodded, her face sad, and reached out to cup my face with her cheek. "Are you content?" she asked me softly.

I didn't answer her right away. I wasn't sure. I put my hand out to touch the sutras again, let my fingers stroke over the familiar pattern of the cover again; I could have drawn it with my eyes closed by now. That was still the work I wanted, the work I could have done with joy. But other people *could* do that work, now. And I had to be glad about that. I'd had to find a way for other people to do it, because if I was the only one, like Purochana had been, the only wizard in a thousand years able to build enclaves of golden stone, then after I was gone—everyone else would go back to the way they already had. They'd start making maw-mouths once again. And I knew that for bloody certain, because they were ready to do it *now*, while I was still right here.

Everyone had joined in to help during that last panic at the doors of the Scholomance, down to the most vicious and self-ish council member in the world, but that was because they'd been trapped in a cavern about to come in on their heads, and it had been a matter of immediate self-preservation. But now—

well, the rulers of forty enclaves had been in that cavern, with unlimited access to their enclaves' mana stores. I didn't know how much mana it had taken to replace all that old stolen power underneath the Scholomance, underneath the other enclaves, but I suspected most of their coffers were empty. And they wanted to refill them.

Literally the morning after, I'd been sitting up in the highest corner of the Sintra gardens, with the dust of the near-collapse still clinging to my skin, when Antonio and Caterina had come to me bright-eyed and eager to ask if I'd be willing to join them as a founding council member in a new enclave they wanted to put up. They wanted to build a sort of wizard daycare, where indie wizards who didn't have extended family could drop their little kids off for the week and pick them up for the weekends and holidays when they had more time to look after them. If it went well, they could start one on every continent! A whole franchise of enclaves!

And they could actually do it, they assured me, because the council members of their two enclaves had offered to give them a *wonderful* rate on the enclave-building spells.

They went on for several minutes just brimming over with grand plans and idealism before they noticed my expression and also the simmer of storm clouds gathering overhead, and trailed off uncertainly. If it had been anyone else, I'd probably have howled them off the face of the earth; as it was, I told them to go and ask Aadhya or Liesel why that was an extremely bad idea, and they nodded and hurried away and left me to seethe my way through realizing that my career goals had gone obsolete.

If they were left to their own devices, enclaves would go on selling the same old spells, because that was how enclaves got loads of their mana. And wizards on the outside would go on buying them, because they wanted huge modern enclaves, and they wouldn't know exactly what they were buying—they wouldn't *want* to know—until they'd already poured half the mana that they'd raised over decades into the price, and couldn't get it back out again. And then they'd get to make Shanfeng's choice: to let their children die in the maw-mouths built by other enclaves, or make a new one of their own.

I'd tried to stop it with words, with explanations. But it was almost impossible even just to tell people about the maw-mouths underneath the enclaves. The compulsion spells were even nastier than we'd realized. All the people in charge of things like, for instance, the *Journal of Maleficaria Studies,* or the secret Facebook group that all the older wizards were in, were *council members,* all of whom had needed to sign on to the compulsions before they were allowed to attain those rarefied positions. And it wasn't just that they couldn't tell other people, they were compelled to *hide* the information. Anytime we tried to post something online, it would get taken down or altered, and our accounts kept getting locked and deleted.

And the harder we tried, the worse it got. I was on my third phone now because the two before had been mysteriously fried shortly after I'd used them to group-text a few dozen people. The only reliable way I'd found for sharing the information was literally for one of us who already knew to personally tell people, face-to-face. And we were already being called trolls and overimaginative children, to boot. It wasn't going to be very hard for people to put that comforting wall back up, in front of their own eyes or someone else's.

I'd tried going at it from the other direction, too. I'd passed the word to every council member in front of the Scholomance gates that I was willing to replace their foundation stones, too, and all they'd need to do was gather the mana to do it with. And I'd passed the word around to all the independent wizards, too, as best I could: I would build them a brand-new Golden Stone enclave with just a few years' worth of mana beneath it.

I'd had a grand total of zero takers so far. To get the mana to replace a foundation stone, most of the enclaves would have to open their doors to three times as many wizards. And one of the little golden enclaves wouldn't have enough room to do more than tuck kids in at night. There were a few wizard circles, mostly ones formed by our classmates, who had *started* on saving up the mana. But all the ones that already had it—well, they were having a hard time agreeing to spend it on a golden enclave, when the old enclaves were offering the spells to build massive modern ones at cut-rate prices.

It wasn't going to stop. It wasn't ever going to stop, not if I *left them to their own devices.* So someone else would have to do the work that I'd wanted to do, the work of building that sang to me, and I would have to go and do the work I didn't want, the terrible work that only I could do.

Because there was one and only one thing that would make enclavers throw their doors wide open to all the independent wizards of the world, replace their foundations, and turn their enclaves into shelter for them all. *Fear.* Of the unknown maleficer, the scourge of enclaves, still roaming the world, about to bring them down. That was why they'd done it in Beijing, and that was why they'd done it in Dubai: because they hadn't had any other choice. They'd had to share or watch their whole enclave go sliding off into the dark. And when that was your choice, suddenly sharing didn't look so intolerable after all. That was how Alfie had talked Sir Richard and the rest of London council around to the urgent necessity of replacing all of those eight remaining maw-mouth foundations: he'd persuaded them that their odds of getting hit *again* were too high for comfort.

So I couldn't do the work I wanted myself, but I could make room for the work in the world: by fulfilling Deepthi's prophecy and bringing death and destruction to all the enclaves of the world. By hunting down the maw-mouths that stood beneath them.

And as soon as I got *close enough* to one of them, once I had a maw-mouth in my sights—then Deepthi, and the four other members of my father's clan who'd inherited some degree of her gift, would *know* which enclave was going to go down when I destroyed it. And then they'd tell the enclave, the way she'd told Dubai, and they'd also offer to come over and replace their foundation stone just in time. The way I'd done in Dubai.

So every time I tracked down a maw-mouth, another enclave would have to open up their doors, and one by one they'd absorb all the wizards who would have built new enclaves. Maybe more wizards would even start to work strict mana, over time: my family would share the spells from the sutras freely, and surely other enclaves would want to have the power in-house. And the more maw-mouths I destroyed, the quicker it would happen.

Deepthi was still waiting for an answer: was I content? I took my hand off the sutras, and left them in her lap. "I'll find a way to be," I said, firmly, and meant it. I'd told Orion as much myself: I was alive, and out of the Scholomance, and so was everyone I loved, and I hadn't had any right to expect even half that much.

So the next thing I did, obviously, was go back to the Scholomance.

I hugged Mum goodbye at the airport; she was going back to Wales. "Maybe you'll have two homes, now," she said to me, smiling through tears, and kissed me. "Come soon." I boarded my own flight to Portugal after she'd gone.

The big placards on the outer walls of the museum park still said CLOSED FOR RENOVATIONS, and there were polite blank-faced guards on the gates making sure no mundanes got inside. But in the gardens the worst of the mess had already been tidied up, statues returned to their proper places—whether that was by repairing them and putting them back into their niches, or by turning them back into people. One mistake had been made in that direction which had resulted in several people getting chased round the garden with arrows until the single-minded Diana in question had been turned back into stone.

The way to the school was temporarily wide open, by which I mean it was only three spells of concealment to work through and then ten minutes slogging through dank tunnels to get back to the entry plaza. But the doors were back on their hinges, and the repairs in the graduation hall were almost completely finished; the sound of work was echoing down the big maintenance shafts from the upper levels, where massive teams of artificers were hard at work installing the new dormitory levels, almost twice the former size. The rooms would be a bit bigger, too, but not for luxury: from now on there were going to be two students to each one.

Shanfeng and Balthasar were in the workshop when I rode the lift up, so I stopped to see if they needed my help for any of the heavy lifting; I'd been able to shave a few solid weeks off their time estimates, just by heaving some of the bigger pieces up the shafts. "No, I think we will not be needing your assistance any further," Shanfeng said, consulting his many diagrams. "The construction process is on schedule. We will be ready by September."

"And the trial run of the new induction spells yesterday

went fine," Balthasar said. Then he paused, and hesitantly told me, "Domina Vance decided to retire. Ophelia's been elected."

I didn't congratulate him; I stomped away seething instead. She'd murdered an entire year's worth of Scholomance students, performed a hideous act of human sacrifice on her own child, and had nearly destroyed us all: obviously the only thing for it was to make her Domina.

I had been trying with some difficulty not to let myself recognize that I was in fact going to be doing exactly what Ophelia had been trying to achieve all along, forcing enclaves to stop proliferating and *share.* Mum had tried to gently reassure me that I wasn't anything like her, and that the means mattered as much as the ends, but that wasn't any help; I already knew. I was just angry. I wanted Ophelia to *pay*, and instead she was getting almost exactly what she'd wanted, and if she was even sorry about anything she'd done, it was news to me and would *stay* news to me, since Deepthi had once again firmly warned me off going to New York and shoving Ophelia's face in a rubbish heap.

The warren of seminar rooms were in the same places they'd always been, meaning that they were in completely different places than any other time I'd been trying to find my way through to any of my lessons. But they didn't feel the same. The cleansing machinery had been updated and refined, and the walls of mortal flame had gone back and forth a dozen times during the tuning. Even the oldest stains had been scorched away, everything clean and bright in the new lighting that had been efficiently strung throughout the place, tiny constructs made of LEDs and mana, vastly cheaper than the old ones. But it wasn't the visible stains that were the real difference.

I'd hated the school ever since I'd first come in, as if all along I'd felt the horrible lie that lived down at the heart of it, the rotting flesh beneath our feet. And now that lie was gone, replaced by that plea we'd all made together: *stay and shelter us.* I was having to *work* at hating the place, dredging through all my worst memories of being jumped in this corner or that one, sneered at here or there.

I sullenly shoved my way into the gymnasium. I was so determined to hate *that,* at least, that I didn't even notice the tiny palm-sized digester that peeled itself off the wall and flung itself towards the back of my head. Stupidly; it hadn't got halfway when it was snagged out of the air and vanished with a snap, and I jerked round with Orion grinning at me smugly. "I'm opening up a lead," he said.

I glared at him. "You're *not* opening up a lead, you wanker; you'll be the rest of your life catching up to me." He only beamed at me, undampened.

We weren't sure how he was still able to suck mana out of the mals, now that his inner maw-mouth was gone. The only plausible explanation had come from him: he'd shrugged and said, "I've always been able to do it," with the faint air of wondering why we found it surprising. That was the kind of belief that could let you do almost anything. Orion wasn't being held up by a maw-mouth anymore, but he *was* still connected directly to the void: we'd just built him a golden new place to stand.

With the Scholomance and a dozen other enclaves piled up on his shoulders like Atlas, except he didn't seem to even notice the weight was there. All was right with the world again, as far as he was concerned. The bastard wouldn't even be mad at *Ophelia.* I'd had to stop talking to him about it. The morning after the fighting, he'd told me earnestly that she'd made a terrible mistake and she'd apologized to him and asked him to forgive her and *he had,* and I'd nearly gnashed his entire face off in frothing rage. I'd have considered forgiving her after she'd spent the rest of her life scrubbing out the toilets of the families of every last wizard child she'd killed, only I wouldn't really.

I'd made him come with me to Wales and spend as long as it took to unearth his trauma by talking with Mum and going out with her circle and taking long walks in the woods. After three days, Mum had sat me down firmly and told me that Orion had been distressed for a very good and concrete reason, which I'd *fixed,* and it was all right for him to be just fine now that it was gone, and I needed to stop trying to make him be traumatized, and also *I* was the one who needed some treatment. I ended up spending several weeks trudging around the commune with Mum myself, instead, before I couldn't stand it anymore and wrote to Liesel in desperation to get some work to do.

"What are you doing here anyway?" I added. "There's not a single child in the school to guard yet, you don't have to lurk in here like a goblin."

He said mildly, "I like it here. Anyway, it's too hot outside," which was absolute nonsense. It was indeed too hot outside, because it was a sunny day in the middle of August in Portugal and I'd nearly had heatstroke just getting from the palace to the well, but that wasn't the shadow of an excuse for *preferring the gym,* even if at the moment it was full of huge old trees rustling softly in a faint breeze, and a wide stream running the whole length of the chamber, up and down a hill and gurgling over grey rocks, with a perfect little red arch of a bridge leading to the pavilion.

We went and sat on the steps together. There was a jug on the table inside with cool water, and one bowl full of fruit, a second one full of edamame.

"How many maw-mouths do you think there are, out there?" Orion said.

I half shrugged one shoulder. I didn't really want to think

about the numbers. When the maw-mouth was killed, the enclave came down in a crash, but it didn't happen the other way round. Enclaves could be lost from the world, forgotten, their entrances blocked up, their wizards killed or tumbled away in the void. The maw-mouth they'd made didn't vanish at the same time. It kept creeping on round the world, still endlessly hungry. And how many enclaves had been made in the last five thousand years, all of them set atop lives crushed down into the void? Hundreds at least. And the maw-mouths would all be hiding from me as hard as they could.

But I'd have help, at least. Aadhya had taken Liu home to her place in New Jersey, to get a bit more rest—and an enormous amount of feeding-up—before we started, but the plan was, once the school was well on its way, we were going to meet in Cape Town. There had been seventeen sightings of maw-mouths in South Africa in the last month. Jowani was waiting there for us.

Liesel would be sorting us out a network from London, or rather two of them. The first one was officially a public maw-mouth survey meant to help people avoid them, now that they were attacking wizards more aggressively: people all over the world would be sending reports of maw-mouth sightings to her. The second network was going to be a small and carefully handpicked group of our schoolmates scattered round the world, and they would all be in on the actual project. They'd help get our little hunting party quietly in and out again, ideally no one else the wiser, and also file false sightings of the late unlamented maw-mouths afterwards, just in case we'd been spotted, and in various other ways throw a veil of confusion over my activities.

All very clever, but I was fairly sure that people were still going to work it out sooner or later. Later, most likely, because we'd just packed a decade of upheaval into a single fortnight, and everyone was still reeling. Even most of the people who'd joined the chain of mana down in the cavern didn't fully understand what exactly we'd done. They'd come into the working because they'd seen Shanfeng helping us, or Ophelia, or because they'd been terrified of having the roof fall in on their heads, and mostly they'd come away with the idea that Shanghai and New York had made peace, and as part of the terms, they'd saved the Scholomance together.

But a fair few people had seen me kill a maw-mouth by now, or knew that I could do it, and every council member knew what was holding their enclaves up, after all. Eventually, someone hostile would put those two things together, and I hadn't the shadow of an idea for what I'd do then. Shanfeng and Ophelia might be all for my crusade, but it was easy to feel that way when you were at the top of the world's most powerful enclaves. Other enclavers would be more than a bit put out.

I'd suggested to Aad and Liu that maybe they ought to just go home and not get too involved, but Liu had said, "No," firmly and immediately. Which would have been understandable if *home* had been Beijing enclave, but it wasn't anymore. Shanfeng had made a quiet arrangement with the new council they'd elected: Beijing had taken in seven of Shanghai's own long-term hirelings—still several years away from earning places and fully willing to settle for a bit less room—and Liu and her immediate family had been given places in Shanghai enclave instead.

"What about Yuyan?" I tried—Liu had already put her on the list for Liesel's second network—but Liu had just smiled at me a little watery and said, "Maybe after Shanghai replaces their foundation." I couldn't exactly argue that, could I.

And practical Aadhya had just shrugged at me and said, "El, I'm not a crazy person, so I'm not going to spend the rest of my life doing this. But I'm ready to spend *some* of my life doing this, because it's worth doing, and right now is when you're going to need the most help figuring out how to get it done. Anyway, if someone's going to try to get at you through me and Liu, they'll do it whether we're with you or not. That was the price of admission when we put our names up on the wall. However," she added pointedly, "I'm stipulating right now, no more youth hostels. That place smelled like the boys' bathroom back at school. You can sleep on the floor in my hotel room if you need to demonstrate your asceticism."

Liesel only sniffed when I tried it on her, too. "If you try to do this all alone, you will certainly expose yourself within three months, and then all of us will be targets at once," she said. "If we aren't prepared to sever ties with you completely, we are much better off helping you while we strengthen our own positions," meaning she *wasn't* prepared to do that, even though it was obviously the most sensible option.

"Watch out, Mueller, I'm going to start thinking you like me," I said.

"You already know I like you," she said brusquely. I heaved a deep beleaguered sigh and hugged her. "Thanks," I said. "I like you too."

"Yes, yes, don't be mawkish," Liesel said, but she gave me a hug back.

I'd told Deepthi I'd find a way to be content, and I would. Maybe I hadn't *wanted* to go in for a career of hunting mawmouths, but it *was* work worth doing. A good life's work. And a few days from now, I'd go and start on it, with my allies and my friends helping.

And Orion would start on his own good life's work, here in the Scholomance, guarding the gates. He'd keep the doors clear, and the agglos out of the cleansing machinery, and blithely slaughter all the mals that came to feed on the children, and the mana would flow through him to keep the

Scholomance up, keep it running. A shelter that would now in fact protect *all* the wise-gifted children of the world.

Orion picked off the last of the edamame and stretched long and lanky and sprawled back over the steps. He'd traded in his crisp clean tailored clothes for an outfit that he might've been wearing anytime in the last four years of our lives: cargo shorts and a Queen T-shirt that had been new three days ago and now was already faintly aromatic and had acquired three small burn holes near the hem from some poor hapless mal.

"When the kids go home for the summer, I'll come out and help you hunt," he said. "It'll be fun."

Spoken exactly like the solid block of wood who'd once told me the Scholomance was the best place in the entire world; it was like he hadn't learned a *thing*. "It will not *be fun*," I said peevishly. "Hunting maw-mouths isn't *fun*."

"It'll be great," he said, grinning up at me, refusing to yield. "We'll go all over the world—"

"—to find the most horrible monsters and kill them?" I snapped. "Yes, a delightful holiday; lying on a beach, a trip to Paris, they really can't compete—"

His smile was only widening as I went on, a shining in his face like golden light as he looked at me, the wanker, and I tried to keep going but I couldn't help it; I leaned over and took his face in my hands and kissed him, again and again, there in the Scholomance gym, with the birds going in swoops and the tiny butterflies poking among the wildflowers, and the school sent a soft cool fragrant breeze in our faces, full of the scent of wildflowers and peaches.

It was, actually, a bit nice.

About the Author

NAOMI NOVIK is the *New York Times* bestselling author of *A Deadly Education* and *The Last Graduate*, the award-winning novels *Uprooted* and *Spinning Silver*, and the Temeraire series. She is a founder of the Organization for Transformative Works and the Archive of Our Own. She lives in New York City with her family and six computers.

naominovik.com
TheScholomance.com
Facebook.com/naominovik
Twitter: @naominovik
Instagram: @naominovik

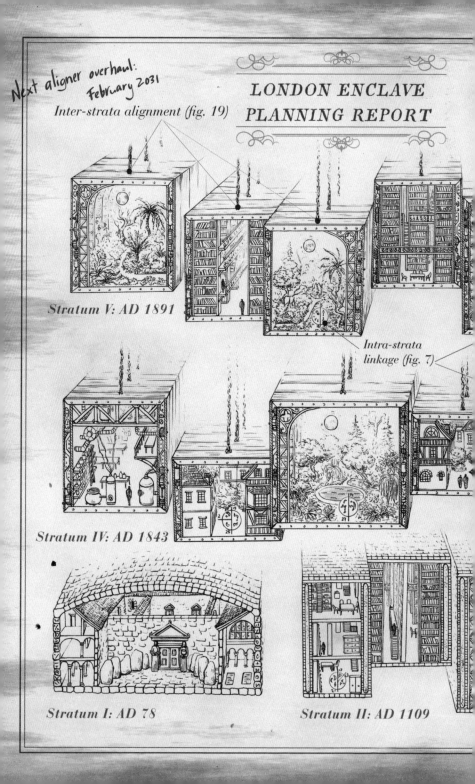

Next aligner overhaul: February 2031

Inter-strata alignment (fig. 19)

LONDON ENCLAVE PLANNING REPORT

Stratum V: AD 1891

Intra-strata linkage (fig. 7)

Stratum IV: AD 1843

Stratum I: AD 78

Stratum II: AD 1109